A SEASON OF THUNDER

An unsolved crime. A father's secrets. A quest for the truth.

ALEX GERRICK

A Season of Thunder: An unsolved crime. A father's secrets. A quest for the truth.
© Alex Gerrick 2025

A Season of Thunder is inspired by real events, but I have chosen to fictionalise certain elements of the story. Apart from my parents, siblings and known historical figures, the book's other main characters are fictional, with no connection to any real person. Certain places described in the book, such as the Eriksen Hotel and Scandinavian Prince Hotel in Copenhagen, as well as Neptune's Table in Marathon, are also fictional. My description of events in Šibenik, Croatia, where my parents lived during the Second World War, is based on their recollections, my personal research and fictionalised additions.

Editor: Candice Holznagel
Cover Design: Ocean Reeve Publishing
Design and Typeset: Ignite & Write Publishing

Published by Alex Gerrick at Alex's Books
www.alexgerrick.com.au

ISBN: 978-1-7637561-0-6 (Paperback)
ISBN: 978-1-7637561-1-3 (eBook)

A catalogue record for this book is available from the National Library of Australia

For John Clements (1965-2024) and
Bill Crane (1961- 2023)
–friends gone, but never forgotten.

Author's Note

A Season of Thunder is inspired by real events, but I have chosen to fictionalise certain elements of the story. Apart from my parents, siblings and known historical figures, the book's other main characters are fictional, with no connection to any real person. Certain places described in the book, such as the Eriksen Hotel and Scandinavian Prince Hotel in Copenhagen, as well as Neptune's Table in Marathon, are also fictional. My description of events in Šibenik, Croatia, where my parents lived during the Second World War, is based on their recollections, my personal research and fictionalised additions. The views espoused by some characters in the book do not necessarily reflect my own.

For the sake of consistency across two separate time periods, I have utilised the metric system of measurement throughout the book. Where appropriate, I have used the Serbian or Croatian spelling of specific places, names and titles.

Yugoslavia under the Italian Occupation - 1941-43

The Four Seasons of Life

The Season of Thunder, which reveals the circumstances that led to your birth and defines the events of your early childhood.

The Season of Fire, which draws upon those flames of passion that burn inside your soul as a teenager and turns you into the person you eventually become.

The Season of Clouds, when your capacity for happiness as an adult is temporarily consumed by the storm clouds in your life.

The Season of Wisdom, when you successfully defeat the Clouds and finally discover true peace and contentment.

As described to Alex Gerrick by Brother Rojo, Manila, 2001.

Prologue

Canberra, Australia
September 2022

A violent clap of thunder rescues me from my latest batch of nightmares. Overwhelmed with confusion, I jolt upright in my chair, my eyelids frozen, unable to open, my cheeks flushed and laden with sweat. Outside, the rain and lightning dance together in brutal harmony, their movements choreographed by a band of restless spirits determined to wreak their vengeance upon the world. Fully awake at last, I am momentarily captivated by the storm's alluring beauty before the suspicious growl of our young beagle, Louie, returns me to reality.

Ignoring the mindless chatter from the TV, I rub my eyes to the cadence of a ticking clock, furious that, for the third time this week, I've managed to fall asleep in the middle of the same documentary. I keep reassuring myself that I am not getting old, but these unwanted 'grandad' naps are now a regular intrusion in my life.

'It's okay,' I comfort Louie softly. 'It's just a thunderstorm.' From the sanctuary of our leather couch, he considers me with those huge, doleful eyes that always look thoroughly miserable. Perhaps he is waiting for the tasty treat that must surely be coming his way. But when my arthritic fingers snatch at the TV control instead, he wearily drops his head back into his snow-white paws and offers me a contemptuous stare.

Unperturbed, I begin to surf impatiently through the endless channels on my pay TV service, like I do every night, convinced that I won't find anything that can hold my attention for more than twenty minutes. If it isn't the sound of a football being kicked or a cricket ball being hit, it doesn't interest me anymore. Maybe this is a side-effect of PTSD I have never countenanced.

Frustrated, I finally land on one of those real-life crime shows. It piques my interest for several lobotomised minutes. The story involves a spaced-out waitress from the American Deep South (naturally), who dreams of becoming an actress (naturally) and then gets run over by her jilted lover (naturally).

It bumbles along nicely until just before the first commercial break when we are lumbered with the usual family member bemoaning what a great person the spaced-out waitress was, despite her insidious cocaine habit and subsequent jail time for pushing this shit out to local school kids. *What a cop-out!* Just once, I wished someone would admit that the victim was a complete douchebag and that the world was now a far better place for their demise.

Flabbergasted by the darkness of my heart, I switch the TV off and stagger into the kitchen to fix myself a drink. This is our little secret, of course. I tell everyone who cares that my love affair with alcohol is a thing of the past. But hidden in the back of the cupboard, behind that two-year-old packet of cereal, proudly stands the bottle of whiskey that I keep for emergencies. Just a tipple to see me through my next trip to Hell.

I take it how I like it: a couple of ice cubes in a small glass and two, maybe two and a half nips. The first swig burns my throat, but it somehow reassures me that I'm still alive. Of course, being alive is so much better than being dead, but it does have its drawbacks.

I stumble back into the lounge and focus on a white folder sitting on the coffee table. It stares at me with its hypothetical sharp, gleaming teeth, an unrepentant albatross stuck forever around my neck, devouring everything in its path.

Yes! That manuscript that I can never finish. A Season of Fucking Clouds.

I completed the first draft three years ago, just before the Covid-19 pandemic took over the world. Or so I thought. Bumping into my ex-girlfriend Eleanor in Potsdam, Germany, in September 2019 changed everything. Just seeing her again convinced me that I had become a victim of my own vanity and that the book was still incomplete. My mind swirling with self-doubt, I decided that I had one more chapter to write, one last attempt at justifying why I had been trapped inside the clouds for so long and how I had allowed my PTSD to almost destroy me.

But before I could even contemplate its implications, the evil curse of writer's block intervened. No matter how many times I tried, all that awaited me was a blank computer screen and piles of discarded paper. Even though my wife Miriam insisted that I push through my usual self-imposed dramas and finish it on time, that she would leave me if I didn't at least try, I was still looking for an excuse to throw it all away.

And for a man who ate excuses for breakfast, I had my pick at what came next. First, it was Covid. I mean, how could I finish my book when the world was immersed in so much death and misery? I had other commitments to fulfil during this awful time, other people who needed my help. But the world eventually found a vaccine, and we eventually grew the balls to live our lives again. How convenient, then, that Martina, the young Bosnian woman who stole my conscience on a faraway Greek island in 1995, suddenly became the next excuse. *You must understand,* I convinced myself every night as I stared at my computer screen, *I can't write that last chapter until I know what happened to her.* It's a deal-breaker —perhaps the biggest deal-breaker of them all.

So, four months ago, once the borders had reopened, I followed my heart to Edinburgh and Copenhagen in one last effort to find her. But like all those other times, all those other wasted trips, the trail went ruthlessly cold just when it looked promising. Having tempted fate too often, I returned to Australia ready to face an uncertain future, when, as if by autopilot, I became obsessed with the next big distraction.

Yes. Kandos. So many years ago.

I return to my lounge chair and gulp down the last droplets of whiskey. Its warmth slowly consumes the strands of fear churning inside my stomach. Eager to feed my paranoia some more, I pick up a copy of *The Australian* newspaper from the floor. It is the same one that I have doggedly kept for the past few weeks. Just to amuse myself, I re-read the article about the Croatian Six and their fight for justice. *The Croatian Six from Lithgow, New South Wales.*

I was sceptical at first. What did this long-forgotten case have to do with what happened to me in Kandos? It was the failure of another generation, irrelevant to the machinations of my past. My situation was more complex, more speculative. Yet if he were still alive, I am certain Brother Rojo, my Filipino mentor from another time, would reassure me that this was the key to everything. 'Follow your instincts, Alex,' he would have said, even though he understood my frailties better than anyone.

I slam my empty glass on the coffee table in front of me and watch the pockets of lightning seep through the kitchen blinds, announcing my pain in headlights to the world. *Remember,* it screams. *That mystery from your childhood. The shooting. The pain. The betrayal. Kandos! An hour's drive from Lithgow.*

I think back to everything Brother Rojo taught me about the Four Seasons, especially our discussion that morning in Manila, the last time I ever saw him. How he encouraged me to search for the truth, regardless of the implications. Even at this precipitous hour, his enduring wisdom from that day sustains me. The pathway he created for my personal redemption has made such a difference in my life, and there is far too much at stake to change direction now.

After all, it wasn't my fault that his love for me was eternal; how, even in death, he had given me the perfect excuse to further delay work on my book. For there is still so much of the puzzle that doesn't make sense. So many false diversions that lead to nowhere. No matter which path I choose, the lingering shadows that destroyed my innocence on that fateful day in Kandos continue to tighten their grip on my soul. If I am truly meant to reclaim my childhood after all these years, there is only one course of action left open to me.

I must return to Croatia and finally uncover the truth about the Season of Thunder.

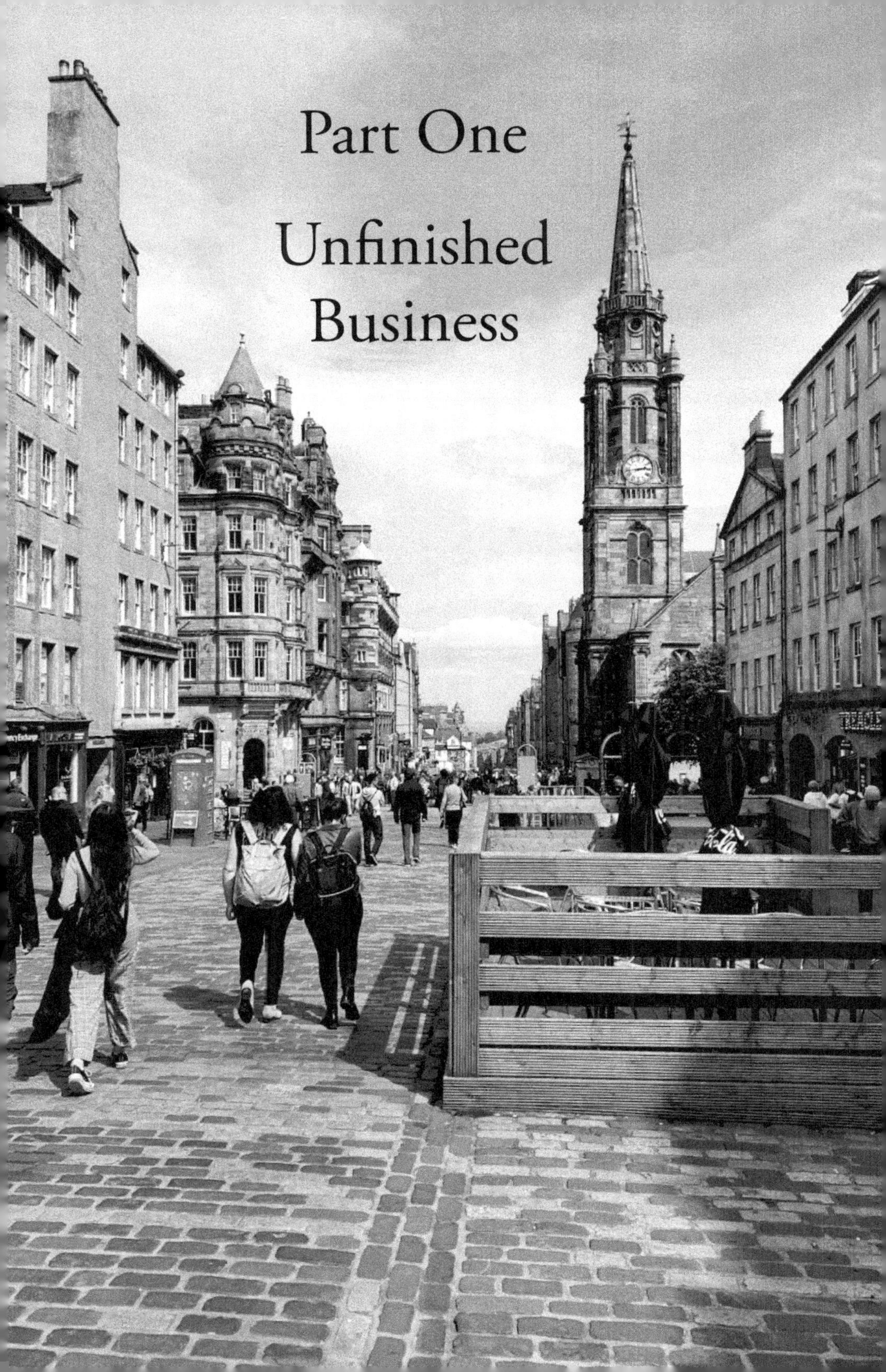

Part One

Unfinished
Business

Chapter One

Four months earlier
London, United Kingdom

'Welcome to our hotel, Mr Gerrick.' The pretty young receptionist behind the desk of the Heathrow hotel casually inspected my passport photo. 'Is this your first time with us?'

I waited until she returned my passport before answering her question. Given that I had been to London so many times in my life, each trip melted into the next. *Possibly. Probably. Who knows?* Honestly, I was just grateful to be standing in England again after three years of imposed frustration. There was a time last year during all those ridiculous lockdowns and border closures when I seriously believed that I would never travel overseas again.

'I am pretty sure I have,' I began cautiously, 'but unfortunately, the pandemic turned my brain into a block of Swiss cheese.'

'Excuse me, sir?'

'You know, full of holes.'

My joke wasn't especially funny, but she giggled anyway. I hadn't acquired too many life skills over the years, but making a woman laugh was one of them. After she complained that her boyfriend had been stuck at home for several days with the virus, the receptionist quickly attended to a few things on her computer, asked me to sign a piece of paper, and then handed me a room key. 'Enjoy your stay, Mr Gerrick, and if there is anything I can… ' Blah, blah, blah.

A few minutes later, I was huddled like a frightened turtle underneath a warm shower, hoping to dredge out the last remnants of fatigue accrued by a seventeen-hour trip from Darwin. Normally, my dodgy back and even dodgier right shoulder would have enjoyed a premium economy or business class ticket for such a long journey, but those seats had long been sold by the time I booked my flight. Luckily, I was able to secure the best seat in economy—the middle aisle behind the bulkhead—and the flight turned out to be a reasonably comfortable affair. I even managed to get a few hours of sleep, which was rare for me during a long-haul international flight. However, wearing that goddamn mask for the entire flight was mere torture. At some point over the Indian Ocean, I was ready to tear it into little pieces.

After I finished showering, I shaved, threw on some fresh clothes and readjusted my watch to London time. It was barely seven in the morning and way too early to enjoy the fruits of central London. Although I was not especially hungry, I decided to waste an hour or so at breakfast, perhaps sipping at an endless cup of coffee while reading the latest Charles Cumming spy thriller, which I had begun on the plane. But when I finally located the dining room after navigating a maze of hallways, I found that every seat in the house had already been taken by other guests. Accepting defeat at last, I wandered down the platform that led to Heathrow Terminal 2 and soon found myself at a café in Arrivals, happily gorging on a cinnamon scroll.

I returned to my hotel room just after nine o'clock, brushed my teeth, and then examined myself in the bathroom mirror. Old age was beginning to catch up with me. The hair was now completely grey, the black eyes drained and weary from the long flight, the face rudely corrugated by the odd wrinkle. In a further blow to my vanity, just before last Christmas, I mysteriously began to lose weight. I didn't feel unwell apart from the usual aches and pains, and my doctor was at a loss to diagnose a cause after doing the necessary tests.

But whatever was wrong with me, my cheeks had now lost some of their middle-age robustness, giving me a haggard, sallow look that I thoroughly despised. Even so, I still looked younger than the average fifty-eight-year-old man, and that gave me some solace. 'Looking young is in our genes,' my mother proudly said to me just before she died, and for one of the few times in her life, she may have been right.

I locked away some valuables in the safe and thought about taking a nap but decided to head into the city instead. In years gone by, I would have stayed at a hotel in Bloomsbury or near Trafalgar Square. However, during my last trip to London before Covid, I discovered that the Heathrow Airport hotel chains usually offered much cheaper accommodation than the city. With the advent of the Heathrow Express, the journey from the airport to Paddington Station was a guaranteed fifteen-minute ride, making the thirty-pound return fare and the cheaper hotel excellent value.

Twenty minutes later, I was sitting inside an express train adjacent to a young American couple on their honeymoon. Without offering an opportunity to escape to another compartment, they began to bombard me with a million excited questions about visiting London. As always, I tried to be polite and rattled off some bland insights about the usual attractions. Eventually, they realised that I wasn't really wired for small talk, and so when we cruised into Paddington Station, they quietly grabbed their suitcases and slithered off into the distance without even bothering to say goodbye.

After disembarking, I quaffed down another extra hot latte—my third for the morning—then skulked towards the entrance to the London Underground. Not knowing what to expect in the new post-Covid underground world, I diligently flicked on a face mask as I went in search of the Bakerloo line. I was surprised to see that no one else was wearing a mask when I clumsily fell inside the next train.

A bald, middle-aged guy with a neck tattoo of a rattlesnake made his views known immediately. 'Nowt gives a fuck about Covid anymore, sunshine,' he reassured me in a tense, cockney accent while pointing at my face. Emboldened by his caring and sensitive nature, I ripped off my mask and lazily smiled at the air. Having felt the man's unremitting gaze for several more minutes, I was somewhat relieved when I made it to Charing

Cross tube station unmolested. After negotiating several sets of stairs, I finally tiptoed into the waiting spring sunshine.

Ah, London! There was something about this incredible city that still beguiled me after all these years. The crisp, cool breeze that caressed my cheeks, the irreverent sound of those famous London cabs bellowing their horns at the universe, the chimes of unfinished history singing sweetly in the distance, all rolled into one absorbing riddle. Despite my aching body, I was like a child at Christmas, waiting to open that new present, exploring that next new secret. The city's understated charm suddenly thawed my disposition, and I realised that even at this late stage of my life, I still had so many more adventures to look forward to.

I negotiated the mid-morning traffic surrounding Trafalgar Square and slowly made my way towards Piccadilly Circus. As I solemnly walked past the National Gallery, my thoughts turned to the events of 1999… my God, was it really twenty-three years ago? I had been on a self-absorbed holiday in the United Kingdom and had met two incredible women who changed my life forever. Eleanor, the beautiful but ethereal Austrian history teacher with whom I had a brief but passionate affair, and Danielle, her best friend, a French woman so stunning that in ancient times men would have fought wars over her. In their own way, each woman taught me how to appreciate myself, a virtue that probably saved my life after I attempted suicide in 2016.

Suddenly, my heart yearned for even more of their memories before realising that this would only lead to unwanted feelings of regret and guilt. *I really don't have time for this,* I thought. Scolding myself, I quickly shuffled along Haymarket Street, before landing at a lovely little café near the Eros Statue. Soon, I was gratefully pouring myself a therapeutic cup of tea. Sometimes, revisiting the past was exhausting.

I finished the morning by raiding the history section at my favourite London bookshop in Piccadilly Square. Satisfied I had enough reading material for the next two weeks, I sneaked in a last-minute haircut, unashamedly grabbed a greasy hamburger for lunch, and shuffled back to

Paddington station. By two o'clock, my jet lag finally caught up with me and I was soon snoozing on my hotel bed, satisfied that everything with my trip had gone to plan so far.

I woke up just before five thirty, to be greeted with a sniffling nose and a brutal sore throat. *Fuck it*, I screamed into my pillow. *After avoiding Covid for so long, I've now caught it on the first day of my trip!* Furious at my ill luck, I quickly unwrapped one of the oral Rapid Antigen Tests (RAT) that Miriam lovingly packed in my suitcase and nervously sucked on it for thirty seconds. As I waited impatiently for the result, I calmly thought through the implications. Everywhere I turned for reassurance, I came out with the same morbid conclusion: if I had Covid, I was screwed.

Prior to the pandemic, I regularly travelled overseas by myself. Miriam had sanctioned these annual two-week 'man trips' in 2012, soon after I became a senior leader in the federal public service. She understood that my work was highly stressful and that I often needed my own time to chill out. We believed that a good marriage was about respecting the individual lives of your partner. My idea of relaxing involved watching my beloved Liverpool Football Club, visiting a range of European historical sites and sometimes meeting long-forgotten relatives in Croatia.

Loving her space like she did, Miriam would use my absences to renovate our ageing house, engage in some spring cleaning without male interference, and spend quality time in the garden. When the time was right for both of us during the year, we would take a holiday together for several weeks and always enjoyed ourselves immensely. It was slightly unorthodox, but we were merely being truthful to ourselves.

But then my trips began to take a dark turn. Following my falling out with *The Spiders* in 2016 (a shadowy group of corporate and political highflyers I occasionally did work for), my mental breakdown and subsequent attempted suicide, I began looking for answers to the questions that had plagued my life through both childhood and adulthood. Top of the list was discovering the truth about Martina, the tragic young Bosnian woman I had befriended during a visit to the Greek Island of Samos in

May 1995. The story she told me about being gang raped by soldiers near Sarajevo had opened long-forgotten cracks in my own traumatic life that had conveniently laid dormant since my childhood.

My betrayal of her trust, when I refused to answer her desperate phone calls after I returned to Australia several weeks later, sparked an endless spiral of guilt inside my conscience that lasted for the next twenty years, especially after I discovered that she may have committed suicide. Motivated by the work I was doing on my book, *A Season of Clouds*, I became obsessed with finding the truth about Martina. It slowly became obvious that if I failed, the lessons from *Clouds* that I wanted to share with the world would become worthless.

I started my search for Martina in September 2016 after consulting a prominent war crimes investigator in Berlin. Over the next three years, under the mask of watching Liverpool play at the height of their powers, I trampled aimlessly across Europe, secretly following every tiny morsel of information about Martina I could find. As one trip followed the next, I slowly exhausted every tenet of patience that existed within my heart before I finally reached the proverbial dead end while visiting Athens in April 2019.

Fearing retribution as a result of my constant lying to Miriam and my friends, I finally decided to give up the trail for good, even if that potentially meant throwing my manuscript into the bin.

But in late January 2020, I received a tip from an overseas contact who knew about my previously failed search and desperation. The contact pointed me in the direction of a man called Marković. He had apparently worked for a refugee agency in Switzerland, helping women who were sexually assaulted during the Bosnian War, which spanned from 1992 to 1995, have their day in court. According to my source, there was a very good chance that he may have become aware of Martina's case. Most importantly, he would know whether she was still alive or not. And so, on the dubious premise that I wanted to see Liverpool win its first English title in thirty years, I managed to lie to everyone again and booked a business class ticket to Zurich, departing on 15 March 2020.

Of course, by then, someone in China had supposedly eaten a bat, and the whole world turned upside down in the very week that I was scheduled to leave Australia. The Australian Prime Minister, Scott Morrison, soon closed the international borders indefinitely, and my hopes of travelling to Switzerland and resolving this issue once and for all were immediately dashed.

Despite a series of flustered emails sent across several months, any thought about contacting the mysterious Marković dissipated as hundreds of thousands of people across Europe died from or with the coronavirus. It was a dreadful time for everyone.

And so, on that fateful day in London, I picked up the RAT, closed my eyes in a temporary gesture to wish away the inevitable, and then calmly assessed the result. Thank God. That ominous squiggly line we all loved to hate was absent. A reprieve of sorts. But everyone knew that these tests were barely foolproof. There was still a risk that I could be infectious. And there was still a risk that I could be stuck in this hotel room for days and miss out on my final chance to locate Marković. Putting my short-term health aside, I couldn't let that happen under any circumstances.

So, let's get things clear now, God. I'm seeing this to the bitter end, even if you have to send me back to Australia in a box.

Chapter Two

London, United Kingdom
May 2022

My throat felt like I had swallowed a glass of unused razor blades. It was seven thirty in the morning, and despite ten hours of uninterrupted sleep, my body wanted to go on strike. Unimpressed, I picked up my travel thermometer from the side of the bed and grudgingly stuck it under my tongue. Thirty seconds later, I was looking at a temperature of 37.2 degrees Celsius. *Is that a fever?* I had no idea, so I consulted my phone. No need to be worried yet, the words on the screen read. Hit 37.5, and you may have an issue.

I made it to the shower and tried singing a Taylor Swift song that had been in my head ever since I landed in London. After the first line, I began to cough up a pile of yellow pus from my chest. *No offence, Taylor, I think you're terrific, but maybe I should quit singing before I do myself more damage.* I finally managed to do another RAT without keeling over and once again hit the negative payload.

Perhaps this was just a minor head cold, after all.

I reluctantly skipped breakfast and, instead, spent valuable time raiding the Boots pharmacy at Terminal 2. I swallowed two painkillers with sparkling water and then bought several packets of cough lozenges—lemon, honey, berry, take your pick. They were not going to work, but at least I was pretending to find a remedy.

I spent the next few hours trudging around the Strand and Pall Mall. After every second or third breath, I swallowed hard, checking to see if my sore throat had mysteriously disappeared. But it was never going to be that easy. In fact, as the hours slowly passed, my cold, or whatever it was, grew progressively worse. I tried visiting the Tower of London, but I bailed out before I could even say hello to the nearest Beefeater. Pretty soon, I was back on the Heathrow Express and headed for my hotel.

When we finally arrived at Heathrow, I felt my back pocket vibrate. I pulled out my phone. Just as I thought, it was a text message from *her*. Another relic from my trip to Greece in 1995.

'Assume you made it to the UK safely?'

Straight to the point, just as I remembered.

'All good, apart from a cold. Still fine for Thursday?'

I didn't get a response from her until I stumbled into my hotel room.

'Wouldn't miss it! BTW, if you have Covid, stay away! I don't want to catch it again.'

Yeah, I figured that part out already. As I kept reminding myself, if indeed I had Covid, it would ruin everything. Well, for this trip, at least. *And I promised Miriam that this would definitely be the final trip.*

I waddled into the bathroom, took another RAT, got another negative result, and then checked my temperature—37.6, which didn't surprise me. It felt like I had a fever, which was never a good sign, especially when you might have Covid. I held that thought long enough before I collapsed underneath my sheets and blissfully fell asleep. I didn't feel all that much better when I was woken up several hours later by the sound of people arguing loudly in the outside hallway. Unperturbed, I watched Liverpool beat Southampton on my phone and then swallowed several painkillers. I eventually dozed off again while reading the introduction to my new book on David Stirling, the founder of the SAS.

Wednesday morning welcomed me with the obligatory coughing fit, but after it disappeared, I was surprised to find that I felt much better than the previous evening. The sore throat was still lingering, but my temperature was back to 36.8, and my body no longer ached. One last negative RAT convinced me that I could travel, so an hour later, I was lining up with my luggage at the British Airways business class counter at Terminal 5.

It was her idea to meet in Edinburgh, not mine. 'I'm there for a conference, so take it or leave it,' she had said to me.

To be fair, I didn't need much convincing. After all, I loved Scotland as much as any country I had visited, and Edinburgh was one of my favourite cities in the world. What better place to come face-to-face with my past? To set my eyes on the woman whose provocative laugh teetered on the edge of my memory even after all these years.

The flight from Heathrow to Edinburgh was mercifully short. Sitting next to Wee Hamish McStink would have been an unpleasant experience at the best of times, but it was an absolute killer when recovering from a respiratory illness. His beer gut spilt into my seat, and his body odour hovered over my head like a putrid veil of thick smoke. It was so strong that even a stuffed nose couldn't offer any respite.

The kindly head purser noticed my discomfort and, to her immense credit, asked me if I wanted to sit in the opposite aisle seat next to the nice lady with the pink jacket. I didn't think twice about it. Still, the foul BO followed me all the way to my new seat, the toilet, the aerobridge and finally to the baggage counter. Thankfully, by the time I entered a taxi, it drifted off to launch a surprise attack on a group of unsuspecting schoolkids.

The driver was a friendly chap looking for a chat, and we spent the thirty-minute trip to the Mercure Haymarket Hotel talking football. His team, the Glasgow Rangers, were playing in the Europa Cup final that week, and Scotland was gripped with football fever. I gave him a healthy tip when we arrived at the hotel so he could buy that extra pint while watching the game. It was two o'clock in the afternoon when I checked into the hotel.

As soon as the door to my room closed behind me, my lungs exploded into a chorus of coughing and wheezing. The virus was obviously planning a counterattack. One look at the king-sized bed and cluster of soft pillows convinced me that the only way to defeat this curse once and for all was to have an extended afternoon resting with no distractions. I soon collapsed on top of the doona and drifted off into a deep slumber. I woke just prior to sunset, and after a quick trip to the nearest pharmacy, I gargled furiously for twenty minutes before falling back to sleep.

Incredibly, I fell out of bed the next morning to find that my cold had miraculously disappeared overnight. I felt like a new man. Gargling that honey and warm water, with a little splash of apple cider vinegar thrown in, had obviously done the trick. The colour had finally returned to my cheeks, and although it may have been my imagination, I looked fuller in the face than at any stage in the past three months. It was almost as if God wanted me to look my best for today's meeting. If that was the case, then I took back everything I ever said about the guy.

We were scheduled to meet right on five o'clock at a popular bar close to Edinburgh Castle—after she attended the closing session of her conference. In anticipation, I looked at my watch and calculated that I had about seven hours to kill. As a historian who completed one of his majors in Scottish history, there was always something in the Edinburgh district to keep me occupied. Within the hour, I was boarding a train to Stirling. Upon arrival, I jumped into a taxi and asked the driver to take me to the Bannockburn Visitor Centre.

Over the next two hours, I completed the guided tour of the famous fourteenth-century battle, walked solemnly across the battlefield from east to west, then north to south and took several selfies standing in front of the statue of Robert the Bruce. When I finished fighting the English, I ambled back towards Stirling Railway Station—a good five-kilometre walk—and grabbed some lunch before catching the two-fifteen return service to Edinburgh.

After arriving at Waverly station an hour later, I walked to Edinburgh Castle and took in some of my favourite views of the city from the steps of its medieval battlements. If this was meant to negate the butterflies swarming inside my stomach, I had completely miscalculated. As it got closer to our rendezvous time, all I could think about was whether I was doing the right thing by seeing her again.

I reminded myself that she was the one who had initiated the first contact, not me. Towards the end of the previous year, I took to social media to provide a progress report about *A Season of Clouds*. To my shame, I used every opportunity on every platform to provide excuses as to why I still had not finished the book. It was the least I could do after creating so many false expectations with people. That night, while I was making a coffee, I heard several loud buzzes from my phone, indicating that someone had messaged in response to my post.

At first, I couldn't believe that it was her. But after twenty-six years, here she was, hoping that I was well, congratulating me on my book and wondering whether I had based a character on her. Before I replied, I quickly pulled up her social media profile. Her picture showed a much older woman than the one who had briefly touched my life all those years ago in Samos. Her blonde hair, once long and bountiful, was now cut to a sassy shoulder-length bob. Those incredible sapphire eyes that had mesmerised me with their spontaneity now conveyed a refined weariness, while her smile seemed both forced and constrained. But she was still very much a beautiful woman. Confident, successful and, judging by her followers, incredibly well-connected.

None of this surprised me, of course. Out of those incredible six women I met overseas during my thirties, all who had left a lasting impact on my future self, her formidable spirit and kindness of heart had resonated with me the most. Not in a sexual way, of course; despite the endless flirting and one whimsical kiss, nothing physical ever happened between us. Yet for a moment in time, on a ferry in the middle of the Aegean Sea, we willingly shared the same hopes and dreams, the same black sense of humour, the same oblique way of looking at the world, and the same unfettered devotion to the mysteries of desire. It was a connection that I could never fully expunge.

During the next few weeks, we had contacted each other several times. After the third exchange, I agreed to send her a copy of the first part of my book, in which both she and Martina had played prominent roles during my cataclysmic visit to Samos.

They had been adversaries at first: two beautiful young women who thought they owned the world and who strangely saw the other as a competitor for my affections. But during a chaotic party on my last night on the island, where I lost my dignity and eventually my mind, the two women had curiously bonded, perhaps for no other reason than to prove that opposites do attract. Her cultured pragmatism complemented Martina's manic self-destruction. In retrospect, she was the friend Martina needed at the time, not me.

In a bizarre way, I hoped that she would hate the book and demand that her character be withdrawn. Indeed, I saw this as another reason to throw the manuscript underneath the bed where it could gather dust forever. But to my despair, she emailed several days later and exclaimed excitedly that she loved what I had written so far and how I had portrayed her role in the story. She wanted me to retain her anonymity, of course, as her husband and children didn't need to know that she was chasing some deluded Australian guy on a Greek Island when she was in her mid-twenties. But like Miriam, she encouraged me to finish the book upon pain of death. Another devotee to my mindless excesses.

Over the next several months, our topic of conversation inevitably turned back to Martina. She did her best to understand my obsession with her. She also tried to convince me that I was being too hard on myself, that Martina was a hand grenade ready to explode at any moment, and that I was never responsible for her feelings or actions. But in the end, she accepted that I was on a one-man demolition mission, so she decided to limit the damage as much as she could by helping me locate the enigmatic Marković.

Her role as a senior partner in one of the major accounting firms gave her access to numerous European networks. *Leave it with me*, she had demanded. Within a week, she sent a text with encouraging news.

'I have found him. But I can't tell you anything over email or online. We must do this in person.'

And so here I was in Edinburgh, trapped by the miscalculations of my past and the impossibilities of my future.

It was now quarter-to-five, so I took a few more snaps with my phone and then walked the short distance to our designated bar. Happy in the knowledge that I was the first one to arrive, I quickly made my way to the gents for one final check of my appearance. Yes, my hair was perfectly ruffled, and I convinced myself that my nose had shrunk over the past few hours. Satisfied that all was in order, I made my way back into the main bar.

Oh my God, there she is! She was sitting quietly at a table, inspecting her phone, when fate told her to look upwards. Our eyes connected, and she immediately released that beautiful smile that had once beguiled me as a younger man. I giddily rushed over towards her and extended my hand.

'Oh, don't be so formal,' Lottie laughed before she stood up and embraced me. The warmth of her gaze momentarily made my heart skip a beat.

'You look amazing,' she said with that cool Dutch accent as we pulled away from each other. 'Ten years younger than what you really are.' Perhaps she was lying just to be nice, but with Lottie, one never knew.

'So do you,' I replied with a smile. And she did. Everything about her, from her blue woollen jumper to her black chequered business skirt and pantyhose. She was elegance personified. That profile photo didn't do her justice at all.

'I bet you say that to all the girls,' she laughed.

'That's not me anymore,' I reassured her. 'I am a happily married man.'

'Of course,' Lottie replied with a dubious frown. 'What was I thinking?'

I ordered some drinks for us; a glass of white wine for her and a boring soft drink for me.

'Still as cosmopolitan as ever,' Lottie teased as she pointed at my glass.

'Old age,' I replied earnestly. 'I've become a boring old fart.'

We made small talk at first, about our families, our careers, that sort of thing. I discovered that her parents, whom I had also met all those years ago in Greece, were still alive, living in a retirement village outside of Amsterdam. Her son, Willem, had just finished his law degree, while her daughter, Sonja, had dreams of becoming a ballet dancer. She said little about her German husband Kurt other than that he was currently in New York on business. Whether it was a happy marriage or not, I could go either way, but it really was none of my business.

Just when we had run out of things to say about our families, Lottie reached into her handbag and slid a brown envelope across our table towards me.

'Here, take this,' she ordered.

I wrapped my fingers around the edge of the envelope and stared blankly into her eyes. 'What is it?'

She folded her arms and considered me with that facetious girlish scowl she had perfected when we first met. 'What do you mean, 'What is it?' I have arranged a meeting for you with your friend Marković. That's what you want, isn't it?'

I was too stunned to answer her at first. 'The details are inside,' she continued. 'In essence, you need to get yourself to Copenhagen by next Thursday.'

'Copenhagen?'

'Yes, you know, Copenhagen? The capital of Denmark? *The Little Mermaid*? Vikings? Princess Mary? That sort of thing!'

'I know where Copenhagen is,' I grizzled back at her. I leant into my chair and watched while she casually stroked her hair. 'I don't know what to say.'

'How about a thank you?' she replied sarcastically.

'Thank you, Lottie.' A veil of silence consumed the air around us. Eventually, I asked, 'How did you find him?'

'A friend of a friend of a friend who works with Amnesty International called in some favours. Marković did contract work in Europe over the last few years before disappearing off the grid once Covid arrived. They didn't tell me how they found him, and I am wise enough not to have asked.'

I shuffled my legs from side to side. 'Why couldn't you tell me all this over email, text, or phone? I mean, why all the cloak and dagger stuff?'

Lottie shrugged her shoulders and helped herself to a mouthful of wine. 'Those were the instructions that I received. Anything less and the deal was off. Apparently, our Mr Marković is a secretive man.'

Something didn't feel quite right, but this wasn't the time or place to feed my ongoing paranoia. 'And he has met Martina?'

'That I can't help you with.' Lottie now sighed and bent her neck towards me. 'I am just the messenger, the go-between. Do you understand? You must find the details out for yourself. But if he is willing to speak to you, then that's a promising start.'

She suddenly made a grab for my hand, and it melted between her long, smooth fingers. 'Listen sweetheart, I warned you weeks ago that once you stepped on that plane, there was no turning back. But perhaps I was mistaken. You still have a choice, even at this late stage. If this meeting doesn't feel right for you, then don't go through with it. It's no skin off my back.'

I offered her a nervous laugh, an unfortunate by-product of my flailing false bravado. 'You seem worried, and in the short time I knew you in Samos, I never saw you worried about anything.'

Lottie coughed into her wine glass. 'Look, this guy has gone to great lengths to keep his whereabouts private. My experience is that people who make it hard to be found do so for a reason. Just be careful, that's all I am saying. And while you are at it, you need to work out whether finding Martina is worth this chaos in your life.'

She hit an especially raw nerve, and we both knew it. If truth be told,

I had asked that very same question every night for the past six years, convincing myself that growing old and dying was perhaps my only way out of this mess. But something mysterious I couldn't explain kept driving my obsession into new, darker pathways. I simply didn't have the courage to stop. No, I had to see this through to the end, even if it meant destroying everyone around me. 'This is the last chance saloon,' I lied. 'If Marković becomes yet another dead end, then I am finished for good. Trust me.'

Lottie released her hand from mine. 'That's a promise you should be making to your wife, not me.'

Ignoring her retort, I stuck the envelope into my coat pocket, and thankfully, we dropped the subject for good. For the next ten minutes, we fumbled around the delicate question of whether to have dinner together and finally, after much mutual flagellation, we decided that we should. She suggested a nearby Italian restaurant, and we were soon tucking into some antipasti. I even treated myself to a glass of red wine—a Bordeaux, I think—and for once, she complimented my choice.

Everything about our conversation was dignified and innocent until our main courses arrived. As Lottie carelessly twirled her fettuccine around her fork, I could sense that the unspeakable storm cloud that had hovered over us all night was about to burst. And when it did, a sheet of ice-cold raindrops came tumbling down on top of me.

'Did you ever regret that we didn't become a couple?' she suddenly asked, her fork now pointed horizontally at my head.

'I thought we agreed not to talk about this,' I replied.

'Indulge me, nevertheless.'

My experience was that when a woman asked you to indulge her, it was time to run for your life. But there I was, trapped in the corner of a cosy restaurant, a fork targeted at my beady eyes and nowhere to turn.

'That was a long time ago, Lottie. So much has happened in our lives since then.'

'You can do better than that.' She sounded deadly serious.

'After we said goodbye in Athens,' I reluctantly began, 'I carried a dagger in my heart for you for weeks. But I returned to my boring life in Australia and moved on, just like you asked me to.' I paused for a few seconds to see her reaction, but her eyes remained blank. 'I would often think of you and wonder what you were doing. And the memories of our time together helped me survive the most difficult period of my life in 2016. But apart from that, I'm not sure what else you want me to say.'

She rubbed a finger around her glass of wine. Despite the slight curl of her lips, I couldn't tell whether I had offended her or not. 'I'm not sure either, to be honest,' she finally said. 'I always considered our time together unfinished business, something that I never fully understood. Over the years, you became this mythical figure in my imagination, a lonely man walking across an endless field, like an unplanted seed forever blown across the world by the wind. Despite everything, I was desperate to know where you landed.'

'Now you know,' I replied with a smile.

She picked up her wine glass and clinked mine. 'Yes, now I know.'

'Perhaps that's what fate always planned for us.'

She threw me one of her dazzling smiles. 'Yes, perhaps.'

We hurriedly made it through our desserts and coffee with idle chitchat, both trying hard not to take the night into more forbidden corridors. As soon as I finished my cappuccino, I jumped up to pay the bill. Then we walked out together into a brutally cold Edinburgh night. We stood there aimlessly for several seconds, looking at each other with weary intent, not knowing who should make the next move or even what the next move should be.

Finally, Lottie took the initiative and dragged me towards her. I felt her sweet breath on my skin as she wrapped me in a huge bear hug. 'I have enjoyed seeing you again, Alex,' she smiled before tucking her handbag firmly under her armpit.

'Same here.'

'Promise me that you will be careful in Copenhagen,' she insisted. 'If something doesn't feel right, abort the meeting, jump on the next plane to Australia, and forget about Martina for good.'

'I promise,' I replied. She looked so beautiful at this juncture; her elegant body silhouetted perfectly against the backdrop of a brilliantly lit Edinburgh Castle. For a moment, I was taken back to that night on the ferry from Samos to Piraeus when she startled me with a kiss from nowhere that almost split my heart in two. A tiny part of me was still that same person, a hopeless romantic who saw the world through the unpredictability of a woman's heart. But over time, everything had become lost inside my own madness, and I was nothing more than a broken man with a broken past.

'Will we ever see each other again?' I asked her softly. It seemed the appropriate thing to say, despite the precariousness of the situation.

'Probably not,' Lottie replied sadly. 'But then again, we said that once before, didn't we?'

Before I dared work out what she meant, Lottie blew me a whispered kiss from the corner of the street curb, and without saying another word, one of the most intriguing women I had met in my life quietly disappeared inside a rising fog.

Chapter Three

Edinburgh, Scotland
May 2022

When I returned to the privacy of my hotel room, I immediately opened the envelope that Lottie had given me, pulled out a sheet of crisp A4 paper and scrutinised its contents. The typed instructions in fourteen-point Times Roman were simple and to the point—Marković would meet me at seven o'clock next Thursday evening at the main bar at the Eriksen Hotel in the centre of Copenhagen. He would be wearing a black leather jacket and dark blue jeans. I was to address him only as Josip and come to the meeting alone. Any deviance from these instructions and our appointment would be terminated without prejudice.

I casually waited for the instructions to self-destruct in ten seconds like they always did in the *Mission Impossible* action movies, and when they didn't, I laughed at the stupidity of it all. Upon scrunching the paper into a ball, I tossed it into a nearby bin and then reached for my phone. I logged into my airline app and booked myself a return business class fare from London to Copenhagen, leaving on Wednesday week. After making myself a cup of tea, I pulled up a map of central Copenhagen to locate the Eriksen Hotel. I wasted several more minutes searching for accommodation in the same neighbourhood and then decided that this would be a foolhardy option.

Didn't you learn anything from your time with The Spiders?

I expanded my reach on the internet map and found exactly what I was looking for. The city of Copenhagen is basically two islands separated by a harbour. The Eriksen Hotel was on the northern island; I needed something on the southern island.

One can't be too careful, especially someone with my secrets.

I skimmed through four or five online properties and landed on the Scandinavian Prince. It looked perfect for my needs, a high-class four-star hotel with all the right facilities, so I booked three nights and fell back onto my bed.

I tossed and turned all night. My mind alternated between Lottie's impugned indiscretions and the impending meeting in Copenhagen with Marković. During the times that I did manage to fall asleep, I seemed trapped within a reoccurring dream, full of dark, foreboding skies and obscene gargoyle-like characters from my past. I finally woke up just before six thirty, one skinny leg hanging over the side of the bed, a shaking hand clutching at my phone. If this was how my mind was going to work for the next week, then I was in for a miserable time.

Thankfully, things panned out quite differently. Over the next few days, I spent an idyllic twenty-four hours in York, watched Liverpool FC beat Wolves 3-1 at Anfield in the last game of the season (although we sadly lost the title by a miserly point), and then pottered around numerous London bookstores and antique shops. By the time I boarded my flight to Copenhagen, my body and mind collectively felt the best they had for several weeks.

I arrived at the Scandinavian Prince just after two thirty. The hotel was exactly what I had envisaged—modern, spacious and busy. The friendly and helpful reception staff only reaffirmed that I had made the right choice. Given that it was my first time in Copenhagen, I politely asked the concierge for directions into the city. In perfect English, he outlined the journey, which would take no more than twenty minutes on foot.

I changed into some fresh clothes and, with map in hand, I carefully followed the concierge's instructions. Not long afterwards, I was having a refreshing beer at a sumptuous little bar on the northern side of the harbour. Man, it tasted damn good. So damn good, in fact, that I quickly ordered another one. *I am going to like Copenhagen very much.*

After I spent another hour exploring the CBD, I came to two quick conclusions: Copenhagen was an extremely beautiful city, and everyone was incredibly friendly. I returned to my hotel just before six, happily whistling *Wonderful, Wonderful Copenhagen* in my head and looking forward to exploring more of its treasures during my stay.

I always said that if you want to understand a new city, particularly its dangers and annoyances, you should talk to a taxi driver, a hairdresser, or a barman. After I offered a cursory wave to the concierge, I made my way to the bar, where I was greeted by Thomas, a handsome and friendly young barman from Finland with cropped blonde hair and vicious blue eyes. He stared at my new Liverpool FC hoodie that I had bought the previous Sunday at Anfield and cautiously smiled. 'You're a Liverpool fan?' he asked in brilliant English.

'Too right I am,' I replied sadly. 'Still getting over last weekend.'

'Me too,' he laughed. No surprise: we Liverpool fans were everywhere. I ordered a lemonade, and we quickly dissected Liverpool's chances in the Champions League final on Saturday against Real Madrid. Although football remained the overwhelming topic of conversation, Thomas also provided me with a snapshot of life in Copenhagen. The economy was still slow but picking up; no one wanted to talk about Covid anymore, and there was some disillusionment within the country over immigration. Other than that, Thomas reassured me, Copenhagen was a confident, progressive city where everyone looked out for one another and where the women were incredibly beautiful.

Exactly what I want to hear—well, the first bit, anyway.

The bar quickly began to fill, and before I knew it, I was greeting five middle-aged Swedish workmates in town for a conference. They seemed nice enough, and once they discovered that I was Australian, they settled into the chairs next to me and ordered a round of beers. Pretty soon, I was doing a one-on-one with Agnetha—a rather buxom forty-something from Stockholm with long, curly blonde hair and a cigarette-stained smile. She had the look of someone intending to have a quick, meaningless fling while away from home. In fact, all five Swedes looked like they were intending to have a quick, meaningless fling while away from home.

As the night progressed, so did their outlandish behaviour. Inga and Peter happily commenced proceedings by 'pashing' in a dark corner of the room after they finished their chocolate mousses. Their sordid slurping only encouraged Sven to grab Lara around the waist, and with a nod and wink to the rest of us, as if we were the reason they had delayed their indiscretions for so long, they scampered, arm in arm, to the nearby lifts. *Sorry to have wasted your time,* I thought. This left me with Agnetha, a party of South Koreans and a bemused Thomas, keen to see how this was all going to end.

To give Agnetha her credit, she went straight to first base. 'I could do with a night of guilt-free sex,' she admitted, landing her hand on my knee. I stared curiously at the wedding band on her finger and wondered if it was time I started wearing mine again.

'Really?' I replied, pretending to be shocked. 'Do you have anyone in mind?'

I heard Thomas laugh from behind the bar, and Agnetha gave him a horrid frown. But my quip did the trick. Without even fluttering an eyelid, she immediately engaged me in a conversation about alpine skiing and after forty minutes of this nonsense, we both departed to our respective rooms.

I slept well for a man on the brink of his destiny. Indeed, I jumped out of bed just before seven o'clock the next morning, feeling naturally apprehensive but relieved that by the end of the day all my questions about Martina would finally be answered. I had my schedule planned out in detail, so after breakfast, I casually walked back into the city, gripping my *Lonely Planet* guide.

Doing the occasional job for *The Spiders* taught me many things—one of them being that if you want to hide your true purpose when visiting a strange city, act like a tourist for as long as you can. And for the next seven hours, that's exactly what I did. First, I picked up a three-hour walking tour where I got to see some beautiful old churches, the seat of Danish democracy at Christiansborg Palace and a fantastic Viking exhibition at the National Museum. From there, I wandered through the majestic Tivoli Gardens, a nineteenth-century version of Disneyland.

There were rides, street food, cake stalls and music. I gobbled down a bratwurst with sauerkraut, a piece of mouth-tingling apple strudel and then stupidly jumped on a ride where we plunged one hundred metres to the earth at supersonic speed. Once I eventually found my stomach behind a couple of seat benches, I slowly walked back to my hotel room.

I won't lie—the closer it got to my rendezvous with Marković, the more nervous I became. I tried to catch a quick afternoon nap to ease my burden but became distracted listening to a Foo Fighters album. When I was ready to leave, I picked up a plastic bag, stuffed my Liverpool hoodie inside, and then shuffled back into town.

I arrived at the Eriksen Hotel just before six o'clock. Situated near Tivoli Gardens, it was a stylish and handsome building. Marković had chosen well. I slipped into the old-fashioned lobby unnoticed and immediately found what I was looking for. To the left of the main entrance, I noticed some visitor chairs. Trying my best to look inconspicuous, I pulled out a book from my plastic bag and quietly slumped into an empty seat, all the while keeping an eye on the entrance.

You see, this was something else I had learnt from experience. If you are concerned about meeting someone suspicious for the first time, come to the venue they have chosen early and see what you can find out. Over the next twenty minutes, I took in every valuable bit of information I needed. The vicinity of the toilets, the location of the lifts and how many fire exits I could count. The number of staff servicing the reception desk was important, too, including making a quick assessment on whether the concierge could be depended upon to help me out if required.

Finally satisfied, I relaxed in my seat and cautiously watched the front entrance while pretending to read my book. As usual, my suspicions were right when, just before six thirty, a grey-haired man in his early to mid-fifties, wearing a black leather jacket and blue jeans, slowly strolled into the lobby. *That's him! Marković! At last!*

Once he reached the reception desk, he did a mini-twirl towards the lifts and then closely watched a group of strung-out potheads argue with the concierge over the price of some theatre tickets. Figuring that no one was watching him, he reached into his jacket and pulled out a phone. He tapped a few keys, held the phone close to his mouth and then, several seconds later, calmly returned it to his jacket pocket. One of the girls behind reception caught his eye and asked whether she could help him, but he arrogantly ignored her and stormed off towards the bar. As he walked past me, I carefully produced my phone and took a couple of quick photos. Perhaps they would come in handy.

Confident that he didn't see me, I dropped my book back into the plastic bag. Tiny goosebumps snapped at my skin, but I tried to focus on what I had learnt about him so far. First, like me, he knew what he was doing. He had come to the hotel early to take control of his environment. He would undoubtedly pick a table at the bar that suited his needs and afforded him that extra bit of advantage over me. It might be the positioning of the booth or how close to the entrance he would sit in case he had to leave in a hurry.

Second, he had an accomplice. That much was obvious. Who else would he have been talking to? Just a quick call, I imagined, confirming that he was inside the hotel and to remind his accomplice to remain vigilant. 'I will be ready,' he undoubtedly reassured Marković.

Third, I could always tell that someone was dangerous simply by their appearance. Over the years, as I travelled across the world, I had seen every type of cutthroat on offer, and rarely had I been wrong about their intentions. I was under no illusion that this guy looked the business. The arrogant swagger, the black eyes, the scar on his nose. *The scar on his nose. Why does that ring a bell?*

A part of me wanted to leave while I still had the chance, to bring this obsession of mine to a final conclusion and quietly depart Denmark in one piece. But then I realised there was one thing Marković hadn't planned for. *I'm just as smart as he is.*

I lifted myself from the chair and silently walked toward the men's bathroom. Once inside, I found myself an empty cubicle and removed the green jumper I was wearing. After readjusting my t-shirt, I grabbed my Liverpool hoodie and slipped it gently over my head. There. Should something happen to me tonight, everyone at the bar and reception would recall seeing the tall Australian wearing the distinctive red Liverpool hoodie. *Brilliant, even if I say so myself.*

I remained hidden in the cubicle for twenty more minutes before I flushed the toilet and walked back outside. I sent the photos of Marković to one of my rarely used email addresses and then deleted them from my phone. Satisfied that I was ready to go, I said a loud hello to the reception staff so that I was noticed, asked them if they could kindly look after my plastic bag for a while, and then wandered off to the bar to meet Marković.

There he was. Just as I thought, Marković had selected the furthest table from the main bar. His chair also faced the entrance. He wanted full control, as I knew he would. His eyes immediately fixated on me, and I pushed myself confidently towards the spare seat that leant up against the other side of the table.

'Josip?' I casually asked.

'Mr Gerrick, I see,' he replied with a heavy accent. His voice sounded gravelly and strained, definitely not an indication of friendliness. He extended his hand, and I reluctantly accepted. As ultra-tough guys normally did, he squeezed it extra hard to assert his authority over me, but I gave no quarter and squeezed that extra hard back. For a moment, our eyes locked together. He raised a brow in a sign that he had misjudged me already, while I continued to stare at the jagged scar on his nose. *What is it with that scar?*

I slumped into my seat, wary that if I needed to leave quickly, Marković could easily stand in my way. One nil to him. But I would have to manage the situation the best I could.

He clicked his fingers at a waiter and ordered us some drinks. I grabbed another soft drink while he chose a beer. Like Lottie did at dinner, he smirked at my choice and then pointed to my hoodie.

'A Liverpool supporter, my man,' he casually remarked. Somehow, I knew that he had never seen a game of football in his life.

'We all have our burdens.' I smiled back at him.

'I'm a fan, too, my man. We win the title, no?'

'Yes, we did,' I replied, perhaps a little too hastily. Of course, Manchester City won the title this year, not Liverpool, a fact obviously lost on Marković. I was correct in surmising that he had no real interest in football.

'Are you a Croat?' I asked as the waiter delivered our drinks. He took a mouthful of beer and smacked his lips in appreciation before considering me with a frown. 'No, no, no. I am Bosnian, my man,' he defiantly revealed. I pondered how many more times I would allow him to call me 'my man' before he wore my soft drink over his pristine leather jacket.

We made small talk about Copenhagen for several minutes before he folded his arms against his chest. 'Let's get down to business, my man. I understand you are looking for a woman called Martina, who you think was raped during the Bosnian War.'

I stared at him coldly. 'I don't think that she was raped; I know she was raped.'

'She told you this?' he asked brusquely. 'This girl you call Martina?'

'Yes.' I briefly explained to him how I met her on Samos Island, how we quickly became friends, and how, under the pretext of a silly game during a day trip to Ephesus, we agreed to tell each other our biggest secret. While mine was something pithy and disingenuous, hers was a horrific story about mistaken identity and being gang raped by a dozen Serbian soldiers.

When I finished, Marković offered me a callous smirk. 'What's so funny?' I asked him angrily. 'From what I was told, you help women who were raped during the war find justice.'

'Of course,' he replied. 'But I tell you this, my man. After years of bitter experience, it is impossible to believe every story I am told. I normally … how do you say in English? Do my own sniffing around before I decide to take a case like this Martina.' He laughed at his own bellicose response before adding, 'Battling so many governments isn't easy, my man, so these things have to be watertight.'

'That's sensible for a man in your role,' I admitted. 'But I know when someone is lying to me, and I am certain she wasn't.' It was obvious to him that I was getting increasingly pissed off at his attitude, and we both knew that this left him with a distinct advantage over me.

To my surprise, however, Marković suddenly became smirkingly agreeable. 'Please, Mr Gerrick.' He lifted his hands until they touched the top of his chest. 'I do these things for a very long time. Yes? You must excuse me if I sound like a big pain in the arse.'

'Okay,' I grumbled into my drink. 'But you're obviously an important man.' *That's right, stroke his ego, Alex.* 'I was led to believe that you might have come across Martina in the course of your work.'

He launched into his beer for a good ten-second swill. 'In 1997, I meet a woman called Martina in Rome who said she was raped by some Bosnian Serb soldiers. But whether she is your Martina, I am not sure.'

'I have a photo,' I replied hesitantly. I opened the photo app on my phone and then clicked on the only picture I had of her, the one I accidentally took at the Ephesus Amphitheatre on that fateful day she revealed to me about her rape. With my heart bouncing inside my chest, I slid my phone across the table towards Marković. As he picked it up to examine the photo, twenty-seven years of frustration and guilt swelled in my throat.

'A beautiful woman, my man,' Marković said, laughing at his own malice. 'She good in bed, yes? Does things for her man, like a good Bosnian girl?'

I wanted to grab this slimy bastard by the collar and slam his head into the table. But incredibly, I somehow held my nerve and replied, 'She was my friend, nothing more. Now, please take another look at the photo.'

He stared at the picture again for what seemed like an eternity, his trembling fingers scratching at the phone screen. *My God, he recognises her! There is no doubt about it!* I wanted to dance a jig of delight, even for a solitary moment.

'No, no, no,' Marković repeated in a mild panic, placing my phone onto the centre of the table. 'That's no good, my man. It cannot be her.' My body froze deep into my seat as I considered his uncertain response. *He's lying! He must be! I saw it in his eyes! He bloody well knows her!*

'Are you sure?' I pestered him again. I offered him my phone once more. 'Take another look.'

'I don't need to look again! It's not her! I tell you this already! You will believe me now, yes?'

I could tell immediately that Marković was lying, but if he refused to admit that he knew her, what could I do? As much as I wanted to, I couldn't put a gun to his head and force him to tell the truth. Suddenly, I felt like the biggest idiot in the world… and the most impotent. All the money I had spent to make this trip possible, all the lies I told Miriam, all the sleepless nights. And for what? To be screwed around by this deceitful, lying prick.

'I tell you what, my man, I will make some enquiries for you,' he casually blurted out. 'I have many friends who know many people.' He pushed out a piece of paper with his mobile number scribbled across it.

'Send the picture to me now.' I clicked a couple of keys on my phone before both of us heard the inevitable *whoosh*. Some might wonder why I had given a dubious character like Marković my mobile number, but they needn't be concerned. I had sensibly changed SIM cards before I left my hotel room. The number now appearing on his phone was from some local card I bought for ten Euros at reception. When he examined my text message, Marković immediately realised I had tricked him. The resigned nod he offered me almost had a tinge of respect behind it.

'I will be in contact,' he assured me. 'Perhaps we will find your Martina.'

I wanted to tell him to take his phone and shove it up his arse, but sometimes discretion is indeed the best part of valour. 'Yes, perhaps,' I replied seditiously. I got up from my seat to leave, but his steel-like hand gripped my elbow and guided me back to my chair. 'Why are you in a hurry, Mr Gerrick? Finish your drink, and let us talk for a while.'

We looked at each other like two gunslingers squaring up in Dodge City. 'I'm not sure we have anything else to talk about,' I began. 'I'm not all that interesting.'

He laughed. It was a rasping, dangerous laugh, too. 'I think you're wrong, Mr Gerrick. I naturally did my research before I agreed to this meeting.'

'Naturally.'

'If you must know, I find that you're a very interesting man,' he continued. 'Five degrees, including a master's degree acquired in the Philippines. A former military officer, political adviser and senior civil servant. A CEO, mind you, of a charity as well.'

'Congratulations,' I remarked brusquely. 'You've read my profile on social media.'

'And some of the things you experience in your life,' he replied, ignoring my initial riposte.

'Nothing all that important,' I muttered.

'Oh, hardly, my man,' he guffawed. 'Held at gunpoint during a military coup in the Philippines. And shot in the front yard of your house when you were a four-year-old boy.'

For a moment, I wondered how he obtained this information, but I then remembered that an internet search would bring up several videos and podcasts where I discussed these matters openly and in great detail.

'All in the past,' I replied. My right leg began to twitch nervously. *Where the fuck is he going with this?*

'I'm very curious about this shooting,' Marković said, the lines on his face crinkling in cadence. 'Did they ever find the culprits? These bad people who try to kill you?'

A cold sweat dribbled down my forehead. *The Spiders* had used my shooting to blackmail me for years. 'We know who shot you,' Funnel Web Spider, the head of *The Spiders*, had warned me several times whenever I needed to be brought into line. He liked to pretend that they were the only ones standing between me and the shooter. But in the end, I realised that he was lying to me like so many others in my life. Like every other lie he had told me, it was all bullshit designed to control me. But I had escaped from all that nonsense years ago.

'No,' I finally answered. 'Just another mystery that will never be solved.'

Marković laughed again. 'Perhaps you should have asked your father. Anton was his name, yes? A good Chetnik like him. Or did you ask him, and now you want to keep his answer a secret?'

His words tumbled into my face. *My father? Why did he mention my father?* 'I don't know what you are talking about,' I replied. 'My father has been dead for over thirty years.'

'Yes, he died from cancer, didn't he? Very sad, my man.'

Marković had finally succeeded in unnerving me, which I guess was always his intention. It was obvious to me that his entire persona was a ruse. Oh, the social worker malarky might have been a successful cover story, but most likely, he worked for an unfriendly spy agency or perhaps a highly sophisticated criminal organisation. In the end, did it even really matter? On the basis that he already knew too much about my life, it was time to leave before the walls permanently closed around me. I had a wife, a dog, an extended family and lots of friends who cared for me. My main priority now was to get back to them safely. However, there was one last thing I had to test just to confirm my suspicions.

'I need to take a leak,' I told Marković as I carefully stood up, my hands slightly shaking. He stared at me as if his entire plan had now come crashing down on top of him. 'Please,' I said politely. 'I have to go. I will be right back.' He grunted something underneath his breath, moved his chair to allow me to pass, and I stumbled briskly towards the toilet.

Once inside, I splashed water over my face and counted to thirty. I realised that leaving my glass unattended in any European bar was extremely risky. But there was a method to my madness. If he insisted immediately when I returned that I finish my drink, then it was very likely that during my absence, he had slipped me a drug like Rohypnol. That would then confirm that this whole meeting had been a set-up from the start. For Lottie's safety, that was something I desperately needed to know.

I returned several minutes later, whereupon Marković immediately ushered me to my seat. He didn't waste another second. 'Why not finish your drink, and I will get you another, my man?' Bingo. *As usual, my instincts were correct.*

'I think it's time for me to leave, Mr Marković.' I managed a courageous smile. 'I have another appointment at eight o'clock, and if I don't turn up, there will no doubt be hell to pay.'

'What is the harm of finishing your drink?' he insistently asked again.

'Oh, I think we both know the answer to that, don't we?'

The jig was up, and we both knew it. This time, Marković dispensed with all the niceties. 'You should have stayed in Australia, Mr Gerrick. Poking your nose into things you don't understand is really stupid.' His legs now braced against mine, and for the first time that evening, I was afraid that he would use physical violence against me. 'Now, once again, you must finish your drink.'

Of course, I didn't appreciate it at the time, but it's amazing how the odd coincidence can change the fate of your entire life. Here I was, threatened with violence and with no obvious way out, when, from nowhere, a rather buxom blonde walked straight into my line of sight. Without hesitating, I leapt from my seat in a single bound and grabbed the blonde by the arm before she had time to protest.

'Agnetha!' I cried out. 'Fancy meeting you here!'

She gave me a quizzical stare before her face flushed in recognition. 'Oh, Alex! How nice to see you.'

While keeping a wary eye on Marković, I guided Agnetha to the bar, my hands gently brushing the side of her leg. Yes, I was trying to mark my territory like any man looking for a night of fun would, without being too obvious about it. If Agnetha took offence, she could sue me for sexual harassment afterwards, providing Marković hadn't killed me first. 'Would you like a drink?' I eventually asked in a pathetically disguised suggestive tone.

'Er, I am waiting for some people from the conference.' She seemed reluctant to indulge me at first, but when she saw the stress in my eyes, she instantaneously nodded her head. 'But I am sure we have time for one.'

While we walked arm in arm to a spare table on the other side of the bar, I turned to face Marković once again. His demonic eyes were glaring at me with intense hatred, his head seconds away from bursting into flames. A waiter took our order, and I pretended to listen as Agnetha prattled excitedly about her day. Given how many times her panty-hosed legs seemed to rub up against mine, I realised that my invitation for a drink had worked better than I ever expected. Hoping to keep the pretence up as long as I could until Marković left the bar, I did my best to act interested as she bombarded me with several anecdotes about several people in Stockholm whom I would never meet.

Twenty minutes passed, and Marković was still irrationally glued to his seat. His face had now turned a morose shade of purple, and if looks could kill, I would have been dead already. Even so, I now began to panic, realising that once Agnetha's friends arrived, my excuse for a one-on-one conversation would evaporate. I would be back to being inside the bar by myself, an easy target for Marković's next move.

However, when her friends started to arrive minutes later, Agnetha begged me to stay, and so I quickly made myself the life of the party. When I needed to be the life of the party, I could come out with the bullshit in spades. Happily, in the middle of these celebrations, Marković threw a paper napkin onto the floor in exasperation and then angrily stomped towards reception. He seemed a beaten man. Job done.

Unsurprisingly, I didn't take things for granted. I stayed with Agnetha and her friends for another hour before I excused myself to go to the bathroom. On the way, I passed through reception and reclaimed my plastic bag. I casually swapped jumpers once inside the bathroom and then flicked out my phone to check my messages. As expected, there was an unread message from Marković.

'Go back to Australia, Mr Gerrick, before you regret it.'

My response was brief but straight to the point.

'Fuck you, my man.'

After I sent the message, I double-checked that I had forwarded his photos to my email address and then ripped out the temporary SIM card. Twirling it between my fingers for old times' sake, I quickly flushed it down the toilet and slipped my normal SIM card back into my phone. Once I was online, I nonchalantly walked out the front entrance of the hotel, keeping my eyes focused on any inconsistencies.

It wasn't hard to find him. Middle Eastern in appearance, he was a smallish man, perhaps no taller than one hundred and seventy centimetres, with a distinctive mohawk haircut and a three-day growth. He was standing about two hundred metres along the road, sipping on a soft drink, pretending, I guessed, to be waiting for a friend. As if by instinct, he casually turned his head towards me, gave me a cursory glance, and then became distracted by a pretty young woman walking her dog. Of course, he was waiting for a man leaving the hotel wearing a distinctive red Liverpool FC hoodie, not a dark green jumper, and having been your typical run-of-the-mill henchman, he wasn't smart enough to notice my plastic bag and discern what might be inside it.

But just to be sure that I was not getting too cocky, I circumnavigated the block where the hotel stood and then backtracked my movements. When I approached the hotel from the opposite direction, I found the henchman staring blankly into thin air. Satisfied that I was in the clear, I hailed a taxi, and ten minutes later, I slumped on my bed, an ice-cold sweat pouring down the back of my neck. I wanted to be sick, but I calmly swallowed some painkillers, reached for my phone and belted out a text with trembling fingers.

> 'Lottie, meeting didn't go to plan. Marković not trustworthy. Break off all contact. Alex.'

I waited for an hour, glued to my bed, every crazy, paranoid scenario playing out inside my head. Finally, she replied.

> 'I'm so sorry, Alex. Don't worry about me. Forget about Martina and return safely to Australia. Take care. L.'

I sat underneath the hot shower for fifteen minutes, tried to watch CNN and then somehow drifted off to sleep. I dreamt of monsters, huge flesh-eating spiders, large rivers of blood and my father crying out to me from another world. When I woke up just after two in the morning, I pulled my sheet around my naked chest and suddenly remembered the significance of the scar on Marković's nose. Now that it all made sense, I wondered how I would have a peaceful sleep ever again.

Chapter Four

Canberra, Australia
September 2022

Once the storm finally ends, Louie emerges from his slumber and demands to go outside. We creep through the back security screen together, his twitchy nose ever alert for any scrap of food that might be lying around. While he does his business, I think back once more to the events in Copenhagen.

After I worked out Marković's true identity on that fateful morning, I had this absurd desire to track him down and make him pay for what he did. But if I understood how he worked, he would have caught the first plane from Copenhagen to whatever destination he now called his home. There was a reason why he didn't want to be found, why he wanted to meet in a city like Copenhagen, and we both knew it.

Rather, I had spent that Friday, my last day in Denmark, like the anonymous tourist I always should have been. I walked down to the Little Mermaid, took a few selfies, and then posted them on social media. I caught a tourist bus back to the Tivoli Gardens and pigged out on more hotdogs, cream puffs and fairy floss. Later that evening, I picked the most expensive restaurant I could find and celebrated my stay with all the arrogance of a self-delusional fool.

Over the next few days, I quietly made my way back to Australia. The trip, for the most part, had been a disaster, and I knew that it was time to draw a line in the sand. As much as Martina's story still ripped at my heart, I finally had to put this obsession behind me. There were far too many people like Marković in the world, trying to hide their dirty secrets, and I was too old and too tired to take them all on by myself. Besides, I was now confronted with another mystery that began to consume me during the flight home.

Even when I was safely ensconced in Canberra, I couldn't let it go. My shooting, as a four-year-old, had set in train a series of events that had shaped my life; it had been like a prison sentence from which I could never escape.

I never believed that the shooting was an accident. Even at a young age, I knew there was more to the story; something my parents or the police weren't telling me. However, I never once made a specific connection to my father or his wartime service. Surely, too many years had passed for anyone to delve deeper into these allegations. After all, I was just a lonely kid in a town that time had now forgotten.

No, I couldn't possibly investigate such a complex mystery by myself— not after the personal tribulations involving my empty search for Martina. But shortly after I arrived back in Australia, in the middle of my daily walk with Louie, I suddenly thought of my friend Belinda.

I first met Belinda Rice at a PTSD conference in 2018. The two of us had shared a podium together during a plenary session on the importance of exercise and diet in PTSD management. We had hit it off immediately. Over time, we became good friends. I learnt more about her stellar career as a detective in the New South Wales Police Force and grew to admire her passion and integrity. Belinda had been involved in several high-profile criminal cases and was destined for higher promotion before she retired early as a result of her own battles with PTSD. Since leaving the police force, she had graced the speaker circuit, encouraging people through her own lived experience to act quickly over mental health issues.

At first, I didn't know how to broach the topic with Belinda. But after several cups of coffee at a little café in Sydney, I casually raised my story with her. The fires of intrigue immediately filled her startling blue eyes, and I knew that she was about to grasp my predicament with both hands. 'Everything can be investigated,' she reassured me as she sipped her water several times. Who was I to contradict one of New South Wales' top police investigators?

And so, the wheels were in motion, and despite my previous vows, I would soon return to Europe and pick up the trail once more. As always in my life, before I could finish one story, I had to start another.

Part Two

Private Investigations

Chapter One

Dubrovnik, Croatia
October 2022

I think it was George Bernard Shaw who once wrote, 'If you want to see Heaven on Earth, come to Dubrovnik.' His eternal words aside, there can be little doubt that this beautiful historical city, tucked beneath the sanctuary of the Dinaric Alps, is the sparkling jewel of Dalmatia, thought to be the most scenic stretch of coastline in all of Europe.

But, of course, I was incredibly biased. After all, Dubrovnik was in my blood, a beguiling heritage bequeathed from my father that I could never escape; an irresistible force that kept calling me back year after year and would probably do so until the day I died. Dubrovnik, despite its hidden secrets, was my spiritual home, the only place in the world where everything in my life made perfect sense.

Stretching out a stiff back courtesy of the short flight from Athens, I muttered something to myself as I twisted my way through the packed Dubrovnik airport in search of my driver. I quickly manoeuvred my head in between a pair of muscular Greek surfers and targeted a tall, gangly kid carrying a white cardboard sign with '***Alex Gerrick***' scrawled in thick, black pen. When I made myself known to him, the kid excitedly shook my hand and proudly introduced himself as Luka.

'Just like Luka Modric, the football player,' he beamed, just in case I didn't know the identity of Croatia's most famous sportsman. We walked slowly together towards the Aegean Airways baggage reclaim area and waited several minutes before my blue suitcase came tumbling down the conveyor belt. After flexing his muscular arms, Luka grabbed my bag in one swoop. Soon, we were driving down the main road towards Dubrovnik in his shiny black SUV.

To help pass the time, he pressed a few buttons on the dashboard, and the raucous sound of a local Croatian punk rock band screamed out from his car's twin speakers. 'You like?' he asked hopefully. To his relief, I nodded politely. Of course, the music was plain ugly to me, but it was way too late in the day to start offending the locals.

Instead, I found other distractions to pass the time, given that the trip from the airport to Dubrovnik was one of the most scenic drives in the world. As Luka steered the SUV past a series of winding, weather-beaten cliffs, my eyes became transfixed on the crystal-clear ocean glittering in the late afternoon sunshine. Then, as if by providence, the scene I had been waiting for with anticipation since I left the airport unfolded before me. Yes! There it was in the distance! The grey walls of the Old Town glistened like diamonds inside a delicate blue sky, welcoming me back after three years of travel restrictions and Covid insanity.

'I never get tired of that view, Mr Alex,' Luka said with an unworldly grin.

'Me neither, mate,' I replied truthfully.

As if to signify this experience with the dignity it deserved, Luka suddenly turned off the excruciating Croatian punk music. We both stared wondrously into the distance, two strangers uniquely bonded by Dubrovnik's exquisite magic.

During my last visit to Dubrovnik in April 2019, I stayed several nights at the wonderfully luxurious Hilton Imperial Hotel, barely five hundred metres from the Pile Gate, the main entrance to the Old Town. However, as much as it was my favourite hotel in the world, my needs on this trip were vastly different. I needed somewhere less tourist-focused and more private, a place where I could come and go as I pleased and not be beholden to the demands and inanities of other people.

Luckily, Dubrovnik was full of spectacular self-contained villas that could give me everything I needed. For several weeks, I had been tracking various options on my large collection of hotel apps before finally settling on Villa Spirac, located near the entrance of the famous Dubrovnik cable car. The feedback from patrons on the hotel sites was incredibly positive, and when I booked an apartment for four nights, something in my heart convinced me that this was *the* place.

'You will love your room!' Luka reassured me. 'The views from the balcony of the Old Town and the ocean are simply amazing!' Given the sincerity of his enthusiastic smile, I had no reason to disbelieve him.

After Luka dropped me off outside the villa, I was greeted by Filip Spirac, a typically handsome Croat in his early thirties. His tanned, chiselled face offered a welcoming smile as he lifted my luggage. Filip beckoned me down a flight of concrete steps and through a security gate. After showing me the numerical code for my apartment several times, he quietly invited me inside and allowed me to take stock of my surroundings.

What could I say? Everything I read from satisfied customers didn't come close to doing the apartment justice. The layout was large and modern, while the kitchen and lounge room contained every gizmo and contraption you could ever imagine, including two large TVs, a myriad of different blenders and a snazzy high-tech stove, which you needed a university degree to work out. Although Luka had prewarned me, it took me several more hours before I could begin to fully appreciate the spellbinding view of the Adriatic Sea from the apartment's balcony. It was a picture that could have been painted by van Gogh himself.

Filip took me through the six million channels on the TV before providing a thirty-second rundown of the local restaurants and a nearby convenience store where I could buy everyday necessities like milk and bread. We swapped numbers on WhatsApp, and he reminded me, one last time, to call him if I needed any assistance.

Once Filip left, I shuffled some clothes from my suitcase into the bedroom wardrobe, charged my phone for fifteen minutes, and then slipped my leather jacket over a crumpled black t-shirt. After running a dry razor over my chin, I collected my phone, double-checked that I had locked the security gate properly and stumbled into a cool Dubrovnik autumn evening.

The initial part of my journey took me past dozens of goggle-eyed tourists, the cable car entrance and several enticing bars and cafés. At one point, I flirted with the alluring aroma of a rustic-looking pizza bar decked out with dark blue drapes and black tinted windows but dutifully resisted the temptation for other delicacies that awaited me in the Old Town.

When I reached the fire station at the bottom of the street, I made a sharp left turn and walked through an underpass before reaching the top of Ulica Svetoga Dominika. I tentatively stared down the hundreds of steps that would guide me into the Old Town itself, conscious that walking up and down flights of ancient stairs was all part of the unique Dubrovnik experience. Unperturbed, I flexed my leg muscles as if I was about to commence a marathon, ran a hand through my hair and, five minutes later, found myself mingling among hundreds of other tourists out for a fun night.

First stop, as always, was the beautiful St Blaise's Church, where I briefly prayed to the Holy Mother for her protection and wisdom during my stay in Croatia. Once satisfied that all was well with my inner spirit, I checked out a couple of nearby restaurants before settling on a bistro that served most of the traditional Croatian fare that I usually loved. A pretty young waitress wearing cut-off blue jeans and a white tank top immediately offered me a seat outside, and to her amusement, I quickly ordered some *ćevapi*—a traditional Balkan dish of minced meat beloved by all Slavs— before she had time to even offer me a menu. Content with everything so far, I sipped at my sparkling mineral water and casually watched the nighttime shadows as they bounced along the shiny pavement.

I don't know why I suddenly became so obsessed with the Australian family of four sitting at the table next to me, munching on several large pizzas. Maybe it was their constant farting and burping. Or maybe it was because they collectively reminded me of something from a B grade horror movie.

Look, whenever I am overseas, I try very hard to avoid other Australians, and I never, never eavesdrop on personal conversations. But on this occasion, the urge to pry simply overwhelmed me. The mum and dad, both in their late thirties, uncannily resembled the pizzas they were eating—large, oily and very thick in the middle. The daughter, probably around eight or nine, would undoubtedly become a lovely-looking young woman one day if only she avoided all the carbohydrates her mother was force-feeding her.

'You are never going to have a great figure and become a film star if you don't eat your plate of chips,' the mum declared angrily. As parenting goes, this was a pretty low comment to make to your eight-year-old daughter.

But it was the son and his loud, whiny pre-teen complaining that really put me into a foul mood.

'I want to see the Walk of Shame,' he kept insisting to his parents while streams of soft drink dribbled down his stained, white t-shirt. 'Do you hear me? I want to see the Walk of Shame! Now!'

For those who have never watched *Game of Thrones*, it might do well to explain that many of the King's Landing scenes in the mega-series were filmed in Dubrovnik. Probably the show's most famous scene occurred in Season Five, when arch-villainess Cersei, played by the beautiful English actress Lena Headey, was forced to walk naked amongst a baying crowd of onlookers as punishment for her many crimes. The actual walk itself commences at the top of the elegant Jesuit Staircase, situated on the south side of Gundalic Square, and winds through some of the city's most scenic streets. Thanks to this wonderful television series (yes, I am a huge fan), it is now probably one of the most famous and alluring walks in Europe.

Perhaps I was overreacting, but the smell of the family's hillbilly farts and the kid's constant, loud moaning made me feel nauseous, so I wondered whether I should restart the evening elsewhere. But as I contemplated my next move, I wanted to rail against the ignorance of every tourist who visited Dubrovnik for the wrong reasons. As much as it's all-important to celebrate local success stories like *Game of Thrones*, it should never be at the expense of the city's extravagant beauty and history.

As I grizzled into my drink, I realised that most of the tourists around me were nothing more than characters in a sideshow. Dubrovnik was always destined for the glitz and glamour, even when it was under threat by its enemies. It was a place where dreams were made and destinies fulfilled. It was also a city that somehow transcended the historical events that swirled around it.

Most historians agree that Dubrovnik was established in the seventh century by settlers seeking sanctuary from the Barbarians. It soon became an independent and prosperous sea-trading city, even when bludgeoned by local bullies, such as those power-hungry Venetians from across the Adriatic Sea. By the mid-fifteenth century, it had repositioned itself as the capital of the Republic of Ragusa, complete with its own flag, currency and army. It also became a place where literature, the arts and architecture prospered. Put simply, it was the centre of culture in a region known for its backward, violent way of life.

Both the Ottomans and Venetians eventually coveted Dubrovnik's strategic position on the Adriatic Sea as they battled each other for hegemony in the area. Then a devastating earthquake in 1667 virtually destroyed the entire city, and it subsequently slipped into a period of destitution and poverty.

Next came Napoleon Bonaparte and his destructive European wars. For a time, the city was occupied by the French, losing forever its unique status as an independent city state. After Bonaparte's defeat at Waterloo, Dubrovnik was merged into the Kingdom of Dalmatia, serving fealty to the Austro-Hungarian Empire until the end of the First World War.

By the end of the nineteenth century, Serbia—which had won its full independence from the Ottoman Turks in 1878—was leading a push to bring all Serbs living in the Austro-Hungarian Empire under its control. Serbian settlements stretched throughout different parts of wider Croatia, as well as Bosnia, which Austria-Hungary had annexed for themselves from the fading Ottoman Empire in 1908.

Tensions were running high in the region as Serbia acquired more territory during the Balkan Wars of 1912-13 while happily fermenting internal unrest in Bosnia with its latent support of pro-Serbian terrorist groups opposed to Austro-Hungarian rule. Around the same time, various political activists began discussing the potential unification of all Slavs in the region—Serbs, Bosnians, Croats, Slovenes and Montenegrins—under a Serbian monarchy. How that was going to work, God only knew.

The region ultimately became a tinderbox of intrigue, and it only needed one spark to ignite a catastrophe. That spark was lit in Sarajevo on 28 June 1914, when Gavrilo Princip, a young Bosnian with links to Narodna Odbrana, a Serbian nationalist group, assassinated the heir to the Austrian crown, Archduke Franz Ferdinand, and his wife, Sophie, precipitating a mad sleepwalk into Hell called the First World War.

This was the world at play when my father Anton was born in Dubrovnik on 8 March 1914, three months before Princip's fatal call. Understanding these political machinations and the influence they eventually had on my father was the main reason I had chosen to start my Croatian journey in Dubrovnik. Although there was already much I knew about Dad's early life, I wanted to confront the intricacies of Dubrovnik's past in the forlorn hope that more of his secrets would be revealed.

My ancestry on Dad's side was indeed a fascinating one; a mixture of diverse cultures and beliefs all melded into one beguiling storyline. Like generations before him, my grandfather—Dad's father—was born on the beautiful and historic Island of Korcula, situated about one hundred kilometres north of Dubrovnik. Renowned mainly for its hard-nosed seafarers and stonemasons, Korcula also boasts an impressive cultural history, producing many famous local artists and musicians. Having visited Korcula several times, all I ever saw were men who looked exactly like me—tall, lean and tanned, brushed with an aura of unstated self-confidence.

Despite my obvious Slavic attributes, people sometimes mistook me for an Italian. Therefore, I wasn't entirely surprised when I recently discovered that I had Italian ancestors on Dad's side of the family, who came from Venice. My oldest sister, Dubravka, and I also learnt through DNA testing that we possessed Iranian genes as well, a by-product, we think, of what was once a flourishing Slavic community inside the Persian Empire. So, if one needed any more proof, I was the ultimate mongrel; a fascinating human melting pot of Slavic, Italian and Iranian blood— no wonder life had been so damn confusing!

Dad's lineage was also blessed with generations of artistic talent. My great-grandfather, for instance, was a renowned local artist who acquired a handsome reputation for his exquisite religious frescos. From an early age, his son—my grandfather—also showed a remarkable talent for both painting and sculpting. Such was his ability that in his late teens, he was awarded a scholarship to study in Florence. There, he continued to develop his skills under the supervision of some highly regarded tutors before finally deciding to focus his life's work on his true love, the delicate world of sculptures.

He quietly emerged as one of Dalmatia's brightest young talents, much to the delight of his family. To enhance his career, he left Korcula and settled in Dubrovnik, where he eventually met my grandmother. After an appropriate courtship, they married and had three children, all two years apart; Ina, the oldest girl; my dad Anton, who was the middle child; and Lucia, the youngest.

In 2001, after I completed my master's degree in the Philippines, I travelled to Croatia for the first time and met my Aunt Lucia in the beautiful seaside resort town of Cavtat, a thirty-minute car ride south of Dubrovnik. She was eighty-five years old at the time, a wonderfully robust and kind woman who cried tears of joy when she met me and then wouldn't let go of my hand until it was time for me to leave. Through my cousin Chistina, who spoke perfect English, I was able to glean some fragments about Dad's early life.

Dubrovnik was thankfully immune from the worst of the violence during the First World War. Even so, much of Dalmatia experienced significant economic hardship throughout those years, and life inevitably became a struggle for survival. Although my grandmother came from a well-to-do family, she and Grandad apparently lived a simple existence, doing their best to become financially independent through what Grandad earned through his sculptures and tutoring. As was the case with most Croats, day-to-day life consisted of your obligations to the family and the Catholic church. If you remained faithful to both institutions, happiness was surely guaranteed.

For a brief period, at least, life for the family was as good as it could have been under the circumstances. Grandad and Grandma loved each other and their children dearly. The family eventually settled in Cavtat and found a comfortable apartment near the town square. They had sufficient money to put food on the table, clothe the children and give what little was left to the church. If they could hold on until the war was over, then better times surely lay ahead.

Then, just before Lucia was born in 1916, the family was touched by tragedy. On a peaceful, sunny morning, Grandma and Grandad took Ina and my father for a quiet walk along the beach. It was a family ritual, a routine zealously kept several times a week. As always, Grandma, who was heavily pregnant with Lucia, shuffled slowly with careful steps, hand-in-hand with Ina, while Dad and Grandad drifted ahead of them, eager to see the early morning tide crash into the waiting rocks. For a moment, Grandma lost sight of her husband and son as they disappeared behind a bend in the coastline. When she reached that same position with Ina minutes later, the boys were nowhere to be seen. This had never happened before. Where were they?

As time melted inside a glaring sun, Grandma grew more frantic as she ploughed her naked feet into the warm sand, a confused Ina pulling at her skirt. Suddenly, she saw a figure in the distance slumped on the ground. When she and Ina staggered forward to investigate, they found Grandad's lifeless body pointed at the sea, his two-year-old son crawling happily over his spindly legs, a new game to be enjoyed as the excited seagulls screeched above him. Grandad had died of a heart attack, aged only thirty-three.

Back in the present, I paid my bill, and with the nighttime breeze caressing my face, I slowly headed back to Villa Spirac. In front of me, a young Croatian girl with gloriously tanned legs deliberately spilt some ice cream over her boyfriend's arm and giggled wickedly while an old woman wearing a crimson scarf cried bleakly at the half-crescent moon.

I thought back to my dad as a toddler on that lonely beach playing with his dead father and reminded myself of my own traumas as a child and how they impacted my life. As my therapist Roy used to say, most people carry their childhood traumas with them into adulthood without truly understanding the consequences. How a person responds to this realisation is critical to sustaining a happy life.

In my case, I had spent most of my adult existence pretending that certain things never happened and nearly paid a hefty price. But how Dad reacted to his father's death remained a mystery to me; he never once discussed his childhood, nor did I ever expect him to. He simply wasn't the type of man to release his burdens on another person. That would be admitting failure, and men from my father's generation viewed failure as a weakness.

Even so, perhaps the trajectory of his early life revealed some worthwhile clues. Forever heartbroken by the loss of her one true love, Grandma never remarried. It was said that before she died, she had asked to be buried next to Grandad in the local Cavtat cemetery with a small brown box. Inside were bundles of love letters that the pair had written to each other before and during their marriage.

Her devotion struck at a vulnerability hidden by the passing of time, but she was also a strong woman who sacrificed everything for her children. Luckily, Grandma's family was able to provide her with the financial support she needed to raise her family. However, life would never be the same again, especially after the war finally ended in 1918, and the Slavic states, courtesy of the Treaty of Versailles, amalgamated into one country, which would eventually be called Yugoslavia.

As Lucia explained, the loss of Grandma's beloved husband at such an early age made Dad the centre of the family's attention. As he moved into his teenage years, Grandma doted on him incessantly, providing him with the love and affection she knew he needed if he was to succeed in life.

Despite his mother's support, my father enjoyed living life on the edge. Everyone seemed beguiled by his charisma, his sporting prowess and his ability to talk himself in and out of trouble with relative ease. But Dad's lifetime weaknesses—his penis and an inability to handle money—already began to emerge as a teenager. In the future, there would be accusations of stealing, gambling debts and affairs with older married women. Even as a seventeen-year-old, having been told all his life how special he was, Dad couldn't resist the youthful temptations that greeted him wherever he dared look, even if it meant upsetting his beloved mother. Consequences never mattered to him because God would always find a way to make it right. Luckily, he had one ace up his sleeve—the navy. The decision to join the armed forces almost certainly kept him out of jail.

As my eyes drew westward towards the unforgiving darkness of the ocean, I remembered how Dad would angrily lecture me over my own childish transgressions with that deep, menacing voice that I grew to fear. There was the *Penthouse* magazine he found underneath my mattress, the time I failed a maths exam in Year Five and the bottle of Jim Beam bourbon whiskey someone had hidden in my school bag. In many ways, he acted like the moral guardian of the universe, a figure of virtue and integrity I was meant to follow for my own salvation. So, it was especially ironic when I discovered before he died that many of his own personal intrigues were fallacies he had created inside an unwieldy imagination aimed at justifying his hypocrisy.

After I entered my apartment, I poured myself a glass of water and quietly strolled onto the balcony. The dizzying lights of Dubrovnik began to dance across my naked arms as I casually slumped onto a deckchair.

I love Dubrovnik so much, I reminded myself as I watched a falling star disappear into the horizon. For some reason, I thought about my father once more and the many secrets he had kept from me. How often did I curse his name so I could justify my own frustrations with the world?

There were times shortly before his death when I caught him glancing in another direction after I asked him an important question. Whether he was hiding something to protect me from an unforeseen evil, I could never tell, but I always retained the feeling that there were parts of his life he didn't want to remember himself.

What was that famous old saying from Winston Churchill about the Soviet Union? *A riddle wrapped inside an enigma.* I began to laugh. Yes, that described Dad perfectly. But with so much of that riddle still tightly guarded, I knew that I could never rest until the secrets it jealously guarded were finally revealed. Whatever I hoped to find in Dubrovnik, I prayed that I would find it soon.

Chapter Two

Dubrovnik, Croatia
October 2022

I woke up the next morning just in time to witness a flock of seagulls initiate a series of intricate somersaults outside my bedroom window. Still half-asleep, I casually opened the balcony door and was immediately entranced by the beautiful, cloudless Dubrovnik morning. After a quick shower, I helped myself to a bowl of local cereal that I bought from the convenience store and then quaffed down a couple of fresh blueberry muffins. I thought about making myself an instant coffee but decided to finally get off my arse and get a proper one in the Old Town. *Life is too short to waste on shit coffee.*

Fifteen minutes later, I ordered an extra-hot flat white from a little takeaway café at the bottom of Ulica Svetoga Dominika, then found an empty seat near the Revelin Fortress, overlooking the city's main harbour—another *Game of Thrones* landmark. I spent the next half-hour clearing those overnight messages on my phone and watching the early morning ferries dart across the calm tabletop ocean.

Not long afterwards, I walked back to the Pile Gate and paid the standard two hundred Kuna entrance fee to access Dubrovnik's famous old walls. Yes, more bloody steps to negotiate, but I knew that it was all part of the experience. When I reached the top of the stairs and took a moment to consider the bewildering view of the ocean and Old Town that greeted me, the nerve-splitting pain in my legs was immediately forgotten. Satisfied with my morning's work, I gathered my bearings and treaded slowly towards Fort Bokar as an increasingly hot sun gnawed at the back of my neck.

Before I knew it, I was surrounded by a group of excited tourists, many of whom were experiencing this amazing spectacle for the first time. For a moment, I became jealous of their astonished cries, of their sudden realisation that they were indeed witnessing the true hand of God. To escape their wretchedness, I made good time towards a small bar at the top of the wall, where I rewarded myself with an ice-cold mineral water. Having frequented the bar many times before, I knew exactly where to find a lonely patch of railing that overlooked the ocean. Soon, I was stretching my legs towards the fierce morning sunshine.

The Adriatic Sea was everything to the inhabitants of Dubrovnik. It guided the city's culture, history, successes and failures. It also gave those who honoured its sanctity endless opportunities if they were brave enough to take the risk. Thankfully, Dad had heeded its call and, for a while at least, grabbed his own opportunity with both hands.

Dad believed that there was little difference between a life of crime and the pursuit of military service; in both scenarios, he once explained, you take orders from those higher in the food chain, you relentlessly pursue your mission to the end, and then you ask no questions afterwards. Notwithstanding the irony, the navy actually worked for Dad and undoubtedly set him on a more virtuous path.

For the first time in his life, he was given a structure, a purpose, a way forward. Supremely talented with his hands and a mechanical genius in the making, Dad prospered in the navy from an early age. Training as a marine engineer, he completed his apprenticeship with flying colours. Although Dad served on many different vessels, he once told me that he loved working on destroyers the most. There was something noble about serving on a destroyer that he couldn't explain, but his eyes lit up whenever he spoke about his experiences at sea. While he was never one for specifics, I was able to glean that he had sailed back and forth across the Mediterranean several times, battled a hurricane off the Scottish Coast and wined and dined beautiful French women while on leave in Marseille.

A talented sportsman and a strong swimmer, Dad represented his country at water polo and played competitive soccer. Stirringly handsome and dashing, with deadly hazel eyes and an impressive mane of thick black hair, he was the life of every party, a man dedicated to the women who flocked to him in droves. He had the world at his feet, confirmed by his eventual appointment to the officer ranks. You could argue that Dad became the epitome of the local Dalmatian made good, a new breed of Croat that was out to take on the world.

So why the fuck did he join the Serbian Chetniks during the Second World War?

Specks of yellow light bounced off the table towards me, so I pulled out some sunburn cream from my pocket and applied a tiny squirt onto my face. Identity was everything in the mad world of Balkan politics. If you were a Croat, if you were a Serb, if you were a Slovene, it all meant something different. But Dad clearly wanted to be someone else, and I could never understand why.

I paid my bill and stepped cautiously around an Italian family taking snaps of the city's ageing rooftops. Whatever the reasons for Dad's identity crisis, it somehow had followed me for much of my life. Growing up with a funny-sounding wog name made me the subject of pitiless jokes and, dare I say it, just a little prejudice and bullying. I mostly laughed it off, of course; I wanted to be accepted, and sometimes to do that, you had to dispense with your vanity and learn to play along. But during college, the jokes became a little too personal, and I started to erroneously believe that every misfortune that came my way was because of my unique background.

When I reached my twenties, I decided to do something about it. I was now master of my own destiny, and I was convinced that to get ahead in life, I had to first anglicise my identity. 'Gerrick' sounded so much better than a funny-sounding Yugoslav surname. But all this did was add to the confusion I was experiencing. *Am I a Yugoslav, an Australian or a Croat? Who the fuck knew anymore?* And when the Wars of Independence broke out in the former Yugoslavia in 1991, all I could do was sit back and wonder whether I, too, was at war with myself.

Then along came *The Spiders*. I was in my late twenties, living in Brisbane when they first approached me. I was on the verge of a new life I had created for myself after years of neglect and failure, so their intervention came at an opportune time. They promised to mentor me and open the doors for guaranteed success as long as I moved to Canberra. Once I arrived in Australia's capital several months later, they revitalised my public service career, supported my pursuit of an army reserve commission and showed me a future of endless possibilities should I stay true to their cause.

It all seemed so innocent at first; writing policy papers in my spare time, helping their migrant colleagues assimilate to the Australian way of life, doing the odd job while on holidays overseas. Then, in 1997, they ordered me to deliver some business documents to a colleague in Belgrade, Serbia's capital city. The trip involved catching a train from my base in Vienna to the Hungarian capital of Budapest, where I would then obtain a fast-tracked Serbian visa before proceeding to Belgrade. I had just completed a two-week tour of Eastern Europe with my girlfriend at the time, Rachel, and we had decided to separate for a few days before meeting up again in Paris. I had the perfect opportunity to make a mad dash to Belgrade, and no one would have known otherwise.

As I made my way towards the Serbian Embassy in Budapest that fateful morning, my stomach churned with fear. Was I really going through with this? Every doubt about my heritage, every confused thought I had since I was a child, flooded my brain. When I finally reached the embassy security gate, I took one look at the burly Serbian soldier on guard, mysteriously connected with his black, threatening eyes, then turned on my heels and ran away as fast as I could. When I reached the entrance to my hotel some ten minutes later, I couldn't tell whether I had run away from my newfound fears or had simply run away from my past.

Later, I made some pithy excuse to *The Spiders* about being struck with a stomach virus, and they arranged for another courier to deliver the documents. I may have fooled them, but the entire episode reinforced the confusion I felt about who I was, as well as the underlying impact of my father's legacy. I knew that one day, I would have to atone for his sins or forever become a slave to my own.

Chapter Three

Dubrovnik, Croatia
October 2022

After I finished exploring Dubrovnik's walled city, I grabbed some lunch at an Italian restaurant before returning to Villa Spirac. During my short walk home, my thoughts suddenly turned to Martina, as they often did when I went searching for my soul. Out of nowhere, her beautiful, lonely face soon became my erstwhile companion. Everywhere I turned, every young woman I passed along the way bore a mystical resemblance to her.

That long black hair that swept the crevice of her back, those dark liquid eyes that scrutinised your every thought, those slender, long legs that left you wanting for more. Like a Homerian siren, she was everywhere but nowhere, a fallen bystander along the road to purgatory. For even here in Dubrovnik, I could not seem to escape her memories nor her vengeance, and I began to wonder whether she was trapped with my father beyond a fallen star, their heads shaking in laughter, plotting the next stage of my inevitable demise.

Later that afternoon, I contacted a man called Bruno, who agreed to show me some of the local sites made famous thirty years ago during the Homeland War. I wanted to understand the mindset of a Dubrovnik citizen during wartime, their motivations, their belief systems and why they fought with such passion and intensity. I also hoped that a man of Bruno's experience could provide some crucial insights into why someone like Dad spurned his ancestry during the Second World War and fought for an opposing cause.

That night, I dreamt about Martina. I was resting on a seat near

Revelin Fortress, staring into the cobalt-blue sea, when out of nowhere, a young woman began to hover innocently above the water's edge. As I admired her ghostly beauty, she carefully lifted her white dress towards the sun and, without saying a word, floated onto the seat next to me. At first, I didn't recognise her beneath the crimson veil that covered her face, but once she grew into the sunlight, I finally remembered that beautiful smile.

'Hello, Alex,' she said softly.

'Hello, Martina,' I replied. 'You have come back for me.'

'But I never left you.' She placed a hand on my knee, and I began to shiver at the coldness of her touch. 'You believe that, don't you?'

'I'm not sure of anything anymore,' I protested.

'But I am telling you the truth.' She repeated those words over and over again until I finally relented.

'I believe you, Martina.'

'That's all I ever wanted, Alex. To be believed.'

'What do we do now?' I asked as the sun lost itself behind a brilliant rainbow.

'We sit here and wait.'

What we were waiting for, I never found out. But it didn't seem all that important. Instead, I sat quietly beside her, content to watch her long, dark hair blow freely aside an ocean breeze. Then, without warning, she turned to face me, the sadness in her eyes magnified by the swirling colours of the rainbow. She hesitated slightly, as if she was first seeking confirmation from another entity, before she gently manoeuvred her lips onto mine. The perfection of her kiss sent me floating into the sky like a balloon at a country fair. It felt so beautiful, so magical, and I begged Martina to join me.

'Please!' I cried out a million times. 'Don't leave me now!' But before she could answer, Martina's shallow face, stained with an unswerving love that I never truly understood, began to slowly melt in front of my eyes until all that remained was decayed flesh and bone. There was nothing I could do but scream.

Nooooooooooooooooooooooo!

That's when I woke up. For a moment, I could see Martina's shattered face tattooed across the bedroom ceiling. Riddled with guilt, I reached for my phone and immediately called Miriam. She was busy at work, so we couldn't talk for long. In hindsight, it was probably fortuitous that she ended the call when she did as I was still traumatised by my dream. After I checked some more overnight messages, I showered and dressed, then helped myself to some homemade bacon and eggs. By nine thirty, I was lining up for a ticket at the famous Dubrovnik cable car.

The ride up to the top of Mount Srđ—the low, steep mountain that guarded the city of Dubrovnik like an ancient giant—usually lasted fifteen minutes. But for some painful American tourists who shared the car with me, you would swear it was a five-hour trawl through *The Towering Inferno*. We were barely off the ground—maybe one hundred metres or so—when they started to squeal and shout in abject terror. 'Oh my God,' one overweight, pale-skinned twenty-something roared into the wind. 'Why are we so high up?'

I wasn't quite sure what he and his ridiculous friends, with their purple hair and powdered noses, expected to see when they jumped into a cable car, but their over-the-top theatrics were pissing me right off. For a moment, I wondered how much jail time I would face if I threw them all out of the car onto the cliff face below us. Thankfully, the cable car operator, sensing my annoyance, offered a sympathetic grin while pointing at his watch. *We are almost there!* With his unwavering support, I somehow made it to the top without committing mass murder.

My first task upon alighting the cable car was to pay my respects to the famous White Cross, originally built in 1935. For me, this majestic stone crucifix aptly commemorates the sacrifices of those who fought and died for the Croatian state. From this vantage point at the crest of the mountain, which stands around four hundred and twelve metres high, you have an incredible view of Dubrovnik, Lokrum Island and the Adriatic Sea. Unfortunately, it is also the perfect position from which to lay siege to the city below. And that's exactly what happened during the Homeland War.

Following Croatia's declaration of independence from Yugoslavia in June 1991, the new government declared that Dubrovnik was a demilitarised city, believing that this would exempt it from the escalating hostilities between Croatian forces and the Serbian-led Yugoslav People's Army (JNA). However, the Serbs and their Montenegrin allies argued that they were under no obligation to comply. As far as the Montenegrins were concerned, Dubrovnik historically belonged to their country even though most local residents identified as Croats.

The JNA commenced a siege of Dubrovnik on 1 October 1991, which lasted seven months. They ruthlessly used the heights surrounding Dubrovnik to conduct a relentless artillery barrage against the city. The Old Town suffered at least six hundred and fifty hits during this time, while one hundred and fourteen local citizens were killed as a result.

A Croatian military operation beginning in May 1992 eventually cleared Mount Srđ of the enemy, but it took another five months of fierce fighting in the surrounding terrain before the JNA finally retreated. Despite universal condemnation from the international community, the JNA continued its artillery bombardment of Dubrovnik well into 1995. Visitors to Dubrovnik can still see the remnants of these attacks within the walls and streets of the Old Town.

'Hello, sir,' a deep voice blared at me. 'Can you be Alex?'

I turned to face a bald, muscular man in his early fifties. A deep, crooked scar bulged from under his left eye and twisted all the way to the dimple on his chin. He looked like he could take a bull out to piss before breakfast and have a cup of tea while doing so. Despite his rugged, threatening appearance, I casually smiled at him.

'You must be Bruno.' When we shook hands, he almost twisted my arm out of its socket, such was the power of his grip. Maybe he was on the verge of apologising, but I suspected he also understood what an insult to my manhood that would have been.

Despite our inauspicious start, I warmed to Bruno quickly. He was one of those typical alpha male Croats I had met in the country from time to time, initially guarded at first but eager to open up once he gained your respect and trust. Perhaps it was my knowledge of the Homeland War or my enthusiasm for the Croatian football team and its chances at the World Cup later in the year; either way, there was an instant connection between the two of us that was strangely compelling.

Over the next two hours, beneath a gruelling autumn sun, Bruno led me on a fascinating walking tour of the Mount Srd battle sites. We sifted through various artillery positions, talked about hand-to-hand combat and discussed the tactics deployed by both forces during the worst days of the Dubrovnik siege. When we entered the Homeland War Museum at the Fort Imperial, close to the entrance of the cable car, Bruno quietly revealed what I had already suspected—he was a sergeant with the Croatian Army during the height of the battle for Dubrovnik. Bruno didn't need to regale any more war stories for me to understand that I was standing next to a local war hero.

After I bought Bruno lunch and a well-earned beer, he offered to take me for a drive across the Dubrovnik hinterland to show me some more battle sites. I became so captivated by his husky accent and insightful storytelling that I lost all track of time. Before I knew it, my watch hit three o'clock. While I was having a splendid time, I was still no closer to the answers that I had hoped to find when I left the villa that morning.

Bruno was wise enough to notice my change in demeanour. 'You seem quiet, my friend. What is the matter?'

At first, I wasn't sure how much I should tell him. How might he react to the complexity of my background? But what the heck, I wasn't responsible for the choices my father made during his life. So, I let it all out—how my Croatian father fought for the Chetniks during the Second World War, why I was trying to understand his motivation for doing so and whether any of this may have contributed to my being shot as a four-year-old boy.

If I thought these revelations might change Bruno's views about me, then I was happily mistaken.

'You have an interesting story to tell, no doubt,' he said after stopping at a pedestrian crossing. 'We all have our demons, no? I try to hide mine from my family, but they still haunt me every day. I suspect that yours are very real, eating you up inside. Am I right?'

'Yes, you are right.'

'In times like these, men must face their fears in the company of other men. How would you like to have a drink with my friends?'

It sounded like a smashing idea to be honest, for no other reason than after five hours of touring, I had inherited an incredible thirst. So, he made a couple of calls on his phone, and we soon arrived at a crowded open-air bar situated barely two hundred metres from my villa. After I bought two Nova Rundas—a wonderfully delicious local pale ale—we were soon joined by Bruno's two friends, Zlatko, a squat, black-haired man with tree trunks for forearms, and Igor, a man mountain with charcoal eyes and tightly cropped grey hair. Both served with Bruno during the war, and it was clear to me immediately that the trio were very close, perhaps more like brothers than merely friends.

Both men spoke English fluently, with the occasional grammatical flaw, although Bruno explained my story to them in Croatian. Of course, I could pick up bits and pieces of their conversation; despite their unemotional grunts, they seemed accepting of my presence. After the obligatory small talk about Australia, we happily eased into our conversation with no preconceived ideas of where it would land.

'I was a carpenter when the war broke out,' Zlatko began, his beer almost disappearing inside his huge hand. 'Like most of my family, I wasn't interested in politics. I couldn't care if you were Croat, Serb, or Martian. As long as you were an honest man, true to those you loved, and worked hard, you were okay with me. This how I live my life. You see, Alex?'

'You had many Serbian friends?' I asked naively.

'Of course,' he laughed. 'Montenegrins, too. In fact, one of my best friends was a good Montenegrin plumber. We sometimes work together, he and I. All these experts who tell you that the war was caused by historical hatreds lasting centuries have no clue. They know shit, these people. The truth is much harder to understand.'

He told me how, before the war, he and his friends would meet for a beer at this very same bar every Friday afternoon. Politics was never discussed. Their conversations always centred around fishing, football and females, in that order. They laughed, drank, swapped stories about the women they fancied or screwed, and then went home. But once Croatia claimed independence in June 1991, everything changed. It was like everyone had to select sides or be ostracised by their respective communities.

'One Friday afternoon, Slobodan, my Serbian friend, and Mira, my Montenegrin friend, just didn't turn up for drinks,' Zlatko said. 'Why don't they turn up? I tried calling them, but they don't answer the phone. Days later, I bump into Mira inside the Old Town, and he just walks past me like I was a ghost. Damn fool.'

'That would have hurt.' It was all I could say.

'It wasn't so much that,' Zlatko said. 'It was more that both Slobodan and Mira were ordered to end their Croatian friendships, and they didn't even have the balls to tell those idiots to fuck off. And then, to make things worse, some skinny white-collar fucker from Split comes to my house weeks later and tells me that I can't have Serbian friends anymore. Who is he to say that?'

Zlatko took several more sips of his beer and looked me straight in the eye. 'If you want to know why I pick up a rifle and shoot those fuckers, it was because of this reason. No government had the right to tell us who our friends should be or how to live our lives. I rebelled against this stupidity and wanted to end the war quickly so we could all get back to normal life again. I still say that it was a good thing to fight for.'

I nodded my agreement. 'Yes. Nationalism is a toxic concept. It forces you to choose both your friends and enemies in a climate of fear and retribution.'

'Yes,' Zlatko replied. 'Unfortunately, some politicians are good at twisting people's minds. They toy with your insecurities, your religious beliefs and the many jealousies you have, then twist them for their own vile purposes. That is how the war really started.'

I recalled Martina saying something similar to me all those years ago in Samos at the height of a bewildering sunset. War always began with the politicians, but how it was fought was left to the devices of ordinary men and women.

'My story is different,' Igor soon began. His English was much more refined than Zlatko's. 'I come from a little town, not far from Dubrovnik. You like football, Alex?'

'Love it,' I replied with a grin. 'It means everything to me.'

'And me.' He smiled for the first time, realising, perhaps, that he had met a kindred spirit. 'I was a gifted player as a child. I played central midfield, similar to the role that Ivan Rakitic used to play for Croatia. You must have heard of him?'

'Of course,' I said. 'One of my all-time favourite players.'

'That is good.' He smiled again. 'I did well at youth level and was even scouted by Hajduk Split. To my great delight, in my eleventh year of school, I was selected in the Yugoslav under-16 training squad. We were a great group of boys comprising of Croats, Serbs, Slovenes, Montenegrins, the whole damn lot.'

'You all got along?' I asked casually. I knew enough about the history of Yugoslav football to understand that ethnic tensions usually bubbled inside their national teams.

'Absolutely. Never a problem. And if something did come to the surface, we resolved the problem immediately.' He paused. 'All except for one kid. Let's say that his name was Radovan. He also came from the same town as me; it was unusual to have two players with similar ability grow up together. I never understood what was wedged up his arsehole, but he had it in for me from First Grade. He was one of the few non-Croats at our school; his father was some big wig party official. To compensate for his lack of humility, he would push his way around with the weaker kids. I hated bullies, and we were destined to clash. One day, in Fourth Grade, I think, I had enough of his shit, and I gave him a bloody nose in front of the entire school. One which I maintain he deserved.'

'I suppose he never forgave you,' I observed dryly.

'Never,' Igor replied. 'We were like two bantam cocks, always weighing each other up, looking for the perfect time to strike.'

'Yet you played in the same football team?'

'Yes, we did.' He shook his head in despair. 'What a disaster that could have been. The two-star players of the same team absolutely hated each other. Yet, as God is my witness, we had this strange connection on the field. He was a centre forward, and I must have assisted him for sixty per cent of his goals. But he never thanked me once.' He placed his beer on the table and looked wistfully at the ceiling. 'Never.'

'What happened when you both made the Yugoslav side?'

'The prick went out of his way to undermine me. He lied to the other players that my parents were right-wing Croatian nationalists and that I was following in their footsteps. All bullshit, of course, but mud sticks.'

'It sure does,' I replied in agreement. I had been the victim of scurrilous rumours myself at the workplace in 2016, and it took many months before my reputation was restored. Of course, that paled in comparison to being labelled a right-wing terrorist.

'It eventually got sorted by the coach, and Radovan was eventually dropped from the squad. He, of course, blamed his demotion on me and began to hate me even more.'

'I have a nasty feeling that your paths crossed again during the war as adversaries.'

'Yes, but I will come to that in a moment,' he replied impatiently. In other words, he was telling me to stop interrupting.

'There was this pretty girl at school called Maria,' he continued. 'All the boys, including me, were infatuated with her. I tried my hand in Eighth Grade and got humbly rejected, but we remained the best of friends. Her parents were extremely strict Catholics and wouldn't let her out of their sight. Of course, our friend Radovan had a crush on her, too. During the normal schoolboy banter, especially in our final year, he would often tell us what he wanted to do to her. His biggest fantasy, he shared with us, was to rape her while her parents watched.'

'Charming,' I replied blankly. Igor seemed bemused by my nonchalance, as if he correctly assumed something nefarious from my past.

'He asked her out many times but always got the same answer. One sensed he didn't like rejection, especially from a female Croat whose family he considered to be inferior to his. It was a situation that was destined to end in tragedy once the war commenced.'

I squeezed my hands tightly. I could tell Martina's story was about to be repeated all over again, and understandably, I was overwhelmed with fear. A part of me wanted to leave the bar immediately before I was burdened with yet another woman's tragedy.

'After we declared independence, I knew my football career was over.' Bruno quietly placed a comforting arm around his friend's shoulder. It was a tender gesture that only men who had faced death together could offer. I thought it polite to disconnect with Igor's tear-stained eyes as he continued his story.

'My new country came first, don't you see? So, I joined the army and learnt how to kill. And I was damned good at it, as it turned out.'

'Igor was awarded several medals for bravery,' Bruno interrupted.

Igor's face turned a bullish red. 'Our army was full of brave men, Alex. But I am sure Bruno has explained that the JNA occupied some of the hinterland around Dubrovnik, including my hometown.'

'Yes, he did,' I offered sadly.

'It was a very hard time for me personally, especially when I heard that my old friend Radovan was in command of an enemy attachment that occupied the area. You see, like me, he was quick to exchange a football for a rifle. The fuckers even made him an officer, a situation helped no doubt by his father.'

'Jesus.'

'I'm pretty certain that Jesus never visited my hometown during the occupation,' Igor hissed. 'If he had, he obviously didn't have any influence over Radovan. You see, the bastard used his new powers to revenge every slight, real or imagined, he believed was perpetrated against him as a teenager by the Croatian townsfolk.' All three Croats suddenly shuffled uncomfortably in their seats, an indication of what we all knew would come next.

'Maria?' I finally asked.

'Unfortunately, yes,' Igor replied. 'Remember the fantasy that he spoke to us about in high school? Well, I was told that he spent an entire afternoon acting it out inside Maria's family home. And when he was finished, he then passed her off to his men. Two days later, overcome with shame, her body having been torn to pieces, Maria found her father's gun inside his closet and shot herself.'

It would have been easy to think about Martina again, but this latest story impacted me in other ways. Even though I had never met Maria or had any idea what she looked like, I could now picture this innocent, young girl and the torment and loneliness that tore at her soul before she decided to take her own life. As such, I wanted to bury my head in shame at the brutality of it all. *What the fuck is wrong with some men? Why did they turn into wild animals as soon as they put on a bloody uniform?*

'I am lost for words,' I eventually coughed. 'It's such a horrible story.'

'Yes, possibly the most horrible story of the war, if it were possible to actually rank such things. But in a strange way, it sustained me during my darkest times.'

'How so?'

'You want to learn what drives a man to war? Is this right? Mark my words, you would be foolish to fall for all the usual cliches one hears. Fighting a war has nothing to do with national pride or whatever you want to call it. Rather, it is a personal choice, the chance to avenge whatever affliction is devouring you at the time. For me, it was avenging

Maria's rape and death and all the other crimes that Radovan and his men committed in my hometown. I did it all for them, do you understand? A burning sensation inside of me made me fight like a wild dog, encouraged me to take risks that I would normally never take, without any fear of death. The day I led the liberation of my town was the greatest day of my life, and it fulfilled every aching desire that drove me forward to that point. After that, the war was an anti-climax, and I cared not if I lived or died. I hope you understand.'

'I think I do,' I replied. And I did. How many times over the past twenty-seven years had I dreamt about avenging Martina's gang rape? It was a feeling that never left me. 'What about Radovan?' I finally asked.

The three friends shared a secret smile with each other. 'Oh, he got his—how do you say in English? Yes, just desserts.' Igor released a thunderous laugh. 'But that is another story.' I quickly got the message. It was a story that I was not encouraged to pursue.

'Don't be too judgemental about your father,' Igor then added. 'After we fight a war, we all try desperately to resume life with a clean slate. I'm sure he convinced himself that what he did was right. Try not to make assumptions that are blurred by an unforgiving history. Understand the man, then you can understand his reasons.'

Good advice.

We sank some more beers, deliberately allowing the conversation to drift to other matters, like football and the general state of the world. I enjoyed their company very much, particularly their honesty. I found Igor particularly appealing; there was a shrewdness and kindness behind those craggy features that belied his obvious, fierce reputation as a war hero. But having lulled me into a false sense of security, I was totally unprepared for what he said next.

'Can I ask you a question?'

'Sure. Anything.'

'You are obviously a man of good intentions who loves Croatia, especially Dubrovnik. I can see it in your eyes.'

'Yes,' I replied softly. 'The city and its people are very special to me.'

'Then why didn't you come to Dubrovnik during the Homeland War and contribute to the fighting like some other Australian Croats?'

His question initially rattled me. It almost felt like the entire afternoon had led to this juncture, and whatever answer I now provided would forever dictate Igor's final impression of me. But as I stared deeply into his grey eyes, I realised that I had misinterpreted his intentions. He was not here to judge me but to genuinely understand my own motives.

To be honest, it was a question that I still thought about every time I visited Dubrovnik. For a man acutely aware of his surroundings, it was very hard not to. As I mentioned previously, there are constant reminders throughout the Old Town of the fighting; the fragmented bullet holes in the walls and shop entrances, the plaques of those who had fallen doing their duty. Yet, for someone who called this country his second home, I was absent at the time of its biggest crisis. Did I have the right to lay claim to my heritage when so many other men made the ultimate sacrifice?

I was at the peak of my physical prowess at the time, a recently commissioned army reserve infantry officer, no less, who could have made a difference with my military skills and leadership. And to be fair, one rainy Canberra afternoon in 1993, I even seriously considered it for about ten seconds. Sadly, my first marriage was failing, and the thought of losing oneself in a foreign war seemed like the perfect 'get out of jail free' card from all the emotional repercussions. I also had a Croatian friend at the time who was always badgering me to join him in the fight. 'Come on, Alex,' he would say every time he saw me in the street. 'We must go and fight together for our brothers and sisters!'

However, his own limitations didn't inspire any confidence that he would meet his side of the bargain. 'I was going to go last week, but I have a bad back at the moment,' he would often explain. Then, at another chance meeting, 'I was definitely heading off next week, but I just remembered that I have a skiing trip booked.' I soon realised that he was living inside his own fantasy world, a Walter Mitty character who hadn't the foggiest notion of what it meant to fight a war. Following someone as flaky as him was a one-way ticket to disaster.

Besides, I held no animosity towards the Serbian community whatsoever, and from a young age, I had always respected their culture and religion. Some of my closest friends in Canberra were Serbs, especially a wonderful couple I worked with who doted on me like a wayward son. And, of course, how could I disrespect my father's wartime legacy in such an ungrateful and unforgiving way?

No, I wasn't going to risk everything by paying lip service to a hatred that didn't exist within me. I was a first generation Australian, and my unswerving allegiance remained with the country of my birth. Furthermore, I thoroughly disapproved of people bringing their traditional rivalries and disagreements into our country. Australia was a melting pot of all nationalities, joined together by a common cause, and I would always fight to keep it so. My real bitch was with extreme nationalism and racially based violence, a feeling enhanced whenever I saw the television footage from Sarajevo and Dubrovnik.

So, as the hostilities in the former Yugoslavia continued, I contributed the best way I could by giving money to charities, sponsoring Croatian and Serbian refugees and attending protests that railed against the attacks on Dubrovnik's historical treasures. But I suspected that this wouldn't be enough to satisfy Igor, so I rolled out the usual, standard excuse that I gave to people like him.

'It was impossible,' I began. 'I was an Australian Army officer at the time. If I left to fight in Croatia, I would have been arrested, court -martialled and jailed upon my return.' A fair call, but Igor saw right through it and, therefore, right through me.

'Before you focus on your father,' he said wryly, after mulling over my response, 'perhaps you should first reconcile your own motivations for pursuing this quest. I am certain once you do, it will make things easier.'

He bought me another beer and then slapped me on the back, indicating that there were no hard feelings on his part. But as I very gingerly walked back to Villa Spirac later that night, half-drunk, and bedazzled by a radiant full moon, Igor's words kept rolling inside my head. He was right, of course. This quest I had undertaken was just as much about me as it was about my father. If I failed to understand my past and the burdens I had carried with it, there was a real danger that my time in Croatia would become yet another meaningless distraction in my pursuit of the truth.

Chapter Four

Dubrovnik, Croatia
October 2022

I stayed up later than usual that evening in anticipation of an email from Belinda. Over the past few days, she had been interviewing my other sister, Rosemary, about the shooting, and I was keen to know the outcome of her discussions. Rosemary was only eleven years old herself when I was shot, but perhaps she remembered something from that day that was crucial to our investigation. Belinda had waited until I went overseas before she approached her; she was adamant that any contact I had with her beforehand could potentially contaminate or influence her evidence.

'You need to stay well away until I have the chance to form my own conclusions,' Belinda had warned me before I left Australia, and I wasn't about to contradict her. She was a professional who knew her business, and I was grateful to have someone reputable like her on my side.

When Belinda first agreed to help me, she revealed that in similar cold cases, investigators like her initially looked for two things—what did any witnesses see or hear at the time, and what did the wounds on the body reveal about the shooting itself. While we were unable to confirm as yet whether any police records about the shooting still existed in Kandos after fifty-six years, the only 'live' witness to the shooting itself was me, and I couldn't remember that much.

One minute, I was playing by myself in our front yard; the next minute, I was writhing on the ground in agony as blood gushed from my arm. I recalled the local doctor wrapping a huge, grey bandage around my elbow and my father telling my mother that the police thought the shooting was an accident. 'It was just a couple of children playing about,' Dad had told her. 'Very unlikely we will ever find out who they were.'

For some reason, Mum and Dad accepted this version unreservedly, and the family rarely discussed the incident.

'I find it difficult to believe, myself,' Belinda had proffered a few weeks before in the Qantas Club while we waited to board our respective flights. 'Even in the 1960s, the shooting of a child was a big thing. You just wouldn't brush it aside without first conducting a thorough investigation.'

'This was Kandos,' I had replied. 'It was nothing more than a small factory town where everyone knew everyone else's business. Perhaps the police thought someone would eventually own up to the shooting when they were ready.'

'Perhaps,' Belinda had said wistfully before pointing at my arm. 'Now, show me your scars.'

'What?'

'You heard me. Show me your scars.'

In front of bemused onlookers, I proceeded to take off my shirt before silently handing over my left arm to Belinda. After she had examined it several times, her poker face casually connected with mine.

'These wounds don't make any sense.'

'What do you mean?'

'The way your entry and exit wounds are positioned seem to indicate that the bullet came tumbling downwards at a rapid speed, entered your arm and then came out near the top of your elbow. I would like to consult a ballistics expert, mind you, but to me, this suggests that the bullet took a deflection first before hitting you.'

What that meant in the bigger scheme of things, I had no idea, but when Belinda's email finally arrived just before midnight, I knew immediately that it would contain fascinating new evidence.

Dear Alex,

I hope you are enjoying Dubrovnik. What a beautiful place!

Anyway, this is just a short note to let you know that I have some big news. I have now spoken to your sister and also located and talked to Matt White, your neighbour in Kandos, who was the first person to reach you after you were shot. What they have revealed is a game changer.

I first interviewed Rosemary; she has a great memory and an eye for detail. She remembers two things very clearly that I think are important. First, you weren't wearing your cowboy costume like you insisted. In fact, you were wearing your combat uniform, complete with a plastic helmet that was too big for you. The front of the helmet apparently protruded just above your eye line. Rosemary remembers that a policeman told your father that the bullet had hit the tip of your plastic helmet before tumbling down into your arm. If that's true, then it would solve the riddle of the deflection that we recently spoke about. It is very important that we confirm this with a ballistic expert. Unfortunately, if I am right, this would also indicate that the shooter was aiming directly for your head. Therefore, the shooting was no accident, Alex, and what Matt then told me has only confirmed that.

In my opinion, Matt is the key to this whole thing. He was the first person who reached you after you were hit, so his evidence of what you said seconds after the shooting carries the most weight. He is in his seventies now but very fit and healthy for his age. He was very keen to help because he has never quite forgotten the shooting. I asked him to take his time and try to reconstruct the afternoon as he remembered it. And wait for it, he called me back today and confirmed that when he asked you what had happened, you replied, 'Two men in a car drove past the house, and one of them stuck a rifle out the window and shot me.' Matt is also certain that he then told your father what you said to him.

I can't tell you how huge this is. I also can't explain, if your father told the same thing to the police, why they didn't conduct a full investigation into the matter. Please wrap things up over there as quickly as you can and get back to Australia soon. We have much work to do.

Yours, Belinda.

Perhaps I should have been stunned by this new information, especially about the two men in the car. Yet strangely, I took it all in my stride. Even though I couldn't remember every detail from that afternoon, I always knew that the 'kids' theory was bullshit. Who would seriously believe that a teenager had ambled down the street in broad daylight with a fully loaded .22-calibre rifle by his side (without being seen by anyone) and then accidentally fired a shot that hit another kid playing in his front yard? No, I never truly believed that scenario for a second.

Some people might ask why I didn't approach Rosemary or Matt earlier in my life, but I was conditioned by my parents not to speak about the shooting at all. It was like it never happened. They were only too pleased to whitewash the entire incident whenever I raised it with them as a younger man. Without confessing any details about what they actually knew, they simply encouraged me to forget about the entire episode and carry on with my life. And so, after a while, I did what they asked me to do.

But I was a different person now, someone who had belatedly discovered a thirst for the truth to the point of obsession. My instinct told me that I was on the right track and that the shooting was somehow connected to my father's wartime service. I was determined more than ever to keep going until I found the answers I was looking for, even if it meant staying in Croatia indefinitely until I succeeded.

I spent the next day in holiday mode, given that I desperately needed a mental health break. After fifty push-ups and the usual extra hot latte, I took an early morning ferry ride to Cavtat, something that any traveller visiting Dalmatia must experience before leaving. Although the journey lasts no more than forty-five minutes, it meanders through the stunning southern corridor of the Adriatic Sea, offering incredible views of the rugged coastline and its surrounding mountains. You could take a hundred random photos of this scenery and turn any of them into picture postcards.

Most tourists visit Cavtat for the beauty of its harbour, the idyllic walks, the allure of its golden beaches, the hip restaurants and bars and its historical architecture. Of course, I loved those things, too, but Cavtat was also part of my heritage. Several of my cousins from my father's side of the family still lived inside the Old Town. Indeed, whenever I visited Cavtat, it felt like I was walking in my father's lonely footsteps.

Over the next few hours, I strolled around Cavtat's pristine streets, paid my respects to the stretch of beach where my grandfather had died, prayed in the beautiful St Nicholas Church and ate loads and loads of *palačinke*, a wafer-thin Croatian crepe.

Later that afternoon, I returned to Dubrovnik and enjoyed dinner at my favourite seafood restaurant near the Pile Gate. Soon after the entree, I introduced myself to a lovely middle-aged Hungarian couple seated at the table next to me. This was their first night ever in Dubrovnik and they were out to enjoy themselves. Given that the husband was a dead ringer for Bela Lugosi, the American-Hungarian actor best known for playing Dracula in the 1931 movie of the same name, I had no option but to invite them to join me. Soon, the three of us were enjoying several bottles of local wine and solving the many problems of the world. As last nights in Dubrovnik went, this one couldn't have been better, especially when the stunning Mrs Lugosi told me in the most incredible Hungarian accent imaginable that I was one of the most charming men she had ever met.

I awoke early the next morning with a slight headache and Mrs Lugosi's musty perfume still painted on my cheek where she had kissed me goodbye. Desperately needing a coffee, I managed one last walk to the Old Town before returning to pack my suitcase. After admiring the balcony view for the final time, I said a sad goodbye to Villa Spirac and hustled out onto the busy street, where I waited several minutes for my chauffeur service to arrive.

The only downside for me when visiting Dalmatia is the paucity of available flights between Dubrovnik and the region's largest city, Split. The usual options for a tourist in making their journey to Split are either by ferry—noting that services can be limited towards the end of peak season—or by bus.

Prior to 2022, the four-hour bus trip involved a detour across the border and through a narrow Bosnian corridor before returning to Croatia thirty minutes later, a burden highlighted by the usual passport controls.

However, thanks to Chinese investment, a much-needed bridge connecting the Pelješac Peninsular to the mainland by road, thus bypassing Bosnia, had recently opened to travellers. The Bosnian Government was understandably concerned that the new Pelješac bridge would further isolate the country and impact on the profitability of local businesses dependent on the tourist trade that the detour had provided them. However, none of that was really important to me now; I just wanted to get to Split as quickly as I could. And the best way to do this was through a relatively inexpensive local chauffeur service.

Right on ten thirty, a black SUV pulled up alongside me. *What is it with black SUVs in this country?* In broken English, the driver told me his name was Goran and then ordered me to put my bag in the boot. After I dropped into the front passenger seat, he offered me a bottle of mineral water. 'You drink,' he demanded. I leant back comfortably against the headrest and watched while he fiddled around with the gearbox. 'We will be in Split by two thirty,' he promised, which suited me just fine.

The trip was mainly uneventful, although crossing the new bridge was a welcome distraction. Goran especially was extremely excited when signs for the bridge came into view. 'We build good bridges,' he boasted once we made it to the other side. Thinking about the mindless destruction in Europe during the Second World War, I agreed with him that building bridges was much better than blowing them up. He looked at me funnily, as if I had just landed from Mars, but laughed along with me anyway. After an hour and a half of more stilted conversation, I needed to pee desperately, so we stopped at a service station in the middle of nowhere, where I bought Goran a coffee and snacked on some delicious hot chips.

In a courtyard next to the service station, a large group of people were sipping beers on several rickety tables in between singing Croatian folk songs in tribute to a newlywed couple standing proudly in front of yet another black SUV. There was something about their raucous melodies and infectious laughter that convinced me that I really did belong in Croatia, after all. Overcome by a desire to join the celebrations, I was disappointed when Goran reappeared with a grizzled smile and politely insisted that it was time to leave.

We arrived on the outskirts of Split just before two thirty. For some reason, Goran's navigation device suddenly turned to shit, but he reassured me that the building which housed my hotel was just to the front of us. I tried to explain to him that the hotel I had booked was supposed to be near the waterfront and the famous Diocletian's Palace, and as far as I could see, we were nowhere near the waterfront or the famous Diocletian's Palace. We soon entered a standoff where neither of us wanted to agree with the other person's position. In the end, I realised that I was going to lose this one by some distance, so I let myself out of the car after giving Goran a generous tip.

Dragging my luggage behind me, I lumbered towards the entrance of the building only to be told by the security guard that I was right the first time; I was indeed several kilometres away from the waterfront and Diocletian's Palace. *No shit.* The security guard smiled brazenly, as if he was used to seeing tourists being fucked about, and generously ordered me a taxi. A half-an-hour later, I was checking into my new hotel, which, I would soon discover, was a miserly five-minute walk to the main city area. My room wasn't as salubrious as the Villa Spirac, but it was neat and comfortable and contained all the modern amenities. Exactly what I needed for the next four days.

This was my fourth visit to Split, a beguiling, historic city that has a reputation for attracting some of Europe's most beautiful people, especially in summer. It may not possess the majestic charm of Dubrovnik, but in many ways, it's a more cosmopolitan city compared to its feted rival. No matter what time of day, you can take a walk along the main promenade, and you will find a strip cluttered with an eclectic range of buzzing cafés, restaurants and shops. Watch carefully as hordes of bronzed people wander idly past you before gazing longingly at the melting sun or a nearby ice cream stand. Then, park a curious eye towards the Adriatic Sea and stare wistfully while a large cruise liner returns from the nearby island of Brač, carrying tourists from every corner of the world.

When you are ready, leave the main thoroughfare and walk down the city's backstreets. Somewhere along the way, you will perhaps see a haggard old cobbler displaying his latest treasures to an elderly couple; maybe a brash male barista concocting a special brew for the young woman he obviously fancies. Take a leisurely stroll down to the Green Market, where you can enjoy the frantic chatter of market life while taking your pick of the best cheese, fruits and cured meats.

And then there is Diocletian's Palace itself. Built in the fourth century as a leisure palace for the Roman Emperor Diocletian, it is the shining beacon for every tourist who visits Split. Spend at least two hours there if you can, using every moment to absorb its many treasures. The experience will remain with you long afterwards.

Its aesthetic wonders aside, Split figured prominently in my father's life. He was posted in Split for several years with the navy and undoubtedly enjoyed the city's vibrant social life before the war. Characteristically, he fell head over heels with a local woman and was engaged to her for a short time before abruptly ending the relationship. The reason for his change of heart was unclear, but it obviously had something to do with meeting my mother, who lived in the coastal city of Šibenik, situated approximately sixty kilometres to the north. After they were married, Dad and Mum would live with her parents in Šibenik for much of the war.

Dalmatia was initially occupied by the Italians following Yugoslavia's defeat to Germany in April 1941 and quickly became an epicentre for anti-Fascist resentment in Yugoslavia. What role Dad may have played in this movement was critical to uncovering his wartime secrets. But all I had for the moment were snippets of random conversations I stole from my parents before they died and the childhood memories of my oldest sister, Dubravka. Somehow, I had to link these disparate pieces of information together and mould them into a coherent narrative.

Luckily, I was a gifted problem solver. My capacity to deconstruct and resolve complex issues had won me many plaudits during my career in government. So, before I left Australia, I spent many hours refining my approach. My first priority was to identify the main military, social and political events that occurred in Dalmatia during the Second World War. By linking these seminal events with what I already knew about my family's activities, I hoped to create a comprehensive timeline that would reveal the full extent of their life during this period. With a bit of luck, this knowledge would help me unravel the murky bits of Dad's life that continued to tease me.

Okay, it didn't sound like much of a plan. But with so much at stake, something told me that once I opened the Pandora's box containing my family's past, anything was possible.

Chapter Five

Split, Croatia
October 2022

To help get me started, I contacted a local expert, who tantalisingly called himself Professor Peter. He was a credentialled historian with a keen interest in the Chetniks. I met him at a waterfront café the following morning; he was a small, wiry man in his mid-forties, with oval-rimmed John Lennon glasses and a wispy moustache that needed urgent trimming. His frigid black eyes considered me carefully for several minutes as if he suddenly remembered me from a most-wanted poster. But once I paid his consultation fee in US dollars, he relaxed a little more.

'Before we start,' he began with a sheepish smile, 'I would like to know whether you have any biases on these issues.'

'What do you mean?'

'Do you have any preconceived views about blame or guilt, or a personal grievance concerning the former Yugoslavia?'

'Not really.' I shook my head. 'I am simply here to enhance my understanding of the war, nothing more. And please be reassured that I always keep an open mind to new information.'

'Good,' he said calmly. 'We live in a world where everyone wants to contradict the past. And, of course, it's the victors that write the official histories, not the vanquished.' I nodded politely and he smiled back at me. Maybe I had just passed his first test.

He waited for me to pull out my notebook and pen, and then, with a cappuccino attached to his skinny hand, he proceeded to lecture me on Yugoslav history. Peter believed strongly that the Kingdom of Yugoslavia was always destined to fail once the Second World War began. At a time when Europe was under siege from totalitarianism, the internal political tensions caused by competing ethnicities and cultures became more intense. The country's plight wasn't helped by its complex political system.

Following the assassination of the Serbian King Alexander in 1934 by the Ustaše—a Croatian paramilitary and ultranationalist terrorist organisation—his son and heir, King Petar II, was considered too young to rule. As a result, Alexander's cousin, Prince Paul, assumed the regency until such time Petar came of age.

By 1941, Yugoslavia was a fractured country beset by uncertainty. Its Serbian-dominated government often rankled the other states within the federation, especially Croatia, which resented how its political independence, religion and culture always seemed to be neglected. To complicate matters in Croatia, the Ustaše threat continued to hover menacingly in the background.

Their leader, or *Poglavnik*, Ante Pavelić, was hiding with his wife in Fascist Italy, waiting for events to conspire his way.

Meanwhile, his benefactor, the Fascist dictator Benito Mussolini, had set his own eyes squarely on the Dalmatian coastline, a region he and many Italians firmly believed belonged to Italy. He secretly disapproved of a separate Croatian state, but for the moment, he would watch and wait.

If that wasn't troubling in itself, Prince Paul soon had Adolf Hitler breathing down his neck. The Regent had declared his country's neutrality at the beginning of the Second World War, but the Nazi regime wanted Yugoslavia to become a formal ally. Hitler was obsessed with protecting his southern flank from British attack. From his perspective, there was much to gain from a formal treaty with the Yugoslav Government, such as raw materials for Germany's wartime industry, as well as access to several deepwater ports. With the impending invasion of the Soviet Union, the last thing Hitler needed was a military conflagration in the Balkans. So, he began to pressure Prince Paul and his government into signing a pact.

Prince Paul was faced with an unenviable dilemma. His government had recently initiated reforms that gave Croatia some level of increased autonomy, but tensions inside the federation remained. To aggravate the Nazis in any way would potentially leave the door ajar for Pavelić to return. There was also the spectre of an overly aggressive Italy having already invaded Yugoslavia's neighbours, Albania in 1939 and Greece in 1940. Despite opposition from several high-profile politicians, Prince Paul finally decided that Yugoslavia had no option other than to accede to Germany's demands. On 25 March 1941, his two principal ministers travelled to Vienna and formally signed the Tripartite Pact.

'This created an immediate shitstorm, especially in Serbia,' Peter said. 'Many Serbs opposed Nazi Germany and now felt that the government had betrayed them. Thousands of protestors lined the streets of Belgrade, crying out the famous slogan, *Bolje grob nego rob, bolje rat nego pakt.*'

I nodded my head. 'Better the grave than a slave, better a war than the pact.'

Peter offered me a smile. All of a sudden, there was a sign of respect behind his dead-fish eyes. 'You do know your stuff,' he acknowledged.

'Some of it,' I replied politely.

'Then you know what happens next.'

'Yes,' I said. 'Two days later, military officers stage a coup in Belgrade, and Prince Paul flees into exile. The teenage King Petar assumes the throne.'

'A Serbian throne,' Peter reminded me. 'Although the new government doesn't withdraw from the pact, the coup is viewed by Hitler as a personal insult and an indication that Yugoslavia will eventually join the Allies. A week later, he unleashes the full extent of his military fury upon our country. The Germans obliterate our forces within ten days, and King Petar escapes to London, where he eventually establishes a government-in-exile. Meanwhile, many Croatian and Slovenian soldiers refuse to fight due to their hatred of Serbia. It's a complete debacle.'

'Sometimes, doing the right thing doesn't pay.'

Peter toasted me with his cup of coffee. 'You're a philosopher, I see, Mr Gerrick.'

'No, just a realist. What else could they have done in the circumstances?

The mere thought of bowing down to the Nazis was simply abhorrent to those Yugoslavs who believed in freedom.' A reflective pause. 'And please call me Alex.' I produced a forced smile before adding, 'I broadly know the next part. Germany divides the spoils with its co-conspirators. It takes over much of Serbia and Northern Slovenia. Italy occupies Dalmatia and parts of Montenegro. A Croatian puppet-state, including large areas of modern Bosnia, is established under the Fascist rule of Ante Pavelić. Other bits and bobs are given to Hungary and Bulgaria.'

'The complete destruction of the state first envisaged by those fools at Versailles,' Peter snorted. 'Some might say we were never meant to be a united country.'

'Perhaps,' I replied. 'But it didn't justify the brutality that followed.'

'No, it didn't,' Peter agreed.

Immediately after the dismantling of Yugoslavia, the true horrors began. Once Pavelić took power, he and his Ustaše followers quickly turned Croatia into a model dictatorship. Basic human rights and freedoms were virtually suspended overnight, while Serbs, Jews and Roma were indiscriminately targeted. Within months, a large concentration and extermination complex was established in the area around Jasenovac, an hour's drive from the capital, Zagreb.

In the pantheon of brutal death camps during the Second World War, this one obtained an especially sadistic reputation. Those who survived Jasenovac would later recall in vivid detail the heinous crimes committed there—torture, rape, mutilation and murder of the most obscene kind. Women, children and the elderly: no one was spared during the camp's darkest times. While the number of people killed at Jasenovac is still debated to this day, for many, its name remains synonymous with cruelty and horrific violence.

Some Axis soldiers deployed to the Independent State of Croatia in support of the Ustaše regime became so appalled by the savagery they witnessed that they requested to be transferred to other theatres of war, including the much-feared Eastern Front. Nevertheless, the mass killings, the forced conversions to Catholicism and the resettlements continued unabated.

In response to the escalating violence that gripped Yugoslavia, two separate resistance movements soon emerged: the Royalist Serbian Chetniks and the Communist Partisans, led by a Yugoslav left-wing radical named Josip Broz, more commonly known as Tito. While both groups coducted guerrilla operations against the Germans, Italians and Ustaše, they were also at loggerheads with each other in a vicious civil war. You see, it wasn't just about this war, but who would rule Yugoslavia when it was over.

At first, the British government, at the behest of King Petar, supported the Chetniks, commanded by the enigmatic army officer Colonel Draža Mihailović. Over time, that support would be redirected to the Partisans.

Although I had read countless books about the war in Yugoslavia, they often contradicted each other, leaving me thoroughly confused. As a result, I found it difficult to distinguish the good guys from the bad guys. Unsurprisingly, Peter seemed nonplussed when I raised the issue with him.

'First rule, Alex: don't try to make sense of everything that occurred in Yugoslavia during the war and especially don't believe everything that you read on the internet. It will drive you insane. There are no patterns to follow and no obvious rationale for why people did the things they did. For instance, the Chetniks and Ustaše might negotiate a local agreement to fight the Partisans together one day, but then start killing each other again twenty-four hours later. It's like those Russian babushka dolls. Once you unearth one doll, another one awaits to torment you.'

'I get that,' I replied blankly. 'I am not here to write the definitive account of the civil war or the history of the Chetniks, but rather to ascertain the validity of Dad's story.' I proceeded to explain to him what my father had told me about his war when he was alive. About how he claimed to have worked for the British, how he became a Chetnik guerrilla commander, how he was a Croat by birth. Peter wrung his hands gently and then offered me a smile.

'I find your father's story about working for the British very believable. As a former navy officer loyal to the King, his background was exactly what the British Special Operations Executive (SOE) were looking for. You said he lived in Šibenik during the war? Certainly, the area between Šibenik and Split, due to its geography and cultural importance, was a hotbed for anti-Fascist activity.'

'But I still don't understand how Dad became a Chetnik,' I pleaded. 'I thought it was exclusively a Serbian organisation. Dad was born a Catholic Croat, not an Orthodox Serb. Man, his oldest sister spent most of her life in a Zagreb convent.'

Peter scratched his chin. 'Many people like you who come to me inquiring about their family histories think the same. But in actual fact, there existed a small number of Croatian Chetniks, like your father. If you supported King Petar, there was pretty much nowhere else to go.' He picked up his notebook. 'Your mistake is assuming that the Chetniks were one single entity observing a defined, coordinated chain of command. Far from it. The Chetnik movement was unbelievably complex and multifaceted, with different factions and local units operating throughout the country.'

'Why, in Croatia alone,' Peter continued, 'I have identified at least twenty different units who called themselves Chetniks during the war. In reality, some Chetnik units reported to Mihailović in name only and acted independently of his command. Having spent much of the war trapped in Eastern Bosnia and Serbia, he actually wielded less control over the wider organisation than people think. The old saying went that the further away you were from him, the less authority he had.'

'I always thought he was the main man.'

'He was for much of the war, but by the time the Partisans took control of the country, his influence and authority had abated.'

'But didn't Mihailović release a manifesto in late 1941 that guided his Chetnik followers throughout the war? From memory, it was a controversial document, calling for a greater Serbia that was simply for Serbs and no other races.'

'Yes, I know the document you mean – the so-called Directive 20,' replied Peter. 'But we need to be very careful here, Alex. It's true that many Chetniks were fighting for a separate Serbian state. However, having spent many years researching this issue, I personally doubt whether the document in question was indeed authentic or if it was, that Mihailović actually signed it. As Mihailović said at his trial, he was a soldier and not interested in politics. If you ask me, I believe that he was a decent man with mostly noble intentions who opposed unnecessary violence, a point which he also emphasised at his trial. However, various historians have condemned him for not preventing some of his more aggressive commanders from acting unilaterally.'

'Even so, he eventually lost the support of the Allies,' I remarked.

Peter sighed heavily. 'Mihailović was in a very difficult position for much of the war. The reprisals against Serbian civilians by the Germans in response to Chetnik attacks always played heavily on his mind. For a time, he focused on building his forces and capabilities for a major action against the Germans, a strategy that King Petar and the Allies had initially supported. But as the war continued, he gradually came to believe that the Allies would ultimately win, so his main objective was to ensure that his country didn't submit to communism. Fighting the Partisans became the main game in town, then the Ustaše. As a result, he perhaps dropped the ball on some other issues and didn't always exert total control over his forces, especially in Montenegro, where Pavle Đurišić ran his own race. And, of course, he and the Chetniks had to fight persistent accusations of collaboration.'

I quietly gathered my thoughts as Peter momentarily sipped at his coffee. Dad and I rarely spoke about those accusations when he was alive, but I knew how much he resented them. He may have been many things, but he was never a collaborator. On this issue at least, his heart was entirely pure; I was sure of it.

'I know I said that I didn't have any preconceived views about the war, but Dad urged me to ignore the history books when it came to the subject of collaboration in Dalmatia,' I began. 'He agreed that the Italian army and the Chetniks sometimes shared a commitment to fight the Partisans during the occupation, but this never amounted to full-scale collaboration as he understood the term.'

Peter wanted to interject at this point, but I raised my hand in defiance, and he humbly allowed me to finish. 'As Dad once said, if you decide to fully collaborate with another party during wartime, it means that you fundamentally agree with their ideology and strategic aims. Dad wasn't a Fascist or a Nazi; he firmly believed in democracy and freedom, as did other Chetniks he fought alongside. Why would they fall into line with their occupiers, countries whose ideologies were repugnant to them? He would get very angry whenever someone contradicted him or if he watched a movie or documentary that claimed that all Chetniks were Fascist or Nazi sympathisers. As Dad recalled, he spent much of his war conspiring against the Italians, not helping them.'

Peter shuffled uncomfortably in his seat, perhaps knowing that he had to choose his next words wisely to avoid offending me. 'I think your father described the situation rather elegantly, although some historians would argue that several formal agreements between the Italians and the Chetniks existed in Dalmatia at the time. We must remember, too, that soldiers on the ground, like your father, had little say on these matters as they involved orders from above.'

'Surely there were Chetnik units who were genuinely opposed to any form of cooperation with the enemy?' I interrupted.

'Of course there were,' Peter replied. 'But more broadly, we are talking about survival here. Sometimes, you had to fight alongside people you didn't like just to make it through the next day alive. I am a Croatian historian, but when it comes to the Second World War, even I hate the word collaboration; it's a lazy way of explaining a complex situation and at times, can be so misleading. I prefer to use the term 'operational necessities' when describing those situations.'

'War is not a linear concept,' the military historian in me offered.

'Sometimes you have to be agile and adaptable to survive, even if it means readjusting your relationships when you need to. Friends today can be your enemies tomorrow and vice versa. History is full of such examples. Ho Chi Minh and the Americans fought the Japanese together during the Second World War. The Afghan Mujahideen, supported by American funding, defeated the Russians in the 1980s, long before 9/11. People forget that the Soviet Union signed a non-aggression pact with Germany in 1939 and then joined the Allies two years later. Heck, some of Tito's deputies even attempted to reach an agreement with the Nazis in 1943 but were rebuked.'

Peter looked at me goggle-eyed as he played with his notebook. Perhaps I sounded a bit too defensive about an emotional issue that continued to elicit historical debate. Hiding my embarrassment, I sheepishly ordered another coffee and then asked a further question, just to change the subject. 'My mother told me that Dad turned his hand to guerrilla warfare with the Chetniks in late 1944 after running afoul of the local Ustaše. Furthermore, he was wounded in a major battle north of Šibenik in late November, early December.'

'Ah yes,' Peter replied knowingly. 'That would be the Battle of Knin, which involved a famous Chetnik encounter in the village of Padene.'

'What happened there?'

Peter held up his hand. 'To understand Padene, let's backtrack first to 1943. The Italians, as you know, surrendered to the Allies in September of that year. That had two main implications. First, things suddenly got a lot worse for those Serbs living in Dalmatia. The Italian army, in the main, loathed the Ustaše and had given sanctuary to many Serbs who had escaped persecution in Croatia. With the Italians now fleeing in droves back to their country, those Serbs faced an uncertain future. Some of them joined the Partisans; others joined the Chetniks. Did it tip the balance in the civil war? I am not sure, but it's worth pondering.'

'And second?'

'Yes, this is most important. You see, most of the weapons that were given up by the Italians quickly found their way into the arms of the Partisans.'

'How did the local Chetniks respond?'

'As best as they could. But their effectiveness slowly began to wane, mostly due to a lack of weapons and ammunition, falling morale and a number of desertions. With the Germans and Ustaše now replacing the Italians in Dalmatia, and the Partisans getting stronger every day, the Chetniks were slowly being squeezed from all sides. Then a major bombshell. At the Tehran Conference in late 1943, the Allies agreed that the Partisans would be provided with more supplies, equipment and operational support at the expense of the Chetniks. Pro-Partisan elements inside British intelligence and SOE convinced the British Prime Minister, Winston Churchill, that Mihailović needed to be dropped from the team. They pointed to accusations of Chetnik collaboration with the Germans and also questioned their military effectiveness when compared to their Partisan counterparts. Some might say it was the ultimate hatchet job.'

'The Chetniks lost the public relations war, as well as the guerrilla war,' I said bleakly.

'That is one way of looking at it,' admitted Peter. 'But the die was cast. The Chetniks were slowly discarded, and in August 1944, King Petar and his government-in-exile finalised an agreement with Tito, calling on all Croats, Slovenes and Serbs to join the Partisans. When Mihailović refused to adhere to this request, King Petar unceremoniously dumped him several weeks later. The Communist Partisans were now recognised by the King's government-in-exile as the official royalist fighting force in Yugoslavia.'

'And the Chetniks were now on their own, hunted by both the Partisans and the Ustaše, and ignored by almost everyone else,' I concluded.

'Pretty much,' said Peter disconsolately.

'I recognise that he was a great wartime leader, but my father always despised Winston Churchill for his role in abandoning the Chetniks.'

'Most Chetniks I met felt the same way,' Peter acknowledged. 'But to be fair, by the war's end, he understood better than anyone the impending Communist threat to Eastern Europe. Unfortunately, by that time, it was too late for Yugoslavia. Furthermore, some historians still argue that Mihailović was culpable for his own demise by refusing to join the Partisans in a united front against Germany when he had the opportunity, thus further perpetrating the narrative that he was a collaborator who didn't want to fight the Nazis.'

'You obviously refute that argument?' I asked.

'To a large degree, yes. As I said before, perhaps the main reason he promoted restraint against the Germans was to stem the number of reprisals against Serbian civilians, which were excessively brutal. I mean, the accepted practice was one hundred Serbs shot for every German killed by a Chetnik. How could any military commander live with that on his conscience? No, his main priority in the summer of 1944 was to defeat the Partisans, that much is clear. He simply couldn't understand why his government and King Petar were wanting to make deals with Tito. Given what was at stake, the future of post-war Yugoslavia, Mihailović's stance took courage.'

'You sound like you admire him,' I replied with a smile.

'Perhaps I do,' he eventually said after giving my comment some thought. 'As a historian, I try to look at the facts and then make an informed assessment. It doesn't matter to me what other historians think about my views.'

His last sentence was mumbled out with an accusing frown, and I wondered if I had somehow offended his intellectual pride. That's why I quickly asked him another question before he had time to give my unintended impertinence another thought.

'So, tell me more about the Battle of Knin,' I asked.

'Let's go for a ride first before I tell you that story,' he suggested wistfully.

'A ride? Where to?'

'Knin, of course.'

Chapter Six

Split, Croatia
October 2022

In keeping with the local vibe, Peter directed me to his—you guessed it—black SUV. He kindly showed me how to find my seatbelt before landing his car radio on some local hip-hop station. He didn't strike me as a rap music sort of guy, but there he was, tapping away on his steering wheel to a song about some Croatian gangster who missed his 'bitch'. Obviously, 'woke culture' had yet to find its way to the Dalmatian Coast.

Twenty minutes outside of Split, we began to discuss the Battle of Knin. 'Knin is a very historic city,' Peter began. 'During the Middle Ages, it was known as the 'City of the Croatian Kings' before the country was subsumed by the Hapsburg Empire.'

'What about the Second World War?' I asked.

'After Yugoslavia was defeated by the Axis Powers, Knin fell under the jurisdiction of the Independent State of Croatia, although the Italians had a large military presence in the area throughout their occupation of Dalmatia. However, over time, Knin became a Serbian Chetnik stronghold.' He coughed a few times before adding, 'As it was during the recent Homeland War.' Indeed, Knin, the capital of the Serbian independent state of Krajina, was the site of several brutal engagements between Croatian and Serbian forces during that conflict.

As if to confirm that point, Peter gestured towards a deserted, broken-down house standing idly along the road. 'After we proclaimed victory in August 1995, many Serbian families were forcibly removed from this area. That house to our right is a reminder of those traumatic times.'

Peter repeated the last sentence in a forced whisper, an indication, perhaps, of his overall indifference to the Serbs' plight.

'But back to the Second World War,' he continued. 'The Partisan 8th Dalmatian Corps had first taken Split on 26 October 1944, and then liberated Šibenik a week later. It was now early November and the Partisans were on the cusp of securing the entire region.'

'And the Chetniks decided to fight them at Knin?' I jumped ahead.

'Not only the Chetniks but the Germans as well.'

'Really?' I was readily surprised. Dad never once mentioned that he had fought alongside the Germans. 'Are you quite sure? I mean, Dad loathed the Nazis with a passion. As a kid, I wasn't even allowed to have German friends.'

Peter smiled politely at me. 'Once again, you are forgetting our golden rule. None of this makes any sense. It was just the way it was. Operational necessities, remember? The enemy of my enemy is my friend. Just because they fought next to each other doesn't mean that they had to like it. The Chetniks were fighting for their own survival, Alex, not for the glory of Adolf Hitler and the German army. Never forget that. As you said yourself, sometimes in war, temporary alliances like this have to be negotiated in order to survive.'

'Sure,' I muttered. Then it occurred to me. *What else hadn't Dad told me about his war?* 'So, who was in charge of the Chetniks during the battle?'

'Momčilo Đujić, perhaps the most effective of all the Chetnik commanders.'

'Wasn't he a Serbian Orthodox priest?'

'Yes.'

I nodded my head. 'Interesting. My oldest sister Dubravka, who was only four at the time, remembers a high-ranking Chetnik general showing her considerable kindness during a field visit. Perhaps it was him.'

'More than likely. He was a very charismatic leader, feted by his troops and their families, reviled by his enemies. By 1944, his Dinara Chetnik Division was responsible for the majority of Chetnik operations in Northern Dalmatia. Importantly, he was able to commit around four and a half thousand troops at Knin.'

'Including my father,' I whispered.

'If your mother's recollection of events is correct, almost definitely.'

As Peter navigated us through the outer suburbs of Knin, he became lost in his own thoughts. I asked him a simple question about the city's population, and he ignored it with a strange mixture of self-absorption and impunity. It was as if an apparition from his past had suddenly seized his living spirit. However, once we hit the city's central business district, he became conversant once again, pointing out some key landmarks as we slowly drove past them; a cathedral here, an old marketplace there, a statue of some local identity in front of us. Finally, he twisted his head towards me. 'Knin has a long history with death. First, the fierce battle in 1944, followed by Operation Storm fifty-one years later. Sometimes, I feel as if the souls of the dead are watching me here.'

He wiped his brow with a tissue and then provided me with a thorough analysis of the battle, including details about a heroic stand and breakout by Chetnik forces at Padene. As I became more immersed in Peter's story, I tried to visualise my father caught inside this unremitting hellhole, fighting tooth and nail for his life and for the lives of his men. It was a scene I could barely imagine, let alone understand. As I contemplated each new detail of the battle, the missing gaps in my parents' timeline that had confounded me for years finally began to connect. At last, all the anecdotes, all the whispered references, they all made perfect sense. In many ways, their story had always been in front of me, demanding to be told, but I had simply chosen to look in a different direction.

That night, as a show of my appreciation, I bought Peter dinner at a popular seafood restaurant in Split. It was mainly a dour affair. Peter tried his best to make interesting dinnertime conversation, but, unlike Bruno and his friends in Dubrovnik, he lacked any semblance of personal warmth.

At one point, he was at pains to remind me about the precarious nature of my quest. 'Just remember, Alex. The civil war was an extremely brutal affair, and all sides contributed to that brutality. Don't be surprised if you find out something about your father's wartime service that shocks and abhors you.'

I wanted to explain that this was indeed the whole point of my quest, but sometimes it's best to leave sleeping dogs lie. Seemingly caught inside his own personal minefield, the horrors of war that Peter freely spoke about had left a permanent scar on his conscience. His life had become nothing more than a seismic reflection of every battle fought inside his homeland. As he farewelled me after dessert, I was overwhelmed with a sense of pity that he would never be able to escape the scars of his country's volatile past and live the cherished life that he deserved.

Perhaps that's God's plan for all of us who become beholden to the past.

I woke up later than usual the next morning, conscious that I had another busy day in front of me. Just before ten thirty, I boarded a bus to my mother's birthplace of Šibenik. The trip took about eighty minutes, winding through another glorious stretch of the pristine Adriatic coastline, including the incredibly beautiful seaside town of Trogir.

Despite my mother always waxing lyrical about her beloved Šibenik, to my shame, I never held the same affection for the city that I did for Split and Dubrovnik. Šibenik has a fine harbour and is steeped rich in history, while in modern times it has always served as a key transport hub. For this reason, it became a natural target for enemy forces during wartime. Peter told me over dinner that at the height of the Second World War, Šibenik had the dubious honour of being one of the most bombed cities in Europe, while during the Homeland War, it was attacked several times by the Serbian Navy.

As I walked along the main promenade from the bus station towards a strip of packed cafés and restaurants, I wondered whether my coldness towards Šibenik reflected the unhealthy relationship I had with my mother. Mum had admitted to me several times during my formative years that I was a clear mistake; that she never planned to have a child in her middle-aged years. The circumstances of my birth, therefore, mainly caused the barrier between us to grow wider the older I became. I can't remember how it was first presented to me, but when I found out that she had pushed for an abortion during her pregnancy, it simply reinforced a feeling that she never loved me. Throughout my young life in particular, I always believed that she resented having to look after a young child well into her fifties.

I think that's how it started for me; her failure to acknowledge the issues that were important to my life, her ignorance and her constant criticism of my ability, my looks and my character. 'We spent all this money on your education, but you never finish anything,' she once said to me just before she died, not bothering to realise that I had completed two master's degrees, a graduate diploma and two undergraduate degrees. She was also nonplussed with the career I had chosen, never fully recognising or trying to understand any of my many achievements. Although I cried when she passed away in 2011, I wasn't devastated by any means—it was more a relief that I didn't have to try anymore.

Ironically, I was closer to her in personality than I was to my father. My mother and I both shared the same self-deprecating sense of humour, a love of history and horror films, and an obsession with how we presented ourselves to other people. She also told me many things about the war during a holiday we took together to the United Kingdom in 1996 that made me realise, probably too late, the full horrors of her life journey. Given where I had now landed in my quest, I had a unique opportunity to understand her more in death than I ever did during her life.

Despite my indifference to Šibenik, it is an attractive city in its own right, and has a wonderful medieval heart. My first stop, the beautiful St James' Cathedral, is a perpetual reminder of Šibenik's impressive cultural heritage. Completed in 1536, its classical architectural style is augmented by a frieze of seventy-one heads on the exterior walls at the rear of the building. They represent a diverse cast of characters from different ages, where life meant something different and where community, family and church prevailed above all other distractions. Within this sea of faces, I pretended that I could see an outline of Mum and Dad staring at me from the ceiling, beckoning me to join them. It was fun while it lasted until a grumpy-looking priest gestured for me to move along.

Apart from its beauty, St James' Cathedral has a significant connection to our family. It was here where my parents were married and Dubravka was baptised. However, like everything in our family, these events hid the true story. Under regular circumstances, I doubted whether Mum and Dad would have lasted a casual one-night stand, let alone marry and have kids. Dad was too urbane, worldly and charismatic for someone of Mum's sheltered upbringing.

While I had never connected with Mum's side of the family, it was true that her background was even more fascinating than my father's. Her ancestry linked back to a time when Croatia was an independent nation, long before it was incorporated into the Hapsburg Empire. Her maiden name was synonymous with an influential clan that was close to the Croatian monarchy, even establishing its own coat of arms. Mum often liked to boast about how she came from a higher class than Dad, and in many respects, she did.

Her father, Mateo, typified this elevated status. He was a well-known, respected and successful local businessman who wielded significant influence within the Šibenik community. Despite his Croatian heritage, he was extremely supportive of the monarchy, the Yugoslav state and the traditional values of religion and family.

And these reasons alone probably explained why Dad thought it was a good idea to marry Mum after all. That, and one other important detail. You see, they really never had a choice. All I know is that they met each other one night at a dance in Šibenik. Mum had just split up from her fiancé, while Dad was most likely out for a quick bit of action. What happened next left little to the imagination but was summed up comically by Mum. 'It was late at night, and your father wanted to show me something, and boom, the next thing I knew, I was pregnant with your sister.'

Of course, there was no going back in those days. If you got someone pregnant, you had an obligation to do the right thing. While Dad didn't always do the right thing, on this occasion, he did. But then, this 'noble' gesture did come with some advantages. For a start, he was marrying into a well-off, middle-class family, which meant he could leave the navy and pursue the luxurious lifestyle he always coveted. He also found himself a cushy job at the local aluminium refinery, which paid well and conferred upon him instant status. Say the right things, keep up the pretences, and you never know, you might even be able to squeeze in a quick fling in Split every now and then.

Perhaps I am being too harsh on him, I admonished myself, as I slipped some Kuna into a nearby donation box. It was not as if I had lived my life as a celibate monk, either. Whether I accepted it or not, my father had a weakness that would hound him relentlessly for the rest of his life. Regardless, my pernicious judgment of his character was completely irrelevant. It explained a lot, but not everything.

Upon leaving St James' Cathedral, I lost myself down some hidden side streets before finding a sign to my next destination, the mighty St Michael's Fortress. I headed north towards Trg Pavla Subica and then turned right onto Ulica Kralja Zvonimira. I walked a further two hundred metres before reaching an intersection. From there, I cautiously followed the directions towards one of the steepest hills I had ever encountered in my life before finally reaching the summit some twenty minutes later. The unintended physical exertion I had put myself through left my chest heaving for air and my aching bones cursing the tendrils of a chilly afternoon wind.

St Michael's fortress was built around the eleventh century and has been used for many different purposes over the years, including as a military strong point, a prison, and a storage facility. Its position, at the apex of the hill overlooking the city and the sea, gives it a commanding view over the rest of the world. Indeed, as I now embraced a mysterious horizon, I could hear the imaginary whispers from another time as they floated past my face.

Hidden beneath the white-tipped roofs below me lay the secrets of my family's past, secrets that now demanded to be unravelled. With so much at stake, I was suddenly consumed by their honesty and raw power. The picture I could never unveil before now silently illuminated my heart like a thousand lights, and I thanked God for taking me this far.

After searching for most of my adult life, all the strands had finally come together. It had been both a frustrating and emotional experience, but I was ready to tell my parents' story if time could only do it justice. With the knowledge I had obtained over the past few days, I felt a deeper connection to my heritage than ever before. And if nothing else was achieved, I held onto the hope that, at last, scattered amongst the ashes of this tragedy, was a pathway to what really happened to me in Kandos.

Part Three

Anton's War

Chapter One

Split, Croatia
April 1941

Anton sat nervously at the table as he waited for the pretty young waitress with the seashell-coloured eyes to return with his coffee. For a moment, he wondered if the constant tapping of his fingers, the frequent inspections of his watch and his occasional glances at the gloomy afternoon sky made him look suspicious. If it did, it would have defeated the whole purpose of choosing this secluded café in the first place, an old watering hole he had discovered by chance when he was stationed in Split with the Royal Yugoslav Navy two years before.

Back then, he had used the café, on several occasions, to initiate his many illicit trysts with the staggering array of married women he had met during his posting, the names of whom he could now barely remember. 'My husband would never be seen in a place like this, so we are perfectly safe,' a certain blonde heiress had convinced him before they disappeared into a nearby hotel. And how right she was.

Tucked away on the corner of a tiny cul-de-sac behind Bacvice Beach, barely noticeable even to the discerning visitor, the café was a sanctuary for every local cutthroat, smuggler or Lothario who wanted to spark the fires of an intimate stranger or trade their loathsome secrets to a higher cause. More so, it definitely wasn't the place to be seen if you lived a normal, mundane life, a cause that Anton had willingly accepted since his marriage to Vuka. For that reason alone, he wondered whether playing roulette with his past was the right thing to do, given what was at stake.

A car backfiring in the distance temporarily startled him before he lifted his eyes across the outside courtyard towards the café's only other patron. Dressed in a torn black suit, his hands fumbling over a bottle of red wine, sat a single man in his late forties, his shiny, bald scalp glistening inside a speck of yellow light, the sallow jowls on his face melting into his half-filled glass. Perhaps the unbridled tension was now playing tricks on him, but Anton was sure that the peculiarities of the man's downtrodden profile were familiar. Was he someone he had served with in the navy? Or perhaps the husband or boyfriend of some floozy he had bedded years ago? Whoever he was and whatever his story, Anton's paranoia wanted the man to magically disappear before his companions arrived, for no other reason than to mitigate his strained nerves.

The waitress finally returned with a large cup of black coffee. She tried to smile as Anton nodded his thanks, but it was more out of politeness than desire. He certainly didn't judge her, even though he could have done with a bit of harmless flirting, given the circumstances. But with the country on high alert after the events of the past week, it was hard to approach life with anything other than pessimism and despair. Yugoslavia was on the brink of catastrophe; everyone Anton had spoken to since the coup expressed the same sense of foreboding.

This wasn't the time for flippancy or procrastination. Decisions were being made; alliances were being sought. Whatever options were available to Anton over the weeks ahead, he felt obliged to meet with Duško and the Englishman first before deciding on his next move.

It was Duško's idea to meet in Split. He was a former naval colleague of Anton's who now worked for military intelligence in Belgrade. They had once been friends, drinking partners, men about town. But that was in 1939, when the world was a different place. With Europe now consumed by war, everyone had become hostage to their own individual priorities. Anton's priority was to make sure that the aluminium factory ran efficiently every day; Duško's priority was to stumble inside a murky world where no one understood the rules or the consequences of the end game.

As for the Englishman, all Anton knew was that he was an army officer who had come from Cairo to meet people like him—supporters of the crown who could see that war was coming to Yugoslavia very soon. It was rumoured that the English had facilitated the coup in Belgrade last week. If so, they had got what they wanted. But at what cost? And what would that mean for the future of his country?

Damn it, he felt compelled to look at his watch once more. *One thirty. Already fifteen minutes late.* Anton had made some pithy excuse to his supervisor about why he had to travel to Split that afternoon. In retrospect, his story was hardly believable, but then, the supervisor, aware of Anton's military past, also knew not to ask too many questions. 'Make sure you're back by four thirty,' he had barked. There was a bus that left for Šibenik in an hour and a half, and Anton was determined to be on it. Regardless of what had made Duško and the Englishman late for this appointment, he wasn't going to wait for them for much longer.

Anton reached inside his coat pocket and pulled out a packet of cigarettes. His father-in-law, Mateo, hated smoking, especially inside the family home, so to keep the peace, Anton would sneak outside every night and gasp out two or three cigarettes before going to bed. It was not ideal for a packet-a-day man like Anton, but it was the way it had to be.

Despite some minor disagreements, Anton had an excellent relationship with his father-in-law. Vuka often growled that he liked her father more than he liked her. Perhaps there was an element of truth behind that remark. Mateo was a successful and principled entrepreneur who knew everyone and owed no one. For whatever reason, his hard exterior was frequently softened by Anton's swirling charisma and zest for life. And, of course, Anton was Dubravka's father, so that put the cherry on top of the cake.

While marriage curtailed the carefree life he once enjoyed, Anton knew that it had its advantages, and having a father-in-law who admired him certainly helped. He was living a comfortable life that befitted his ambitions, and he wasn't prepared to give it up so easily. But with war inevitable, maybe he wouldn't have any choice in the matter. *Damn those fucking Germans.*

Anton carefully snapped out a cigarette from the packet and placed it between his cracked lips. But before he had a chance to fumble around for his zippo, a flickering shadow appeared at his table.

'Here, let me do that for you,' said the black-suited Wine Man, who now stood over him like a clumsy bear. As if by magic, he produced a lighter from nowhere, and a single orange flame flicked at Anton's cigarette.

'Thank you,' Anton said curtly. He took several seconds to study the man's face. It betrayed no emotion other than an effortless stare. 'Do I know you?' he finally asked.

'Perhaps you do,' Wine Man replied. 'But now is not the time for reminiscing, is it?' He took a deep breath. 'Please listen. At the top of the street, a car is waiting for you. Please make yourself known to the driver. He will take you to Duško and the Englishman. Now, finish your cigarette quickly and get moving.'

Anton didn't like taking orders from people he didn't know. He felt like grabbing this obnoxious man by the neck, pinning him up against the wall and demanding some answers. But all he could think about in between bursts of white rage was that damned bus to Šibenik.

'Okay,' he muttered bleakly, angry at his own impotence. He immediately delved into his back trouser pocket in search of his wallet, but Wine Man lifted his arm in protest. 'I will take care of the bill. Just get moving.'

Anton stared coldly at Wine Man one last time before he kicked away his chair in disgust and made his way briskly to the top of the cul-de-sac. Sure enough, there sat a black Mercedes Benz 770 parked alongside several carefully manicured oak trees.

He peered nervously through the front passenger window where a young man, dressed in a striped suit and boasting a brutally short haircut, gestured to the back of the car. Anton casually nodded his head, opened the rear door and slumped onto the firm leather seat. The car exuded an air of elegance and sophistication he had rarely experienced before in this part of the world.

'You're taking me to Duško?' he finally asked the driver politely in Serbo-Croatian. The young man either didn't speak the language or pretended not to understand. Without raising an eyebrow, he signalled to Anton to close the door. Whether he liked it or not, Anton was now trapped.

For the next ten minutes, Anton sat nervously as the driver navigated a series of winding streets towards the safe house. He had been waiting for this meeting for days, ever since he had received that cryptic phone call from Duško. But the confusion of the sudden change of plans only enhanced the palpable tension swirling around him as they made their way deeper into Split's hidden neighbourhoods.

Anton tried to pass the time by mentally preparing for the questions he was certain that Duško and the Englishman would ask him. Whether he had the answers to satisfy them, he didn't really care. He had left the navy twelve months ago, mainly because he couldn't stand the bullshit any longer. If Duško was out to offer him more of the same, then he could forget it. Anton was his own man now, capable of making his own decisions, and he didn't need anyone telling him how to fight the next war.

The driver finally stopped in front of a freshly painted apartment Anton had never seen before. 'In there,' he suddenly snapped at Anton in English. He pointed an ugly black fingernail towards the front door of the apartment. 'Do you understand?' Anton had visited the United Kingdom and Ireland on several occasions during his naval years and had become reasonably fluent in English—something that he often downplayed for his own security.

'Yes,' he replied indignantly before opening the car door.

Satisfied, the driver offered him a lazy frown. 'I will wait for you here.'

'Enjoy yourself, won't you?' Anton replied sarcastically, closing the car door behind him. After stretching his legs on the footpath, he strode towards the front patio, the early afternoon sunshine caressing his pale cheeks. Making doubly sure no one else in the neighbourhood was watching, he swallowed some warm spring air, calmly opened the unlocked door and walked inside.

He was greeted by a narrow hallway that mysteriously led to an old, creaky staircase. Anton wondered at first whether he was meant to navigate the stairs at his own peril, but a garbled speck of noise now echoed softly from the first door on his right. As always, he followed his natural instinct, blew out some more air, and then quietly entered a large living room.

Surprisingly, it was far more sophisticated than what he had expected. He first noticed the walls, which were expertly painted in a swirling array of beige and cream hues. Matching these colours, the floor was covered by a patterned carpet, which added warmth and grace to the room. A small fireplace guarded the entrance to an adjoining passageway, while a large mirror with yellow-gold frames hung opulently from above.

In the middle of the room stood a handsome coffee table made of polished wood with curved edges and sleek lines, accompanied by three sturdy chairs. The table was decorated with several porcelain vases filled with fresh flowers, an overturned notebook and a decanter of brandy supported by three glasses. All things being considered, it was rather upmarket for a safe house.

'Anton, my dear fellow,' a deep, soothing voice bellowed from the corner of the room. 'Welcome to our humble abode.' Anton twisted his neck sideways to greet a tall, rugged-looking man in his mid-thirties.

Duško.

Happily, his friend still possessed that fierce look that never changed even when he smiled, while his muscular build was the result of many years of hard physical work. As was his style, Duško's hair was skilfully unkempt, and he wore a tattered suit that had been patched up one too many times. Nevertheless, he carried himself with a quiet confidence, the trait of a man destined to do remarkable things with his life.

A second man soon emerged from the dazzling light behind him. He was of slender build, with blood-shot, rapier-like eyes that seemed to stare straight through you. His chiselled jawline and stern expression gave the impression of a man who had already seen too much of the war and didn't enjoy the experience. Even so, the man moved with the grace of a leopard.

'My name is Major Eric Stubbs from the British Army,' he announced in perfect Serbo-Croatian. After shaking his hand, Anton turned towards Duško, and the two old friends embraced.

'Good to see you, my brother,' Duško said warmly. 'Marriage suits you!'

Anton didn't know whether his friend, the permanent bachelor, was having a joke at his expense or not, but then, one never really knew with Duško.

'You too,' Anton replied. 'It's been far too long.'

Stubbs interrupted the reunion by coughing impatiently several times. 'Of course,' Duško laughed. 'We must get down to business.' He beckoned to the table and invited his companions to avail themselves of the brandy.

Anton rarely drank alcohol during the day, but nevertheless, he poured himself a half-filled glass before taking his seat. After everything he had gone through so far that morning, a drink seemed an appropriate distraction.

Duško smiled at Stubbs, as if the pair had rehearsed this whole scene beforehand. 'Anton was an exceptional engineer in the Royal Yugoslav Navy with an impeccable service record,' Duško began.

Well, not entirely true, Anton thought. *There was that issue with the commanding officer's wife that almost led to my dismissal from the navy.* If it weren't for his mother pleading with them to give him another chance, he would have been ousted without a second thought. But Duško, who indeed knew about the scandal, was remarkably forgiving about such things. In any case, Stubbs seemed thoroughly unimpressed with Anton so far, as he considered him with his rapier-like eyes.

'What do you do now?' he finally asked with an attempted smile. *As if you don't already know.*

'I am the boiler room supervisor at the aluminium factory near Šibenik,' Anton replied. 'I keep the boiler room running, manage the water-testing facilities, all the important things that the big wigs know nothing about.'

'Sounds interesting.'

Anton frowned at what he assumed was a backhanded retort. 'Not as challenging as living inside an engine room on a destroyer, but interesting enough,' he replied bluntly. He was already starting to dislike the Englishman but was determined to keep his mouth shut out of respect for Duško.

Sensing this, Duško suddenly leant forward and refilled Anton's glass. 'My apologies for the change in plans, Anton, but we have to be careful. There are Ustaše spies everywhere.'

Anton said nothing at first as he sipped at his drink. The brandy burnt his throat. 'I am sure they are,' he coughed. 'It is a natural reaction to what is about to happen.'

'And what is about to happen?' Stubbs asked quizzically.

'I don't think I have to explain that to you, Major.'

'Try me.'

Anton sighed. 'I expect the German Army to invade any day now. And when they do, we will not be able to withstand them for more than a week.'

'You underestimate the Yugoslav Armed Forces.'

For the first time, Anton noticed the Englishman's scuffed silver cufflinks. For some reason, they didn't seem to match his stifling arrogance. 'No, I don't,' Anton replied brusquely. 'If anything, you English have overestimated our fighting capabilities. And despite celebrating the outcome of that damn coup, you won't be in a position to help us for much longer.' For a moment, a steely silence gripped the room.

'Perhaps you're right,' Duško finally intervened.

'We all know that I am,' Anton replied. 'We also all know that as soon as the government capitulates, the Ustaše will take control of Croatia and we will have half the Italian Army deployed on the Dalmatian coastline, just like they have always wanted. There is nothing anyone will be able to do—not the English, not the Russians, not anyone.' He paused to catch his breath. 'Tell me that I am wrong.'

Duško and Stubbs shared a reflective glance. Anton probably didn't realise it yet, but he had definitely passed their test.

'And what are you personally going to do when they invade?' Duško asked.

'Fight, of course,' Anton replied curtly. 'What would you have me do?'

Duško reached across and grabbed Anton's arm. 'Of course, my friend. You are a patriot, after all. But first, you must think carefully where your talents could be best utilised before rushing your decision and doing something that you may regret.'

'I don't know what you mean,' said Anton honestly. *Damn you, Duško. What are you playing at? Spit it out, for God's sake.*

'I'm just saying that joining an army that is about to get crushed may not be the wisest decision for you to make at this point in time.'

Anton felt a flush of anger thump against his chest. What did they expect him to do? Sit back and watch his country be destroyed without lifting a finger? For all of his faults, Anton was not a coward. If there was a fight to be had, he was determined to be in it.

'I am not sure what other options I have,' he finally retorted. 'You think poorly of me, Duško, if you suggest that I should step back and do nothing.'

Duško's unforced frown was flushed with exasperation. 'That's not what I am asking you to consider,' he snapped.

'Then what are you asking me?'

Duško folded his arms and stared impatiently at his friend. 'Perhaps we should first tell you who we represent.'

'That would be a good start.'

'I currently work for a man called Ilija Trifunović-Birčanin. I take it you have heard of him?'

'Of course I have,' Anton nodded. 'He is a Serbian hero of the Great War.'

'One of the famous Chetniks who helped save our country against Austrian aggression,' Duško added proudly.

'A worthy man to work for,' Anton said jealously. Being able to recite the Birčanin legend and the sacrifices made by the Chetniks during the Great War had almost been compulsory during his time in the navy.

'Yes. He and I have been working together now for several weeks to establish guerrilla cells that can be activated in the event of an enemy attack. With things currently at a flashpoint, we are starting to make our final preparations.'

'And what of him?' Anton pointed rudely at Stubbs.

The Englishman quickly held up his hand before Duško had an opportunity to respond. 'Anton,' he paused to catch his eyes. 'May I call you Anton?'

'Of course,' Anton grumbled in response.

'I work for an organisation called the Special Operations Executive. It was established last year by Prime Minister Churchill. Our role is to take the battle to the Nazis by helping our allies in occupied Europe. We provide resistance groups with training and equipment to help undertake intelligence gathering and sabotage operations. To quote old Winston himself, we want to set Europe ablaze and give the Germans the bloodiest nose imaginable. So, to answer your question, I am here in Yugoslavia on behalf of SOE to help make the Birčanin proposal work.'

Anton tried very hard not to laugh. 'Once the Germans destroy my country, I am not sure how many of us will still be alive to do the bidding of the British Empire, Major Stubbs. Perhaps Mr Churchill's time would be better spent sending us your planes and tanks before the German invasion actually commences.'

'You know that is not going to happen,' Duško intervened quickly before Stubbs could respond. 'Whether we like it or not, going underground and fighting the way we know best will be our only choice, just like the Chetnik guerrillas did in Serbia during the Great War.'

'And you want to bring this guerrilla war to sleepy old Šibenik?' Anton asked caustically. 'I applaud you.'

Duško barely batted an eyelid. 'Establishing a resistance movement in an important coastal city like Šibenik will be vital to our success. To begin with, it's a logistical pathway to the Northern Dalmatian Coast and Italy. And aluminium is critical to the Axis war effort. You know this more than I do, Anton.'

Anton rubbed his chin. 'So, if I understand you correctly, you are asking me to spy for the British after we are defeated by the Germans and living under Italian occupation?'

'Not only the British but the Chetniks as well.'

'The Chetniks?' Anton laughed. 'You are already calling yourselves Chetniks?'

'Of course. What else would you suggest we call ourselves?'

Anton shook his head. They obviously took him for a fool with these insane plans and catchy names. Understandably, his face began to betray every one of his wavering doubts.

'Maybe I was given the wrong information, but I was led to believe that you support King Petar and the monarchy.' Stubbs spoke with an air of lofty superiority, as if he was addressing one of his downtrodden corporals on the parade ground.

'Of course I do,' Anton replied angrily, offended by the question. 'God willing, the monarchy is the one thing that has protected my country from the Ustaše and the threat of communism. If there is an alternative for me, I have yet to hear of one.'

'Then join us,' Duško encouraged. 'A man with your skills and ambition is too valuable to spend the rest of the war in a brutal prisoner of war camp, or worse still, in a coffin. And you should think of your wife and daughter and what is best for them.'

Although Anton tried not to show emotion, Duško's mention of his family struck a raw nerve. Even though his friend was correct—there was a strong chance he would end up dead if he joined the fighting—it was still a course of action he was willing to take. He couldn't leave the war for other people to prosecute. How could he look at himself in the mirror? More importantly, what would he say to those people he knew who had sacrificed their own husbands and sons for the cause of freedom?

Yet, hidden behind that desire for action, that longing to be part of something historic, Anton was flooded with conflicted feelings about leaving his family, possibly forever. His physical desire for Vuka had worn out many months ago, and he had recently discovered the full extent of her emotional frailties that weren't apparent before their marriage. He just accepted that sooner or later, he would seek another woman's bed. In a place like Šibenik, such a scandal could never be kept secret and would undoubtedly destroy his reputation.

But his daughter, Dubravka, was altogether something else. *Something special.* Despite the growing concerns he now possessed about his marriage, he was exceptionally proud to be a father. Just watching his little one sleep silently in her crib, oblivious to the machinations of the deadly world she had been born into, made him feel strangely contented. How could he possibly leave such a delicate little creature, barely five months old, to the mercy of the Nazis or Ustaše?

Do I really have a choice? Or is Duško giving me a perfect way out?

'What do you want me to do?' he finally asked the two men as he squeezed a hand around his now empty glass.

'Nothing for the moment,' Duško replied. 'Return to Šibenik this afternoon. Don't tell anyone about this meeting; go about your daily routine. When the storm comes in the next few days, stay close to your home and family, even if there is fighting in the city. Most importantly, do not broadcast your political views to anyone you don't know or reveal that you were once a navy officer unless you have to. Keep a low profile, do your job quietly and become indispensable at the factory. It's important that you can move about town without arousing too much suspicion. When we are ready to use your services, your handler will contact you with further instructions.'

'And who is my handler?' He paused to emphasise the point. 'I would like to know his identity, given that he has my life in his hands.' It seemed a reasonable request, considering the risks Anton was taking.

'You have already met him earlier today,' Stubbs said brusquely.

Wine Man. Anton wiped his brow. 'You mean that grubby fellow I met back at the café?'

'Yes,' Duško replied. 'That grubby fellow back at the café.' He paused to wipe his mouth with a napkin before adding, 'You would be unwise to pass judgement on him so quickly based on appearances. He is a formidable agent, one of the best we have, and also a local Croat. He has been shadowing your movements for several days, making sure that the Ustaše have not been following you. Consider him your new guardian angel.'

Shadowing me? Perhaps that's where he had seen him before, skulking around in the corner of some unknown alleyway with all the other night crawlers. Anton wasn't someone usually fooled by first impressions, but back at the café, Wine Man had conjured up a black cloud inside Anton's mind that he couldn't explain. Perhaps it was nothing, or perhaps it was something. But if Duško vouched for this man, then he would just have to accept him for who he was.

The three men spoke about the political situation for another fifteen minutes before Duško raised his hand once again. 'Time for you to go, Anton.' They stood up at the same time, and Duško surged forward to offer his friend another warm embrace. 'You are doing the right thing, my friend. We need good people like you in the Chetniks.'

Anton managed to laugh. 'This is going to be a Serbian fight, Duško. We both know that. At the end of the day, I am a Roman Catholic and a Dalmatian Croat and unlikely to be ever fully trusted by the Serbs. Perhaps that's why I am valuable to you and your British friend—no one will ever suspect that a Croat is working for the Chetniks.'

The disconcerting thing was that Duško didn't deny his accusation. 'Don't think too much about that, my friend. You have already served the monarchy well.' He suddenly put a reassuring hand on Anton's shoulder. 'You may not realise it yet, but you were born for war, a natural leader if I ever saw one. Men will follow you to the ends of the Earth without even questioning why. We both know that. When the time comes, the love you have for your country will undoubtedly prevail.'

'And what about you?' Anton asked his friend with concern. 'When will I see you again?' There was a strained silence as Duško considered the question with a raised eyebrow.

'Perhaps after the war,' he said honestly. He now tried to offer Anton a reassuring smile. 'Until then, we must do our best to survive.'

'And if we don't?' Anton asked grimly.

'Then I am afraid there won't be much left of this country for us to worry about.'

Chapter Two

Šibenik, Yugoslavia
September 1941

On 6 April 1941, two days after Anton met with Duško and Stubbs, the German-led attack on Yugoslavia began. The hostilities commenced with a ruthless aerial bombardment of Belgrade by the German Air Force, (Luftwaffe). The Yugoslav Air Force and its ground defences were destroyed within hours. However, as the foreboding sounds of the German Stuka dive bombers howled mercilessly from above, hour after hour, it was the civilian population that would suffer the most. By the end of that first attack, beneath the endless piles of rubble and debris lay four thousand dead men, women and children. It was warfare at its most brutal.

Hitler had aptly called this exercise in terror *Operation Vengeance* for a reason. Maddened that his 'Balkans problem' had delayed his long-awaited invasion of the Soviet Union, the Führer had promised his generals that he would destroy Yugoslavia with 'merciless brutality'. It was a promise delivered with furious intent.

On 17 April, after only eleven days of fighting, Yugoslav officials signed an armistice agreement, confirming that its armed forces had unconditionally surrendered. It was an abject humiliation for the Yugoslav state, who thought it could defy Hitler and not suffer the severe consequences.

As Duško had predicted, the only option that remained for the new government-in-exile was to continue the war through an organised insurgency. From the moment the official armistice was formalised, and the victorious Nazis began dismembering Yugoslavia, sharing the scraps with their vile allies, members of the armed forces loyal to King Petar, led by Colonel Draža Mihailović, started to organise resistance groups in the mountains of western Serbia.

The war came quickly to Šibenik. First, the Stukas arrived, destroying selected targets and causing fear and panic among the population. Following the proclamation of the Fascist Independent State of Croatia in Zagreb on 10 April 1941, Ustaše supporters and Croatian soldiers belonging to the local Šibenik Army Garrison effectively took control of the city. Some fanatics wasted no time in rounding up perceived political enemies, mostly prominent Serbs who had been on their watch lists for years. One by one, people began to disappear into thin air without even having the opportunity to say goodbye to their families and loved ones. Within days, rumours of murder, rape and helpless children crying in despair for their missing or murdered parents surfaced throughout the city.

And this was only the beginning.

As Šibenik wilted under the strains of war, Anton could do nothing but sit helplessly inside the sanctuary of the bedroom he shared with Vuka. At any moment, he feared the sound of a heavy knock on the door and some Ustaše thug demanding his presence. On the third night of the occupation, with a revolver he had stolen from the navy by his side, he confided with his father-in-law that should he be arrested, he would go down all guns blazing. However, to Anton's surprise, Mateo's eyes had lit up with incandescent rage as he thumped his hands hard against the kitchen table.

'In this house, I am responsible for the safety of my family,' Mateo warned. 'So, you will do nothing that compromises that situation. Do you understand, Anton?'

Not wishing to sour the good relationship he had with Mateo, Anton had garbled some swear words under his breath and then quietly returned to his bedroom, ignoring Vuka's usual nightly screams as she followed him inside. Her mother had warned Anton that Vuka was suffering from the usual mood swings some women experienced after giving birth, but the strains of war had taken her frustrations and outbursts to a new level. If it wasn't bad enough being trapped inside this house, with a possible target on his forehead, he also had to share his precious time with an emotionally unstable wife.

What the hell had he got himself into?

That night, Anton fell inside an endless labyrinth of torment as he grappled with the agonising question that had weighed heavily on his mind for days—had he put the entire household in peril by agreeing to spy for the British?

As the nighttime shadows danced provocatively across his bedroom ceiling, Anton fell in and out of a troubled sleep, barely able to differentiate between his subconscious and reality. When he finally emerged from yet another self-induced nightmare, he knew it was time to act. Not only was he a danger to himself, but he was also a danger to everyone around him, especially his beloved daughter. Her chances of survival would increase substantially if he only followed his original plan and escaped into the mountains to join the resistance.

Mateo would ensure that Vuka and the child would be looked after properly should anything happen to him. He was a proud man who would put things right, if not merely to protect his own reputation and standing in the local community. And while he could sometimes appear pitiless towards his family, Mateo loved his little granddaughter with all his heart. Now that the war had consumed Šibenik, she had become his obsession, his main connection to a happier life.

As for Duško, fuck him. He was a fool to believe that Anton would idly sit by and allow the Ustaše terrorists to do what they liked. And why should he trust this Wine Man fellow? A man who looked like he could barely dress himself in the morning, let alone run a spy ring for the British. No, he was a man who looked after his own destiny; he wasn't beholden to some half-drunk brute who stank like a piggery.

But by morning, Anton's demons had seemingly deserted him for another day. He tried to calmly rationalise his options. In the end, he had made a promise to Duško, and now he had thought it through some more, he was determined to keep it. There was no guarantee that the Serbian resistance would accept a Roman Catholic Croat like Anton if he simply appeared to them unannounced. He desperately needed Duško's patronage; that was made clear to him when they met in Split. Nevertheless, the waiting game was killing him, the daily stress unbearable, and who knew when he would see Wine Man again, if at all.

His anxiety eased later that morning when the oldest of Mateo's three daughters, Jelena, arrived at the house with some news. Five years older than Vuka, Jelena was undoubtedly a more attractive and sophisticated version of Anton's wife. Her brown eyes danced seductively whenever she spoke, and her long, curly auburn hair gave her a distinct Hedy Lamarr look that Anton found bewitching. Much like Lamarr, the famous American actress and inventor, Jelena was as sharp as a knife. Curiously, Jelena and Anton shared a special bond, although he strongly suspected that underneath that vivacious exterior, she was a practising Communist.

Married at seventeen, the family of Jelena's husband were working-class people who opposed everything that her traditional, conservative upbringing stood for. Mateo had disapproved of the marriage and was hurt by his daughter's regular subversive utterings about his bourgeois lifestyle. The desultory look she gave her father whenever the topic of politics came up surely gave her secret away.

But for now, she excitedly gathered Anton, Mateo, Vuka and her youngest sister, Ruža, around the kitchen table and, without pausing to catch her breath, told them what she had just heard. Jelena had been the only family member who had so far ventured outside to see what was happening for herself, which was entirely consistent with her intriguing personality.

'I was just speaking to my friend, Mario, the policeman. He told me that the Italians are arriving in Šibenik today and taking control of the city. The Ustaše are not happy about things but have been told by Pavelić himself to back down.'

Everyone took a moment to consider the implications before Jelena added, with a slight frown, 'This has to be good news, surely?'

Mateo placed an arm around his daughter, a gesture that caught everyone by surprise. It wasn't every day he showed such affection to his children.

'We don't know that for sure, my child. The Italians felt cheated after the last war when Dalmatia was not absorbed into their country. They are bound to be just as harsh as the Ustaše, perhaps not with the same levels of cruelty, but harsh, nonetheless. We just have to see what happens.'

They didn't have long to wait. Later that afternoon, the much-vaunted 17th Italian Army Corps seized control of Šibenik. Several days later, the Italian Grado naval infantry battalion landed at Šibenik harbour. The city was now firmly in the hands of the Italians. The Ustaše, caught within their own circle of violence, begrudgingly handed over the reins of power before they could do more damage. Within the blink of an eye, Šibenik became subsumed by the contradictions of war.

Unsurprisingly, Mateo's warning proved to be prescient. Although Šibenik thankfully escaped the full extent of the Ustaše's wrath for now, life under the Italian occupation remained extremely harsh. Within days, a series of repressive measures were introduced by the occupiers, such as curfews, forced labour, ongoing surveillance and strict controls over personal movement and association. Several concentration camps were established across Dalmatia, including a notorious prison run by the Ustaše on the island of Pag in June 1941. Thousands of prisoners, including Jews, Serbs, Roma and political dissidents, were incarcerated in the camp infamously known as 'Slana' (which translates to 'Salty' in English). The appalling conditions of the camp undermined the island's natural beauty.

While the Italians feasted on their military success, Šibenik's residents suffered regularly from food shortages, while buying basic items such as clothing and medical supplies often became a daily struggle. Travel in and out of Šibenik was heavily restricted, given the strict military control over the roads and its modern seaport. In addition, the Italians introduced a number of policies aimed at Italianising the region. They changed Šibenik's name to Sebenico, promoted Italian culture in every facet of life, including within the education system, insisted that people spoke Italian in public and discriminated against the local population wherever and whenever they could. It was as if Šibenik's proud history, which had stoically withstood the cumulative pain of centuries, was to be wiped clean forever.

Although the Italians were dismissive of the Ustaše and were eager to exclude them as much as possible from any meaningful decision-making, they maintained a menacing presence in the region. The local population remained fearful of their retribution; even those Croats who may have supported independence but were opposed to the Ustaše's questionable methods didn't feel safe.

A reminder of their mendacity occurred on 27 August 1941, when a group of Ustaše soldiers murdered thirty Serbian civilians in the village of Civljane, a short distance from Šibenik. This was in reprisal for the killing of an Ustaše officer by Communist guerrillas a few days before. To the horror of those who actually cared, the victims were mostly women, children and the elderly. This wasn't warfare; it was a pathway to annihilation. And make no mistake, more was to come. The Italians might have treated the Ustaše as an irrelevance, but the locals knew better.

As much as possible, Anton tried to take these unfolding events in his stride. He wasn't happy, of course; in fact, as a proud Yugoslav and Dalmatian, it hurt him deeply to see his beloved country systematically dismantled. He dreamt only of revenge. How he wished that the British would soon give him a task worthy of his talents before he took matters into his own hands.

Yet, if he was being honest with himself, Anton was surviving better than most people in Šibenik. Mateo had such a good reputation within the community that even the Ustaše left him alone. And despite the city's severe economic constraints, Mateo's local restaurant thankfully began to thrive once again, mainly due to the patronage of cashed-up Italian soldiers. Suddenly, nights within the household became less stressful.

Once the Italians occupied the city, a group of industrialists arrived from Rome and immediately took control of the aluminium factory where Anton worked. The unfettered production of aluminium had to be maintained at all costs. Realising that they needed the assistance of experienced men like Anton to run the factory's daily operations, he was quickly given the status of an essential worker and then ordered to return to his job.

His position at the factory came with some privileges. Most importantly, it meant that Anton was able to leave the house during the week, erasing the severe claustrophobia he had experienced during those initial days of the occupation when the fear of being arrested and Vuka's constant tantrums had driven him to the edge of madness. And it also enabled him to move freely around the city without attracting too much attention from the authorities. After a sustained period of unbridled tension, Anton finally felt in control of his own destiny.

The aluminium factory was situated in the small village of Lozovac, about thirteen kilometres to the east of Šibenik. It was a particularly picturesque part of Yugoslavia, surrounded by thick, dense pine forests and coarse, rugged peaks that snaked invitingly towards the sky. Close by, the crystal sounds of the famous Krka waterfalls gushed in cadence with the ever-present birdsong, even while the terrors of war threatened to expose its untouched beauty. It was said that both the Chetniks and the Partisans roamed the nearby mountains, but for the workers like Anton, the Lozovac factory offered a welcome respite from the drudgery of Šibenik's daily tribulations.

By the end of summer, Anton's days had fallen into a monotonous routine. Every morning, just before seven thirty, he would kiss Dubravka goodbye, mutter something unflattering to Vuka, and then quietly stroll down the esplanade towards the main Šibenik bus shelter, where a fading, grey-coloured coach waited for him and some of his coworkers.

After the same group of disinterested Italian soldiers conducted the obligatory identity checks, this strange cohort of blue-collar workers would sit silently in their seats, their arms folded protectively against their chests, while their weather-beaten faces strained to look at the person sitting next to them. Mercifully, the trip was a short one and they usually arrived at the main security gate just before eight fifteen.

After more security checks, the workers were driven inside the compound and eventually released near the main administration building. As if they needed reminding of their precarious situation, an obese, balding army major with an over-exaggerated limp would greet them every day at the same time to explain that resistance was indeed futile. They were here to do the bidding of the Italian empire, and if they wanted to survive the war, they should gratefully remember that. Occasionally, a low-key grumble from some half-wit would leak out from the back of the group, but more often not, the men would just sigh loudly in indignation, as if it was their only form of protest, and then wander off to their workstations.

If they were lucky, they might stop for twenty minutes just after midday to eat their packed lunches and take a leak, but other than that, they worked solidly until five thirty, when that infernal grey bus arrived once more, this time with the factory's night shift employees. For many, it was boring, back-breaking work, but it was better than living like a cockroach inside a slave labour camp.

Anton's small office was situated next to the boiler room. His first task upon arrival each morning was to read the overnight production reports and then consult with his foremen on the current state of the boilers. Providing that there were no issues, he would then trudge across to the laboratory to oversee the daily water testing. Regular water testing, in conjunction with necessary treatment and maintenance, ensured that the boilers operated safely, efficiently and reliably, minimising the risk of damage and potential safety hazards.

Prior to Anton's employment, the factory's boilers frequently experienced stage-one corrosion, caused mainly by the rapid mixture of dissolved oxygen and a collection of various minerals. The time spent remediating the boilers heavily impacted on production costs and delivery. Indebted as he was to his on-the-job training in the navy, Anton was an expert in mitigating metal corrosion. Within months, his expertise came to the fore, and most of the systemic problems had been quickly eradicated, much to the delight of the factory owners. If he didn't know already that water testing was the most important part of his job, his supervisor, Mr Vlasic, would constantly remind him. 'Test, test, test, Anton!' he would shout at least once a day. 'That's what it's all about!' As if a man of Anton's experience and ability had to be reminded.

Once the stress of the water testing was over, Anton would spend the rest of his day troubleshooting, catching up with more paperwork, or offering some technical advice to one of his workers. His final appointment of the day usually involved his verbal report to Vlasic, a task that he rarely relished.

Some of Anton's coworkers joked that Vlasic looked like a senile, balding baboon, perhaps a worthy description if you bothered to take a look. While they laughed at Vlasic behind his back, Anton always observed the utmost respect in his interactions with him. He was his boss, after all, even if Anton couldn't work out how he could wear that same miserable three-piece suit every day, especially during the peak of summer. Vlasic's secretary argued that her boss was capable of the odd, witty comment, even though Anton never saw him actually laugh. But in the main, Vlasic was an officious bureaucrat whose sole purpose in life was to seek favour from those above him. He had sauntered into a new relationship with the Italians more seamlessly than others gave him credit for, which made Anton believe that the rumours suggesting he was a closet supporter of the Ustaše were probably true.

Although Vlasic genuinely liked Anton—mainly because of his knowledge and efficiency—Anton knew that his boss couldn't be trusted. Apart from his possible Ustaše connections, Vlasic was the ultimate corporate manager and Anton was under no illusions what would happen to him should he ever screw up. As such, he could never relax.

By the beginning of October 1941, as the cooler autumn winds began to meander through Šibenik's medieval streets, Anton was starting to feel restless. Occasionally, if a problem occurred with one of the boilers, he had the authority to stay behind with the night shift to supervise the necessary maintenance. These nights gave him the rare opportunity for some quiet isolation inside his office, his thoughts often lost on a burgeoning war that he desperately wanted to be part of.

It was over six months since his meeting with Stubbs and Duško. As instructed, he had sat patiently on his arse inside Mateo's opulent house with his young family, eating good food and drinking reasonable wine while others risked their lives fighting for his freedom. The pangs of guilt that had eroded his conscience ever since the invasion began were now starting to fray at his nerves. He knew that he couldn't live like this for much longer. It was time to make some decisions, to plan ahead for all eventualities.

If I can't find Wine Man by Christmas, I will volunteer with a local Chetnik unit. What other choice do I have?

But just when Anton decided that he would try and find Wine Man, Wine Man suddenly stepped out of the shadows and found him.

To keep the pretext of being a hard-working Catholic family man, Anton would attend mass every Sunday morning. Church was one of the few activities enjoyed by the local residents, and the Sunday morning services were always full of devoted parishioners. Attending a Catholic mass was actively encouraged by both the Italians and the Ustaše. Of course, Anton doubted they had the people's spiritual wellbeing in mind; rather, it was a way of exerting further control over the community while also providing an opportunity to identify possible dissenters.

The Ustaše, in particular, was often suspicious of any local not regularly attending church services; that could mean they were a Serbian Orthodox churchgoer in disguise. For those extremists, there was nothing better than a forced conversion under the threat of a rifle on a beautiful Sunday morning.

St James' Cathedral was a two-minute walk from Mateo's house in Šibenik's Old Town. Before the war, the Cathedral had been a cornerstone of Anton's life. While not especially devout himself, attending church had at least given Anton a temporary sense of peace and fulfilment, feelings that were now missing from his life. Sometimes, in that solemn interval between the gospel reading and holy communion, Anton would transport himself back to his childhood in Cavtat and the love that was bequeathed to him by his mother and sisters. For a moment at least, he was consumed by a rare happiness that perhaps he would never find again.

On an overcast Sunday morning in mid-October, Anton woke up early, ate his breakfast, and then readied himself for church. Dubravka had been up all night with a nagging cough, so he encouraged Vuka to catch up with her sleep, given that the child was now finally settled. Neither Ruža nor Jelena was interested in accompanying him, so just after eight forty-five, Anton put on his blazer and grey fedora and casually walked along the ancient steps towards St James. As usual, the Cathedral was overly crowded, so he decided to hover inauspiciously towards the back until a spare seat became vacant. Once the priest slowly walked up the aisle to welcome his flock, Anton saw some space in the second last pew and dropped himself next to a middle-aged couple whose drawn, pale faces wilted in the sunlight.

It was only after the first reading from the Old Testament that another man politely forced himself into the same pew and squeezed next to Anton. A familiar stench of cigarette smoke and alcohol wafted from the man's coat. It was enough to make the lady in the row in front of Anton turn her head towards the ceiling and snarl at the putrid smell that surrounded her. Anton hated the feeling of being hemmed in, so when he felt the man's legs suddenly shift into the bottom of his hip, he turned his head to protest at this intolerable intrusion.

To Anton's credit, his face barely flinched when confronted with Wine

Man's facetious grin. However, he battled gamely against his first impulse, which was to grab the lapels on his rival's filthy coat and drag him outside. Thankfully, common sense prevailed, and Anton soon relaxed into his seat, the twangs of built-up excitement ripping at his sides. Wine Man's sudden appearance could only mean one thing: it was time.

The rest of the church service became muddled inside Anton's rising sense of anticipation. As holy communion was coming to an end, Wine Man leant forward to fiddle with his shoelace and casually slipped a small piece of paper into Anton's side coat pocket. Anton watched the whole event in stunned silence, as if it was deliberately being acted out in slow motion. With a slight wink for the benefit of the nosy woman sitting in front of Anton, Wine Man suddenly lifted himself out of his chair just as the last communion hymn had finished. Then, like a character from a children's fairy story, he trundled out into the aisle and disappeared into a haze of smothering bodies, now returning to their seats.

Ten minutes later, Anton slipped into a side alley and carefully pulled out the piece of paper from his pocket. First checking to see that he was alone, he unscrambled the note and carefully read its contents.

> *Anton—at the back of the bus terminal, there is a set of stairs that leads to a cleaner's room. Make sure you get there at exactly ten thirty, knock three times, and I will let you inside. Tell no one of our meeting and destroy this note immediately.*

Anton checked his watch—it was ten fifteen. He had to get moving. He ripped the note into tiny strips and then stuffed them into a nearby bin. Scared that he was in danger of missing his deadline, he took a shortcut he knew through several backstreets and thankfully reached his destination just in the nick of time. The terminal was more or less deserted for this time of day, apart from some local derelicts and an Italian soldier who seemed more interested in a flock of seagulls chipping away at a crust of bread rather than looking out for suspicious people.

Confident that he wasn't noticed, Anton swiftly negotiated the stairs that led to the cleaner's room, knocked three times as instructed, and waited for a response. Several seconds later, a grinning Wine Man opened the door, his ruddy cheeks glistening in the dimming light as he beckoned Anton to come inside.

Surprisingly, it was indeed a cleaner's room, complete with a robust collection of brooms, cleaning liquids and buckets scattered across a narrow corridor. The only things out of place were two small wooden chairs facing each other in the middle of a dusty floor. The lack of windows or any other source of ventilation gave rise to an obscene odour that permeated every nook and cranny it could find. It was as if someone had spent the entire night holed up inside the room farting their arse out. But then, with Wine Man, anything was possible.

'Nice room,' Anton remarked facetiously as he dropped himself down onto one of the chairs.

'It serves a purpose,' Wine Man said as he sat down opposite Anton. They were now so close to each other that Anton could smell Wine Man's vile garlic breath.

'Better not let the Ustaše find out about this place,' Anton began. 'You might have some explaining to do.'

'Oh, they already know that I use it for my work,' Wine Man offered with another grin. 'I pay a weekly stipend to a local Ustaše official just for the privilege. Lovely fellow—apart from the occasional blood-thirsty atrocity.'

'You work for the Ustaše?' Anton asked, bewildered by the thought. *What the hell is going on?*

'They think I work for them,' Wine Man replied. 'To survive, one has to sometimes walk with the Devil. I do what I have to do.'

Anton's back stiffened in his chair, and he felt his hands turn to ice. 'How do I know that you're not really an Ustaše informer?'

'Because you would be dead by now, that's how.'

Anton let Wine Man's response slowly worm its way through his troubled mind. Eventually, he grudgingly accepted that Wine Man was telling the truth.

'What do I call you?' he finally conceded, his arms dropping cautiously to his sides.

'How about Max?'

It was Anton's turn to laugh. 'You don't look like a Max.'

'And you don't look like a Chetnik either, but who's quibbling?'

'But I am not a Chetnik yet,' Anton replied, as if the mere suggestion had somehow offended his sensibilities.

'We all have our crosses to bear, Anton,' Max began. 'It's far too early in the war for you to deny yours.'

More silence before Anton intervened. 'I've been waiting to hear from you for nearly seven months. I was on the verge of losing patience. Where the hell have you been?'

'God forbid that I have kept you waiting.' A pause. 'Suffice to say, Anton, it's not all about you.' Max scratched his face with a dirty index finger. 'I have been doing some work for Duško in Zagreb,' he began to explain. 'Fortunately, the Ustaše let me come and go as I please. Although, to be brutally frank, after the things I have seen and heard, I wished to God I never left Split.'

'Is the situation in Croatia that bad?' Anton asked.

Max nodded wearily. 'Not just in Croatia, but across Yugoslavia. Worse than you could ever imagine. Thankfully, there are still decent people from all ethnic persuasions, including many Croats I know, who are appalled by this never-ending spiral of violence.'

'I am aware of the rumours,' Anton admitted. 'Is it true that they are building a huge concentration camp outside of Zagreb? And that they are ruthlessly killing Serbs on a daily basis?'

'Yes. A death camp has been constructed at a village called Bročice near Jasenovac. More are being built along the Sava River. This first camp has only been opened for business for a few weeks, but ...'

To Anton's surprise, Max suddenly appeared to be consumed by emotion, which completely contradicted his usual phlegmatic personality.

'Let me tell you one particular story that illustrates perfectly the inferno that is now spreading across the country.' He took a deep breath, leant back into his chair, and stared into Anton's blazing eyes. 'I am not sure where in the Bible it says that raping and murdering your enemy is acceptable in wartime. But in war-torn Yugoslavia, as long as you carry a weapon, anything goes. Raping schoolgirls can be fun if that takes your fancy. Or maybe it turns you on to see a father forced to rape his youngest daughter or a son made to rape his mother or sister.'

'I don't know what to say,' Anton replied. 'Of course, I have heard of such things.'

'You have heard nothing,' Max replied angrily. 'But I digress. Back in August, the Ustaše entered the village of Prebilovci in Herzegovina, where, over several days, they systematically killed nearly every Serb they found. Why? Because apparently in the last war the village provided twenty volunteers to the Serbian army. I mean, twenty fucking volunteers! In the process, they turned a local school into a temporary torture chamber, a right proper charnel house. A local Serbian teacher called Stana refused to leave her pupils and was taken back to this school. By all reports, she was well respected by everyone in the village, a very fine teacher indeed. But being a good teacher matters nothing to the Ustaše.'

'Jesus Christ,' Anton sighed. He knew where this was going.

'Normally, I detest blasphemy, but on this occasion, it's warranted, given what occurred,' Max replied sadly. 'You see, the Ustaše guards proceeded to gang rape Stana in front of her pupils and the remaining prisoners. They didn't care how many people watched. The more the merrier, in fact.'

Max's voice suddenly dripped with sarcasm. 'It was a right party, Anton. Don't you get it? I even heard that some of the boys were ordered to join in.' Max paused to catch his breath once again. 'After everyone got their ends in, they slaughtered Stana and her students like wild animals.'

'Barbaric behaviour,' was all Anton could say.

'An apt description, perhaps.'

'Yes.'

'But a Bosnian preacher I know and once respected told me just yesterday that what we are seeing is a spritual cleansing of the nation: God's true work at hand.' Max now coughed into his hands. 'Happily, there are many decent clergymen of all faiths across the country who do not share his philosophy and are trying to fight back.'

Anton was unable to speak. Now more than ever, he felt a deepening shame that he had not yet lifted a finger in anger during the war. But as of today, things were going to change. He would not prevaricate any longer. He was now committed to taking a stance against those who perpetrated this evil, those who turned their backs on justice and freedom. The Allies had to win the war, and he was going to help them with all his might. For all the Stana's being brutalised every day, for the sake of little Dubravka, for the future of his country—the wicked stain of Fascism had to be eradicated before it was too late for all of them.

'Listen, Max,' Anton finally said. 'We cannot afford to lose this war. So, let's get down to business. First, where is Stubbs?'

'Ah, good question,' Max said. 'After the Yugoslav government capitulated, most of our British friends, including Stubbs, were forced to flee the country. Wasn't quite what we expected, mind you, but you can't win them all. Here in Dalmatia, we have had sporadic contact with them over the past few months, not helped by the fact that the wireless sets they provided us have all disappeared.'

'What do you mean, disappeared?'

'I mean, disappeared, along with their trained wireless operators.'

'Sounds like an absolute farce if you ask me.' He studied Max's face for a reaction, but there was none. Just that same insolent smile.

'However, there is some encouraging news,' Max finally chirped.

'What exactly?' Anton asked curiously.

'An Allied delegation recently entered the country to confer with Colonel Mihailović. I am told that Stubbs is with them. We expect to see him soon, maybe even tomorrow.'

'Well, that's a positive, at least,' Anton replied. 'What about Duško and Trifunović-Birčanin?'

'Duško is working for Mihailović now in Serbia, as are the Chetnik cells he helped create prior to the invasion. Birčanin is hiding somewhere in Split, but we hear that he will soon take command of all Chetnik operations in Dalmatia.'

For the first time since he entered the room, Anton was able to relax in his chair. At least Duško was still alive, and that was a good start. 'Thank you for taking me into your confidence, Max,' said Anton. 'And now, if you will permit me, I want to start fighting Fascists.'

'Ah, I like your enthusiasm,' Max said, blinking with honest approval. With a twist of the neck, he considered Anton closely. 'How easy would it be for you to travel to Split this week?'

Most men in Anton's position would have thought the question thoroughly stupid, given the travel restrictions between the two cities. But rather, Anton sat back quietly in his chair, stole a lungful of putrid air, and then tugged at a loose flap on his coat. 'I think I could manage it,' he finally said. 'I have already been granted a special pass by my new Italian masters in case I need to travel for a work emergency. And it just so happens that one of my boilers needs a new water pump. I have been complaining to my supervisor about it for several weeks now. If it's not replaced soon, the water circulation will stop, causing the boiler to overheat and fail.'

'We can't have that,' Max said grimly. 'What would the Italians say?'

'Not a lot,' Anton replied sheepishly. 'They depend on me and a few others to keep the factory operational. That's why they have no choice other than to let me buy a new pump. Of course, the type of pump we use for our boilers can only be purchased in Split.'

'Rarely have I seen so many coincidences come together.'

'Call it the luck of the Devil.'

'Or maybe simply beginner's luck,' Max replied with another irrepressible smile. 'Just one more question, if I may. How well do you know the waters around Brač?'

This idyllic Adriatic paradise, situated about seven nautical miles from Split, is the largest of the central Dalmatian group of islands. Before the war, it was a popular tourist destination for many holidaymakers, especially Italians. The main town on the island is called Supetar.

'Very well,' Anton began. 'Are you aware that I was stationed in Split for two years with the navy?' Before Max could reply, Anton added, 'I often visited Brač in the conduct of my duties. I know the island like the back of my hand.'

'Could you navigate a motorised boat on a moonless night from Split to the northern side of the island?'

Who was Max to ask such an impertinent question?

'Blindfolded,' Anton boasted.

Max clapped his hands together with such force that some of the wooden shelves inside the room began to rattle. 'Excellent news! Just what I wanted to hear.' He leant forward and placed a welcoming arm around Anton's shoulder. 'You want to know something, my friend? I trust my instinct above all other things. It has served me well over the years, kept me safe. And my instinct tells me that you and I are going to make a great team.'

Anton now forced out his own hand and the man he had once sarcastically referred to as Wine Man shook it fiercely. 'For both of our sakes,' Anton finally grinned, 'you better be right.'

Chapter Three

Split, Yugoslavia
October 1941

As Anton had predicted, it didn't take much for him to convince Vlasic to sanction his trip to Split, although he was tentative at first.

'Why can't Sumic or one of the other boilermakers go instead? You are needed here.'

When Anton had to use his charm, he could manoeuvre into overdrive at a whim, and this was one of those occasions. The ease with which he could flatter someone without appearing sycophantic amazed even him.

'Mr Vlasic, sir,' he had begun. 'As you know, I would never do anything to compromise your impeccable reputation, especially one that has been so diligently acquired.' Scarlet rose in Vlasic's cheeks; whether he was embarrassed or genuinely touched by Anton's comment, who really knew? But he voraciously lapped it up, like Anton had predicted.

'That is why I have to make sure that we get the right pump and that it is appropriately tested for our needs before we buy it,' Anton continued. 'It would devastate me if you personally took the blame because the wrong purchase had been made.'

'I see,' Vlasic had replied.

'Also,' Anton whispered, stepping closer to Vlasic, 'my cousin Ilsa lives in Split, and I have not heard from her since the occupation. I am very worried about her. She suffers from colitis, you see, so I would like to check on her while I am there. If you would permit me to stay overnight in Split and return the following morning, I would be very grateful.'

'Of course, of course, Anton. We must all look after our families during these dark times.' He began to wring his hands as if they had just been burnt on a kitchen stove. *Something else was now coming*, Anton could feel it. 'And perhaps you might also find me some bottles of Rakija while you are there? I find that a tipple or two at night helps me relax from the pressures of work.'

'Indeed, I shall,' Anton grinned sheepishly. 'It would be my pleasure.'

To Anton's relief, Vlasic had cleared the travel arrangements with his Italian superiors by lunchtime. Vlasic even arranged for his own driver to accompany Anton to Split. 'You look after me Anton, and I will look after you,' Vlasic had reassured him. Much to Anton's relief, everything had gone better than expected.

When the work bus returned to Šibenik station later that afternoon, Anton disembarked without even saying goodbye to his work colleagues and quickly made his way to the bathroom. Checking first that no one was using either of the two cubicles, he stepped up to a spare urinal, unzipped his fly and began to pee. Several seconds later, Max walked in wearing the same tattered trench coat as always and hovered over the urinal next to him.

'We have to stop meeting like this,' he joked.

Anton smiled. 'Wednesday is confirmed.'

'Good,' Max replied. 'That's perfect. Where are you staying?'

'I was thinking of the Bellevue.'

'Out of the question,' Max said. 'The Italians have claimed the hotel for themselves. You would be shot as soon as you entered reception. And for God's sake, stay away from the Hotel Palace as well. The Italians have established their command headquarters there.'

'You are not doing a very good job of selling this mission to me.'

Max laughed. 'I guess not. However, if you must know, Split has become the playground of the Italian *intelligentsia*. It is also teeming with Ustaše, waiting for the day they can take over for good. You will have to be very careful. Strangers stick out like a sore thumb. You can't even take a shit in a public toilet without someone noticing.'

'Don't worry, I will be discrete,' said Anton. He then nodded his head wearily. 'What about the Ragusa Hotel, near Bacvice Beach?'

'Perfect,' Max finally agreed. 'I will meet you at our favourite café at four o'clock for a drink. Does that give you enough time to buy your damn water pump and visit cousin Ilsa?'

'More than enough.'

'Okay,' Max laughed as he zipped up his fly. 'Oh, and by the way, pack some dark clothing for the operation.'

'I figured that part already,' Anton said.

'As always, one step ahead.' He cracked one last smile, although it was delivered more cautiously than usual. 'Good luck, my friend. God willing, I shall see you in Split.'

'God willing,' Anton confirmed with a shake of his head.

If convincing Vlasic was easy, convincing his wife, Vuka, would be less so. And she didn't disappoint him.

'Why do you have to go to Split?' she screamed at him later that night. 'Do you have another woman there? Are you going to see your former fiancée?' This was standard operating procedure for Vuka. Whenever in doubt, she would hang his past engagement to Lucia over his head like a vengeful sword of Damocles.

'Don't be so stupid,' he replied scornfully. 'I haven't been in contact with Lucia for over eighteen months. If I don't find the right water pump, they will blame me if something goes wrong with the boilers. I don't want to go to Split, but I have no choice.'

'Oh, for God's sake, Vuka,' Mateo intervened irritably. 'Give your husband some peace; we are talking about his profession here. Unless you want the Italians to arrest him one night in front of dear Dubravka, you will keep quiet now and help him prepare for his journey.'

Thank God for Mateo, Anton thought. He was always the beacon of common sense in a household full of overwrought women. Oh, except for Jelena, of course, who was visiting with her three children.

'You're not getting up to mischief in Split, are you, Anton?' she asked cheekily.

'I don't know what you mean,' Anton replied somewhat brusquely.

'Oh, I think you know exactly what I mean,' she laughed before skirting off to the kitchen to help her mother with dinner.

On Wednesday morning, Anton woke up earlier than usual, packed his duffel bag with some clothes and toiletries, took a warm bath and kissed Dubravka one last time. He didn't want to admit to himself that this could be the last time he would see her. That thought remained in the back of his mind for the rest of the day, especially during the bus trip to the factory.

After Anton completed his normal morning checks in the boiler room, he was approached by Boskic, Vlasic's long-suffering driver. His overly crumpled trousers and the cigarette stains on his faded white shirt indicated a certain disillusionment with life.

'I am here to take you to Split,' he grumbled. 'Are you ready to go?'

'In five minutes,' Anton replied, probably too bossily. He stepped inside his office, grabbed his bag, and wrote down some last-minute instructions to Tomic, the night shift supervisor. Satisfied that he had thought of everything, he rejoined Boskic, and the two men soon found Vlasic's prized Chevrolet parked opposite the administration building. It was a stunning autumn morning, and the sound of the wind creasing the nearby pine trees somehow gave Anton a sense of impending freedom.

The journey to Split was mainly incident-free. There were the occasional roadblocks and security checks that had to be navigated, but for most part, they travelled largely unbothered. Boskic tried to keep the conversation going for the first half of the journey but gave up when he realised that Anton wasn't all that interested in talking about football, the weather or women. *These navy types*, he figured, *totally up their own backsides.*

Although he personally thought Boskic was an idiot, Anton was not being deliberately rude. Rather, he was trying to settle his nerves. The implications of what he was about to do had suddenly become a reality. There was a strong chance he might get killed tonight, so the last thing on his mind was whether Hajduk Split should be forced to play in the Italian Football League. He just wanted to get to Split quickly, complete his mission, and return to Šibenik with his head still attached to his shoulders.

They arrived at the Ragusa just before eleven o'clock. After Boskic parked the car in front of reception, he tumbled outside to open Anton's door in a vain attempt to make some pointed working-class missive. 'Always at your service, Anton,' he said sarcastically.

Anton ignored him. Instead, he lifted his duffel bag from his seat and stepped into a cool but cloudless Split morning. 'What time do you want me to collect you tomorrow morning?' Boskic growled. He began to wonder whether Anton's main purpose in Split was to screw some hot broad behind his wife's back. He looked the type, after all.

'Make it nine thirty, if that's not too much trouble.'

Boskic doffed his cap in feigned deference. 'Anything for a man like you,' he sneered. There wasn't time for a last-minute retort, so Anton glared defiantly at Boskic before entering the hotel. After negotiating an early check-in with the disinterested woman at the front desk, Anton signed some papers with a half-chewed pen and was given a key to room 215.

The Ragusa had always been a working-class hotel, even before the occupation, frequented mainly by drifters, casual workers and those wishing to have a wild fling after a drunken night out. The rooms were overly spartan, containing nothing more than a single bed, an ivory-coloured washbasin, some towels and a small cupboard. In normal times, Anton wouldn't have been seen dead here, but these were far from normal times.

His appointment with the engineering firm that sold the water pumps he needed was scheduled for one thirty. The firm was located at the edge of the main central business district, perhaps a fifteen-minute walk at best. He had two hours to spare, more than enough time to pay a quick visit to Ilsa and then buy those damn bottles of Rakija for Vlasic.

From memory, Ilsa barely lived four hundred metres away from the Ragusa, in the same crumbling one-storey apartment with the half-mangled outside toilet that she had inherited from her now deceased aunty. Of course, Ilsa wasn't really his cousin—just an old flame that he had grown particularly fond of in between his broken engagement with Lucia and his marriage to Vuka. Ironically, the only reason he had gone out that night he met Vuka was because Ilsa had stood him up earlier in the evening for some rich kid from Dubrovnik—a fact he was intending to remind her about should she ever stop swearing at him.

'Fuck your mother,' she screamed at him through her screen door. 'Go and fuck Hitler!'

'Will you please calm down, Ilsa?' Anton implored. 'You will bring down the entire Italian Army upon us if you are not careful.'

'Good! Nothing would give me more pleasure than to see them hang your scrawny neck from my ceiling,' she screamed.

It went back and forth like this for several more minutes; Ilsa was thoroughly determined to invoke every insult about Anton's mother that came readily to mind. Eventually, the last strain of anger evaporated through Ilsa's heaving breasts. She frantically opened the door with trembling hands and then smashed into Anton's confused face with a thousand wet kisses.

'I missed you, you bastard,' she finally conceded before they fell onto the floor in a wild embrace. Afterwards, as they lay naked on her double bed, sharing the same slimy cigarette she had just lit, Ilsa asked Anton the million-dollar question. 'Is this the first time you have cheated on your wife?'

'Yes,' Anton finally admitted. 'But I don't think it really counts as cheating. You know, because of the war and everything.'

Ilsa laughed cruelly. 'You always were so full of shit, Anton. It's going to catch up with you one day. You know that, don't you?'

Anton tried to ignore her while sweeping his hand clumsily through her curly blonde hair. He wasn't in the mood to receive a lecture from a woman who was so careless with her own morality; all he wanted was a distraction to calm his nerves before tonight.

Was that too much to ask?

'I really wanted to see how you are, Ilsa,' he lied. 'I have been worried about you.'

Ilsa laughed once again. 'Oh, come on, Anton. Please don't treat me as a fool. We both know you better than that.'

'No, really,' Anton protested. 'How have you been? Are you surviving the occupation?'

'How is anyone surviving these horrid times?' she replied. 'You wake up in the morning, you bathe, you get dressed, you go to work, you make sure you're back well before the curfew, and you say nothing to anyone in fear of reprisals, not even to your own mother. Not much of a life, hey?'

'You deserve so much more,' Anton said wistfully.

'Even if you didn't really mean that, you're incredibly sweet.' She reached over and kissed him softly on his lips. 'At least they didn't kill you, Anton. I would have thought those damn Ustaše would have had you clearly in their sights. A navy hero like you.'

'I thought they may have come for you, too. The famous Ilsa who once claimed to have screwed the Yugoslavian Prime Minister when he visited Split. '

'You still don't believe me?' she teased. To be honest, Anton didn't know what to believe when it came to Ilsa. That she was a beautiful woman was never in doubt; those sultry green eyes, her honey-ladened lips, that incredible figure. She would have turned the head of any sane man that came her way. That's why, during this morning's journey, he suddenly realised how useful she could be to him and Max over the coming months.

'What I do believe is that you have enormous power over men, and they end up succumbing to your wishes like lovesick puppies. But I also know how much you hate the Ustaše. You made that very well known before the war.'

'What if I did?'

'Nothing,' Anton whispered. 'If the Ustaše murdered my father, I would have wanted revenge as well.'

Ilsa's Serbian father, David, had been a popular local politician in the early 1930s. A gregarious and generous man, he loved his only daughter passionately and made her the centre of his life. He taught her politics, how to form an opinion and to think for herself. Ilsa adored her father in equal measure and told everyone she knew that one day he would become Prime Minister of Yugoslavia. Unfortunately, that day was destined never to arrive. After King Alexander was assassinated in 1934, her father led several public meetings throughout the country denouncing the Ustaše. It was dangerous work, but he felt compelled to do it for Ilsa's future more than anything.

After one late-night event in Zagreb, David hurried out onto the street to find a taxi when an anonymous figure crept out from the shadows and fired two bullets from a revolver into his face, killing him instantly. Several hours later, the Ustaše claimed responsibility, leaving David's nineteen-year-old daughter fatherless and completely devastated.

David's murder changed Ilsa forever. She immediately quit her promising nursing career and sought work in several upper class Split hotels, hoping to engage with rich and powerful men that could do her bidding. You see, Ilsa had a burning desire to strike back at anyone who contradicted her father's legacy, even if that meant using her body to get her way. Her targeted affairs with several local heavyweights who were critical of David after his death not only destroyed their marriages but also their careers. Anton knew that the matter of her father's death was still a sensitive topic for Ilsa and the main driving force in her life.

Realising that Anton was trying to elicit a reaction from her, Ilsa sighed menacingly in his direction. 'You didn't come all this way to remind me of the past, did you? You know how much that upsets me.' She grabbed the last puff of the shared cigarette and squashed the butt into an over-used ashtray sitting on a set of nearby drawers. 'If you must know, I hate the Bolsheviks even more than I do the Ustaše. And mark my words, they plan to take control of this country once this fucking war is over.'

'You think so?' Anton asked churlishly.

'I know so,' she replied bleakly. 'Split is full of them. They are living right under the noses of the Italians, and those idiots don't even realise it yet. But their time is coming soon. Power to the workers and all that shit.'

'Well, we better stop them, don't you think?'

Ilsa sat up on the bed and slowly crossed her long, smooth legs, just for Anton's benefit. If he didn't have to see a man about that damn water pump in twenty minutes, he was sure he could go another round with her. 'Well, what do you know?' Ilsa smiled. 'My Anton is working for the Chetniks. I knew you were up to something the moment I saw you. You can't help yourself.' She chuckled loudly, as if it was a shared joke that they would take to Hell together.

'Can I trust you then?' he asked cautiously. He knew he was taking a risk, but he figured it was a risk worth taking. Ilsa could become a treasure trove of information if properly motivated. Max would be thrilled!

'Of course you can,' she said. 'But you didn't tell me all this just to impress me. You want something, am I right?'

'Do you still work at the Bellevue?'

'Yes. I am one of the few local staff that has regular access to the building.' She paused and offered Anton a knowing smile. 'I think the Italians like having me around.'

I bet they do.

'Then you must see many things; perhaps hear many things as well.'

'It depends. Strangely, my memory always seems to improve when the word 'money' is mentioned.'

'And I thought you were a patriot.'

'Even patriots have their price.'

Anton quietly swung his legs over the side of the bed and put on his trousers. After flexing his biceps for Ilsa's benefit, he reached out for his wallet and pulled out some Italian Lira.

'Hear, take this,' he said flippantly as he tossed the notes onto the bedcover. 'I can get you more later on, but I must speak to someone first. In the meantime, keep your ears open for any information that you think might interest me, especially about our Partisan friends.'

'My ears open, as well as my legs?'

Anton shook his head at her impertinence. Inevitably, it always came back to sex with Ilsa. 'I will leave that to you and your natural ingenuity.'

'Bastard,' she scoffed. She licked her fingers and then carefully counted the notes to make sure that they were real. 'And how do I get this information to you?'

'I am very sure that my factory will soon have some more problems with our water pumps. Hopefully, another trip to Split beckons in the next few weeks.'

After Anton finished dressing, they fell into each other's arms one last time and kissed like two sex-starved adolescents. 'If you do this for me,' Anton began, once he had released her from his grip, 'maybe you can live out the war in style.'

'And if it all turns to shit and the Bolsheviks take over?' A streak of mascara flushed down Ilsa's right cheek. 'What then?'

'Then wherever I go, I will take you with me.'

'I will hold you to that.'

As Anton stared at Ilsa blankly, his thoughts consumed by the weight of the promise he just made to her, a wave of uncertainty washed over him. The solemn words he had spoken, promising to aid her escape one day, echoed in his mind. A profound sense of responsibility mingled with the flickering flames of fear that danced within his heart. Anton knew the risks involved, the perils that now faced Ilsa should she ever be caught. Did he have the right to place her life in jeopardy as the result of a half-baked idea that came to him during a car ride?

Yet, in this moment of contemplation, Anton somehow felt a glimmer of hope, an unwavering belief in the indomitable spirit of humanity. As he surveyed the room, his gaze fell upon a recent photo of Ilsa and her mother, her eyes brimming with determination and vulnerability. For some reason, this one photo had encapsulated everything in Anton's world that was worth saving. Yes, Anton now knew that he would honour his promise to Ilsa at all costs, for the bond they had immediately created with this new partnership transcended the boundaries of fear and desire. In that instant, he resolved to become the irresistible force that would help Ilsa and others like her navigate the treacherous path towards freedom.

Chapter Four

Split, Yugoslavia
October 1941

'You're a damn fool, Anton,' Max grunted as they drank their beers. 'Who the fuck gave you permission to recruit this woman?'

In Anton's short experience with Max, he rarely got angry, but he could now literally see the steam pouring out of his rat-like ears.

'I need permission from you to fight the Fascists?' he asked gruffly. Just like their initial meeting at the very same café back in April, the two protagonists had the entire courtyard to themselves. Despite its unflattering reputation, it remained one of the few backstreet cafés still open in Split since the occupation. It was as if the Italians were completely ignorant of its existence.

'When you work for me, yes, you do.'

'But I don't work for you. I work for the British and Duško.'

'I am happy for us to continue this discussion with Major Stubbs if you like. I am sure he can straighten out the situation for you.'

An uneasy silence surrounded their table. Maybe Max had a point, Anton finally conceded to himself. Perhaps recruiting Ilsa was a little above his station.

But the advantages of having a mole inside the Bellevue far outweighed the negatives. Surely Max would eventually see things his way?

'Look,' he finally began. 'I understand your frustration, but you needn't worry. I know Ilsa well. She is as cunning as a snake. The quality of information she might be able to provide us is incalculable.'

Max sighed loudly. 'This is not about what she can or can't provide us, Anton. This is about you keeping your end of the bargain. You were told by Duško and Stubbs to follow instructions, but you decided to ignore them. Your activities for the British must involve maximum discretion or else I am compromised too.'

'What do you mean?'

'Are you so stubborn that you can't see the bigger picture? Or are you just plain stupid? The Ustaše think I work for them. They have most likely seen us together; trust me on this. If some floozy rats you out to the Ustaše, they will then come looking for me with a noose.' He took another swig of his beer. 'Or worse.'

'She will not rat on me,' Anton said defiantly. 'Her father was killed by the Ustaše when she was a teenager, and her hatred for communism borders on fanaticism. She's a royalist through and through.'

'That might be the case, but she is a risk I can't afford. I will have her followed by one of my contacts to test her bona fides, and if she so much as wiggles her pretty arse the wrong way, I will put a bullet in her brains myself. Understood?'

Anton gazed into his beer glass, his face contorted by fragments of his own stupidity. 'Yes, understood,' he finally grumbled.

'Good,' said Max. 'And, in future, if you have any more fantastic ideas on how to win the war by yourself, let's talk about them first.' He paused to allow Anton the opportunity to stew in his own remorse before adding, 'You're a good man, Anton, but your compulsive behaviour will get you killed. Think about that the next time you put both of us in the shit.'

The proprietor of the café briefly came outside to check over his only two patrons before trudging back inside. The pretty young woman who had served Anton back in April was nowhere to be seen, and he guessed what might have happened to her. So many good people were disappearing without any questions being asked.

'If you are through berating me,' Anton began softly, 'perhaps you can now explain to me what I am doing here. I am rather keen to demonstrate my true worth to you.'

Max let the last comment slide before inspecting his watch. 'In thirty minutes, I am catching the last ferry to Brač to visit my mother and younger brother in Supetar. You, meanwhile, will go back to your hotel room and change into your dark clothing. Leave behind any personal identification. At seven thirty, you will casually walk to the alley behind the hotel, where you will be met by a man called Sukevic.'

'Sukevic,' Anton repeated.

'Yes,' said Max. 'He is one of the most formidable Chetniks in all of Dalmatia, and he does not suffer fools. So, watch your tongue.'

'I think I can manage that,' Anton replied caustically. 'And what then?'

'He will take you to a safe house in Podstrana, just south of Split, where you will be further briefed by our old friend, Major Stubbs.'

'He's in Podstrana?'

'Apparently so, and I am sure he will be delighted to see you.'

Anton couldn't work out whether Max was being sarcastic or not, but he had other concerns on his mind. 'So, my next question. You want me to navigate a motorboat from Podstrana to Brač? For what purpose?'

'As I said, you will be further briefed by Major Stubbs.'

'And when do I see you again?'

'Perhaps sooner than you think. Now, finish your beer and get going. I will leave several minutes after you.'

This time, Anton did what Max instructed and quickly made his way back to the Ragusa. Once he secured his personal belongings inside the cupboard, Anton changed into his 'spy' clothes—dark khaki work trousers, an undershirt and a black woollen jumper. He tried to relax by taking a soldier's nap on his bed. Of course, that was never going to happen. Instead, he spent the next hour watching a fly negotiate countless laps around the tattered ceiling above him while his restless mind sped in seven different directions.

Embroiled by the tension that was gnawing at his bones, he finally jumped out of bed at seven o'clock, did his ablutions and then splashed water over his face.

Satisfied that it was too late to turn back, Anton calmly locked the room door behind him, twisted the handle several times to ensure that it was secure, and strode downstairs to the hotel lobby. Ensuring that he avoided the attention of the reception clerk as he sneaked out the door, Anton stopped momentarily to gaze ruefully at the cloudless night sky and then tip-toed his way to the back of the hotel, where the man he assumed was Sukevic was standing idly against the hood of a black Sedan.

Max was right; Sukevic was a beast of a human being. Standing well over two metres, his scalp was completely shaven. His face exhibited a tortured nose, hollow, pale cheeks and pugnacious blue eyes that betrayed little if no emotion. His huge body somehow melted into an overly tight woollen suit, making it difficult for Anton to discern his actual age. One thing was certain, however, he looked like a killer. Although Anton was generally a fearless man, he immediately felt uneasy in Sukevic's presence.

'Anton?' he asked coldly.

'Yes,' Anton whispered. 'You must be Sukevic.'

Sukevic grunted. Clearly, he wasn't someone who concerned himself with everyday pleasantries. 'Lie on the back seat and put that blanket over you,' he ordered. 'Do not say a word during our trip, and keep your body under the blanket at all times. If we are stopped by anyone, leave things to me. Okay?'

'Okay,' Anton assured him. With Anton safely secured, Sukevic closed the back door with an ear-shattering thump. Meanwhile, Anton gently squeezed his head against the seat cover and slowly counted to ten before Sukevic slammed his foot on the accelerator. In between the numerous bumps and the occasional cursing, Anton—without daring to check his watch out of superstition—estimated that the trip to the safe house took about twenty-five minutes. Sukevic obviously knew his way around the silent backstreets of Split without being seen.

Although the adrenalin was madly pumping through his body, something about the warmth of the blanket sharpened Anton's focus. By the time Sukevic ushered Anton towards a small wooden cottage overlooking a rocky promontory that connected with the ocean, he felt perfectly indestructible.

'They are waiting for you inside,' Sukevic said when they reached the front door to the cottage. He then removed a pistol from inside his coat and swung it across his chest. 'I will keep a lookout.'

'You do that,' Anton snapped.

He walked straight into a small, grey living room that was devoid of any meaningful furniture save for a dirty second-hand sofa, a few scattered pictures of the sea, and a small pop-up table that looked totally out of place. Major Stubbs and a tall young man around Anton's age were standing in a corner next to an empty bookcase, drinking coffee. The young man was dressed as a civilian but wore a traditional Yugoslav Army woollen pullover with a captain's insignia attached on his shoulders. Anton couldn't be sure, but he had a feeling that their paths had previously crossed.

Stubbs met Anton halfway and immediately greeted him with a warm handshake and a slap on the back. Given that they hadn't actually hit it off back in April, it was perhaps a conciliatory gesture. However, it didn't take long for Anton to decide that Stubbs looked rather haggard and weather-beaten compared to their last meeting. Hopefully, it was not an indication of how the war was really going for the Allies.

'Good to see you, Anton,' Stubbs said in Serbo-Croatian. 'How are you?'

'I am tired of being shoved into the back seats of cars for secret meetings, but apart from that, I am well.'

'Quite, quite,' Stubbs replied all too seriously. He pointed to the other Yugoslav. 'Can I introduce you to Captain Mario Ilic, Royal Yugoslav Army, now working with the Chetniks?'

Ilic also offered his hand to Anton and smiled. 'You may not remember me, Anton, but we once clashed on a football field a few years ago.'

Anton nodded with a grimace. *Now I remember.* 'Ah, yes! In the Navy versus Army match. I was playing left back, and you played on the right wing. We had quite a tussle, if I recall.'

'Almost came to blows,' Ilic laughed. 'But now we are fighting together for the same cause.'

'I am so pleased.'

Stubbs didn't invite Anton to sit down but offered him a mug of coffee, which Anton accepted gratefully. 'Get this down. It's going to be a long, cold night.'

'Thank you,' Anton replied. 'Colder than Cairo, I imagine.'

'Indeed,' Stubbs replied with a smile. 'But it's good to be back.'

Anton took a moment to explore his new surroundings. 'You seem to have an endless supply of safe houses, although this place is less appealing than the last one.'

Stubbs nodded. 'You can thank Max for that. This house belongs to a Serbian music teacher who was arrested by the Ustaše back in May and taken to God knows where. Max convinced the Ustaše afterwards to hand him the keys for safekeeping—just in case she ever returns.'

'That Max.' Anton smiled. 'He's incorrigible.' He quickly scoffed down the last of the coffee and gently placed the mug on the table. 'Now that I am here …'

'Yes, we should get down to business.' Stubbs reached for an unfolded map sitting on top of a backpack and carefully placed it on the table. 'What do you know about the situation on Brač?'

'Not much,' Anton replied truthfully. 'I know that the Italians are ruling the island with an iron fist, and there are rumours of a growing insurgency. But that's about it.'

'More than rumours,' Ilic added. 'We are giving the Italians a hell of a time.'

'We?' Anton asked carefully.

'Yes. We. The Chetniks.' Ilic looked mildly offended.

'I have heard that it's the Partisans that are giving the Italians a hell of a time.' Anton didn't feel obliged to say anything other than the truth. 'As well as giving the Ustaše and the Chetniks a hell of a time too.'

If I am going to risk my life for you lot, at least spare me the bullshit.

'Alright,' Ilic finally admitted. 'We have not made quite the impact we would have liked. But there are reasons for that.'

'Such as?'

'Such as a lack of weapons,' Stubbs intervened. All of a sudden, he sounded exceptionally weary. 'Getting them to Brač has proven to be difficult.'

'But not for the Partisans?'

'They seem to have better supply lines than we do,' said Ilic.

Anton's bemused face betrayed the scepticism that he clearly felt. 'Look,' Stubbs began. 'The truth is that our operations here in Split are in disarray at the moment. I understand that Max has told you about the wireless sets?'

'Yes, he has.'

'Damned ill luck, to be sure. So, to spout an English phrase, we don't know Arthur from Martha.'

'Thanks to Max's intervention,' Ilic added, 'we have only recently been able to establish direct contact with our people on the island.'

'I see,' Anton replied grimly. 'And now that contact has been established, you want me to deliver a cache of weapons to Brač on a moonless night in a motorboat that I have never seen before.'

'Exactly!' Stubbs meekly clapped his hands. 'Two crates of Lee-Enfield rifles, including several boxes of .303 ammunition, to be precise. Courtesy of the British Government. And a new wireless set as well. You will have some help, of course.'

Ilic suddenly pointed to a window. 'Sukevic will go with you. He's one of our best operators.' He paused. 'Oh, and I am coming too.'

'Good to have you on board,' Anton said cautiously. 'And Max?'

'He will meet us in Brač,' said Ilic. He passed Anton a piece of paper. 'These are the coordinates for our rendezvous with him. We will meet him at a little cove halfway between Supetar and Sutivan.'

'He is always on time,' Stubbs enthused.

Anton took one look at the piece of paper before giving it back to Ilic. 'I know the cove you mean. And if I am being honest, every gunrunner and pirate on the Dalmatian Coast knows it as well. But at this juncture, I am more concerned about the Italian patrols.'

'You won't have to worry about them,' said Ilic abruptly. His eyes dropped to the floor, deliberately trying to avoid Anton's stare.

'What do you mean?'

'We have an arrangement with the Italians tonight. Their navy patrols will turn a blind eye for a couple of hours, although the soldiers occupying the island may be less receptive if they see us. We will have plenty of time to drop the goods off and then return home safely.'

Anton didn't understand what he was hearing, so he poked the bear one more time. 'You have an understanding with the Italians? Our enemy? The people who are brutally occupying Brač, as well as the rest of Dalmatia?' He looked across at Stubbs, a British officer, for God's sake, who seemed suitably embarrassed. *It wasn't my idea*, he seemed to be saying.

'When fighting a guerrilla war, you have to be flexible,' offered Ilic, albeit not convincingly. 'We want to be in a position on the island where we can counter the growing influence of the Partisans should the need arise.' Ilic paused and took a deep breath. 'We will deal with the Italians all in good time, I can assure you.'

'Does Colonel Mihailović know that we are canoodling with the Italians?'

'He understands the pressures we are facing,' said Ilic smugly.

In other words, he doesn't.

Anton shook his head. 'Let me get this right. The Italians are helping us to smuggle weapons onto the same island that they are currently occupying. Aren't they just a little bit concerned that we will use these rifles against them as well?'

'We both share the same concerns about the Partisans, Anton,' Ilic replied. 'Come to think of it, they don't like the Ustaše all that much either.' The Chetnik officer didn't really answer Anton's question and both men knew it.

'It's just a temporary measure,' Stubbs finally intervened. 'Colonel Mihailović and Tito, the leader of the Partisans, are still trying to find a way to work together in defeating the invaders. Until such time that they do, we must plan for all contingencies. Therefore, the priority tonight is getting those rifles to Brač through whatever means available.'

Anton didn't know whether to laugh or tell them to go screw themselves. He was a royalist through and through, but in no way was he a collaborator. Indeed, he would shoot anyone who dared to accuse him of such a heinous insult.

'One last question.' Anton began, raising a palm towards both men. A cold rush of air rattled his teeth. 'Why me? I mean, there are dozens of willing men here in Split you could have used for this mission. Instead, you have dragged me, a total stranger with no experience in gunrunning all the way from Šibenik. There's something else you're not telling me.'

'It's simple,' responded Ilic quickly. 'We think our gunrunning operation here in Split has been compromised by the Communists. Too many fuckups lately to be only coincidences. Until I get to the bottom of things, I am not taking any unnecessary risks. We need a clean skin for tonight; someone we can trust. And you fit the bill.'

There were more questions Anton wanted to ask, but he wondered whether it would make any difference to the way he was feeling. Probably not, he finally decided. He had no option other than to trust these men, even if it meant his ultimate demise.

Let's just get this fucking thing over and done with.

Over the next thirty minutes, Anton, Ilic and Sukevic undertook their pre-mission preparations, which involved camouflaging their faces, inspecting maps and choosing weapons. Anton and Ilic both chose Browning Hi-Power nine-millimetre pistols, while Sukevic, now dressed in similar black clothing to Anton, pulled out a brand spanking new M1928A1 Thompson submachine gun.

To show Anton he meant business, he lovingly caressed the barrel in front of him for several minutes, like a five-year-old kid with a new toy, before carefully attaching a long, grey sling. Fighting his paranoia, Anton wondered if Sukevic had orders to use that thing on him should he fuck up in some way. But for the sake of mission clarity, he put that thought to the back of his mind. For the time being, at least, there were enough problems with this entire scheme to go around for everyone.

Chapter Five

Podstrana, Yugoslavia
September 1941

'Help me get the boat to the water,' Anton whispered loudly to his two companions. The trio were stumbling around the entrance of a tiny cave at the bottom of the promontory where the boat and its cargo had been hidden for the last twenty-four hours. Although the cave could not be seen from the road that twisted high above it, Anton was still nervous about being discovered by some random observer. The pervading darkness offered some protection, but more so, every little sound they made seemed to echo loudly into the lonely night sky.

After some mild cursing and flexing of muscles, the three men eventually pulled the motorboat into position. While the boat was about four and a half metres in length, Anton wondered at first whether it was large enough to carry three burly men, two crates of rifles and ammunition and a wireless set on a dangerous seven-nautical mile excursion.

But the natural seaman inside of him soon began to relax—he had been involved in all manner of challenges with small vessels during his naval career and easily survived them. Thankfully, the sea that night was as flat as a billiard table, while a silky fog began to rise fortuitously from the water's edge. In many ways, he couldn't have wished for better conditions.

'Are you ready to go now, Anton?' asked Ilic nervously before examining his watch. 'We are eating into the Italians' time. They won't turn a blind eye forever.' From the moment they left the safe house, Ilic had become a different person. Gone was the confident raconteur who was eager to renew his past history with Anton. Instead, a new, officious version, wanting to question every one of Anton's decisions, had emerged.

It was obvious that behind the false bravado, he was scared witless, and Anton wondered whether this made him a significant risk to the mission.

'The Italians are your problem,' Anton eventually said. 'My role is to make sure this boat is seaworthy before we venture out into that pea soup. Now, let me do my job.'

Ilic remained silent as Anton commenced the last of his checks, although his gaze lingered long enough to catch a brief glimpse of Sukevic grinning at him. While the huge Serb demonstrating a slice of human emotion was in itself something to behold, it also indicated to Anton a deeper malaise. Perhaps he was concerned about Ilic as well.

Anton examined the boat for several more minutes before he finally beckoned the others to join him on board. Sukevic traversed the surrounding surf in one giant stride before landing clumsily next to the steering console. He shared a quizzical look with Anton before they both stared back at Ilic, who seemed reluctant to enter the water.

For a moment, Anton seriously considered leaving him on the beach, but before he could put his thoughts into action, Ilic grabbed hold of the port side of the boat and pulled himself through the water. Once safely inside, he cursed his wet boots and then shovelled himself onto one of the boat's two wooden benches.

Anton glanced back in the direction of the cave to make sure that they were still undetected. He then pointed to two small oars packed together next to him. 'One of you, please lend me a hand. We will paddle out for about four hundred metres before we start the motor.'

Ilic immediately protested. 'That won't be necessary. The curfew has now started; there is no one around but us. And the motor has been specifically reconfigured with foam and rubber gaskets to reduce any noise.'

'All engines make noise, even reconfigured ones,' Anton brusquely intervened. 'It's not a risk I am willing to take. If, by chance, a passing patrol somehow detects us, then we are exposed out here in the open. But out there,' he nodded towards the ocean, 'we are protected by this growing mist.'

Before Ilic was able to object any further, Sukevic immediately grabbed an oar with his massive hands and rolled himself towards the starboard side of the boat. After Anton positioned himself directly opposite the huge Serb, they started to hit the water simultaneously with savage strokes while Ilic continued to sulk behind them like a spoilt child. Ten minutes later, the two men dropped their oars in exhaustion while the boat rocked side to side against a moderate night breeze.

Once Anton gathered his breath, he crawled towards the steering console. The rising fog had now completely surrounded the boat, and he was sure that even someone with a keen eye and a set of binoculars standing on top of the promontory would not be able to see them. Satisfied that they were safe for the moment, Anton nodded at Sukevic. 'You can start the motor now,' he whispered.

Sukevic quickly bypassed Ilic, who seemed distracted by a meddlesome insect nipping the side of his neck, and hunched down silently next to the outboard motor. Grappling inside the darkness, his fingers eventually grabbed the pull cord handle on the motor and gave it a firm tug. The pull chord motors of the 1940s could be very unreliable, and sometimes, they required significant strength to engage the engine. Luckily for the team, Sukevic had the strength of an ox, and after his second attempt, the engine suddenly snorted into life.

'Can't you keep that thing quiet?' Ilic barked as the motor spluttered loudly for several more seconds. Anton was desperate to say something in response, given their earlier conversation, but decided to let it go. He had more important things to worry about.

Fortunately, once the motor got into a rhythm, the foam covering took effect, and the noise from the motor abated considerably. Anton now clasped both hands on the steering wheel and manoeuvred the vessel into a southerly direction. *So far, so good,* Anton thought. *With a bit of luck, this foolhardy mission might just work.*

Ilic chose that exact moment to re-exert his authority. He carefully balanced his two left feet towards the steering console before flopping onto his knees.

'I hate the water,' he whispered bleakly to Anton. 'That's why I joined the army, not the navy.'

Anton said nothing at first. Small talk wasn't his thing, especially when he was trying to concentrate on where the fuck they were going. And he really didn't care why Ilic chose the army over the navy.

'How long before we get to Brač?' Ilic continued. Some ocean spray suddenly leapt through the air and splashed majestically against his woollen jumper. Anton wanted to laugh, but he decided to save it for another time, should they all survive.

'Conditions are good; the sea is relatively calm, and we have hit high tide. Given that we are travelling at about twenty knots per hour, it should take us about fifty minutes to get to Supetar, give or take an Italian patrol or two.'

'That won't be a problem.'

'Yes, so you keep telling me.'

Ilic spun his torso towards the sea, his eyes locked onto the gathering mist.

'How do you know where you are going inside this mess?'

'I will let you in on a little secret. I haven't got a clue where we are going.'

'I am being serious,' said Ilic caustically.

'So am I,' replied Anton. He flicked a lock of greasy hair away from his forehead, then added, 'Once we get a little further out, the mist will disappear. Then we will have a clear line of sight to the island.'

'And how do you propose doing that? Need I remind you that there's a curfew on the island as well. How do you intend to see through the darkness?'

Anton sighed. 'Our adversaries are stupid, but not that stupid. They will be operating searchlights all around the island, particularly from their northern outposts. Those lights will help guide us in. Then, it's a matter of following a path out of their reach as we head west towards Supetar. Now, why don't you take a seat and relax for a while? Maybe keep an eye out for any Italian patrols that have yet to hear about our special arrangement.'

Feeling suitably rebuked, Ilic moved back towards the boat and began to fiddle around with the wireless set. Meanwhile, Anton continued to search for a break in the fog, hoping that one would arrive before he had to explain himself to Ilic again. However, once more, luck proved to be a comforting companion; as if by magic, the fog finally lifted above them, and they suddenly found themselves in the middle of the open sea.

This is it, Anton reflected. *If anyone catches us out here now, we are fucking dead.* Ilic seemed to read Anton's thoughts because before he knew it, he was back in that same absurd foetal position next to him, demanding more answers.

'Why aren't you using a compass?' Ilic wanted to know. 'We can't afford to land at the wrong place.'

'I navigate by the stars,' Anton cursed under his breath. For a moment at least, he thought about reaching for his pistol and putting a round straight into Ilic's pathetic dome-shaped head. He was certain that Sukevic wouldn't care if he did.

'By the stars? What do you mean by that?'

'I don't have time to discuss basic maritime navigation with you. Can you please get the hell off my back and do something useful?'

Thankfully, Sukevic came to Anton's rescue. 'Sir, can you please help me with this wireless set? I am a bit confused.' Ilic knew better than to get on Sukevic's bad side. He gave Anton a contemptuous stare, even though it was hidden by the darkness, before crawling to the back of the boat. How Anton wished he had kicked the crap out of him during that football game all those years before.

Grateful for the respite, Anton made a gentle left turn towards Brač and relaxed in his seat as the boat effortlessly glided across the tabletop water. It felt strange to be out here in the open sea, a lone vessel trapped in a ghostly arena where one mistake could cost them their lives. Despite himself, Anton began to reminisce about those halcyon days in Split before the war, when the crystal-clear Adriatic Sea seemed to permanently shimmer under the golden rays of the sun.

When Anton was engaged to Lucia, they often spent their Sunday afternoons cruising the surrounding waters in a little boat he had purchased with some spare money. The gentle summer breezes would tickle their faces, carrying the faint scent of salt and seaweed as they sailed along the dramatic coastline. Anton recounted the joyous laughter of children splashing in the azure waters, the cheerful chatter of fishermen mending their nets, and the rhythmic sound of waves lapping against the hull of his boat. There were also the vibrant colours of the surrounding landscapes to admire, from the lush green trees lining the shores to the magnificent brown cliffs that stood tall against the horizon. It was a time that Anton held dear in his heart, a cherished memory that no war could ever erase.

'Look over there.' Anton's thoughts were interrupted by Sukevic, who was standing next to him and pointing to a collection of lights beaming from a distant shoreline out towards them.

'Searchlights,' Anton nodded. 'This is where the fun begins. Do not use torches or any other external lights on the boat from here on. And make sure that you and the good captain keep your heads down as much as possible until I tell you otherwise.'

Sukevic grunted his understanding and slithered back towards Ilic while Anton began to plot his next course. Despite the moonless night, Anton had a pretty fair idea of where he was. The trick was now to run parallel with the northern face of the island, past the town of Supetar and then sneak into the cove undetected. His plan was to utilise the natural cover of darkness while hugging the shoreline as much as possible. It would take some manoeuvring, but he had the advantage of surprise and a relatively quiet engine. His main concern at this point was Ilic screwing things up with his constant interference.

Even by the night's standards so far, the next twenty minutes were extremely tense. The closer Anton steered the boat to the island, the more chance there was that he would accidentally stray into a slipstream of light, exposing them to instant discovery. Once that happened, they were as good as dead. It was simply a case of reducing his speed and carefully skirting around the pockets of light when they appeared.

It was close to midnight when they reached the outskirts of the harbour that led into Supetar. Unsurprisingly, a large tray of light beamed ominously towards them, but Anton kept his cool and maintained a slow, westerly course. At one point, as tensions continued to grow, he could hear Ilic huffing and puffing behind him. He was acting like he had already been captured by the enemy and was simulating his last request before execution. All Anton could hope for was that Sukevic had the nous to keep the bastard under control before they reached the cove.

After what seemed like an eternity, though it was probably no more than five minutes, Anton's boat finally passed the harbour entrance. Soon, the dark visceral outline of Supetar was mercifully behind them. Everyone immediately took a deep breath and tried to relax, even Ilic, who had the audacity to grumble, 'well done' to Anton.

'We're not out of the woods yet,' Anton said grimly. 'I am not sure what other searchlights have been deployed further along the coast. And I still cannot accept that someone won't have a patrol out here somewhere. So, both of you, keep on your guard.'

As Anton had indicated back at the safe house, the rendezvous point was well known to him, as well as many other people on the island. At the peak of summer, the cove was home to a flotilla of small boats, ferrying people back and forth to the remote beaches on the other side of the island. Given its easy access, he struggled to understand why the Chetniks chose such an obvious landmark for their secret rendezvous. Maybe he should have raised his concerns at the time, but he figured that Max knew what he was doing.

Even so, he was not in the mood for surprises, nor did he want to alert his presence to any hostile force that could be hovering around their landing zone. So, when he estimated they were about five hundred metres away from their objective, he ordered Sukevic to stop the engine.

After Anton established a clear line of direction, he and Sukevic each grabbed an oar and began to paddle furiously in conjunction with the rising tide until they eventually hit a sandbar three metres from the shoreline. To their immediate left was a cluster of rocks jutting out into the water in an inverted 'V' shape, which seemed to be the perfect place to hide the boat while they waited for Max.

'This will have to do,' an exhausted Anton whispered to his colleagues. 'Help me position this thing in between those rocks over there.' The three men quickly jumped onto the sandbar, each grabbing a handful of the boat before skilfully manoeuvring it through the crashing surf and laying it to rest inside the 'V'.

'What about the rifles and wireless set?' asked Ilic as he stood over Anton, his arms folded indignantly. 'You are not seriously thinking about leaving them here?' Anton didn't know what was stewing Ilic this time, but he wasn't in the mood to have him question his decisions any longer.

'Yes, I am. The boat will be perfectly safe; these rocks provide a decent cover in the darkness. We may need to leave here in a hurry, so let's wait for Max to arrive first.'

Before Ilic could say a word in dispute, Sukevic thrust his burly frame into a growing breeze and pointed to the adjoining tree line, which surrounded the beach. 'I agree,' he snorted. 'In the meantime, can we please make our way towards the scrub and wait for Max there? I feel very nervous being out here in the open watching two officers having a pissing contest with each other.'

Without waiting for a reply, Sukevic jumped off the rocks with an almighty leap and darted across a patch of wet sand until he set himself down inside a nearby gully that overlooked the beach. Trying hard not to smile, Anton stared at Ilic and said, 'Shall we?' The three men soon found themselves huddled next to each other in the gully, trying to catch their breath as they fiddled around with their weapons.

After about twenty minutes of waiting, Ilic inevitably began to get twitchy, casting regular despondent glances at his wristwatch. 'Are you sure we are in the right place?' he whispered to Anton. 'It's almost zero one hundred; they were supposed to be here thirty minutes ago.'

Anton tried to hold his temper. 'Of course, we are in the right spot,' he replied abruptly. 'There could be a number of reasons why they are late. Be patient.'

'Or it could be that you're plain incompetent, and all this nonsense about navigating by the stars has compromised our mission.'

Okay, that is it. Anton didn't care if the entire island now heard him; he was going to tear Ilic apart, limb by bloody limb. He had enough of his crap for one night. But just as Anton began to stand up with the intention of grabbing Ilic by his pencil-thin neck and throttling him against a tree, Sukevic pointed to the sky. 'Anton, get down. I can see movement on the beach.'

The three men immediately turned their attention westwards. It took several seconds of targeted squinting before they all saw three separate silhouettes emerging from the darkness. Ilic reached for his pistol and gestured to the others, 'This must be Max. But in case it isn't, stay here and cover me.' Anton's initial reaction was to suggest that Ilic wait until the three figures got closer. *Hey, if he wants to get himself killed, why should I care?*

Ilic quietly crawled out of the gully and then rolled out onto the sand for several metres. But that was about as far as he got. Anton and Sukevic soon watched in amazement as Ilic somehow snagged his trousers on the tip of a fallen branch. Every time he tried to crawl forward on his stomach, Ilic was comically pulled back by the branch's natural force. He looked like a stray dog straining at the leash of its new owner.

'Should we help him?' Anton asked Sukevic ruefully.

'No. Hopefully, one of those fuckers will shoot him first.'

Despite the gravity of their situation, Anton quietly laughed. *Christ almighty, Sukevic has a sense of humour, after all!* Meanwhile, Ilic was completely disorientated. Before he had time to think rationally, a surge of panic coursed through his trembling right hand, causing his finger to involuntarily squeeze his pistol trigger. Much to Anton's dismay, the silent night was suddenly shattered by the sound of a single gunshot.

Right on cue, several tumbling bodies accelerated through the darkness in a wave of desperation until a broad figure, his rifle held tightly in his hands, stood over the ailing Ilic. 'What the fuck are you doing?' asked Max in a cold whisper. 'Do you want to get yourself killed?' Before Ilic could answer, one of Max's two companions, a younger man wearing an oversized peak cap, pointed his rifle towards the outlines of Anton and Sukevic as they slowly crept out of the gully.

'We're with him, unfortunately,' Anton whispered grimly. He walked up to Max and thought about giving him a hug. 'Good to see you, my friend. For a moment there, I thought we had missed you.'

'No such luck,' Max grinned as they shook hands. He nodded to the younger man. 'This is my baby brother, Yuri. Don't be fooled by those angelic looks. He's a fighter. And that hefty specimen over there is Ivan.' An exchange of grunts was all that was required at this point.

Max turned to Ilic, who had finally detangled himself from the branch and was wallowing in self-pity like a schoolboy who had just been caned by the headmaster. 'As much as I like to hear your explanation, we have bigger issues. There's a small enemy patrol not far behind us. They picked up our trail just outside Supetar. We have tried everything we can to shake them off, but they are persistent fuckers. More importantly, I reckon they have now alerted everyone in the area thanks to your little accident with the revolver. We need to leave immediately.'

'What about the weapons and wireless set?' Ilic asked. 'Where do you want us to hide them?'

'We don't have time for that.' His voice sounded caustic. 'Unless you want to be involved in a full-blown battle on this beach by yourself, then I suggest you follow my instructions.'

'But that was the whole point of the mission,' Ilic further insisted, ignoring Max's sarcasm. 'We just can't leave them here to rot in that boat.'

'That won't be necessary,' Anton suddenly intervened. 'It's been a few years, but if I remember correctly, about a kilometre to the west of here and roughly six hundred metres from the shoreline is a rocky islet. At high tide, it's no bigger than two football fields, but it's virtually covered end to end in unspoilt vegetation. We can hide the cargo there overnight, and your people can collect it tomorrow. I will take Sukevic to help me unload the crates.'

'It has been a few years?' Ilic laughed. He obviously decided that the best way to get back in Max's good books was to deride this audacious newcomer. 'What happens if your memory has failed you? My God, what an amateur you are.'

Anton did well to ignore him. There was no time for retributions. He turned back to face Max. 'We are wasting valuable time.'

Max stared at Sukevic, who, to Anton's relief, nodded furiously in agreement. 'Okay, Anton,' Max finally agreed. 'But also take Yuri with you so he knows the exact location of the islet.' He then gave Ilic a contemptuous scowl. 'You come with me and Ivan.'

While Sukevic and Anton raced back to the rock pool to prepare the boat, Max grabbed his brother by the shoulders. 'You be careful now. No schoolboy heroics, okay?'

Yuri's pearly white teeth shone in the darkness. 'Of course not, big brother,' he grinned. 'Where will we meet you when we return?'

'In the valley just behind our mother's house, near the old well.' Max looked at his watch. 'We will try to lose these fuckers inside the forest and meet you there sometime after zero three hundred.' Yuri nodded and then gave his older brother a quick hug. Swinging his rifle over his shoulder, he then swiftly made his way across the beach to join Anton and Sukevic.

Chapter Six

Brač
October 1941

The three men silently pulled the boat through the adjoining rock pools until it was swaying in open water. As Anton had privately feared, a typical Adriatic wind had suddenly whipped in from the south. The tabletop sea they had travelled across earlier in the night was now rippling with white-tipped waves.

'Do you want to paddle out for a while first?' asked Sukevic after the three men were all safely on board.

'No,' Anton replied. 'With this damn breeze and the rising tide, it would take us an eternity to even row one hundred metres. We will just have to risk engaging the motor. If someone hears us, so be it.'

'Yes,' Sukevic said before grabbing the motor with his huge hands. 'We are ready,' he informed Anton a few seconds later. After reciting a quick Hail Mary, Anton thumped the steering wheel twice for good luck before accelerating the boat into the open water.

'We made it,' Yuri said when they finally bypassed the westerly edge of the cove. It was only then that Anton took full notice of Yuri's features, previously hidden behind his peak cap. *Yuri is just a boy*, Anton thought, *probably no more than sixteen or seventeen*. He looked as if he should have been studying for his mathematics exam, not participating in a guerrilla operation.

Although there was obviously a large age difference between him and Max (why, he didn't care to know), they shared the same high cheekbones, withering nose and black almond eyes. If he possessed even half as much courage and common sense as his brother, he was happy to have him on board.

For the next fifteen minutes, Anton continued to hit due west, searching for that elusive islet. The total blackness of the sea, combined with the growling wind, started to screw with his mind. For the first time that evening, he began to question his self-belief and whether he was right about the islet's location. After all, it was so many years ago since his last visit to Brač, at a time when he was head over heels in love with Lucia and not responsive to rational thought. Could he be so sure that his memory was perfect on this occasion?

Just when Anton started to doubt himself completely, Yuri excitedly pointed to a shimmering black object about three hundred metres in front of them. 'Look! Over there! We have found it!' Sure enough, like an ancient mirage in the middle of a desert, the islet magically appeared out of the compressed darkness.

'Thank God,' Anton muttered. He quickly turned the steering wheel to starboard and started to glide around the eastern edges of the islet, with a view to finding an appropriate landing spot on its north side, away from any prying eyes on the main island.

'Get ready,' he finally advised Yuri and Sukevic as he targeted a small opening in between a cluster of rocks and broken driftwood. Twenty metres from his destination, he ordered Sukevic to cut the motor once again, and with the help of the tide, they paddled their way across a narrow sandbank before landing safely on a tiny rectangular-shaped beach.

'Well done,' said Yuri with a smile. He was the first one to jump out of the boat and stretch his long, skinny legs on firm ground. Unfortunately, he was also the first one to notice the blaring white light emerging over the horizon and heading straight towards them. 'Hey Anton!' he yelled, throwing all noise protocols out the window. 'What is that?'

Anton and Sukevic both turned their heads towards the light as it grew larger and larger in front of them. 'Fuck,' Anton muttered to Sukevic. 'It's definitely not our night. That's an Italian patrol boat. Call it a big hunch, but I seriously doubt whether they are aware of our special arrangement tonight or if, indeed, there ever was one. Either way, I am not prepared to find out.'

To Sukevic's dismay, Anton immediately ripped off his woollen jumper and undershirt until he was totally bare-chested and then threw both items to the bottom of the boat. 'What the hell are you doing, Anton?' Sukevic asked. He was even more confused when Anton also shook off his boots and tossed them next to the motor.

'Listen to me,' he finally turned to Sukevic. 'If I am right, that's an Italian CRDA 110t, and it's coming right for us. These vessels are equipped with all the necessary firepower to blast our boat into the next kingdom and beyond. And trust me, once they see us, they won't even think twice about doing it.'

'What do you want me to do?' Despite the timebomb that was approaching them, Sukevic remained annoyingly calm and assured.

'Help me get the rifles and wireless set off the boat.' Anton pointed at the steering wheel, his hands beginning to shake from the growing tension.

'Can you drive this thing?'

'Of course I can.'

'Good. You and the boy take a direct southerly route back to the island. Once you hit the beach, find somewhere where you can hide the boat and wait for me. With a bit of luck, I will meet you there within the hour.'

'You are going to swim back to Brač?' Sukevic asked curiously.

'Well, I won't be flying back, will I?' He realised this wasn't the time for sarcasm. 'Look, don't worry about me; it's only six hundred metres, and I am a strong swimmer. Just have those dry clothes and boots ready for me. I don't want to die of hypothermia.'

'You're a fucking lunatic,' retorted Sukevic with a grin.

'Takes a lunatic to know one,' Anton replied with a twisted laugh. 'Now help me move these crates and get the fuck out of here.'

Everything was done inside a minute. The crates and the wireless set were quickly jettisoned onto the wet sand, and then Yuri joined Sukevic in the boat. As they were about to leave, Sukevic tossed Anton his submachine gun.

'You will need this,' he said calmly.

'Hopefully not. Now get going before I shoot you myself.'

Once Sukevic and Yuri safely departed, Anton commenced the onerous task of pulling the crates from the beach and deep into the thick vegetation. Although Anton was an extremely fit man, it didn't take long for him to realise that he had overestimated his own strength and underestimated the weight of the crates, each containing twenty-five rifles plus several boxes of ammunition.

Although the distance to his newfound sanctuary was no more than fifteen metres, the task became a gruesome struggle against time as Anton battled both the weight of the crates and the unevenness of the terrain. To further shit on his parade, the ground was full of razor-sharp rocks, broken seashells and twisted foliage that immediately tore into his bare feet. After several minutes, he could feel a series of deep cuts stinging between his toes. Blood spilled over his insteps.

Despite pulverising nearly every muscle in his body, he somehow managed to manoeuvre both crates into a tiny crevice wedged between two decaying logs. Mission completed, Anton wanted to drop straight to the ground and rest his exhausted body, but he quickly remembered that he had one more trip to make.

That damn wireless set!

When Anton returned to the beach, he noticed that the small white light dancing on the horizon had now become a huge, luminous bubble that threatened to swallow everything in its immediate path. Anton knew that he only had seconds left to grab the wireless set and make a run for it before he was caught out in the open. His feet ached and his back threatened to crumble where he stood, but he somehow managed to lift the wireless set in one swoop and scamper back into the foliage. As soon as he reached the two crates, he placed the wireless set on the ground next to them, grabbed the Thompson submachine gun and found a hiding spot behind a fallen tree.

Instinctively, he lay flat on his stomach and gently raised the barrel of his weapon blindly towards the ocean. The next twenty minutes were perhaps the longest of Anton's life. His first challenge was the cold. While the daytime temperatures on the Dalmatian Coast during October were still generally warm, weather conditions at night could be a different story. And just his luck, the last few nights had been colder than usual. With the wind now blowing violently through the surrounding bushes, Anton regretted taking off his jumper and leaving it with Sukevic.

Anton had been thinking ahead when he made that decision; once he finished his swim to the island, he would need dry clothing to help stabilise his body temperature. But the cold rarely rewards forward thinking. No sooner had his body hit the ground than he began to shiver violently. Although he attempted to maintain some warmth by rubbing his legs firmly together, it was nothing more than a temporary and unsatisfactory solution.

His next challenge was a tactical one. *What will I do if the Italians organise a boarding party to investigate the islet?* Of course, he had no way of knowing the exact purpose of the patrol. *Have the Italians reneged on their deal with the Chetniks and are now searching for our motorboat? Or is this merely a routine operation that ticks a nightly box?*

Either way, there was a distinct possibility that he would soon be engaged in a major firefight with some Italians, which he couldn't possibly win by himself, even with the element of surprise. He began searching for an escape route that would take him out of the vegetation and to the southerly side of the islet. Once there, he could then disappear into the murky water. The chances of not being seen were perhaps a thousand to one, but what other option did he have?

Suddenly, a heavy glow of light permeated through the undergrowth. Anton tried his best to flatten himself on the ground like a snake, although his forehead was regularly hit by a circular spike of light. He feared the sound of a machine gun spraying rounds into the tree line at any moment. But the longer he held his breath, the more it seemed that the patrol boat was playing a waiting game. Waiting for him specifically? Probably not. But yes, most likely waiting for something or someone to emerge from the shadows.

The longer this game continued, the more determined Anton was to remain locked in the same position, not even daring to change the pattern of his breathing. Although his mind was numb from the cold, he was resolute in his analysis—if he moved even one centimetre, he was sure he would be discovered.

Sometimes, when a person is under extreme duress, minutes can feel like hours. As the searchlights from the vessel continued to bombard the islet, Anton felt like he was frozen in time. There was no certainty that he was going to get out of this situation alive, yet at the same time, his mind was working overtime to ensure his survival. He had waited so long to strike a blow against the enemy that this was simply a further test of his will. Deep down, he knew he still had many more battles left to fight.

Perhaps he had blinked one too many times, or was it possible that he had actually nodded off for a second or two? Because the spiralling streaks of light that had fermented from the north suddenly started to move from left to right. He gently rubbed his eyes just to make sure they were not playing tricks on him. But no, after a second, more thoughtful examination, he was now certain. The Italian patrol boat had decided to turn eastwards, away from the islet!

Anton remained fixed in his spot for several more minutes before he was completely enveloped in darkness. He quietly picked himself up, flicked on the small torch that he kept in his trouser pocket and began to carefully sprinkle some loose branches and leaves over the crates and wireless set. It wasn't a perfect fix by any means, but he doubted that anyone would visit the islet before the Chetniks were able to recover the cargo.

After taking a well-earned piss, Anton carefully placed his gun next to the crates and trampled his way back to the tiny beach. He nervously peered out into black water, still expecting the worst, but was relieved to see that the brutal white light was now stationary and a healthy distance from the islet. It was a close call, but he had prevailed.

'Put your hands up!' a voice screamed at him in Italian from behind.

At first, Anton thought it was Sukevic playing a joke on him, but when he cautiously turned around, he came face to face with two grinning Italian sailors pointing their rifles right at his head.

Fuck, you're kidding, right?

Anton didn't have time for self-recriminations. He had to think quickly, or else he would probably see the end of a noose before sunrise. He knew enough Italian to try and plead his case; whether these men were stupid enough to believe him would be an entirely different matter.

'Please! I am a fisherman!' he squealed pathetically. 'I am hunting for oysters! My friends will return shortly in their boat to collect me!'

One of the Italians, a tubby specimen with an untrimmed goatee, began to laugh wickedly. 'Do you hear that, Guiseppe? He has broken the curfew tonight in order to hunt for oysters!'

Despite the other man's laughter, Anton stamped his foot onto the broken ground as hard as he could and repeated his story again. 'Come, I can show you if you don't believe me.' He gestured towards the foliage, where the crates and, most importantly, his sub-machine gun were waiting. 'It's all in there. I'm telling the truth.'

Please be as stupid as you both look.

Unfortunately, both sailors stared at Anton incredulously, as if he were an escapee from a mental hospital. 'Do you think we were born yesterday, you imbecile?' Giuseppe asked. Meanwhile, Goatee pointed his rifle at their own motorised boat, tucked behind a small dogleg protruding from the main stretch of sand.

'Get on the boat, now!' Goatee screamed. 'You can tell your bullshit story to our commanding officer. Any smart moves and your friends, the oysters, will be dining on you tonight. So, keep your hands where we can see them.'

Cursing underneath his breath, Anton quietly shuffled towards the boat, his hands linked together behind his neck. He knew that once he boarded the Italian patrol boat, he was as good as dead. His only chance of survival was to get into the sea as quickly as possible and hope that the Italians lose him in the darkness.

The sailors ordered Anton to sit in the middle of the boat and then, with a mighty heave, Goatee started the engine. Within seconds, they were steaming towards the main patrol boat, which was probably about four or five minutes away.

Anton knew he had to act quickly. He didn't have a second to spare. There was a chance that the rifles might be discovered, but he was determined not to become an Italian trophy on his first mission for the Chetniks.

Approximately forty metres north of the islet, Anton noticed that a passing shower had temporarily caught the attention of both sailors, who proceeded to peer aimlessly at the sky as if they had never seen rain before. This was his chance! Pushing his legs over the side of the boat in one controlled motion, he threw a loose life raft at Goatee's bloated head, took an extra deep breath, and then propelled himself into the filthy, black water. With a series of savage strokes, he plunged down towards the ocean floor, away from the boat, hoping that the two sailors would dare not follow him.

Anton was under no illusions about his chances of survival. Winter was still a couple of months away, but the water was already painfully cold. As he told Sukevic earlier, he was a strong swimmer having represented the navy in the fifteen hundred-metre freestyle, as well as being selected for the Yugoslav national water polo side. Therefore, the distance of the swim back to Brač didn't worry him at all; his real challenge was swimming in the cold, open sea against a churning current with a couple of demented Italians chasing him.

But first things first. After several minutes of agony, it was time to come up for air. Anton couldn't hold on for much longer and he had no idea how far he had already swum or if the Italians were right behind him. His lungs about to burst, Anton shot towards the surface like a pointed arrow, half-expecting to be sprayed with rifle fire as soon as he emerged in the open. Bobbing his head just above the water line, he vomited out what seemed like gallons of seawater from his chest before slowly catching his breath. With the location of the Italians on his mind, he twisted his head in a semi-circle to look for his pursuers, only to find that the light signifying the larger Italian patrol boat was now once more moving away from him.

What the fuck? You weak bastards! Anton almost felt offended that the Italians had given up the chase so easily. Maybe they just assumed Anton could not survive being in the water for very long, or more likely, they didn't want to explain to their superiors how a lousy oyster fisherman wearing only a pair of trousers had escaped their clutches so easily. So, they returned to the Patrol Boat as if nothing had happened. 'The islet is all clear, sir! We found no one!' *Stupid arseholes!*

But he didn't have time to celebrate his good fortune. He was cold, partly disoriented and had to find Sukevic quickly. Realising that he had somehow drifted to the west of the islet and was directly facing the Brač coastline, Anton quickly hatched a new plan. Given the deteriorating conditions, he would swim diagonally against the fierce current, aiming for a rocky cliff he could now see in the distance. Anton estimated that the swim would take no longer than six or seven minutes. Hopefully, Sukevic would be waiting for him on the beach.

Hopefully.

Anton remained resilient and calm. There was no point fretting about his situation; he just had to convince himself that he would prevail. Despite the intensity of the cold that threatened to tear his lungs apart, he began with a succession of measured strokes, conserving his energy and maintaining a steady rhythm. Even though part of him wanted to scream in agony, Anton's mind remained sharp and focused, analysing the current and adjusting his path whenever he failed to locate the rocky cliff.

Given his past achievements in the pool, he was used to the despair and loneliness of the long-distance swimmer. He knew that patience and persistence were his greatest allies. With each stroke, he pushed through the cold water, feeling the strength within him growing. The cliff somehow gave him a beacon of hope, an unlikely friend guiding his way back to safety. He wanted to think about his mother and his sisters and, of course, dear Dubravka, but these emotional responses would only distract him. His one and only goal was to beat the twin adversaries of the cold and the vicious sea.

Then, without warning, Anton's clarity of thought suddenly became muddled. It was almost as if he didn't know where he was or what he was doing. He tried desperately to battle through the fog that was creeping into his brain by refocusing on the cliff and urging himself forward. But only two hundred metres from the shoreline, Anton's body began to revolt against the cold. His arms withered in painful spasms; his breathing became increasingly rapid. He wasn't ignorant to the situation; he knew the signs of hypothermia from his time in the Navy. He had to get out of the water within the next few minutes, or he was fucked. There was no other way of putting it.

After a further twenty metres of insane thrashing, his arms began to feel like two lead anvils. There was nothing he could do for the moment other than tread water and hope that the tide would somehow come to his aid. How long he could last in this environment was anyone's guess.

Then, just as he was about to black out, Anton saw a blurry object miraculously appear in front of him. Was he so deluded by pain that he was now imagining things?

But no, I can see a light! A torch? Don't tell me that the Italians have returned!

'Anton!' a voice screamed out. 'Can you see me?'

Sukevic!

Anton tried to kick his way through the surf in an attempt to reach the boat, but for some reason, his arms and legs could no longer move beyond a tiny stretch. It felt like he was stuck in quicksand. 'Sukevic!' he yelled back. 'I think I am going into shock! Do you understand? I am going into shock!'

'Oh, don't be so melodramatic, Anton! I will get you out!'

For the first time in his life, Anton contemplated death. How strange it felt, being trapped inside this dark, watery cave, unable to move, while the freezing ocean poked insidiously at his chest. He figured that there were many ways for a man to die in war, but drowning was the least honourable. Perhaps there had always been an unspoken irony to his self-confidence, and now it was finally pay day. It was such a pity that he wouldn't live long enough to give this final epiphany further consideration.

But just as Anton's body began to sink inside a harrowing whirlpool of surf and grime, a pair of strong hands grabbed him around the shoulders and lifted him out of the sea. *Surely, this is the work of God.*

'Grab hold of something,' Sukevic shouted as he pulled Anton towards him. Somehow, Anton recalibrated every last ounce of energy in his body and flipped himself over the side of the boat, landing face-down next to the motor. Checking first to see that he was still alive, he once again coughed out pools of dirty saltwater before turning to face a grinning Sukevic.

'I thought I told you to stay on the beach,' Anton grunted, as his body shivered uncontrollably.

'If you think I would let you swim back to Brač without trying to help you, then you are dog shit crazy.' Sukevic picked up Anton's dry undershirt and jumper and threw them at him. 'Now get these on before you freeze to death.'

Anton reached for a grey blanket that had previously been used to hide the rifle crates and furiously began to dry his upper torso until some warmth returned to his body. Finally satisfied that he wasn't going to die, he slipped on his dry clothes and then stared back at his colleague.

'I owe you a debt of gratitude, so thank you. Er, what should I call you? Who are you really?'

'My name is Stojan, and what you did back there was one of the bravest things I have seen so far in this thoroughly shitty war. So, you're welcome.'

Anton quickly glanced northwards, across the fierce, black sea towards Split. 'What now, Stojan?'

'We are going home. Providing, of course, you can find a safe route back.'

'What about Ilic?'

'Fuck him.'

'He won't be happy.'

'As I said, fuck him. That stupid prick almost got us all killed. I will talk to Birčanin about him later. Max and Yuri will back me up—they can't stand him either.' He now looked at his watch. 'It's nearly zero three hundred, and we have to get back to the mainland before dawn. So as much as I am enjoying our conversation, can we please get fucking moving?'

Anton chuckled softly before he rubbed his tired eyes. 'Just one last thing, Stojan. It's been bugging me all night. This mission doesn't make a whole lot of sense. Why didn't the British just land the rifles and wireless set on Brač by submarine? Surely, they have the means to do so?'

Fortunately, Anton was close enough to see the look of embarrassment on Stojan's face. 'They did. But they dropped them off on the wrong island.'

'Which island?'

'Korcula.'

'Korcula!' Anton exclaimed. 'But that's one hundred and forty kilometres away! How in God's name did they get Brač mixed up with Korcula?'

'You know the British,' Stojan observed. 'Couldn't land a piss in a bathtub.'

'So what poor sod had the task of dragging those crates all the way from Korcula to Split?'

'Me, actually.'

'And did we really have an arrangement with the Italians tonight?'

'God knows, but I doubt it. Ilic and Stubbs are full of shit most of the time.'

Anton shook his head in laughter before grabbing hold of the steering wheel. 'This is one fucked up, crazy war, Stojan.'

Stojan Sukevic gave his new friend a slap on the back. 'Stick around, Anton. Because if I know anything at all, it's about to get a hell of a lot crazier.'

Chapter Seven

Podstrana, Yugoslavia
October 1941

Anton and Sukevic somehow made it safely back to Podstrana with an hour to spare before sunrise. After hiding the boat inside the cave, they stumbled back to the safe house in the dark, their bodies wracked with fatigue, before finally collapsing on the kitchen floor in uncontrollable fits of laughter, a sign perhaps of how close they came to courting disaster.

After the two men warmed themselves up with several cups of vile ersatz coffee, they sat together on the patio, their arms dangling loosely by their sides, awaiting the sun to arrive in all its glory. When the time came to leave, Anton hustled himself in the back seat of the car, swotted the blanket over his body and told his new friend that he was ready. Twenty minutes later, he sheepishly tip-toed past the hotel reception clerk (who decided that it wasn't his business to stare at his guest's bedraggled state) and somehow fell into his room without making a sound.

Once he ran a bath and changed into some clean clothes, Anton allowed himself to fall asleep on the granite-like bed before waking up just before nine o'clock. Gathering his things, including the bottles of Rakija he had purchased for Vlasic, Anton paid his bill and then waited for Boskic and his smartarse attitude to arrive.

Right on time, Boskic magically appeared from behind a row of army trucks, and after a pre-arranged detour to pick up the water pump, they drove back to Šibenik. Within minutes of leaving Split, Anton slumped head-first into his seat, leaving Boskic to curse his passenger's irreverent snoring. But even if Anton had heard him, he would not have cared. The only thing that mattered was how he had survived his first test of the war. The rest of the world, especially losers like Boskic, could go and screw themselves.

*

A week later, Anton was walking home from the Šibenik bus stop after work when a familiar figure slipped into the shadows next to him. 'Need some company?' Max asked with his usual unsavoury grin.

'Do I have a choice?' Anton replied. He affectionally tapped Max on the shoulder. 'I was wondering when I would see you again. For a moment, I feared that I had been dropped from the team.'

'Not a chance. You're our new star.'

'I'm not sure how I feel about that,' Anton admitted.

'Take it as a compliment; you're unlikely to get too many more before this war is over.'

Max nodded his head towards the beachfront, and they soon took refuge on a lonely park bench. 'It's going to get dark soon,' Anton noted. 'Two men having an intimate discussion on a park bench at this time of the afternoon is sure to raise suspicions, don't you think?'

'I won't be long,' said Max. 'I just need to update you on a few things.'

'Be quick.'

'I intend to be.' He bent down to tie his shoelace before raising his head towards the setting sun. 'Thanks to your initiative, our friends were able to retrieve their packages from the islet. Well done.'

'You're welcome. It certainly was touch and go there for a while.' Anton paused, 'What about Ilic?'

'To put it bluntly, he now despises you with a passion. Oh, and by the way, if he ever sees you again, he will probably try and kill you.'

'I see.' Anton frowned. 'Did anyone explain to him that leaving him on Brač was Sukevic's decision, not mine?'

'Of course,' Max replied. 'Several times, in fact. But you were the senior officer, so he blames you. And, of course, you being a Croat doesn't help matters, either.'

'I never thought it would be with the likes of him. So where does that leave us?'

'With you in the ascendancy, Anton. Sukevic and I have spoken to both Birčanin and Stubbs. We all agreed that you are far too valuable to be impacted by Ilic's blunderings. He has been shipped back to Ravna Gora to serve in Mihailović's headquarters. Hopefully, you will never see him again.'

'One could be so lucky.' Anton stretched his arms in front of him. A week after his arduous swim, he was still feeling its physical impact. 'So, what's next?'

'I love a man who is always ready for action,' Max teased. He then pulled himself closer to Anton and whispered, 'Things are about to get complicated, Anton. Discussions between Tito and Mihailović have not gone well. We will soon be at war with both the Partisans and the Ustaše.'

'That was inevitable. And the Fascist invaders? We always seem to forget them.'

'Of course.' Max coughed several times, as if to ignore his own embarrassment. 'For the moment, the British are firmly on our side, but they are pushing Mihailović to be more active against the Axis forces.'

'It doesn't help the situation if we are seen running about with the Italians.'

'As I said, things are complicated.'

'What do you want me to do?'

Max yawned as if he was suddenly bored with Anton's overt enthusiasm. 'There is some talk that the British want to land an army in Yugoslavia next year to help alleviate the situation in the Soviet Union. The Germans are giving the Russkies a right spanking at the moment, and everyone is worried.'

'Interesting, but once again, what do you want *me* to do?'

'Over the next few months, we would like you to gather as much information as you can about the Italian forces in Šibenik and Split.'

'Such as?

'Their intentions and morale, unusual troop movements, who's fucking the local women, plus anything else you think might be valuable for the British planners.'

'Since we are so much in cahoots with the Italians, why don't we just ask them ourselves?'

'Very funny.' Max shook his head in disgust. 'You never give up, do you?'

Anton didn't attempt to hide his smile. 'Will this information only go to the British, or will the Chetniks have access to it as well?'

'For the moment, we are one and the same.'

'Yes, but for how much longer? And how can I be sure that any information I find doesn't get sent right back to the Italians?' Max ignored Anton's latest riposte and pressed an unlit cigarette to his lips. 'Are you finished being a prick, or do you still require some more time?'

'I am sorry,' said Anton truthfully. 'Of course, I will do my best to give you what you need. But I feel obliged to make one final point.'

'And what is that?'

'The British will never send an invasion force to Yugoslavia.'

Max simply shrugged his shoulders. 'Maybe, maybe not. Our role is not to ask questions but to obey orders. You now have yours.'

Yes, Anton did have his orders, and despite his truculent performance that afternoon with Max, he would do everything in his power to honour them. Deep down, he considered himself to be a true patriot, someone who would fight without compunction for his country, even if that meant facilitating his own demise. Everything that was important in his life—his family, his newfound status and his job—were now secondary to the cause.

In years to come, the world would hear about another Yugoslav spy who was born in Dubrovnik. His name was Duško Popov, and his career as a double agent helped change the course of the war. Like Anton, he was handsome, dashing, charming and a perpetual womaniser. An integral part of the famous British Double Cross system, Popov, codename Tricycle, was instrumental in deceiving Germany over the location of the D-Day landings in June 1944.

It was said that Popov was a master manipulator, a high-class actor who could make even the most hardened operator inadvertently volunteer sensitive information to him. Curiously, these characteristics, like so many other similarities between the two men (they even resembled each other in a peculiar way), were evident in Anton as well.

However, while Popov would be feted in popular culture through a series of bestselling books, Anton remained trapped in the shadows. As with so many other men and women from this remarkable generation who fought their own clandestine battles, Anton was destined to take his secrets and deeds with him to the grave.

But that hardly mattered when you stood tall inside a whirlwind. The allure of living a life filled with intrigue, danger and mystery compensated for any public notoriety he may have wished for. In his heart, Anton knew that being a spy was more than just satisfying his own ego; it was a calling, a chance to make a difference and to play a pivotal role in safeguarding his country and its people. For most men, the burden of looking around corners every minute of their existence would have been too much to bear. But Anton revelled in it; in fact, you might say that he never felt more alive than he did during the first half of 1942.

Ironically though, while occasionally he disclosed some useful titbits to Max about the Italians, it was Ilsa who had hit the intelligence pot of gold by penetrating their inner sanctum. Of course, this was a direct consequence of the Italians penetrating Ilsa. Utterly ruthless and devoid of good conscience, Ilsa quickly entered into a series of affairs with a number of Italian officers stationed in Split.

Rather than it being a deliberately targeted enterprise, she had started by screwing an Italian lieutenant who worked as an assistant adjutant to the newly arrived commander of the Italian Second Army, General Mario Roatta, and then slowly worked her way up the chain of command. It was pretty much an effortless process as well, what she aptly described as an 'escalating set of diminishing returns'.

It worked like this. You escort one officer to drinks, he introduces you to his superior, you flirt with him a bit, perhaps steal a last-minute dance, let him nuzzle your neck, and before the night is over, you are having it off with him instead. Without really lifting a finger, Ilsa attacked the organisational chart with such gusto that she was soon sleeping with one of Roatta's chief operational planners, a tall, skinny colonel named Dino, whose pale, cat-like face made him look like some creature from a Brothers Grimm fairytale.

Despite his objectional looks, Dino could go all night, which unduly impressed Ilsa to no end. For a woman of basic instincts, these things meant more to her than rank or privilege. Furthermore, he didn't promise her the known world after the war was over, unlike the previous fools she bedded had done. Neither was she prone to deluding herself about the future; the relationship with Dino was purely transactional. She allowed him to bed her whenever he wanted, and he absent-mindedly revealed information to her that could have had him hung for treason.

Although Anton was jealous at first, he couldn't fault Ilsa's commitment to the Chetnik cause. On his next visit to Split, after a water pump mysteriously snapped in half during the middle of a nightshift, Ilsa was able to reveal intricate operational details about the escalating situation in Montenegro, where the Italian forces continued to be at loggerheads with both the Chetniks and Partisans.

Even Max was impressed by the quality of the information. 'Don't let this woman off your leash,' he had warned Anton with a grin when they met later in Šibenik. 'This is quality material.' Anton wanted to say something caustic in return, to remind Max of all the angst he had given him back in October when he first recruited her. But in the end, he was just grateful that 'cousin Ilsa' was proving to be a bigger hit than he had ever imagined.

By June 1942, the rumours of an Allied invasion of Yugoslavia intensified. Whether true or not, the SOE saw this as an opportunity to force Mihailović to increase Chetnik operations against the German and Italian occupiers. Some British agents were concerned that he was prevaricating at every turn; that he was more concerned about holding ground and fighting Communists than facing the real enemy in real-time. No one seemed to care too much about the horrendous reprisals that were regularly perpetrated against the Serbian population.

Even so, as Split sweltered under a golden summer, the clandestine operations that were being conducted effortlessly in the city's alleyways, cafés and bedrooms continued uninterrupted. Deeply immersed within this flurry of activity was Ilsa, whose sexual exploits in the pursuit of raw intelligence knew no boundaries. It was amazing how potent the lure of a beautiful woman could be, even among tough, war-hardened Italian soldiers. It was like putty in a child's hands.

With almost comic regularity, Ilsa would provide Anton with a never-ending stream of classified documents, the content of which she mostly didn't understand.

'I'm not sure if this is worth anything,' she said to Anton one night, floating a stapled three-page document in front of his face.

Anton had quickly skimmed through the first two pages before offering Ilsa a quizzical stare. 'Where did you get this?' he finally demanded.

'Oh, it was lying around Dino's bedroom, so I just picked it up.'

'You are not lying to me?'

'Why would I lie to you about this?'

What, in fact, Ilsa had given Anton was General Roatta's latest ORBAT (Order of Battle), precisely outlining his army's unit designations, command structure, unit strengths, equipment and capabilities, support elements and key command postings. In wartime, this information would normally be protected at all costs; a detailed ORBAT falling into the enemy's hands could constitute a potentially catastrophic security breach.

Yet Ilsa had found it lying around Dino's bedroom without having to even search.

While Anton's stocks continued to rise with every scrap of paper given to him by Ilsa, so did the number of 'sudden' business trips he had to undertake to Split. At first, Vlasic became understandably nervous at the increasing frequency of Anton's absences. But as Anton explained to him, 'The increased levels of production demanded by the Italians are putting enormous stress on the factory's ageing infrastructure. Things are breaking down far too easily, so we have no choice other than to fix them as soon as they occur.'

Not wanting to contradict his best mechanical genius, Vlasic finally relented and never asked another question about Anton's frequent trips. For that matter, neither did anyone else, not even Vuka or Jelena. But then, just when Anton thought he was in the clear, a fly landed in the ointment. And what an unpleasant, bothersome fly he turned out to be.

'What's his name?' Sukevic asked Anton one hot July morning in Split as they sucked on some ice-cold lemonades at their favourite café.

'Boskic, my boss' driver,' Anton replied. 'He's become increasingly suspicious about my trips, asking me all sorts of questions. He just won't drop it; always on my case. After we arrived at the Ragusa earlier today, he suddenly announced that he was also staying in town for the night. At the same hotel, mind you. I'm naturally wary because he loathes me.'

'Ustaše? Partisan?'

'Just a snivelling arsehole who wants to get in good with the boss.'

'No problems then,' Sukevic said calmly. 'I will kill him later today.'

Anton scratched his head. 'Shouldn't we talk about this first?'

'No. Let's just do it.'

Five hours later, Sukevic met with Anton behind a disused garage not far from Ilsa's apartment. The huge Serb had a wide grin on his chiselled face. 'All done,' he said triumphantly.

'You killed Boskic?' asked Anton nervously.

'Well, he was certainly struggling for air the last time I saw him.'

'Are you sure?'

Sukevic sighed. 'Follow me.' The two friends walked slowly towards

Sukevic's sedan, whereupon he flipped open the boot with a flick of his wrist, ruffled around some plastic bags for a little bit, and then pulled out a severed head.

'Satisfied?'

Anton didn't blink, not even for a second. 'Very impressive,' he added bleakly. 'Except for one thing.'

'And what's that?'

'That isn't Boskic.'

Sukevic examined the head closely. Thick, dark blood oozed from the jagged wound where the head had been severed, staining the sleeve of his shirt. 'What do you mean this isn't Boskic? Of course it is.'

'You see, the last time I checked, Boskic was about forty years old, with a full set of brown hair and blue eyes. This man is about sixty, bald as a football and has brown eyes.'

Sukevic swore loudly. 'Well, if this isn't Boskic, who the hell is it?'

'How the fuck should I know?'

'Look, you told me to kill the guy in room 424, so I did,' Sukevic fumed.

'424? I said, room 442.'

'No, you didn't.'

'Like hell I did.' They stood looking at each other with aimless blank expressions, like two comedians who had somehow forgotten their lines.

'Okay, okay,' Sukevic finally admitted. 'I may have got a little confused. Arithmetic was never my strongest subject at school. You go back to Ilsa's place, and I will see you here in two hours.'

Exactly two hours later, Anton found Sukevic sitting on the bonnet of his car. He looked far less satisfied than he did earlier that afternoon.

'How did it go?' Anton asked sheepishly.

'As good as could be expected.'

'What do you mean by that? Did you cut his feet off by mistake?' Anton tried to laugh at his own sarcasm, but nothing came out.

'No, I didn't,' replied Sukevic glumly. 'Although I may have accidentally lopped off an ear or two.'

'That's good to know.'

'Do you want to have a—'

Anton raised his hand in protest. 'Absolutely not. Let's just dump the body somewhere and get the hell out of here.'

The absurdity of that evening's events typified what Yugoslavia had now become. Life was so damn cheap, the by-product of an operatic comedy made in Hades itself. However, that was little comfort to Anton the following morning when he had to explain to his boss that his driver had mysteriously disappeared. But if he thought that Vlasic would be overly concerned, he was pleasantly surprised.

'People disappear all the time in this country,' Vlasic explained without a speck of emotion. 'Who knows what that rogue got up to in his spare time? Just carry on with your duties. I will send another driver to fetch you.'

Just like that, Stefan Boskic was condemned to the dustbin of stupidity.

As for the other man that Sukevic had decapitated, not one person came forward to raise the alarm over his disappearance. There was no wife to console, no children to support, no friends to reassure, no workmates to pester, no one. His meagre belongings and overdue bills hung aimlessly in the ether like they were the last remnants of some unworldly puzzle that no one would ever solve. Indeed, as far as Anton was concerned, he seemed to be exactly what he had always feared; a lonely old man, minding his own business, who, by chance, came upon a ruthless killer who mistook him for someone else. A philosopher once wrote that lonely men do not deserve to die a lonely death, and on this occasion, it all seemed mightily unfair.

Despite Anton's incessant chest-thumping and patriotic pledges, he soon realised that the country he desperately wanted to save from its enemies had become a failed state. Perhaps he would have been better off if he had conspired to save Yugoslavia from itself.

As the war blundered on, Anton, while not a violent man by nature, became increasingly immune to the escalating inferno that surrounded him. He didn't necessarily view warfare as something he could control but rather as a calamitous journey from A to B where every detour along the way required a calculated decision that ultimately resulted in death and destruction. As long as someone other than Anton had to make that decision, it would absolve him of any personal responsibility.

This sentiment may have explained why Anton often turned a blind eye to things he didn't want to know about, such as the killings of two hundred Croats during a Chetnik operation in Gata near Split in September 1942. (The Gata incident and its victims are still commemorated in Croatia to this day). As Max explained to Anton afterwards, collateral damage sometimes happens in war. For the sake of expediency, that flippant explanation seemed to satisfy both men. Whether their consciences were equally receptive when they were both lying in their beds late at night, trying to fall asleep, was an entirely different matter.

The one issue that continued to gnaw away at Anton, however, was that horrid word 'collaboration'. He didn't accept the reasons why the Chetniks in his circle were sometimes cooperating with the Italians; neither did he understand it. On the one hand, he was risking his life gathering information about the enemy. On the other, he was providing that information to a command structure that was seemingly paying lip service to the very same people he was spying on. Even in the absurdity of Yugoslav politics, this was difficult to fathom, a point he made to a senior Chetnik commander, possibly Birčanin himself, in Split just before Christmas 1942.

'These arrangements with the Italians have saved many Serbian lives,' the commander had responded with a withering retort. 'Remember that for now, do your duty and move on.'

One day, he would indeed accept that proposition and admit to others that his commander had been right. But at the time, his youthful hotheadedness and exuberance wouldn't let the matter go. Even Stubbs couldn't provide him with a straightforward answer.

'Do you actually support this?' Anton asked him afterwards.

'What do you mean?'

'This bullshit with the Italians.'

'It goes into my reports to London.'

'And what the devil does that mean?'

'It goes into my reports to London.'

'I see.' A pause. 'You wouldn't be taking advantage of the situation, would you?'

'How so?'

'It seems to me that any information we receive from the Italians that is then passed onto you is a major intelligence coup for the British.'

'Everything I see goes into my reports to London,' said Stubbs for the last time.

If Anton felt cheated by that response, he didn't have time to reflect. Hitler, fearful of the rumours about an Allied invasion in the Balkans, finally lost his mettle with Mussolini and the Italians and ordered them to make some critical changes in the way they were conducting the war. That included a direction to come down harder on the Chetniks in Dalmatia and Montenegro and forcibly disarm them wherever possible.

Almost immediately, with new, hard-lined officers in place, Anton could feel the difference around the streets of Šibenik. The newly deployed Italian soldiers seemed more irritable and officious than before, while some locals began to openly belittle their presence and stupid rules. Šibenik, like so many other towns and cities within the Italian zone of occupation, increasingly became a powder keg of resentment.

In February 1943, Ilija Trifunović-Birčanin died of natural causes. The death of the legendary guerrilla fighter inevitably created a short-term leadership vacuum at the worst possible time. Anton and Max grew restless as the unresolved issue of Birčanin's replacement festered for nearly two months. They both implored Stubbs to act quickly, to convince Mihailović to intervene while he could, but it seemed that the Englishman was only interested in submitting his reports on time. And Anton was sure that those reports no longer provided a complimentary assessment of Chetnik operations in the region.

Gradually, several leadership candidates emerged—Momčilo Đujić and a failed right-wing politician called Dobroslav Jevđević being the most prominent. Ultimately, it would be Đujić, a proven fighter, who would assume command of Chetnik operations in Northern Dalmatia. Nevertheless, several local businessmen and politicians in Split became increasingly concerned about the growing Partisan threat and asked Mihailović for assistance. In response, he sent one of his closest advisers, Colonel Mladen Žujović, to Split to assess the situation.

At first, Žujović's arrival seemed like a breath of fresh air. His suggestions on how to enhance Chetnik operations in the area sounded reasonable. Max, who had several meetings with Žujović, was optimistic that things would improve. 'This Žujović knows what he's doing,' he observed to Anton during a late afternoon walk in Šibenik. 'We can depend on him.'

In the end, Žujović's intervention came to nothing. On a delicious summer morning in June 1943, the Italian authorities initiated a brutal crackdown against Mihailović's acolytes in Split. In the space of several hours, they arrested Žujović, who had been living in the city under a pseudonym, as well as a number of other high-profile Yugoslav Army officers who were in Split at the time.

Who was responsible for revealing the location of Žujović's hideout? People speculated, but nothing was ever proven. Any false accusations would have surely escalated the violence in Dalmatia to another level, something that had to be avoided at all costs. But for Anton, Ilsa and Max, there was no such respite. For the events conspired by this incident would initiate a maelstrom that would change their lives forever.

Chapter Eight

Split, Yugoslavia
June 1943

'You have to get me out of here!'

Ilsa screamed at Anton as he entered the apartment, her rising fear etched across her beautiful face. It was the day after the mass arrests, and a pervading sense of terror had gripped the streets of Split. Anton was largely ignorant of these events when he arrived in the city earlier that morning to do a personal favour for Vlasic. But once Sukevic had briefed him on what he knew so far, Anton decided to visit Ilsa.

'Calm down, Ilsa,' Anton said softly. 'What is the matter?'

'Don't you tell me to calm down, you bastard!' Ilsa screamed once more. 'This is all your fault. My life is now in danger because of you.'

Despite Ilsa's verbal barrage, Anton reached across to put a consoling arm around her bare shoulders. 'What do you mean? What happened?'

'Haven't you heard? The Italians arrested a number of Yugoslav officers yesterday.'

'So? How does that affect you?'

Ilsa steadied herself against the kitchen table and stared at Anton defiantly. 'I was sleeping with one of them, that's how.'

Now, it was Anton's turn to lose his temper. 'No, no, fucking no!' he raged at her. He dropped his hands from Ilsa's shoulders to ensure that he didn't accidentally strangle her and then silently stared at the mascara that was dripping off her long eyelashes.

'Who was he?' he demanded. By now, there wasn't even an attempt to hide his growing anger. He always knew that Ilsa's bedroom antics would be the death of him, but even he couldn't have predicted such a calamity.

"

'Colonel Marko Antelic,' she replied in between tears. Unsurprisingly, her demeanour had changed in response to Anton's anger. She now played the role of the scared little mouse, hoping for his sympathy and compassion. Anton was having none of it.

'Oh, my God.' He threw his hands suddenly into the air as if inviting someone to shoot arrows at his heart. 'He was one of Birčanin's closest advisors. I have to give it to you. When you choose them, you go big.'

Ilsa reached out to slap him across the face, but Anton grabbed her hand mid-air. 'We have no time for this, okay?' He paused before staring straight into her cold eyes. 'What did you tell him? Did you say anything about me? About Dino?'

Ilsa reluctantly nodded her head. She knew that when Anton was in one of his moods, you didn't screw with him. 'Yes, yes. Well, I didn't tell him your name specifically, just that an ex-boyfriend of mine was working for the British, and I was providing him with secret information.'

'Oh, my God.'

'It can't be that bad, can it?'

Despite the gravity of the situation, Anton could barely contain his laughter. 'Let me be clear, Ilsa. As soon as the Italians threaten to remove your boyfriend's testicles with a knife, he will no doubt reveal to them that his lover was also sleeping with a high-ranking Italian officer.'

'I told you before,' Ilsa began nervously, 'Dino was transferred to Trieste back in April.'

'I don't care if he is doing a one-man singing and dancing tour of the French Riviera,' Anton said. 'They will track things back to him within days. That's after they have tortured every litle bit of information they need from you first. Then they'll come after me.'

Ilsa started to cry, 'I don't want to die.'

'Perhaps you should have thought about that before putting both of us in danger.'

'You wouldn't understand, Anton.'

'Try me,' Anton retorted. 'Because I really want to know.'

'He was good to me,' she sobbed. 'He treated me like a lady, not like a whore. And he was always there when I needed him, something that you wouldn't understand.'

If that comment meant to have stung Anton, he wasn't moved at all. Not in the slightest. 'Jesus Christ,' he blasphemed. 'We are in the middle of a war, Ilsa, not on the set of some Hollywood movie. Your personal feelings don't really matter in the bigger scheme of things; only our survival does. You have compromised that terribly with your naivety.'

'I'm so sorry,' she now blathered, her porcelain face lined with tears. Despite the gnawing sense of panic churning inside his stomach, Anton suddenly realised he was being too hard on her. Nothing would be gained by having a distraught woman by his side while he was trying to sort this mess out. He needed her to calm down.

'Look, what's done is done,' he countered gently, much to Ilsa's surprise. 'I am more concerned about what we do next. We need to act fast. Find your smallest bag and pack only essential items. Make sure that there is nothing left in the apartment that in any way identifies me. No cards, no letters I may have sent in the past, nothing. Assume that you're not setting foot inside this place for a very long time. When you're ready, lock the front door and meet me behind the Hotel Ragusa in an hour. Speak to no one on the way, not even to call your mother. As of this afternoon, you are disappearing off the face of the Earth. Okay?'

'But my mother,' Ilsa began to weep again. 'She's an old lady. She cannot survive without me.'

'I will ensure that she is taken care of,' Anton promised. 'But for now, you have to do exactly what I say.'

After pecking Ilsa on the cheek, Anton slipped quietly out the front door, double-checking that he wasn't being watched. He found Sukevic leaning against an electrical pole a hundred metres down the street.

'Everything okay?' Sukevic asked with a tinge of concern on his bullish face.

'Far from it,' Anton replied before proceeding to tell his friend of the latest drama involving Ilsa.

'Fuck,' said Sukevic almost casually, but it seemed the perfect response. 'Yes, fuck.'

'Do you want me to kill her?'

Anton raised his eyebrows in disdain. 'Are you serious?'

'Of course I am. It would solve a lot of our problems, don't you think? I can make it look like a robbery or perhaps a rape. And I am certain that Max would approve.'

Anton shook his head forcefully. 'Not a chance, Stojan. Don't even think about it. There has been too much senseless killing already in this war, and I'm not going to contribute more to that list. Besides, I promised Ilsa that I would help her leave Split if her cover was ever blown.'

'Promises are made to be broken, Anton.'

'Not this one.' Anton quickly changed the topic by gesturing towards the town centre. 'I am supposed to meet Max in an hour. Given the circumstances, we have to assume that the meeting is compromised. Who knows how much Ilsa really told Antelic about me? You need to find Max before he arrives at the café and warn him of the situation. But be careful. The first sign of trouble, get the hell out of there.'

Sukevic nodded his head. 'What are you going to do?'

'I am going back to the Ragusa to have a quiet chat with Brontic, my boss' driver.'

Ten minutes later, Anton arrived at the Ragusa and found Brontic standing in front of the main entrance, sucking on a Lucky cigarette he must have swindled from some half-witted Italian soldier. He was a small man with a soccer ball for a head and a pair of squinty hazel eyes that looked perpetually lost. Unlike his predecessor, Brontic was a thoroughly decent fellow with a jaunty sense of humour who had developed a good relationship with Anton over the previous year. Just how good, though, was about to be severely tested.

'Hello Anton,' he said, half-swallowing a huge puff of smoke. 'Have you finished your business?'

'Not exactly,' Anton replied. He gently guided Brontic by the arm to the edge of the street. 'Look, Ivan, I don't have a lot of time, and I need to find out now if you are on board.'

'On board with what?'

'It's my cousin, Ilsa,' Anton began with all the false charm he could muster. 'One of the Italian officers here has been blackmailing her for sex. He told her that if she didn't comply, they would come for her mother—my aunty—and she would never see her again.'

'Those bastards,' Brontic said with genuine anger. 'They think they can do anything they want.'

'Indeed. To make matters worse, he has now found some other floozy to enjoy. Poor Ilsa. Word on the street is that she will soon be arrested, just to keep her quiet. God knows what they will do to her. I have to find a way of getting her out of Split today.'

Brontic wasn't a fool; he understood Anton's hidden implication immediately.

'You want us to take her to Šibenik?'

Anton looked like the cat that had just shat all over its master's pillow. 'Grebaštica, actually.'

Brontic rubbed his chin. He knew the serene coastal village of Grebaštica well—it was perhaps fifteen kilometres south of Šibenik. 'It's slightly out of our way, but I guess we can make some random excuse up if we are stopped.'

'Then you will do it?'

'Yes.' He stared at Anton with a wild grin. 'You don't have to humour me, Anton. I guessed some time ago that you were up to no good. All of these strange trips to Split that make no fucking sense. Come on, man.'

'Then I take it that you have no issues with that?' Anton asked cautiously.

'If I did, I would have ratted you out to Vlasic a long time ago.'

'You're a good man, Ivan. I can't tell you how grateful I am. If there is anything I can do for you, just ask.'

'I shall think of something, but first, lets's get back to the car.'

They returned to the carpark and waited patiently for Ilsa to arrive. About thirty minutes later, Ilsa finally appeared from behind the corner of the adjoining street, her golden hair woven tightly in a bun, her hand gripping a small red suitcase. The stylish floral dress she was wearing accentuated her large bustline and shapely legs, and more than ever, she looked like the Hollywood starlet she probably would have been if her life had been different.

'That's cousin Ilsa?' Brontic grinned as she made her way towards the car.

'Yes,' was all Anton could say, red lines of embarrassment streaked across his half-smitten face.

Brontic whistled. 'I wish my cousin looked like that.'

Both men scampered out of the car, wanting to be the first to relieve Ilsa of her suitcase. 'Here, let me take that,' offered Brontic as he flipped open the boot. Ilsa totally ignored him but allowed him the privilege of servicing her needs nevertheless. She then turned to face Anton, her suspicious eyes alight with their usual fire.

'What now?' she demanded. The fragile woman from an hour ago now had a look of steely determination.

'Well, are you going to stare at me or answer my question?'

Anton took a deep breath and pointed to the boot. 'You're getting inside that boot, and then we are driving to Grebaštica.'

Ilsa calmly shook her head. 'No, I am not.'

'What part are you saying no to? The boot or Grebaštica?'

'The boot part, that's what. If you think I am going to curl myself up inside that ghastly little hole, then you have gone completely crazy. In case you haven't noticed, it's the middle of summer. I'm certain it's already over thirty degrees outside. Imagine how hot it will be inside there?'

'I realise that Ilsa,' Anton said impatiently. 'But we have no choice. You don't have any formal authorisation to travel outside of Split, and we are going to have to negotiate at least one roadblock during our journey.'

'I don't care how many roadblocks you fools have to negotiate,' Ilsa replied loudly. 'I am not getting inside that boot.'

Suddenly, Brontic's diminutive body and toothy grin popped up unexpectedly between them, his hand reaching for the air like some frustrated schoolboy wanting to get his teacher's attention.

'Look, if you want my opinion, Anton, she is much better off in the car with us. When we bump into an Italian patrol, I would prefer to spin a tale on why a woman with no papers is openly accompanying us in the back seat rather than explaining why she is hiding like a criminal in the boot.'

'You don't understand, Ivan,' Anton began. 'Pretty soon, every damn Italian soldier in Split is going to be looking for a blonde woman fitting Ilsa's description. We simply can't take the risk.'

Ilsa now puffed out her chest towards both men and smiled. 'Well, lucky for you then that I bought this with me.' She reached into the boot, opened her suitcase, and pulled out a fluffy black wig. After catching a glimpse of her reflection in one of the car's side windows, she expertly manoeuvred the wig to fit her scalp and then triumphantly turned to face both men.

'What do you think?'

At first, Anton and Brontic looked at each other for moral support. Was there any chance that she could look even more desirable than she normally did? The wig indeed fitted her perfectly—unbelievably so—and it changed the entire complexity of her face. With a stream of black hair now flowing over her tanned, slim shoulders, she had virtually turned into a new woman without even trying.

'Man, oh man, you look exactly like Greta Garbo,' said Brontic enthusiastically, while Anton just sighed.

'You're a true gentleman,' Ilsa noted with a smile without bothering to ask Brontic his actual name. 'Unlike some men I know.'

Given the circumstances, Anton wasn't in the mood to escalate this game of sexual cat and mouse, so he quickly coaxed Ilsa and Brontic back towards the car. 'Can we get going? Please? We have wasted enough time as it is.'

After some last-minute grumbling from Ilsa, they all took their seats, and Brontic soon had the car humming along the main northerly road out of Split. Aside from some army trucks, the traffic was mysteriously quiet for this time of day, and they made it to the outer suburbs in good time.

'This is almost too easy,' Anton remarked as he nervously tapped his fingers on the dashboard.

'We will be coming up to a checkpoint very soon,' replied Brontic. 'Pray that our luck holds out.'

Brontic was right; five minutes later, their car joined a small line of vehicles just near a curve in the road. The Italians were generally hopeless at fighting, but when it came to manning checkpoints, they were in a class of their own.

'Leave the talking to me,' ordered Brontic. If he was worried about the impending situation in any way, he definitely wasn't showing it. In fact, he was plain cocky.

'You speak Italian?' Ilsa asked, with that signature creak in her voice.

'I lived in Venice for several years before the war, so I get by. The main thing is to act normal and not give the impression that we are actually shitting ourselves. Just stay calm, and we will get out of this okay.'

They were soothing words, but this didn't prevent Anton from now gripping the dashboard tightly with both hands. If only he had brought his pistol with him, he could have dealt with the Italians by himself. Without it, he suddenly felt naked and afraid.

After the black sedan in front of him was given permission to leave, Brontic slowly pulled up next to a grubby-looking Italian soldier, complete with a dubious page-boy crew cut and a poorly conceived Hitler moustache. The way the Italian carried himself suggested that he was born to give people a hard time. Indeed, he strutted to the car like an officious peacock and, without hesitation, demanded that Brontic produce whatever papers he had with him. Anton suddenly felt the hairs on his arms bristle in anticipation. Again, he silently cursed himself for not bringing his gun with him.

But to his credit, Brontic was calmness personified. Seemingly oblivious to fear, he calmly passed his papers over to Corporal Grubby while simultaneously offering him an audacious smile.

Anton was sure that the Italian wasn't smart enough to actually read, but nevertheless, he spent what seemed like an eternity examining Brontic's travel authorisation. At one point, Anton thought that the soldier was about to reach for his pistol that was strapped around his extra-large gut, but he then dropped his arms to his side. To Anton's relief, the soldier merely grunted and nodded his head.

'Proceed,' he snarled at Brontic before slowly walking to the next car. While Anton and Ilsa held their collective breath, Brontic pumped his foot hard onto the accelerator and sped down the open road in front of him.

'Jesus!' Anton looked inquisitively at Brontic. 'That must have been the shortest inspection I've experienced doing these damn trips. He didn't even bother to look at Ilsa. What was his problem?' He felt like laughing but just couldn't bring himself to do it.

'Who knows? Maybe he's homesick for his family in Italy. Or perhaps he got incredibly drunk last night and is still suffering from a terrible hangover. Either way, I don't really care. I just want to get where we are going as quickly as possible.' He paused for a moment to consider Anton's brooding eyes. 'Where are we going, by the way?'

'Yes,' croaked Ilsa from behind. 'Where the hell are you taking me, Anton? You have said nothing about that so far.'

'I told you before. We are going to Grebaštica.'

'What's so special about Grebaštica?'

Anton sighed and turned to face his tortured lover. 'Not what, but who. Have you heard of Father Stefan Lukic?'

Brontic whistled loudly while Ilsa scratched her chin with a perfectly manicured index finger. 'Of course I have,' she finally replied. 'He is that Orthodox priest from Knin who saved those Jews last year from the Fascists.'

'Correct,' said Anton. 'A remarkable man and a perpetual thorn in the side of the Ustaše. They would have killed him a long time ago if it weren't for the Italians. But after Birčanin died, the Italians couldn't guarantee his safety anymore, or should I say, didn't *want* to guarantee his safety anymore. Not in their best interests to have the blood of someone so popular on their hands, you see. So, they turned the problem over to the Serbs.'

'You're taking me to see Father Lukic?'

'Yes. Given his reputation for saving those in desperate trouble, I am certain he can help you find somewhere safe until things settle down. This is the best I can do for you at such short notice.'

'And how do you know that he will help me? You act as if you know him.'

'I do know him,' Anton replied with a forced grin. 'Not well, mind you, but enough to be confident that he will not turn his back on a good Serbian girl in trouble.'

Ilsa leant back in her seat and momentarily gazed out the window. Everything in her life so far had seemed so rushed, so needless. But in her own perverse way, she had always found a way to survive. Nothing really fazed her once she overcame that initial feeling of panic. However, this was something else—a high jump into another life she never dared to contemplate before now.

'May I ask how you know him?' she finally implored. Her hands began to tremble as she finally understood the scale of her predicament.

'Let's just say that we helped Father Lukic and his family find somewhere safe to live near Grebaštica a few months ago after the Ustaše came looking for him.'

'We?' asked Brontic.

'The Chetniks, of course.'

Brontic laughed. 'Just checking. I wanted to make certain that I wasn't risking my life for a couple of Bolsheviks.'

'Not today.'

Fortunately, Brontic knew a back route along an old dirt road that led straight into Grebaštica from the east. Better still, he was confident that no Italian units were patrolling this remote part of the coastline. If anything, the area was a known Chetnik stronghold, so once Brontic turned off the main road, they could relax a little. Ilsa even found time to have a solitary cigarette.

The road, if you could actually call it one, was like a minefield. Every ten seconds, it seemed that the wheels would bounce and jostle after hitting the next pile of rocks, creating a dust storm that hovered persistently around the car's bonnet.

'Maybe after the war they can do something about our fucking roads,' Brontic muttered. 'I think more people have died from car accidents in Yugoslavia than from the Nazis.'

Anton laughed. Despite the situation, he was enjoying Brontic's company and his sense of humour, more so because it momentarily turned his attention away from Ilsa. He wasn't in love with her … to be honest, he really didn't understand the concept of love and doubted whether he ever would. But she did make him feel incredibly alive and wanted at a time when his world was surrounded only by misery and death. Surely, he had earned the right for this one distraction.

They soon entered a tiny valley on the outskirts of Grebaštica. Much to Brontic's relief, the road flattened, and the bumps and uneven terrain that threatened to destroy his front axle disappeared.

'Do you know where we are, Anton?'

'Yes. We are not too far away from Lukic's house.' He glanced out the passenger window. 'In another five hundred metres, you will see an entrance to a laneway on your right. Follow that down for another kilometre until you get to an isolated stone cottage surrounded by a large steel fence. Park alongside the main security gate and wait for me to return. During my absence, don't get out of the car or do anything that raises suspicion. Otherwise, the car will likely go up in smoke very quickly with both of you in it.'

'Understood.'

When they arrived at the house, Brontic deliberately overshot the driveway by about fifty metres, and then slowly reversed backwards until the car was parallel with the main gate.

'Good luck,' he offered as Anton reached for the side door.

'Thanks, I will need it.' He turned to face Ilsa, expecting some tiny semblance of gratitude for his efforts. But true to recent form, she deliberately ignored him, her ego focused on some imaginary slight that Anton was sure he would soon hear about.

'Okay,' he said to no one in particular. 'I won't be very long.'

Ivan and Ilsa watched closely as Anton banged several times on the security gate. On the fifth attempt, the gate partly opened, and a burly man wearing a grey uniform and carrying a semi-automatic rifle appeared through the dazzling sunshine. After a brief conversation, the guard patted Anton down from chest to foot and then escorted him into the compound.

'That's a relief,' Brontic muttered.

Ilsa barely registered a grunt in response before proceeding to remove her wig. There was no need to play silly games anymore. This was who she was, blonde, beautiful and dangerous, and they could take her or leave her.

Once she carefully unfurled her natural hair, she considered Brontic with a rueful sigh.

'What do you think about all this?' she asked him coldly.

'About what?'

'Anton handing me over to a Serbian Orthodox priest.'

'Honestly?'

'Honestly.'

'I think Anton is a man under considerable pressure, and you have only made it worse for him today with your boorish behaviour.'

Ilsa coughed angrily. 'Maybe you should keep your opinions to yourself in the future.'

'Someone had to say it.'

They now sat together in morbid silence, both eager to escalate the conversation further if the other party pushed it hard enough. But after ten minutes of this childish nonsense, the front gate opened once again, and Anton calmly walked towards the car, his lips curled in a satisfied smile.

'Like I said before,' he told Ilsa through the back seat window, 'he was never going to turn his back on a good Serbian girl like you.'

'Do me a favour, Anton; don't patronise me. I risked my life for you.'

'And I risked mine for you as well. We are even.'

Ilsa stepped out of the car and retrieved her suitcase from the boot. She callously decided not to thank Brontic for actually risking his own life to help her. He had served his purpose; there were other men to now exploit. In a bizarre way, she was even looking forward to it.

'I gather I won't be seeing you for a while,' she growled at Anton. 'Or am I being too optimistic?'

'You never know in this war,' said Anton. 'Crazier things have happened.' He reached out to her reluctantly, his eyes devouring her savage beauty for perhaps the final time. Despite herself, Ilsa felt the raw emotional power of the moment and instinctively fell into his arms. 'You bastard,' she whispered before they kissed passionately, her soul burning with a desire that left them both breathless.

After they peeled apart, Ilsa patted down her dress and snatched at her bag with her dainty little fingers. 'Take care of your wife and daughter, Anton,' she said softly. 'You are all they have. And if there is one thing I have learnt in this war, everyone has to have someone.' Without waiting for a reply, she lifted her eyes to face the glowing sun and then sprinted towards the open gate.

Chapter Nine

Šibenik, Yugoslavia
June 1944

They say that the Devil finds his own luck, even when he tempts fate. Anton had indeed tempted fate by bringing Ilsa into his secret world, but somehow his luck held firm against all odds. Barely two hours after Ilsa had left Split, a squad from the Italian secret police arrived at her apartment with their knuckle-dusters and flick-knives, hellbent on unleashing their sadistic fury on this treacherous Serbian whore.

When they found no one inside, they trashed the place anyway, just because they could.

As for Antelic, well, he sung like a canary, although he really didn't need an awful lot of convincing after they stuck that pistol in his mouth. Within days, Dino was ripped away from the parade ground at Reveille by a gang of uniformed thugs and never seen again. That was life under a fascist regime, and no one really gave it more than a second thought.

Anton's curiosity was one of his better virtues. So, after things died down following Ilsa's escape, he used an unplanned visit to Father Lukic's safe house to enquire about her whereabouts. Lukic was an overweight man in his mid-forties with an elfin-like smile, a neat, flowing beard, and an imploding bald patch at the top of his crown. He was immediately impressed by Anton's sincerity. 'She is with friends,' was all he would say. 'And she is acquitting herself very well in her new role.'

Anton understood immediately what this meant. Ilsa had joined the Chetniks. While they generally didn't allow women to operate on the front line as fighters, Ilsa's training as a nurse would be invaluable to the greater cause.

When he had time to think about it, Anton was surprised, if not disappointed, by this news. He rather imagined, after all his efforts to free her, that a glamourous woman like Ilsa would have found her way to neutral Switzerland, gratefully leaving the war behind her for good. Never in a million years had he imagined that she would trade a life of potential luxury for a clandestine and transient existence where every new day might be her last one. Perhaps he had underestimated the extent of Ilsa's patriotism.

As for Max and his network, it remained business as usual. By pure chance, Sukevic had found Max wandering through an isolated side street by himself, oblivious to the morning's drama. From a secure vantage point, they both reconnoitred the café for several hours, expecting to see half the Italian Army swarm down the road. But it soon became obvious that no one was coming, not even the local copper on his afternoon beat, so they got shit-faced drunk together and reminisced about the good old days before the war.

After a week of careful analysis, it seemed that the Italians had not been able to secure the identity of Ilsa's controller. This was further confirmed when news broke in Split that Antelic had been summarily executed, much to Mihailović's outrage.

Max, however, was extremely irate that Anton had refused to sanction Ilsa's murder. 'You are a romantic fool,' he railed at his top agent a week later in Šibenik. 'When are you going to learn that there is no room for sentimentality in this war?'

'Probably never. You see, I like to remind myself occasionally that I am still human. If that worries you, then perhaps we should part ways.'

'We should have parted ways a long time ago,' Max replied bluntly. 'But it just so happens that you're my best agent, so we have to indulge each other for a little longer.'

And they did, for better or worse. In his later years, Anton would struggle to define his relationship with Max. In many ways, he had loved him like the older brother he never had. But a deeper, silent part of him was repulsed by Max's flagrant disregard for life, his lack of pity for those who didn't share his beliefs, and his propensity for sudden violence. What particularly concerned Anton was how comfortable Max felt about his own shortcomings. There were never any regrets, no remorse over the life-or-death decisions he frequently had to make, no capacity for self-doubt. He was, in fact, a true warrior—determined, motivated and pitiless.

Max, on the other hand, had an overwhelming affection for Anton that transcended normal friendship. No matter what their differences, he firmly believed that the two men were destined to share an unshakeable bond for the rest of the war, an exclusive partnership for the ages that would only come to a natural conclusion once victory was assured. But Max's tragedy was his failure to fully appreciate the existential crisis slowly playing out inside Anton's soul. When he finally realised what was really happening to his friend, it was far too late to intervene.

Perhaps the seminal events of September 1943 provided the first hint of what was to come. Decimated both militarily and psychologically by a war they never really wanted, Italy surrendered to the invading Allied forces. The Italian King finally grew some balls and sacked Mussolini before asking Marshal Pietro Badoglio to form a new government. Under pressure from the Allies, many Italian units simply swapped sides and joined their former enemies without so much as a second thought.

Mussolini was immediately arrested by Badoglio's government but was soon rescued by a crack German commando unit led by the infamous Nazi paratrooper Otto Skorzeny. A much-diminished figure who had become resentful of Hitler and the war, Mussolini was placed in charge of a puppet state known as the Italian Social Republic, its capital located in the northern Italian town of Salò. But everyone, including Mussolini himself, understood that he had no real power anymore, that every crucial decision about Italy's fate rested with Adolf Hitler and his acolytes.

In Dalmatia, many Italian soldiers simply laid down their weapons and fled back to Italy. Others were captured and imprisoned by the Germans. Those who still believed in a Fascist cause, joined the German Wehrmacht to continue the fight against the Allies. However, the new Roman Empire was now in its final death throes, a ludicrous venture that Mussolini had foolishly pursued without any regard for the welfare of his people.

The situation in Split became symbolic of the chaos that ensued following Italy's surrender. Initially, the news of Italy's capitulation was greeted with jubilation by the city's population. Split had been at the epicentre of local resistance to the Italians for the previous two years. Regardless of whether you supported the King or Tito, a victory was there to be cherished.

However, it soon became obvious to the Chetniks, and those who opposed communism, that the victory being celebrated was very much a pyrrhic one. The commander of the Italian Bergamo Division, befuddled by his new obligations, initially decided to give away his weapons to both the Chetniks and the Partisans.

This did not please the local Partisan commander, General Popović, who demanded that the Italians join his army.

'Oh, and by the way, the rest of your guns and bombs? They belong to us, not the Chetniks. So immediately end your negotiations with them.'

News soon arrived that the crack German Waffen SS Prinz Eugen Division was descending on Split. These were serious fucking soldiers, not your everyday Italian conscripts. However, emboldened by their new partnership with the Allies and free from their Fascist masters, thousands of Italian soldiers from the Bergamo Division volunteered to fight the Germans alongside the Partisans. Split was soon swamped by Popović's forces, to be greeted happily by local Partisan supporters.

These developments unnerved Anton for three reasons. First, the thought of the Partisans being so close to Šibenik made him fear for his own safety and that of his family. He knew the repercussions for people like him, patriots who believed in freedom and King Petar, should the Partisans ever prevail. He was especially angry that the Chetnik leadership had recently lost total control of the narrative, allowing the Partisans to become the unchallenged heroes of the people. What made matters worse was that the British were slowly jumping on the Partisan bandwagon as well. Soon, Anton predicted, the Chetniks would be completely abandoned.

Second, once Split was liberated, Vuka's sister, Jelena, quietly disappeared. It was no surprise when a family friend confirmed with Mateo a few days later that she was seen in Partisan uniform, parading through the main streets of Split. Unlike the Chetniks, the Partisans had no qualms about recruiting female fighters. Perhaps that was one of the reasons why they were now growing stronger by the day.

Mateo and Anton had discussed the matter later that night. Mateo was a man usually devoid of emotion, but he cursed the war and what it had done to those he loved. Like Anton, he always understood Jelena's true affiliations, but never once did he think that she would actually act upon them. 'I failed in my duty as a father to protect this family,' he bemoaned, and Anton could only silently hold his hand in support.

Finally, Anton had lost all contact with Max. Sukevic had managed to escape Split just as the Partisans were entering the city, but he could not offer Anton any information on Max's whereabouts or wellbeing. 'If I know Max,' he reassured Anton, 'he would have gone to ground with Yuri somewhere and is waiting for the right opportunity to leave. Those Commie bastards are pretty thorough, though; at some point, they will come looking for him. The sooner he gets out of there, the better.' They even discussed launching a rescue mission, but they both quickly dismissed such a dangerous folly. As much as they detested the thought, all they could do was sit and wait.

In the end, they didn't have to wait very long. The Partisans and Italians were no match for the Prinz Eugen. Within two weeks, the Germans ran the Partisans out of Split, exacting a terrible revenge on those Italian soldiers who had crossed the Communist line. Dalmatia was soon incorporated into the Independent State of Croatia. It was a win of sorts for Pavelić and the Ustaše, although the Germans maintained military control of the region. Yugoslavia had now become Hitler's problem, and he wasn't in the mood for compromises with Pavelić or anyone else.

Several days after the fall of Split, Max returned to Šibenik. His beaming smile was keenly welcomed by Anton, who had almost given him up for dead. 'I always find a way to survive,' Max boasted as he explained how he and Yuri had hidden in a concealed cave on Brač for much of the Partisan occupation. The dialogue between both men seemed unnaturally relaxed, as if the whole episode had been nothing more than a weekend excursion to the beach.

'We are open for business again, Anton,' Max said confidently.

And for a while, they were. As the Germans started to fill the void left by the Italians, the Chetniks initiated a number of sabotage attacks against their new oppressors. Anton was in the thick of the action too, running guns, organising safe houses and making bombs. How he found the time to also meet his work and family obligations was a mystery that even he couldn't resolve.

What the debacle in Split had proven, though, was that the Chetniks were under considerable pressure to maintain their presence in the area. Although Đujić was a fierce warrior, his Dinara Chetnik Division, like other units, were frequently losing men and arms to the Partisans, a situation not helped by what Anton thought was a clear lack of clarity over Chetnik war aims. Who was the real enemy? The Nazis? The Partisans? The Ustaše? Anton honestly didn't know anymore. By now, it had simply become a case of kill or be killed. And despite Max's insistence that his network with the British was still operational, the rumours persisted that the Allies were about to close the door on the Chetniks for good.

Anton wasn't to know, of course, but that decision was effectively made in late 1943 at the Tehran Conference between the 'Big Three'—Britain's Prime Minister Winston Churchill, US President Franklin D Roosevelt and Soviet supremo, Joseph Stalin. The Chetniks were collaborators and brigands, it was claimed, who were, by and large, refusing to take the fight up to the Germans. Tito and his partisans, on the other hand, knew how to fight and how to die with honour. And as for the future of Yugoslavia? Well, as Churchill allegedly said to his key adviser on Yugoslav affairs,

Colonel Fitzroy Maclean, over brandy one evening, neither man was intending to live in Yugoslavia after the war, so what did they care who eventually ruled the country?

Anton tried to raise his concerns with Max in the new year. Perhaps it was time to give up on all the spy stuff and join Mihailović and the Chetnik guerrillas in the mountains of Serbia. Start taking the fight up to the Nazis and the Partisans with renewed vigour rather than running around in confused circles with the British.

But Max was having none of it. 'We have to stay the course,' he kept repeating, more to convince himself, it seemed. After several days of arguing, Anton finally gave up. Father Lukic had told him confidentially that the Chetnik leadership had become increasingly sceptical of the British and their motives. To complicate matters, Max also confided in him that some Chetnik officers coveted access to his secret network so they could use it as a bargaining chip if required, something that he would never countenance. So, Max stubbornly kept the pretence going even though he knew that time was surely running out.

To his credit, it was Stubbs who put an end to things. Whatever Anton thought of him, he turned out to be a courageous and honourable man. Risking capture by the Germans and the Ustaše, he made one last clandestine visit to Šibenik. On a cold, wet March night in 1944, he met Anton behind a dark alleyway just before the nightly curfew began and explained the situation.

'I am leaving Yugoslavia for good and returning to London,' he revealed sadly. 'Unfortunately, my superiors no longer want to do business with the Chetniks. It's all about Tito now.'

It wasn't news that particularly shocked Anton, but even so, he still found such biting words hard to accept. 'I see.' It was all he could say at first, his hands shaking in tune to the crackling wind. 'And just like that, you're handing over Yugoslavia to the Partisans?'

Stubbs didn't even try to make excuses for his government's perfidy. 'I know, it's a bloody disgrace. I am so sorry, Anton. But this war isn't being decided by patriots like you and me. We are at the mercy of politicians who think they know better.'

'They are all fools,' Anton finally replied. 'But then, when you think about it, this war was started by fools, and so it stands to reason that it will be ended by fools.'

'You're no fool, Anton,' Stubbs whispered. 'In fact, you're an incredibly brave man. I can never thank you enough for what you have done for us.'

Anton grasped Stubbs' hand and shook it firmly. 'Just so you know, I don't blame you in any way for this mess, even though I am still curious about those reports you kept sending to London.'

Despite the situation, Stubbs laughed. 'Maybe one day after the war, we will meet somewhere, far from this madness, and over a glass of pinot noir, I will reveal to you what I said. That's if you find it in your heart to talk to me after what we have done to your country.'

Anton tried to return a smile. 'You have a deal, Major. But in the meantime, please don't burden yourself over these matters. You have been a good friend, even though at times I didn't show you the respect you deserved.'

'Thank you, Anton. I appreciate that.' He then braced himself as a stream of cold wind parted his hair. 'What will you do now?'

'I am not sure, and it scares the hell out of me.'

'Take my advice, for what it's worth. Forget about the war. You need to think about your family first and foremost. Yugoslavia will become a Communist state within the year, and the Partisans will then hunt every Chetnik down until there is no one left. Find somewhere safe to go and do it quickly, man. I will do what I can to help. I still have some pull within the right circles.'

'I appreciate your offer, but no,' Anton replied with tears in his eyes. 'This is my country, my home. I cannot leave yet.' There was nothing more he could say to Stubbs without sounding resentful. 'But thank you for risking your life to see me.'

Stubbs, realising the impotence of the moment, said nothing. Instead, he placed a brotherly arm around Anton's tattered woollen coat for a moment, and then silently disappeared into the grey winter rain.

'So, what's next?' Anton asked Max a few days later.

'Fuck Stubbs, fuck the British,' he replied angrily. 'We continue the fight, that's what we do.' Anton had heard the rumours that Max had tried to kill Stubbs when he discovered the grim news that he was leaving Yugoslavia. But given the red streaks of fire swirling inside Max's eyes, Anton didn't dare to broach the subject. It was bad enough that everything they worked so hard for had suddenly blown up in their faces.

Over the next few months, his spying activities mostly on hiatus, Anton began to question every aspect of his life—his identity, his religion, his marriage, his future. His mood was not helped by the deteriorating political situation. Backed by the full force of the Allied war machine, the Partisans were quickly gaining the ascendancy in the civil war.

Furthermore, British and American planes, operating under the absurd banner of the Balkan Air Force, began a ruthless bombing campaign, targeting key Dalmatian infrastructure and communication lines. Given its importance as a logistics hub, Šibenik was bombed regularly by the Allies, its harbour and aluminium factory at Lozovac natural targets for Allied planners.

Fuelled by Max's increasingly incoherent ramblings, Anton had been clinging in vain hope that the Allies would gradually come to their senses and see the Partisans for what they were. But as each day passed, the reality of the situation became clearer—the Chetnik cause was doomed unless something drastic changed. If he needed any confirmation, a secret meeting on the island of Vis further sealed their fate. After months of negotiation, the royal government signed an agreement with Tito outlining how the rest of the war in Yugoslavia would be conducted. Not long afterwards, King Petar dismissed Mihailović as his military chief of staff for not abiding by the agreement and the Partisans were recognised as Yugoslavia's official army.

When Max told Anton the details of the Vis agreement and that

Mihailović had been sacked, it was like someone had stuck a dagger into his heart. He, and so many others like him, had sacrificed their lives for the royal family and this was how they were now being repaid. To learn that the king you loved and followed without question had made a deal with the Communists of all people was just too much. What a treacherous sellout, even by Yugoslav standards. (After the war, Anton would acknowledge the incredible pressure that was exerted on a young King Petar during this time. He would ultimately place the blame for the sellout not on his beloved King but those who convinced him to accept such a terrible proposition).

That night, Anton and Mateo mourned the end of the Yugoslav monarchy over several glasses of Rakija. 'Those fools,' Mateo kept repeating over and over again, a man completely heartbroken for his lost country. By now, he had guessed that Anton was working for the Chetniks, but he had never once intervened in his affairs. After all, like his son-in-law, Mateo was a staunch royalist. But as the night drew to a close, he gently put his hand on Anton's leg. 'When it's time for you and Vuka to leave, you must not hesitate,' he implored. 'Don't die for a cause that is now slowly withering away.'

Mateo's words hung over Anton like a vulture. Never before in his life had he felt so conflicted. Should he stay and fight until the bitter end? Or should he save himself and his family before it was too late? Little did he realise that fate would soon take that decision out of his hands and propel him into an ungodly inferno from which there was no return.

Chapter Ten

Šibenik, Croatia
September 1944

As the Partisans drew ever closer, Anton's days and nights were spent sifting through the rubble at his factory, coordinating some gun-running and helping Father Lukic and his family move to a new safe house in Šibenik. With the Nazis and Ustaše preoccupied by the Partisan threat, Lukic decided that he needed to be located closer to his flock. Many local Serbian Orthodox families had suffered horrendously at the hands of the Fascists since the war began. With a new, ungodly threat approaching in the form of the Communists, these unfortunate souls needed a strong voice to protect them. Lukic was convinced that God had ordained him to fulfil that role.

Over the preceding months, Anton had grown close to Lukic. While Max babbled on about things that were no longer possible, Lukic provided the rational, calming influence that Anton needed. In their intimate moments, he talked to Anton about finding inner peace through faith, urged him to question some of his traditional Catholic beliefs and forgave him for the many sins he had committed during the war, including his adultery. Thanks to Lukic's serene spirituality, Anton began to see himself in a different light. Perhaps he truly was a Serbian Orthodox warrior, accidentally trapped by circumstances inside a Catholic prism that no longer made any sense to him.

Understandably, Max was not a fan of the budding friendship between his top agent and the rambunctious priest. He had nothing against Lukic personally. Max considered him to be a hero who had saved many lives and who continued to faithfully support the royalist cause despite having a price on his head. A committed atheist despite his Catholic upbringing, Max believed that this religious nonsense had muddled Anton's mind, making him doubt his own motives. As far as he was concerned, a spy who began to question everything in their life was not only a danger to themselves but to everyone around them.

However, there was a more pressing issue that worried Max when he first heard that Anton had helped Lukic relocate to a small, run-down apartment in the Old Town. 'Now that he is living in Šibenik, you can't be seen with him publicly,' he told Anton sternly. 'If you are, the Ustaše will put one and one together, and all of our lives will be in danger.'

Anton wasn't stupid; he realised the risk he had taken by personally assuming responsibility for Lukic's move. But so be it! Throughout the war, Lukic had recklessly thumbed his nose at danger in an effort to help those most in need. To those Serbs and Jews who survived persecution and violence due to his intervention, he was their champion, their saviour. If Lukic, through his unselfishness, could hold the world to account during these tragic times, then Anton felt obliged to help him at every turn. What he failed to consider, however, was that his good intentions would inevitably turn to shit. And to the detriment of so many people, that's exactly what happened.

The day that changed everything began with a golden sunrise. It was the last Sunday in September 1944, and Anton had woken up early after an unsettled night's sleep. News that the Partisans were camped on the southern outskirts of Split had reached him late the previous night, hours after a devastating Allied air raid had targeted German ships inside Šibenik's harbour.

In an attempt to reduce civilian casualties, the attacks were usually prearranged like clockwork. They mostly came late in the afternoon once people had returned to their homes or were able to find adequate shelter. It didn't always work, of course; collateral damage was a natural consequence of bombing campaigns, and many lives were needlessly lost. But such were their tedious regularity that life in the city quickly resumed once the raids were over. The locals had become justifiably tired of the war, so much so, that many adopted a policy of ignoring the cascading violence unless it directly impacted them.

Mateo keenly supported this policy. Even though plumes of black smoke had curled their way through the cobbled streets of the Old Town for several hours afterwards, he made sure that his restaurant opened on time. Punctuality led to better business. By seven o'clock, the restaurant was packed with several German officers from the XV Mountain Corps, the usual band of Ustaše sympathisers and their fat, bloated wives and an assortment of well-to-do locals who always seemed to have enough spare cash to splash on a meal. Mateo didn't discriminate who he served — business was business, after all, and he had to make a living to support his family. However, it didn't mean he had to like it.

Anton knew that Mateo hated the Germans and the Ustaše as much as he did but admired his ability to permanently hold his tongue for the sake of the family. Mateo was also a very smart man, and without letting on, he understood how much Anton benefitted from the information he gleaned from drunken German soldiers and boastful government officials. It was amazing what could be revealed if you listened carefully enough. Even though Anton felt repulsed by being in the same room as some of these characters, he maintained the pretence of the dutiful son-in-law, helping Mateo out where he could, keeping his ear to the ground.

Of special interest to Anton were the activities of the German Commander Oberst Otto Ernst Remer (in the German Army, the rank of Oberst is equivalent to a Colonel). Remer was in his early thirties, with an owl-like face, electric blue eyes and a perpetually puffed-out chest. He walked with all the swagger of a Swabian warrior who had been awarded the Knight's Cross for bravery at the Battle of Smolensk in 1941. If Adolf Hitler could choose a German soldier who represented the archetypal Aryan Superman, he could have done worse than to select Remer.

Yet behind the extra-starched uniform and glittering medals, it was obvious that Remer was sick of the war and the violence that surrounded it. One could even say that he was sick of the Nazi Party and the insane chaos that the Führer and his cronies had inflicted across Europe. Anton had heard rumours that Remer often clashed with local Ustaše operatives over their harsh racial policies and treatment of prisoners. Apparently, he wasn't a fan of the SS either, a stance that frightened some of his fellow officers lest he brought their wrath onto them as well.

Although Anton never fell for his propaganda, Remer was one of the few German officers who understood the concept of winning the hearts and minds of the local population. As pompous and overbearing as he could be, for the most part, he came across as a fair and reasonable man who was adored by his troops. Fluent in Serbo-Croatian, he had opened up to both Anton and Mateo on several occasions about his family back in Germany and his aspirations should the war ever end. In many ways he was a hopeless dreamer, who had romanticised the war one too many times, yet Anton never once underestimated him. He was sure that fully motivated, Remer would be a ruthless adversary. Yes, although he liked the man personally, Anton was under no illusions that he might have to kill him one day soon.

On that Saturday night, Remer had been in a particularly reflective mood, announcing to anyone who wanted to listen that the Germans would soon be kicked out of Yugoslavia. Anton knew that Remer wasn't one for big-noting himself or grandstanding. If he was so vocal about their prospects, then there was a good chance that he knew something about the strategic situation that wasn't so apparent to others. Anton was keen to relay this information to Max that morning when they were due for their next meeting.

After sharing a quick breakfast with Vuka and Dubravka, Anton announced that he had to see a friend about work and would be back in time for lunch. By that stage, Vuka, like her father, realised that Anton was helping the Chetniks, although she knew enough about his clandestine life not to ask questions. For the moment, she had other priorities in her life, like looking after Dubravka and helping her parents take care of Jelena's children. But with time running out before the Partisans inevitably liberated Šibenik, she would soon have to pester her secretive husband about his intentions. Even in such uncertain times, she needed some certainty about the future.

Anton left the house just after nine thirty and wandered down to the waterfront. The dying embers of grey smoke from the previous day's bombing still peppered the pale blue sky. Last night, he had overheard one of the German officers telling a colleague that a torpedo boat had been sunk during the bombing raid. From where he stood, he could see two German patrol boats sweeping the outer harbour in concentric circles. They were obviously looking for wreckage or bodies, perhaps both. Something else that might interest Max.

After losing himself inside the distant horizon, Anton was brought back to reality. He examined his watch and cursed out loud. *Damn it, it's already ten o'clock!* His infernal daydreaming had finally caught up with him. He would be late for his meeting with Max. Fearing the worst, he tossed away the cigarette he had just lit and, without trying to draw too much attention to himself, scurried towards the bus station. When he arrived five or six minutes later, he double-checked that he hadn't been followed and then banged three times on the door to the cleaner's room. No answer. He tried again. Still no answer. *Fuck.*

Max and Anton had established an alternate meeting place if either of them ever suspected that their security had been compromised. The agreed plan was to meet at a tiny grocery store, owned by a Chetnik sympathiser, an hour later behind the Old Town. Not wanting to remain inside the bus station any longer, Anton withdrew quietly into the street and then double-backed towards the waterfront esplanade. Had he waited a further thirty seconds, he no doubt would have bumped right into Max, who was just about to enter the bus station from the opposite side of the building. Sometimes, war is guided by the finest of margins.

Oblivious to the mistake he had made, Anton walked briskly past a row of cafés and restaurants before he reached the main square at St James'

Cathedral. Usually, at that time on a Sunday morning, the square would be brimming with people following the end of mass, but today, it was mostly empty apart from a couple of beggars fighting over some scraps of food.

What the hell is going on?

Suddenly, he heard a familiar voice screech above the silent breeze. 'Anton!' He turned sharply to face his sister-in-law, Ruža, standing still at the edge of the square, her pretty face lined with streaks of panic. 'Please come home! There's trouble brewing. We have been told by the constabulary to stay inside our homes until further notice. I have been trying to find you for the last half hour!'

Anton calmly reached across and took Ruža's hands. 'What trouble?'

'Something big is happening at the Serbian Orthodox church!'

This small but historic Serbian Orthodox Church was barely three hundred and fifty metres away. When the Ustaše came to power, they had destroyed a large number of Serbian Orthodox churches in Croatia. However, thanks to Italian intransigence, the local church had survived. The Italians even allowed restricted Sunday services to occur right under the noses of the Ustaše. But when Italy capitulated to the Allies, the Ustaše sought their revenge. Although the Germans ordered them not to destroy the church, local government officials immediately closed its access to the public. Anyone who defied this edict would meet a predictably horrid fate.

Then it hit him. Who would be courageous enough to defy such an edict?

Father Lukic!

The realisation that Lukic was probably in grave danger hit Anton with incredible force. Such was its intensity that it made him completely forget about his obligations to Max. All that mattered was protecting Father Lukic at all costs, regardless of the consequences. The time had come for him to step out of the shadows and make a stand in this fucking war. If he didn't, everything he believed in would be scuttled forever. Without a semblance of concern for Max, Mateo, Vuka, Dubravka, or anyone else who cared for him, he began to run aimlessly towards the church.

'Where are you going, Anton?' Ruža screamed. 'Please come home!'

Ignoring his sister-in-law's plea, Anton barged down an adjoining street like a wild bull, reaching his destination within minutes. To his astonishment, he found a group of about fifty people gathered around the entrance of the church, shouting obscenities at several local policemen. Some of the people he immediately recognised from before the war, regular attendees at his father-in-law's restaurant—God-fearing Serbs from all ages and walks of life who had somehow survived the vicious persecution of their race. Whatever had spurned their behaviour this morning, it was apparent they had now lost control of themselves. This was their day of reckoning with their abusers, and they weren't backing down.

Anton found Maric, a man he knew reasonably well, at the back of the crowd. 'What is going on, my friend?'

Maric shook Anton's hand and then nodded towards the church. 'You may have heard of Father Lukic? Well, he forced open the church this morning and celebrated mass with us. Stanković then arrived not long after with some of his thugs. They kicked us all out but have kept Father Lukic inside. God knows what they are doing to him. And they won't let us back in.'

There were many good policemen in Šibenik who cared for the local people, but Stanković wasn't one of them. He had a reputation for corruption and cruelty—a dangerous mix in wartime. He wasn't a member of the Ustaše; in fact, no one knew for sure if he believed in anything other than his long pockets. If you had to put a label on him, then perhaps he was nothing more than a mercenary who sold himself to the highest bidder. And at the moment, it was the Ustaše who were paying his wages.

'Have the Germans been here at all?'

Maric shook his head. 'No. Probably still suffering hangovers from last night. Besides, they rarely get involved in local spats like this. What do they care?'

Anton placed a hand on Maric's shoulder, a gesture he often did when he wanted to sweet-talk someone into doing something irrational for him.

'Listen, do you know where my father-in-law's house is?'

'Mateo? Yes, I do.'

'Can you get a message to him? Tell him what's happening and ask him to find Oberst Remer and bring him here. The only ones who can stop this insanity are the Germans.'

Maric always respected Anton due to his navy service, but he was sceptical about Remer. 'What makes you think he will come? The Germans hate us.'

'Remer hates the war even more. I am certain he will help us.'

'What are you going to do?'

'It's time that someone in this war holds Stanković to account.'

With a howling wind at his back, Anton pushed his way through the crowd until he came face-to-face with Stanković's men guarding the entrance to the church.

'Where do you think you're going?' asked a tall, skinny policeman carrying a thick, grey truncheon in his right hand. Without even waiting for a reply, he swirled the truncheon menacingly at Anton's face.

'I am going inside,' said Anton brusquely.

'The hell you are! Step back, or I will beat the shit out of you.'

All Anton needed was the flimsiest of excuses to strike first. With reflexes he didn't even realise he possessed, he grabbed the policeman by his skinny arm, twisted it behind his back as far as it would go, and then knocked the truncheon to the ground. Before the policeman's colleagues could react, Anton picked the truncheon up in his right hand and waved it angrily in their direction.

'Be warned!' he shouted, as they individually reached for their pistols. 'Think about your next move because whatever you choose will be remembered by the people of Šibenik for years to come. If you kill us now, you will initiate a blood feud that will last generations. However, should you let me in, then this appalling tyranny will be forgotten by the day's end.'

'Let him in!' a bald man in his late fifties began to chant. Emboldened by Anton's courage and embarrassed by their own impotence, the rest of the crowd joined him.

'Let him in! Let him in!'

Without Stanković there to bully them into action, the policemen stared nervously at the crowd, their scared faces lost in a situation that was fast spiralling out of control. At a time when revenge was implied even for the most minor of offences, talk of a 'blood feud' had turned their blood to ice.

Sensing his opportunity, Anton propelled himself through the main door while the policemen were calming the crowd, slamming it behind him with a fierce shove of his hand. Once inside, he managed a deep breath and allowed his eyes to adjust to his new environment. The church was dimly lit, but the streaks of darkness could not hide what was happening close to the altar. There was Father Lukic lying prostrate on the ground, his hands clutching at his sides, his face stained with blood, while Stanković and his offsider violently kicked him all over his broken body.

'Stop it, you bastards!' Anton yelled as he ran towards his friend.

Stanković was so focused on his brutal assault of the priest that, at first, he didn't comprehend the presence of another man inside the church or that the same intruder had forcibly grabbed him around the waist and thrown him to the floor in one violent motion. Even when he heard the crack of bone-on-bone and saw his colleague writhing in pain on the floor next to him, blood pouring out of his broken nose, his mind remained clouded in disbelief that someone had the gall to challenge his authority.

With both policemen temporarily incapacitated, Anton knelt over his friend and gently placed a hand underneath his body. 'What have they done to you?' he whispered, the cumulative anger of his forefathers now threatening to explode in an orgy of retribution.

'Please go, Anton,' Father Lukic croaked, tears welling in his eyes. 'They will kill you.'

'I am not leaving here without you,' said Anton. 'I will…'

A steel-capped boot connected with Anton's chest, sending him sprawling into a row of wooden pews. Stunned by his own confusion, Anton tried desperately to squat onto his feet before the next attack, but another kick drove into his chest, this one even more powerful than the first. It sent him hurtling back to the floor, causing him to scream out in agony. He had never taken a beating like this in his life, not even in the navy.

The church was momentarily quiet as Stanković stood menacingly over Anton's stricken body and considered him with a tenacious smile. The men were known to each other, but this was the first time they had come face-to-face as adversaries. And without putting too fine a point on it, Stanković held all the cards.

'Well, well,' he began. 'If it isn't the navy hero.' He poked his boot into Anton's unprotected groin. 'Why are you so concerned with this lump of Serbian filth?' He pointed to Lukic, who was coughing up pools of black-red blood all over his white cassock. 'A good Catholic boy like you?'

'He's my friend,' said Anton. He tried to stand up once again, but Stanković obliged by smashing him on the cheek with his truncheon. 'I didn't tell you to stand up, Anton. Now tell me the truth. What are you doing here?'

'I told you, he's my friend,' Anton grunted as he wiped the blood from his mouth. 'You have no right to arrest him for merely doing his job.'

'Thanks to the Independent State of Croatia, I have every right to arrest whoever I want, when I want, particularly if I suspect them to be spies and traitors.'

'He is not a traitor, and nor am I!' Anton yelled defiantly. 'We support the legitimate King of Yugoslavia and his government. Perhaps you need to explore your own loyalties, Stanković.'

The policeman thought about delivering a firm kick to Anton's groin, but instead, he just rolled back his head and laughed. 'Did you hear that, Stimic?' he asked his companion, who was still holding his broken nose. 'He thinks the Chetniks are the legitimate government.' He turned back to Anton. 'That's a spy's confession if I have ever heard one. Perhaps you can discuss the merits of your political beliefs with the Ustaše. I am sure they would find them fascinating.'

After releasing another loud guffaw to reinforce his superiority, he put a reassuring arm around Stimic's shoulder. 'Tell those morons outside to disperse the crowd right away. Should anyone resist, shoot them where they stand. Show no mercy, Stimic! We have been far too soft with these bastards.'

'Yes, sir.'

'Then, after the crowd has been dispersed, get the lorry prepared to take these two pieces of filth back to the jail.'

By now, Anton realised that Remer wasn't going to arrive soon. He contemplated one last attempt at freedom; he was sure he had enough mongrel left in him to take Stanković out with one punch. But the policeman was rat cunning, if nothing else. Not taking any chances with his wounded prey, he aimed his nine-millimetre pistol at Anton's jawline. 'Just one move, Anton, and I will splash your brains all over the altar.'

Any further thoughts of escape dissipated when Anton heard rapid gunfire and screaming from outside the church, followed by complete silence. Several minutes later, Stimic returned with a waspish smile on his face. 'All taken care of, sir,' he said triumphantly. 'Those cowardly wretches fled after we fired some shots over their heads.'

'Good work,' Stanković said. 'Now, let's get going before they decide to change their minds.'

The remaining policemen entered the church and bundled Anton and Lukic into the back of the lorry. A burly thug with a harelip cruelly drop-kicked Lukic onto the floor of the lorry as if he were a deflated football while Anton was made to kneel next to him. Despite the physical torment Lukic had endured over the past hours, his eyes still held a glimmer of resilience. Anton thought they sparkled with a mix of determination and fear, a testament to the priest's unwavering spirit. Even so, it was obvious by his coarse, shallow breathing that he was close to death.

'This man needs urgent medical attention,' Anton shouted at Stimic, who was watching over the pair like a hawk, his pistol lying in readiness on his lap. 'His death will be on your hands.'

'As if I give a shit, Chetnik.' He now pointed at his own twisted, bloodied nose. 'Don't think I have forgotten about this, you prick. I don't need another excuse to shoot you. So shut the fuck up, or you're a dead man.'

At the same moment that Anton was being threatened by Stimic, Max was sitting on a park bench opposite the convenience store, waiting for him to arrive.

Where the fuck are you, Anton?

The news of Father Lukic's arrest had started to spread throughout the Old Town like wildfire. Max had gotten wind of it from one of the fleeing churchgoers, who found temporary sanctuary inside the store. There was also talk of a stranger who courageously tried to intervene on Father Lukic's behalf but had been arrested for his trouble. Max knew that such a clumsy intervention was straight out of Anton's playbook. Such clueless hot-headedness from his friend in the face of adversity was the one thing he always worried about, the one thing that they had always argued about. Anton simply couldn't help himself once his emotions bypassed his rationality.

If Anton had been arrested, then the Max network was finished. Once the Ustaše made the formal connection between Anton and Max, everything would begin to unravel, putting at risk every agent he managed along with their families. The only option open to Max was to avoid capture and literally head for the hills that evening. But that would mean he would most likely never see Yuri or his mother again.

Make no mistake—once he made the decision to join the guerrillas, there was no turning back. With the Partisans seemingly unstoppable, he would either be killed in battle or forced to leave his beloved Yugoslavia forever. No, he wasn't ready to make such a decision just yet, not if there was a slight chance that his assumption about Anton was wrong. Somehow, he had to find out whether or not he had been arrested.

Stanković and his crew arrived at the makeshift jail that had been established by the Ustaše to incarcerate and torture political prisoners. Before the war, it had been a butcher shop, an appropriate connection given the atrocities that had occurred within its walls ever since. There was a saying about the jail that quickly developed around town—once you went in, you never came out.

Both Anton and Lukic were dragged out of the lorry and brutally shoved to the ground. Stimic then handcuffed both men, and they were forced to lie with their faces kissing the dirt. Given that Lukic could hardly breathe, let alone escape, handcuffing him was a completely pointless exercise designed only to aggravate Anton even further.

'Both of you get up,' Stimic ordered. Although his body was wracked with pain, Anton still had enough strength to hop onto his legs and force himself upwards. It took him a little while to find his balance, but he eventually managed to manoeuvre himself into a standing position before coming face-to-face with Stimic's black eyes.

Stanković now appeared from behind the lorry and started to bark out a series of orders to his men. When he completed his tirade, he gazed back at Father Lukic, who was still lying comatose in the dirt, his body having barely moved at all.

'Why is that man still on the ground, Stimic?' he challenged his deputy.

'I have asked him once already to stand up, sir, but the arrogant cock refuses to budge.'

'You know my policy,' Stanković snapped. 'I will not tolerate prisoners who disobey orders.' Without even checking to see whether Lukic was capable of moving, he pulled out his pistol, hovered momentarily over the priest's semi-paralysed body and then fired two bullets into the back of his head. Blood, bone and brains suddenly erupted into the air like an odious funnel before turning the earth around Lukic's still body into a dark crimson quagmire.

'You bastard!' Anton roared in obscene anger, his loud, desperate cries scaring away a flock of nearby seagulls. 'Damn you all to hell!'

At first, Stanković didn't seem to hear Anton, so enamoured he had become with his latest handiwork. But after he grew tired of the priest's lifeless body, he turned his pistol back towards Anton, his index finger calmly stroking the trigger guard.

'I would love nothing more than to shoot you where you stand, Chetnik spy, but even I have to obey orders. As such, I have just spoken to my Ustaše contacts, and we have agreed that you will be shot at first light tomorrow morning. In the meantime, they are sending an interrogation team from Split to meet with you as soon as possible. I am sure they will have some very pertinent questions to ask you about local Chetnik operations.'

Stimic now grabbed hold of Anton's shoulders and marched him towards the entrance of the building. Realising that he might not get another opportunity to exact his revenge, Stimic slammed Anton up against an empty prison cell and aimed several brutal punches to his unprotected kidneys before tossing him inside like a rag doll. Without having his hands to steady himself, Anton easily lost his balance and crashed headfirst onto the concrete floor. Unsurprisingly, Stimic found Anton's misfortune hilariously funny. 'Look like you've lost your sea legs, navy scum.'

As Stimic locked the cell door behind him, Anton lay motionless on the ground, pretending to be unconscious. Now was not the time to aggravate the situation with more feigned insults and threats when there was still a chance he could survive. He had to believe that Mateo had found Remer and was, at this very moment, convincing the German officer to intervene. Of course, if Mateo failed, Anton's road to perdition would sadly reach its final destination. Such a hollow end to a journey that began with so many possibilities.

Years later, Anton tried to remember those dire moments in the cell when he had all but given up hope that he would survive his ordeal. By then, old age had contrived to erase his memories, a consequence, no doubt, of the horror and trauma he experienced that day. Or maybe his forgetfulness was a symptom of a troubled mind that had slowly turned on itself. Either way, all he recalled was lying on that cold floor for what seemed like hours. Then, out of nowhere, he heard a loud banging, some persistent shouting and a lot of swearing. When he finally managed to pull himself up onto his haunches to see what was going on, Mateo's worried eyes were staring at him through the bars of the cell.

'Anton, are you okay?' Mateo looked strained and tired, and Anton immediately felt regret for dragging him into his affairs. But what choice did he have? He knew Mateo would move mountains to save him.

'Mateo! Thank God you got my message. I began to think that no one would ever find me. Is Remer with you?'

'Yes,' Mateo replied cautiously. 'He and Stanković are now having it out. It was getting very unpleasant, so I came inside to find you.'

Seconds later, Stanković and Remer brought their ferocious argument into the jail. Both men appeared overwhelmed with rage, neither of them wanting to back down. Their mutual animosity shook Anton to the core, and he suddenly realised what was at stake.

They are fighting over whether I should live or die.

'Your request is highly irregular, Herr Oberst,' Stanković kept insisting. 'This man has committed crimes against the state. He must remain in our custody until we have the opportunity to interrogate him further.'

'Any rights you have were given to you by the fatherland!' shouted Remer. 'Your Ustaše Government only exists at our pleasure.' He looked like the quintessential Wehrmacht officer in his newly starched uniform and peak cap as if he had just graduated that morning from officer school. 'And need I remind you,' he began, stroking his Knight's Cross for special effect, 'that I am in charge of all military matters in this city. My directions are to be obeyed at all times without question. These arrangements were established when we occupied Šibenik last year. So, are we clear now?'

'What about the Ustaše agents I told you about? They will soon be here. Why not wait for them?'

Stanković was riding on the fact that the mere mention of the blessed Ustaše might send this German upstart packing. But he was mistaken.

'I have no intention of waiting for them; they are irrelevant to me. This man has done nothing wrong other than to protect his friend from being murdered in cold blood. I shall formally raise my concerns about your behaviour to your superiors tomorrow morning so they can be investigated further, but I repeat, you must now release the prisoner into my custody!'

Stanković laughed insanely. 'You're a German officer, and you talk to me about murdering people in cold blood? That has to be the funniest joke of this war.'

'Release the prisoner,' Remer repeated. 'Or suffer the consequences!'

Stanković was many things, but he wasn't a fool. Even though he was prepared to push Remer further out of sheer bloody-mindedness, he knew deep down that he didn't have a leg to stand on. Remer was right— in many ways, he was the real authority in Šibenik, and as much as Stanković was scared of the Ustaše, the Germans weren't to be fucked around with either. Especially not Remer, who had a reputation for ruthlessness. Reluctantly, he nodded at Stimic, who reached for his block of keys and released Anton from the cell.

'And the handcuffs, too,' ordered Remer.

Once Anton was free, he wrung his hands violently to regain the circulation in his arms before glaring at Stanković with a look of pure hatred.

'We will meet again, Stanković,' he said. 'That much is certain.'

'I will be waiting, Chetnik,' Stanković sneered. 'Make sure you come soon.'

'Enough, both of you!' Remer snapped. He gestured to Mateo, who grabbed Anton by the arm and dragged him outside onto the street. The raging afternoon sun temporarily blinded Anton and he took a moment to breathe.

Remer soon joined them, his pale features stained with exhaustion. 'Thank you, Oberst Remer. You saved my life. I am indebted to you.'

The German scowled. 'Don't thank me; thank your father-in-law. He was the one who convinced me to intervene. He is an honourable man. You, on the other hand, double-crossed me with all your talk of peace and harmony. If I had my way, I would have let them execute you for the spy that you are.'

'I understand.'

Remer now pointed his finger at Anton as if he was lecturing a schoolboy. 'If you have any common sense at all, you will leave Šibenik tonight and not return until the war is well and truly over.'

'What about my family?'

'While I remain in command here, they will be safe. But when the Partisans come, and they will come soon, they are on their own like everyone else.'

Anton nodded his head bleakly. It was the best he could expect under the circumstances.

'And one more thing, Anton. If I see you out there in the field, dressed in Chetnik uniform and carrying a firearm, I will not hesitate to kill you. Regardless of what I did today, regardless of any temporary alliance between the Wehrmacht and the Chetniks, you remain my sworn enemy. Remember that.'

'Of course, I will.' Anton desperately wanted to shake Remer's hand to show that he, too, was a man of honour, but he knew that such a gesture would be rebuked. All he could do was nod humbly and allow Remer the opportunity to come to terms with his own demons.

'We must hurry,' Mateo said. 'You have much to do.' Leaving Remer behind, Mateo led Anton on foot back towards the Old Town. Both men realised that their remaining time together was short. But such was the vengeance of war that only one thing was permanently on their minds.

Survival.

Fifteen minutes later, somewhere near St James' Cathedral, as the two men danced between the growing shadows, a figure emerged on the footpath in front of them, blocking their immediate access to Mateo's house. Anton duly recognised the tattered coat, the suede shoes that were rarely polished and the silk scarf the man wore only on special occasions. In his shame, he realised that he hadn't thought about Max at all ever since Lukic's execution. He had become an unnecessary relevance at a time when so many other things had become more important. If only he had seen the signs earlier, it didn't have to end this way. Nevertheless, Anton's guilt now tore into his chest, and he struggled to breathe in response to Max's fierce gaze.

'Max,' he tried to explain. 'I am sorry. Things got out of hand.'

But his controller, his friend, his brother was in no mood for Anton's remorse, no matter how genuine or heartfelt. There was only one thing he wanted to say to his prodigy after everything the pair had gone through together over the preceding three years. And when he finally uttered those hurtful words, there was no coming back for either of them.

'You fool, Anton. You have succeeded in killing us all.'

Chapter Eleven

Šibenik, Croatia
September 1944

The Ustaše were waiting for Max later that evening after he made a foolish last-minute attempt to access his Šibenik safe house. After the shock of Anton's arrest, Max wanted to retrieve some documents that would have further incriminated him as a Chetnik spy. Ironically, the men from the Ustaše internal police didn't need those documents to establish his guilt. His association with Anton was the final evidence needed to confirm what they had always surmised—that Max was playing a double game.

It apparently took four men to hold Max down long enough to bind his hands with piano wire, but the outcome was never in doubt. After dragging him kicking and screaming into the bathroom, they proceeded to beat him with specially made spiked clubs that ripped into his vital organs. Although he put up a brave fight as expected, he was declared dead within minutes.

It was a particularly brutal and agonising way to die for someone who himself had never resisted the temptation to use the most extreme forms of violence when needed. Legend had it that he screamed, 'Long live Yugoslavia!' just as a club came crashing down on top of his skull. Whether true or not, his love for his king and country had been firm to the end.

Afterwards, the Ustaše dumped his body at the bus station, only metres away from the set of stairs that led to the cleaning room. Many believed that this was a message to other Chetnik sympathisers in Šibenik, including Anton, that Max's death would eventually lead to their own discovery. However, it soon became obvious that the Ustaše had been too hasty; that in their rush to kill Max, they missed an ideal opportunity to find out more about his infamous network. In the end, with the Partisans fast approaching, no one apart from the most extreme radicals really gave a shit anymore. The days of the Ustaše regime and the Independent State of Croatia were slowly coming to an end.

That evening, following a tearful dinner with his family, Anton said his final farewells to Vuka and Mateo, promising them that he would return home soon. It was a testament to his ongoing perfidy that neither of them remotely believed him.

One of Lukic's contacts from the Dinara Chetnik Division knew Anton well and agreed to drive him to a secret location west of Knin. When they arrived at the Chetnik camp, Anton was greeted by Đujić's chief of staff, who congratulated him for his bravery that afternoon. You see, word about Anton's attempt to save Father Lukic's life had spread quickly across the Division—by whom, no one really knew for certain. The news made him an instant hero at a time when the Chetniks desperately needed instant heroes.

Much of what was being said by people was grossly exaggerated, but who cared? In such bleak times, the Division could well use a highly regarded local Croat to encourage other supporters of the monarchy to join them. Anton, with his undoubted courage, rugged good looks and charisma, was the perfect candidate—perhaps the only candidate. If you had to twist the facts just a little bit for the greater good, so be it.

Several days later, Đujić met with Anton in his makeshift headquarters and offered him command of a newly formed Chetnik brigade. The brigade was made up of mostly local fighters, along with a healthy smattering of Bosnian Serb volunteers who had nowhere else to go. A Serbian Orthodox priest himself, Đujić, was convinced that anyone who risked their life for a man of the cloth was worthy of promotion. 'We are happy to have you with us, my son,' Đujić enthused, and Anton could tell that his good wishes were genuine.

Even so, Anton tried to explain to his new boss how Father Lukic had changed his views about life and religion and that he was now fighting for him and not for any false political illusions, but Đujić and his commanders weren't interested in philosophical debate for now. All they wanted from Anton was to help them defeat the Partisans and return the monarchy to its rightful place.

It was Sukevic, now the ultimate guerrilla fighter, who broke the news to Anton about Max's death. After they saluted his life with several glasses of plum brandy, they both broke into tears. 'I killed him, Stojan,' Anton had sobbed uncontrollably, but Sukevic was having none of it.

'Nonsense. He knew the risks. You were his best agent, so leave it at that.' Despite the obvious conclusions one could draw about Anton's culpability, particularly if all the facts were known, no one within the Division brought the subject up with him again. After all, the only person within his immediate circle who knew the connection between Anton and Max was Sukevic, and he was steadfastly loyal. Father Lukic's martyrdom and Anton's role in that story had superseded the truth to such an extent that no one dared to question its veracity. And while Anton would always accept responsibility for his friend's demise, the reality was that he now had other things to worry about.

By early October, the Partisans were fast approaching Split from the north and east. Every Chetnik realised that a critical juncture in the civil war had arrived. Anton didn't have a lot of time to prepare his brigade for the impending apocalypse, but after a couple of weeks of fierce training, he had whipped his men into something that resembled a competent fighting force. He was supported by Sukevic, who had been appointed Brigade Deputy Commander, as well as his old friend from the factory, Brontic, whom Anton made his aide-de-camp.

Of course, there was one person missing from this rag-tag bunch, and although Anton never expected to see her again, she suddenly appeared one stormy night like a Botticelli angel.

'Ilsa,' was all he could say at first after she threw herself into his arms.

Even in a drab, grey uniform and with her hair cut ridiculously short, she was remarkably beautiful. She had spent the previous fortnight attending to the wounded near Split, but once she heard that Anton was officially a Chetnik, she was desperate to see him again. All the recriminations about Dino, Antelic and Split could come later, but first, there was a year's worth of carnal desire to resolve. After they returned from a two-hour sojourn from a small clearing in a nearby stack of pine trees, Ilsa strode up to Brontic and kissed him on the forehead. 'I never did thank you for saving me in Split,' she cooed. At last, everything was how it was meant to be.

On 27 October, the day after Split was liberated by the Partisans, Police Senior Constable Josip Stimic was found murdered on the front patio of the house he shared with a well-known Šibenik divorcee. She had come home from the local store to cook him dinner and saw him slumped over a table. Thinking he had suffered a heart attack, she desperately pulled back his head, only to find a single bullet hole between his eyes. Neighbours interviewed by some of his former colleagues talked about seeing four or five shadowy figures emerge from a clump of bushes just after the divorcee had left the house to go to the store. There were no further leads.

Stimic's murder, combined with the inevitable arrival of the Partisans, left Stanković in a mild panic. He had hoped to ingratiate himself with his potential new masters, but over recent weeks, he finally discovered how much he was loathed by the local population and some of his peers. The Lukic killing had not helped matters, for sure. He now wished he had kissed the motherfucker instead of killing him.

Three nights later, Stanković, still in a highly agitated mood, was having a late supper with his wife, Stanica and his sixteen-year-old daughter, Petra. They had just begun to seriously talk about leaving Šibenik in the next few days when they heard a large *bang* from the front of their apartment. Petra, thinking it was her pet cat, jumped up from the table to investigate before Stanković could protest.

Seconds later, Stanica heard another thump. *Oh my God, Petra!*

Four men and a woman dressed in military fatigues and carrying pistols entered the room. The woman had her gun snuggled next to Petra's right temple. The teenage girl began to whimper in fear.

'You!' Stanković shouted at the leader of the group. 'I should have killed you when I had the chance.'

'Indeed, you should have.'

'Please don't hurt her,' Stanica cried at the leader, not knowing what calamity her husband had brought upon them. All she cared about was her Petra. 'She's only a child.'

The leader stepped forward. 'We are not here to harm you or your daughter, so please stay calm. It is your husband we have come for.'

'No!' Stanica cried some more. 'I beg you, don't kill him. Where would we go? What would we do? Please!'

The leader didn't have time for hysterical women. 'Take the mother and child to the bedroom now and keep them quiet,' he ordered two of his men. They nodded their heads and smiled gleefully at each other before tearing Petra and Stanica away from Stanković's worried gaze.

The leader then turned to Stanković. 'Do you know why we are here?'

'Of course I do. You take me for a fool.'

'Good. I want to make this quick. In the name of King Petar and the Chetniks, I condemn you to death for the murder of Father Stefan Lukic.'

'Please don't touch my wife and daughter. They had no part in my crimes.'

'It's a shame you weren't so reflective about Father Lukic, but they have nothing to fear from us.' The leader quietly raised his pistol and, without uttering another word, shot Stanković twice in the head.

'Death to all Fascist pigs,' said the woman.

'The best revenge is to be unlike him who performed the injury,' muttered the leader.

'Who said that rubbish?'

'Marcus Aurelius.'

'Another damn Fascist,' the woman cooly noted.

They were interrupted by the sound of screams coming from the bedroom. The man and woman looked at each other with grim trepidation.

'Those fucking idiots,' the woman finally said.

Leaving the other soldier behind in the kitchen, the leader and the woman raced to the main bedroom. They found their two colleagues attempting to rape both mother and daughter on the double bed.

The leader raised his pistol in the men's direction. 'Get off them now! We are not here to fight a war against innocent women and children!'

'We deserve our fun,' one of the men laughed as he continued to rip at Stanica's blouse. 'Besides, they did much worse things to our women.'

This time, it was the woman who spoke. 'Maybe so, but we are better than them. Well, at least I am.' She meticulously raised her pistol exactly where she wanted and then fired. The man attacking Stanica fell to the floor in one swift motion, blood spilling out from what was now a hollow left eye.

As Stanica screamed some more, the other man dropped a hysterical Petra onto the bed and pressed his arms against his chest in remorse. The man was acutely aware of his leader's fierce reputation for upholding discipline, and he immediately feared the worst. In one swift moment, he was violently shoved against the bedroom wall.

'Please, sir,' the soldier pathetically cried, pleading for his life. 'Don't kill me! I am sorry. He made me do it, I swear. He made me do it!'

'Let me be clear,' the leader raged at his soldier. 'We do not hurt civilians. We do not rob them. We do not rape them. Understand? Our role as soldiers is to protect them, regardless of their nationality or religion. When we get back to camp, make sure you tell everyone what the consequence will be if they ever disobey my orders again.'

'Yes, yes,' the man whimpered. 'I promise.'

Realising that the sound of gunfire would soon bring the authorities to the house, the leader knelt in front of Stanica. 'I apologise for the way my men treated you and your daughter. You are not to blame for your husband's heinous crimes. May both of you find peace elsewhere.' Then, as quickly as they appeared, what remained of the group disappeared into the lonely darkness.

On 8 November 1944, the Partisans finally overcame enemy resistance and entered Šibenik. For Anton, whose brigade had fought bravely against Partisan forces in those last few days, the occupation of Šibenik was the final act of disaster that began with Birčanin's death. How the Allies could allow this to happen was incomprehensible to him. But even if he had to fight to the last bullet, he would never submit himself to Communist rule. After everything he had done over the past three years, Anton's war had now reached its crescendo, and there was no turning back.

Meanwhile, as hundreds of people lined the streets of the Old Town, celebrating their liberation from three-and-a-half years of Fascist rule, a little girl, barely ten days shy of her fourth birthday, peered out of her bedroom window and wondered when she would see her father again. For Dubravka, her war had just begun.

Part Four

A Family Escapes

Chapter One

Šibenik, Croatia
December 1944

Many years later, as an adult woman, Dubravka would put her fear of enclosed spaces down to the countless hours she spent in her grandfather's basement as a little girl during the bombing raids on Šibenik in 1944. They say that when you become an adult, more often than not, the traumas you may have experienced as a child are compounded. What could be more traumatic for a four-year-old girl than the shrieking sound of air raid sirens, the ear-shattering thunder of bombs exploding, the relentless pounding of anti-aircraft fire, and the musty smell of fear that permeated all around her? But then, if you asked her, Dubravka would barely give the tiniest credence to that theory. If anything, Dubravka's wartime memories had made her into the successful woman she became—confident, assertive, always in charge of her own destiny. No, there had to be another reason, something that she didn't quite yet understand.

She couldn't recall exactly when the trips to the basement started or how often they occurred. But she did remember that whenever the bombs began to fall, her grandfather would magically appear out of nowhere, calmly take her hand, and then gently guide her down the rickety, narrow stairs to safety. Of course, there were other people who sought sanctuary inside the shelter with them; her grandmother and mother, for a start, her Aunty Ruža, as well as her many cousins. Sometimes, the family next door and the people who worked for her grandpa's restaurant would join them as well. This made the already intolerable, cramped conditions inside the basement even more uncomfortable and stifling for everyone involved.

But Dubravka rarely noticed those things, for her attention was solely on her grandpa and his magic box of stories.

Once they entered the basement, Grandpa selected an isolated corner where he and Dubravka would huddle together in their own private world, her tiny legs flung wildly across his lap in expectation, her thick blonde hair dangling across his cragged face. While safely trapped in his arms, Dubravka remained oblivious to the cries of fear and anguish that surrounded her. Inside her make-believe world, all that mattered was Grandpa, and he made it clear to everyone else in the basement that all that mattered to him was Dubravka.

Grandpa always seemed to have a new story to tell her. Sometimes, he would regale real-life tales of brave heroes and heroines from Yugoslav history who embarked on exciting adventures in strange, foreign lands. Other times, he would tell Dubravka stories about his own life and that of his family and the lessons he wanted her to learn from them. But the best stories always involved a shared collaboration, where grandfather and granddaughter would allow their imaginations to run wild and create fairytales about imaginary worlds where anything was possible. They would have so much fun together that Dubravka never wanted the bombing raids to end.

When they inevitably did, and it was time to leave the flickering darkness of the basement for the light of day, Grandpa would gently kiss Dubravka on the cheek and say the same words to her every time. 'You are my beautiful, brave Dubravka, and nothing will ever change that.' He would then reach across for the basement door, check that everyone was safely accounted for and brusquely usher them outside. When his other grandchildren—Dubravka's cousins—demanded some solace from their grandfather as well after such a horrifying ordeal, he would wave them away with a shake of his hand and ask his wife to see to their needs.

If this made Dubravka feel bad, she couldn't say. She was too young to understand the feelings of others or why people contrived to do the things they did. All she knew was that her grandfather made her feel special, and it was the best feeling in the world. With so many grownups seemingly mad at each other, her relationship with Grandpa always put everything right, even when her own father suddenly disappeared into the darkness.

Dubravka was always such a happy child; she rarely had time to think about the sad things that were happening around her. Nevertheless, she did miss Tata terribly, especially his handsome smile and soft little bedtime kisses. She didn't understand why he had to go away other than it had something to do with the war. 'He will be back soon,' her mother reassured her on her fourth birthday, not long after Šibenik was liberated by the Partisans. Dubravka was smart enough to know that her mother was only pretending.

As the German bombs began to fall, while they still had to hide in the basement, Dubravka knew that her father was unlikely to return any time soon. But at least she still had her mother, her Aunty Ruža and her cousins, who constantly showered her with love and affection. And, of course, there was Grandpa and his stories and the little pieces of chocolate he used to secretly give her when her mother wasn't looking. Life, for the moment, was as good as it could get for a little girl under such awful circumstances.

It all changed in the first week of December when Aunty Jelena, the mother of her dear cousins, suddenly appeared at their house. Dubravka, of course, was too young to remember when Jelena had left her family to fight for the Partisans. Everything she knew about her aunty was what she had learnt from her cousins, who naturally pined daily for their mother's return. But such was her extraordinary intuition, Dubravka soon realised that even the mere mention of Jelena's name made Grandpa sad. Perhaps that was the reason why he paid scant regard to her children? On one occasion, Dubravka had actually asked Grandpa why he did not like them. Instead of answering her question, he merely sighed, kissed her on the forehead and quietly walked away.

Therefore, it was no surprise that the household was full of tension whenever Aunty Jelena visited. Even Dubravka's normally unflappable grandmother seemed ill at ease during these occasions, although that may have had more to do with her husband's stony moods than anything else. Yet despite those gloomy interludes, Dubravka thought Aunty Jelena was very nice and very pretty, even in that olive-green uniform she always wore. Whenever she spoke to Dubravka, she would take off her hat and allow her luxurious auburn hair to unfurl around her shoulders. 'You're such a beautiful little girl,' she would often say to Dubravka before giving her a huge hug.

But it was during her latest visit when Dubravka realised that something very important was about to happen. Aunty Jelena had arrived just before dinner on that cold winter's evening, a frown etched on her pretty face. Without even lifting her eyes to greet Dubravka, who was playing with her doll next to the fireplace, Jelena slumped onto a dining chair. She was joined by Grandpa, Grandma, Aunty Ruža and Dubravka's mother, who everyone called Vuka. You could cut the tension with a knife.

It was Jelena who broke the silence. 'I have news of Anton's whereabouts,' Jelena said bleakly.

'Why do you suddenly care about my husband?' Vuka asked brusquely. 'If he saw you now, in that ridiculous uniform, he would laugh in your face.'

Jelena's blank eyes betrayed no emotion. She always knew that this would be an overly wrought conversation. 'Despite our political differences, I always liked and respected Anton very much, whether you believe it or not. I suspected that he was working for the Chetniks years ago; I could have easily exposed him at any time, but I didn't. That should explain some things to you.'

'It explains nothing,' Vuka retorted. 'The people you fight for have now put him on a death list, and for that, I can never forgive you.'

'I haven't come to seek your forgiveness, Vuka,' Jelena said cooly. 'This war has asked all of us to choose sides—my decision was determined long before you and Anton even met. My conscience is clear.'

'What is this all about, Jelena?' Mateo interrupted irritably. 'Why do you goad your sister?'

'I am not goading her,' said Jelena, raising her eyebrows in defiance. 'You asked me the other day if I had any news about Anton's whereabouts, and now I do.'

Although she was the youngest of the three sisters, Ruža was also the most conciliatory. Emotional outbursts weren't her style; she preferred to remain calm and composed when faced with difficult situations. And there had been so many awful things to contend with over the past several days. Despite the family always being very close, Ruža now understood that it was on the verge of being fractured forever, and she wanted to avoid this outcome at all costs. She quietly placed a welcoming arm around her oldest sister, someone she had always adored, and encouraged her to continue.

'Please, dear sister, we are listening. What have you found out?'

'You may have heard of a major battle being fought in Knin,' Jelena began. 'After weeks of brutal fighting, the Partisans eventually prevailed some days ago, inflicting a heavy defeat on the combined German and Chetnik forces.'

'The Chetniks fought with the Nazis?' Mateo asked incredulously. 'Don't be silly. That's just Communist propaganda.'

'Anton would never fight with the Germans,' added Vuka scornfully.

'You can believe what you like,' said Jelena ruefully. 'But a fact is a fact. What's left of the Dinara Chetnik Division have regrouped north of Bihać, on their way to Karlovac. If you want my opinion, the Chetniks will have no choice other than to seek sanctuary in either Italy or Austria.'

'And Anton is in Bihać?' Vuka asked

'For now, yes.'

'How do you know this?' asked Ruža.

'We have local spies within the Chetnik ranks. One of them knows Anton personally. He was with him during a brutal battle that developed between the Chetniks and Partisans in the village of Pađene, north of Knin. I am told he fought very bravely but was wounded during the Chetnik withdrawal. He was hit in the legs by artillery shrapnel; superficial wounds, from what I understand. Nothing too serious.'

'Wounded?' Vuka asked in mild panic. 'Then I must go to him.'

'Are you mad?' Vuka's mother scowled. 'Bihać is over two hundred kilometres away. How do you expect to make such a journey? You would be heading directly into enemy territory. I shall forbid it.'

'He's my husband,' Vuka cried. 'I have to be with him. If I don't find him now, I may never see him again.'

'You don't know that for sure, Vuka,' Ruža soothed. 'None of us know how the next few months will unfold. Anton said before he left that he would come back for you and Dubravka, so you have to believe that.'

'You heard what Jelena said,' Vuka replied dispassionately. 'The Chetniks may soon have to escape to another country. So, no, he's not coming back. I knew that from the moment he left this house.'

Everyone around the table now trained their eyes on Jelena, waiting for her to confirm Vuka's remark. 'Vuka is right,' Jelena finally conceded. 'It's time you all accept the reality of the situation. The Chetniks and the Ustaše are finished, and we will soon become the new government of Yugoslavia. The Partisans will pursue Mihailović and his cronies to the ends of the Earth, if need be, to ensure our final victory.'

'What about the King?' Mateo asked with a tear in his eye. 'Has our allegiance to him been all for nothing?'

'Respectfully, my father, the time of kings is over. The sooner you accept this, the easier the transition to a new world will be for you and our family.' Jelena then turned her alabaster face to greet Vuka's hollow eyes. 'There is one more thing I have to tell you and it gives me no pleasure. But please understand, I am doing this because you deserve to know the truth before you make your final decision.'

'What is it?' Vuka asked ominously.

'Anton has been openly seen with another woman; from our reports, they appear to be inseparable. I am so sorry, but it seems that you and Dubravka are perhaps the last things on his mind at the moment.'

Mateo, still reeling from Jelena's comment about the King, immediately thumped his fist on the table, causing Dubravka to drop her beloved doll onto the floor. She had never seen Grandpa so angry.

'How dare you bring idle gossip into this household, Jelena,' he began. 'Perhaps this is part of the Partisan strategy; to destroy the reputation of true patriots like Anton through slander and innuendo. I will not hear any more of this!' He began to stand in his indolent rage, but his wife calmly grabbed his forearm and coaxed him back down.

'Please, listen to our courageous daughter; she is risking her own life by meeting with us, so she deserves our respect.'

'I am sorry, Jelena,' Mateo finally said after a brief interlude of silence, his wife's rebuke stinging him hard. 'Despite our political differences, you have always been a good daughter, and I have treated you unfairly.'

Jelena gently touched her father's forearm. 'It's a difficult time for all of us.'

Vuka now calmly raised her hand, indicating that she wanted to talk. She had always been the irrational one, the one inflicted with insane outbursts of unbridled emotion. But now, a sense of calmness imprinted her face, much to the surprise of her family.

'Unfortunately, Jelena speaks the truth,' she finally admitted. 'We all know that Anton has a weakness for women, and this *kurva* has no doubt taken advantage of my absence. But I will not let this continue. Do you all understand? I would rather die than allow another woman in my husband's bed. I am going to Bihać to find Anton, and I am leaving tomorrow morning.'

Vuka's mother again repeated her misgivings. 'You are not thinking clearly, Vuka. How do you intend to reach Bihać in good time?'

'I will walk if I have to.'

'But that would take several days! Not to mention the inherent dangers for a lone, young woman undertaking such a journey!'

Jelena eased back into her chair. 'I think I can find someone to drive Vuka to Knin, at least. After that, she would be on her own.'

'That sounds good enough for me,' Vuka said defiantly.

There were the obvious murmurings of despair from all around the table, but it was Ruža who raised the most important question.

'What about Dubravka?'

'She is coming with me, of course!'

For once, Ruža lost control of her emotions. Like everyone else, she loved Dubravka like she was her own daughter. She wasn't going to sit back idly and allow Dubravka's safety to be compromised by Vuka's selfishness. 'You can't be serious!' she screamed. 'You would allow your pig-headedness to go so far as to endanger the life of your daughter?'

'We are a family! Do you seriously expect me to run away from Šibenik without my daughter? You think poorly of me if you do.'

'But she's just a child! Think about what you are saying, Vuka!'

'What would you have me do, then?'

'Leave her with me! I will raise her as my own daughter! Then, when you are safely inside another country, we shall send her to you.'

Vuka began to shake her head so violently that Ruža feared she was having a seizure. 'How can I be sure that the Communists would allow her to leave when the time came? No! Without my Dubravka, we are not a family. She must come with me!'

'I will not be party to this insanity,' Ruža shouted. She stared firmly at Vuka. 'The only reason you are taking her with you is because you know that without her, Anton will most likely send you back to Šibenik. Such selfishness I cannot bear!'

Poor Mateo. Having tried as much as he could to keep his family together during this abhorrent war, everything he fought so hard for was disintegrating in front of his eyes. After coaxing Ruža to calm down, he stood up, barely able to balance himself on his wobbly legs, and told everyone that he wanted to speak.

'Enough of this!' he ordered. 'I will not have my daughters squabbling with each other in front of your mother.' He gestured towards Dubravka, who had now lifted her deep, hazel eyes to meet his gaze. 'Do you think for one moment that my heart could bear losing Dubravka forever? But life is not so simple.'

'But father,' began Ruža, 'no child should be asked to take such a dangerous journey in the middle of winter. Surely you can see that?'

'Of course I can, but that decision is neither yours nor mine to make,' Mateo snapped. 'The only person who has any legitimate say over this matter is Vuka. She must make the final decision. And when she does, we must support her!'

After more debate over dinner, it was obvious that Vuka wasn't for turning. She had made up her mind, and nothing was going to change. Ruža continued to agitate and curse like a demented siren, but ultimately, even she realised that it was a waste of time. Vuka and Dubravka would leave first thing in the morning, and there was nothing that anyone could do about it.

Later that evening, while Dubravka lay snuggled in bed, Grandpa visited her for the final time. Choked with a stifling emotion he had never felt before in his life, Mateo was barely able to speak while he held his granddaughter's hand tightly. Even for one so young, Dubravka could tell that he was very upset.

'Why are you so sad, Grandpa?'

He could barely get his words out. 'Did your mother tell you what is happening tomorrow? That you are going on a long journey?'

'Yes, Grandpa! We are going to see Tata!'

'I am going to miss you, my darling.'

'I will miss you too, but we will be back soon.'

'Of course you will.'

Dubravka lifted herself onto her pillow. 'Please tell me a bedtime story, Grandpa.'

Tears now cascading down his cheek, Mateo kissed his granddaughter on her spiralling hair one last time and whispered, 'Not tonight, my child. But I will have the best story you have ever heard ready for when we see each other again.'

Without waiting for his beloved granddaughter's reply, he stumbled blindly out of the room, leaving behind forever what remained of his shattered heart.

Chapter Two

Knin, Yugoslavia
December 1944

'This is as far as I can go,' muttered the Partisan driver to Vuka as he pulled his half-torn woollen mittens over his frozen fingers. An icy wind, fuelled by a sudden sheet of virgin snow, blasted against the side windows of his truck.

Vuka momentarily stared at the obliterated scenery that now confronted her, and for the first time that morning, she felt scared.

'Where are we?' she asked politely. Although she hated the thought of being inside the same vehicle with a Communist, this man had shown her rare compassion during the ride.

'Welcome to Knin,' he said softly. 'Well, what used to be Knin.'

Vuka had visited Knin several times in her life, but this hellhole was completely unrecognisable to her. Everywhere Vuka turned, she could see the visible scars of destruction and devastation caused by the ferocious battle that had occurred during the preceding weeks. The once bustling town centre was nothing more than an avenue of rubble and debris, the scattered remnants of a different time.

'My God, what have we done to this country?' Vuka whispered, as she pulled her coat tightly around her small body.

'In years to come, I am sure someone will make sense of it all,' the man replied. 'But not today.' He turned to Dubravka, who was sitting inside the small compartment behind the driver's seat and smiled. 'However, she is something still worth fighting for.'

Vuka reached into her coat pocket and pulled out some coins. 'I can't thank you enough, so please take this as a demonstration of my gratitude.'

The Partisan lifted his arms in protest. 'No, I cannot take your money. Keep it for your daughter.'

'Thank you,' Vuka replied gratefully. She grabbed her bag, which had been sitting on top of the gearbox, and then casually nodded at Dubravka. 'Get your things, my child, it's time to go.'

Before Dubravka could register Vuka's command, the driver placed a gentle hand on her mother's arm. 'Listen. The area around Knin is not safe, especially for a woman with a young daughter. If you are heading north, stay on the main road; don't go wandering down any side streets. Nothing good will come of it, trust me. There are refugees everywhere wanting to leave Knin, so if you can join a large group, there is safety in numbers. For the moment, the Partisans are happy for people to leave the area, but that could change at any time. The quicker you go, the better.'

'I will take your advice, thank you.'

'If I were you, I would try to reach a small Red Cross station that's been established just north of Velika Popina. It is about forty-five kilometres away, but if you start walking now, you should get there by dinner time.' He paused before continuing, 'Unless the snow gets heavier, of course. Then I'm afraid you will need to find some shelter along the way.'

'The weather doesn't look promising,' Vuka admitted. 'But as an aside, what should I do when I reach the Red Cross?'

'I am told that they are helping people locate friends or relatives in other parts of the country. For how much longer, I don't know, but perhaps they can find you some transport to Bihać. But I must warn you—the area is still full of Ustaše and Germans who don't always appreciate civilians. And without giving too much away, the Partisans will soon be making our presence known in the area. So please be careful.'

Vuka was shocked that the man knew her ultimate destination. *Does Jelena have to blab everything?*

The man could sense Vuka's trepidation. 'Don't worry, Jelena is a good friend of mine; your secret is safe with me. But please, whatever you do, do not tell anyone that you are trying to find your Chetnik husband unless you are certain they are friendly. Mention this by accident to the Ustaše or one of their supporters, and I don't have to explain what will happen to you both.'

The driver then jumped out of the lorry and dashed across to open the passenger door for both Vuka and Dubravka. As the three of them stood shivering in the muddy snow, the driver nodded towards some Partisan soldiers gathered in front of them.

'Stay here while I have a quick word with my colleagues.' As he hurried away, Vuka turned towards Dubravka, who was wiping away some mischievous snowflakes from her pale face. Incredibly, she had not complained once during the trip. Any other child would have been complaining hours ago. Instead, she seemed to be loving every minute of this new adventure.

'Are you cold, Dubravka?' Vuka asked as she gently flicked away the ice from her daughter's woollen coat. For the first time since she made her decision to find Anton, she suddenly felt a nagging pang of guilt for dragging her four-year-old daughter into this harsh, pitiless environment. Was she doing the right thing?

'No, Mama,' Dubravka replied with an extra delicious smile that made her mother relax just a little. She began to twist her tiny backpack around in circles until it settled nicely on her shoulders before adding, 'Will Tata meet us soon?'

'Not yet, Dubravka. We must first walk some distance to another town and find someone who can take us to him. You must be extra brave today because it won't be much fun.'

Dubravka merely nodded her understanding as the driver now returned carrying a bar of army chocolate, probably stolen from someone's pack. Without asking Vuka's permission, he undid the top pocket of Dubravka's coat and placed the chocolate bar safely inside.

'For later, when you are hungry.' He then pointed out one of his colleagues to Vuka. 'Do you see that tall soldier over there with the moustache? His name is Miroslav, and he will guide you to some other refugees further along this road who are also walking to the Red Cross station this morning. You should be safe with them. Good luck.'

Vuka wasn't a philosophical person by any means; she had spent much of her life living a pampered existence where understanding other people's emotions and motivations didn't really matter to her. But within the depths of her despair, she now saw firsthand how kindness in war can appear from the most unlikely sources, and she would forever be grateful for this stranger's thoughtful intervention.

However, if the driver was compassionate and kind, Miroslav was altogether a different breed. Dark and surly, he conveniently muttered several obscenities just so everyone could hear how displeased he was with his new task before ordering Vuka and Dubravka to follow him down a series of broken detours. As far as he was concerned, he had better things to do than play nursemaid to some middle-class wench and her little brat. Even Dubravka's heavenly smile couldn't melt his heart.

Of course, this didn't matter too much to Dubravka, for she was too busy scrutinising her new surroundings. Apart from the daily bombings in Šibenik, she had seen very little of the war and its impacts, nor did she fully understand them. Her family had rightly sheltered her from the violence and depravity as much as possible. But as she held her mother's hand tightly, even her innocent curiosity couldn't mask the reality of the new world she had entered.

In particular, there was something about the huge moon-like craters on either side of the road they were walking on that filled her with dread. She wasn't to know that they were manmade — caused by weeks of incessant artillery fire. Rather, they appeared to her as some violent reincarnation of one of her grandfather's fairytales. She was certain that if she fell inside one of them, she would tumble into an endless darkness and never see her mother again.

As they walked through piles of decaying rubble, Dubravka tried to make sense of what she was seeing. The seemingly endless rows of burnt and desecrated buildings stood as haunting reminders of the war's destructive power. The hordes of miserable people who whirled their arms aimlessly in tandem also transfixed her, searching for their long-lost valuables inside the smouldering rubble. The mere sight of these wretched victims made Dubravka feel dreadfully homesick, and she wondered for the first time that morning whether she would ever see her grandfather and grandmother again.

But there was something else, a strange phenomenon that made her head spin in a multitude of directions. At first, she thought it was the constant smell of acrid smoke that became caught inside the cocoon of a swirling winter breeze. But no, it wasn't that at all. Rather, her senses had become attuned to what she could hear, or actually, what she couldn't hear.

The birds!

 Of course! There were no birds anywhere to be found. To avoid the war, they had all seemingly flown away to another world, possibly forever.

'When will we see the birds again?' she suddenly asked.

Vuka was so caught up in her own nightmare that she failed to understand why this question was now so important to her daughter. 'Hush now, Dubravka,' she replied thoughtlessly as they trudged slowly through another snowfall.

After a further ten minutes of mindless drudgery, Miroslav suddenly called a halt to proceedings and pointed to a group of people hovering around a tiny fire next to a desolate street corner. 'Over there,' he muttered before turning his back on Vuka and Dubravka. Without saying another word, he kicked off the black mud attached to his boots and headed back into town.

Vuka stood motionless as the rag-tag collection of civilians suddenly lifted their hollow, lifeless eyes towards her and Dubravka. Without having time to understand why, a feeling of abject terror encompassed her. For a moment, she thought about lifting Dubravka into her arms, then running down an adjoining street as fast as her legs could carry her, far away from these obnoxious-looking peasants. But she then remembered what the driver had told her: 'Don't go wandering down any side streets.' What then, was she to do?

Her fears, however, melted away when a grey-haired man, perhaps in his early sixties, walked across the potholed road to greet her.

'*Dobro jutro*,' he said softly, smiling at Dubravka's funny little fur hat. 'My name is Miran Radic. Are you coming with us to the Red Cross station?'

'If you will have us,' Vuka replied cautiously. Despite his sallow features and overly manufactured limp, he looked harmless enough.

'You are very welcome, of course. But we leave right on schedule, at eight thirty.' He glanced at his watch before adding, 'In ten minutes.'

Vuka grasped Dubravka's hand tightly. 'How long will the journey take?'

'Normally, on a good day, without a break, it should take around eight hours to walk the distance. But there are twenty-five of us, some of whom are in poor health and cannot walk very quickly. They will need our support along the way. On top of that, my donkey had to be put down yesterday, so we have no cart to carry people's belongings. Everything being equal, with a thirty-minute rest period, we should arrive at our destination just after seven thirty.'

Eleven hours! In this brutal weather! Vuka felt her heart slide into her stomach. She had insisted that Dubravka consume an extra-large breakfast before they left Šibenik that morning, but another five hours without a proper meal? How would she cope? She was only a child, after all.

'What did you mean when you said, 'everything being equal'?'

Miran looked at her curiously. 'We are in the middle of a war, my dear woman. I cannot guarantee that this journey will not be without the usual dangers associated with this madness.' He could sense Vuka's growing despair, so he gently took her arm. 'Look, come join us at the fire and get something warm to drink for your daughter. The sooner we get going, the safer we will be.'

Miran escorted Vuka and Dubravka back to the group, where a diminutive elderly lady, most likely Miran's wife, produced two small cups of steaming hot water from a makeshift stove. Using the tips of her fingers, she then sprinkled a small amount of chocolate residue in each cup. 'Here, drink this, little princess,' she offered Dubravka with a toothless smile.

The child hadn't tasted anything so bland and bitter in her very short life, but nevertheless, she enjoyed the drink's comforting warmth as it surged through her upper body.

As Vuka greedily gulped her substitute hot chocolate down, she quietly inspected the faces around her. Most of them were completely indifferent to the presence of these newcomers, although two of the younger women glared covetously at the quality of Vuka's woollen coat. There was something about the women that was vaguely familiar to her, as if she had seen them recently on the streets of Šibenik. For the moment, though, she would say nothing about her predicament.

At eight thirty, Miran gathered everyone in a semi-circle around him. 'My friends,' he began softly. 'It's now time for us to leave. Please, just take one bag with you; given that I have no cart, we do not have the means to cater for stragglers carrying their excessive loads. You are all making this journey today so you can find your loved ones, but I must insist you follow my instructions at all times.'

He allowed the usual murmuring and grumbling to recede before adding, 'Once we leave the outer limits of Knin, please have your wits about you. The terrain we are walking across can, at times, be dangerous and unforgiving, but we cannot stop regularly to help you. If you are struggling to keep up with the main group, please let me or my wife, Nina, know, and we will assist you the best we can. It is a difficult journey in these conditions, but with the Lord's help and some good luck, we can make it. Any questions?'

Being none, Vuka slid her eyes towards the dark, threatening sky. 'God forgive me,' she moaned softly to herself as her new colleagues solemnly picked up their bags and followed Miran onto the main road.

'Come, Mama,' little Dubravka enthused as she pulled at Vuka's skirt. 'Tata is waiting for us!'

Yes, Vuka thought, *but how happy will he be to see us?* Given what now lay ahead for her and Dubravka, it was something she dared not think too much about.

Chapter Three

Between Knin and Velika Popina
December 1944

After walking for several hours, Dubravka grew bored. Everything seemed like a new adventure when they left Grandpa's house that morning, but now her reality had turned into a mindless prism of pine forests, dirty brown sleet and razor-sharp stones that tore at her feet. To make things worse, there was no one her age to talk to along the way to alleviate the boredom, while her mother, who had detached herself from Dubravka's hand and was walking in front of her, seemed lost inside her own foul mood.

What's more, she was tired—more tired than any little girl should ever expect to be. Apart from her stinging feet, her chest wanted to explode, and an underlying chill tugged at her hair. She still desperately wanted to see Tata, but how she now longed for her soft, warm bed, her toys and Grandpa's reassuring smile.

'Hello,' a voice suddenly emerged from the howling wind. Dubravka turned to face a young boy with the gentlest brown eyes she had ever seen. He was slightly older than her, perhaps seven or eight, and he proudly wore his peak cap over his finely cut blonde hair. She hadn't noticed him before now; perhaps his sullen face had become invisible amongst the sea of desperate adult bodies. But despite herself, his presence immediately lifted her spirits.

'Hello, I'm Dubravka,' she finally replied. 'What's your name?'

'Bogdan,' he said shyly. He tried to smile, but something made his lips stop halfway through the motion. Perhaps it was the unforgiving cold.

'That's a funny name,' Dubravka laughed. She tried to make eye contact with him, but his head dropped in embarrassment.

'I think it's a silly name, too,' he finally said. 'But my mother says that it means I have been sent by God.'

'To do what?'

'I am not sure,' he muttered before kicking at a loose rock on the dirt road. 'Mama says that God will tell me when he is ready.'

'I am sure he will, too,' Dubravka giggled, stamping her right foot on the ground. The pain inside her instep was now excruciating, but even at her tender age, she knew there wasn't much she could do about it.

'Are you okay?' Bogdan asked softly.

'I think so,' Dubravka lied with a forced smile. 'My feet hurt a little.'

'You should tell your mother.'

'Maybe later.'

A stream of unforgiving sunlight crept through the thick clouds and bounced off Dubravka's tiny face. For a moment at least, she totally forgot about the pain in her feet.

'Where are you and your mother going?' Bogdan asked with a tinge of intrigue in his voice.

'We are going to find Tata. That's all Mama will tell me.'

'Did he fight in Knin?'

'I don't know,' Dubravka sighed. 'But I think the Partisans tried to kill him.'

'You know about the Partisans?'

'Yes. Grandpa and Mama talked about them all the time back in Šibenik. They must be very bad people if they want to kill Tata.'

'I hope you find him soon,' Bogdan said gloomily. A veil of sadness suddenly covered his blotchy cheeks. Dubravka could sense that something wasn't right. There was a hole in Bogdan's heart that could never be mended.

'Where's your father?' she finally asked, lifting her head towards Bogdan's mother.

'He died last year,' Bogdan finally replied. 'He was killed by the Ustaše.'

Dubravka was shocked. 'Why would they do such a thing?'

Bogdan blinked wildly, choking back a flood of tears. 'Because they could, that's why.' He paused to compose himself. 'Can we talk about something else?'

Dubravka was angry at herself for making her new friend sad. He seemed so kind and sweet, and she desperately wanted to make it up to him. Without a second thought, she reached into her coat pocket and produced the bar of chocolate that the driver had given her earlier that morning. Ignoring her own hunger pains, Dubravka pointed the bar at Bogdan's midriff and encouraged him to take it.

'But that's your chocolate bar,' he said blankly. 'Why do you want to give it to me?'

'Because I want you to have it,' Dubravka said softly, her playful eyes lifting towards the sky in mild annoyance at the question.

'I am very hungry,' Bogdan finally admitted.

'Then take my bar and eat it. You will feel better for it, I'm sure.'

This time, Bogdan did what he was told and snatched the bar from Dubravka's tiny hands. He greedily unwrapped it with his half-frozen fingers and, without even offering his new friend a solitary piece, gulped the entire thing down in a matter of seconds.

'Good?' Dubravka asked with a smile.

'Good,' Bogdan replied, licking his lips for any last remnants of chocolate.

'I'm glad.'

Little more was said between them for the next kilometre, but when Dubravka once more bent over in pain, Bogdan quickly took her hand and ensured she didn't fall down. Sometime after this, the young boy thought that it was his profound duty to hold little Dubravka's hand even more tightly. Several people in the group forgot about their own travails for a moment and smiled at the joyous sight of the tall, gangly young boy walking in tandem with the beautiful young girl. Something about their innocence gave them a semblance of inspiration and hope that maybe they would survive the rest of their journey.

Unfortunately, not everyone was thrilled. Almost simultaneously, Vuka and Bogdan's mother stared at their children and then at each other. There was a mutual spectrum of fear that connected both mothers, as if their individual predicaments could not cater to their children making new friends. Vuka, in particular, was not happy that some peasant boy was holding her daughter's hand in front of everyone. Who did he think he was?

She was about to say something when she felt a tug on her coat. She turned to find Nina smiling at her. 'Leave them alone, my dear,' she said soothingly. 'God knows when they will have the chance to be children again.'

Normally, Vuka would have given Nina a piece of her mind for interfering, but there was something in the elderly woman's grey eyes that betrayed a conquering wisdom. Perhaps she was right. Perhaps Vuka was being a little too harsh, considering what she had already put her daughter through that day. Nodding her tacit understanding, she shuffled quickly until she was astride Bogdan's mother.

'Let them linger in their world for a little longer,' Vuka suggested and was pleased that her new travelling companion quietly agreed with her.

The unforgiving cold was now relentless, and Vuka didn't know how much longer she would last without taking a break. It seemed like they had been walking all day. She had no idea how some of the older refugees had lasted this long, given the harsh conditions.

'How much longer before we rest?' she asked Nina in between shivers.

'Soon, my dear. Soon.'

Just after twelve thirty, the group approached an acute bend in the road, and Miran, who somehow kept a steady pace leading from the front all morning, lifted his hand and loudly called a halt.

'Over there!' he cried out, pointing to the grass clearing adjacent to the bend. 'That is our rest point. We shall stop for thirty minutes.'

As some people shuffled off into the foliage to urinate, Vuka released Dubravka's hand from Bogdan's clutches and guided her to a fallen log on the side of the road. 'Take off your shoes and show me your feet,' she demanded.

'I don't want to, Mama,' Dubravka replied. For the first time that day, she felt like crying for no other reason than that she did not want to see how bad her feet were.

'Do what you are told,' Vuka demanded once more.

Dubravka knew not to disobey Mama a second time, so she hurriedly bent down and undid her shoelaces. Staring at Vuka with fearful eyes, she somehow managed to shake off her left shoe without screaming in pain. Vuka reeled back in horror when she saw her little daughter's white sock almost completely covered in blood.

'Sweet Jesus, help us!' she wailed as her guilt suddenly intertwined with the horrendous reality of her decision. 'My poor daughter,' she said, gathering Dubravka in her arms before bursting into tears. It wasn't Grandpa, to be sure, but it was the best and most rewarding hug Dubravka had received in a long time.

By now, Nina had heard Vuka's cries and raced over to the log with a look of parental concern enshrined on her face. 'What is the matter?' she asked Vuka as she bent down on her haunches to inspect Dubravka's feet.

'Look, look,' Vuka repeated loudly as she pointed to the blood-soaked sock.

'I don't think it's anything too serious,' Nina said reassuringly. 'Let me see what I can do.' After gently peeling away Dubravka's sock, Nina carefully lifted Dubravka's tiny leg onto her lap. The problem was easily identified. A huge blister caused by excessive walking had exploded on the base of Dubravka's heel. It looked far worse than what it was. Even so, given the long journey ahead, the little one could ill afford to get an infection.

Nina reached into the small bag that hung over her left shoulder and quietly produced a ball of cotton wool and a tiny little glass bottle. She sprinkled some of the liquid contents of the bottle onto the cotton wool and then stroked Dubravka's shoulder. 'This may sting a little, but it will help make the soreness go away. Okay?'

'Okay,' Dubravka said, trying to smile. For some reason, she trusted the old woman with her teacup eyes and gold front teeth and was determined not to cry in front of her.

'What is it?' asked Vuka as Nina began to dab the ointment onto Dubravka's broken skin.

'A special mixture of lemon and calendula residue. It will help negate any infection and tighten the skin around her wound. I will put a little bandage around her heel so her shoes do not rub up against the exposed wound. It's not a perfect solution, but the best I can do under the circumstances.'

'Thank you, you're very kind.'

'That's what I am here for.'

As Nina continued to work on Dubravka's feet, the remaining refugees lingered pathetically around a hastily made fire. Some lay sprawled on the ground, overcome by the physical and mental rigours of the march, while the younger ones among the group tried to refresh themselves with whatever was left of the water. How many of them were going to reach the Red Cross by nightfall was anyone's guess.

Miran began to ponder this question himself as he cast a worrying eye over this desolate bunch of misfits. Ever since the battle for Knin began in early November, he had considered it his duty to lead the town's refugees to relative safety. He had once been deputy mayor of Knin and loved his constituents like they were his own family. But after several journeys over the past week, he could feel his body start to crumble, and his desire begin to wane. He and Nina were getting far too old for this work, even if they had denied the inevitable for so long. And while there was a short lull in hostilities for the moment as all sides took stock of their resources and casualties, Miran knew it would all begin again very soon.

Chapter Four

Between Knin and Velika Popina
December 1944

Maybe Miran had become too engrossed with his own musings to hear the metallic sound of army vehicles bellowing in the distance. By the time the first jeep came screeching around the bend in the road, Miran knew it was too late to warn anyone. He had dealt with these people before, just three days ago, to be precise, but that was at the Red Cross station itself, not out here, in the lonely countryside without any witnesses.

The jeep came to a grinding halt in the middle of the road, adjacent to the now frightened group of refugees. A tall, muscular man wearing the unmistakable black uniform of the Ustaše jumped out from the passenger side of the jeep, followed by a smiling half-dwarf proudly displaying his German SS uniform. The half-dwarf, eager to assert his authority over these *Untermensch,* loudly tapped the stock of his Schmeisser submachine gun.

'Ah, Radic,' the Ustaše officer cruelly laughed. 'Another batch, I see. Sometimes, I wonder whether you are the local reincarnation of Moses himself, leading his flock to the land of milk and honey. Are you sure that you are not Jewish?' The half-dwarf laughed hysterically at the joke, even though he probably didn't know who Moses was from his local butcher.

'Quite sure, Captain Juric,' Miran muttered. His knees wanted to shake in cadence with his growing fear, but he had decided a fortnight ago that he would never allow this beast to intimidate him ever again.

'And what do we have here today?' Juric stopped grinning for once and closely inspected the motley collection of desperate people in front of him. 'More Chetnik filth to be exterminated?'

'Just ordinary civilians trying to reach the Red Cross before nightfall.'

Juric scratched at a mole that sat proudly on his protruding chin and smiled at the half-dwarf. 'What do you think, Leutnant Gross? Do they look like ordinary civilians to you?'

Gross released another one of his rat-like laughs. 'Not sure, Captain, but those two whores over there look decidedly suspicious.' He briefly pointed at the two young women who had stared at Vuka back in Knin and then, in an effort to match his surname, grossly fondled the bulge in his trousers. 'I think we need to take them in for some questioning, don't you?'

'For God's sake, leave them alone,' Miran growled at Juric. 'Show some restraint for once.'

Juric's insane smiling ended abruptly. His right hand twitched against his pistol holster before flicking his eyes in disgust at everyone around him. Nothing would give him greater pleasure than shooting this old fool where he stood, but he knew that Miran still had many supporters inside the Catholic Church who would recoil in horror at his murder. It would only make things difficult for Juric, something he wanted to avoid, given that the Ustaše regime was on the verge of collapse. However, every dog has his day, and Radic's day would surely come before this damned war was over.

'You know the rules, Radic,' he finally barked. 'Line your people up alongside the road in groups of five and tell them to have their papers ready for our inspection. And pity you and your wife if I find that you are harbouring any Jews or Chetnik spies.'

As Miran addressed the crowd, Vuka bent her head close to Nina's as she finished bandaging Dubravka's other foot. 'We have to leave,' she whispered. She could feel herself becoming overwhelmed with panic, but for her daughter's sake, she had to somehow remain calm. 'My husband is a Chetnik brigade commander.'

Nina gave her a tentative frown. 'You might have mentioned that to us back in Knin, and perhaps we could have helped you.' She fell silent for a moment as she carefully replaced the soiled sock over Dubravka's foot. 'Anyway, it's too late for you to do anything now. If you try and leave, they will shoot you. That Ustaše fellow is quite the animal, trust me. He wouldn't even think twice about executing your daughter in cold blood.'

'Then what should I do? I am told that both the Ustaše and the Partisans have my husband's name on a death list. Once they see my papers …'

Nina didn't allow Vuka to finish your sentence. 'You have no choice but to show them your papers and hope for the best. If they challenge you about your husband, deny everything, even if they put a gun to your head. That's your only chance. Even Juric's barbarity has its limits.'

While they continued to talk, a further detachment of SS soldiers arrived in a truck. After Gross shouted out some orders, they disembarked and started to separate the refugees, designating two soldiers to each block. Vuka and Dubravka soon found themselves together with the two young women and a middle-aged carpenter called Drusic.

'Do not say anything about your Tata to these bad soldiers, or else they will stop us from ever seeing him again,' Vuka whispered to Dubravka. 'Do you understand?'

'Yes, I understand, Mama.'

'Be brave now, little one, and leave the talking to me.'

Although she was scared and wanted to cry, Dubravka decided that she would save her tears for later. For the moment, all she could think about was what was happening to Bogdan and his mother. There was screaming and yelling and crying everywhere she turned, and Dubravka knew that somehow, Bogdan was trapped inside that wall of terror.

The soldiers on Vuka's block were soon shouting the usual profanities at Drusic. Still, he continued to hold his nerve in response to their abuse, calmly waving a solitary piece of paper at their faces until they both lost patience and ushered him through to the other side of the road. The soldiers muttered to each other in hushed tones and then called the first of the two young women to approach them.

'Wait!' The soldiers and the woman, whose name was Maria, turned to face a grinning Leutnant Gross, who had casually made his way over to their position. His covetous stare at Maria's lithe body and silky blonde hair was delivered with more than an obvious hint of sexual intent. To put it bluntly, he wasn't going to let his two prized assets escape his clutches if he could help it.

'I will conduct the rest of these interviews,' he barked at the two soldiers. 'Stand back and await my orders!'

'Jawohl!' The two soldiers snapped to attention, as if following the SS code still meant something out there in the wastelands. Then, like a couple of hapless jackals, they gratefully shuffled behind the two women, occasionally glancing at Vuka and Dubravka.

Gross was salivating. 'Your papers, fräulein! Now!'

By this stage, Maria was petrified, and she could hardly move her hand inside her coat pocket to collect her documents. The more she tried to manoeuvre her half-frozen fingers, the more she fumbled around like a lost child.

'What is wrong with you? Should I strip search you myself?' Gross grinned wildly as if his lust for her had turned him completely insane.

'Here!' Maria screamed as she finally whisked out her papers and flung them into Gross' pitiful little hands. 'Please don't hurt me!'

Whether Gross could actually read Croatian or not was of no importance. He took several seconds to casually stare at the papers, more for the benefit of his soldiers than anything else and then became fixated on Maria's left index finger.

'What is that?' He pointed at a simple bronze ring.

'It's my wedding ring,' Maria gasped.

'Yes, I can see that, you stupid woman. What I want to know is, who are you married to?'

Maria had obviously rehearsed her response many times before that day.

Yet, when the time finally came, she could not stop herself from stuttering and coughing, making her performance seem totally unbelievable.

'My husband died in a bombing raid in Šibenik,' she implored. 'He was a carpenter.'

'A carpenter? Is that what they call traitors these days?'

'He is not a traitor!'

'Is? I thought you said your husband died. Make your mind up, wench. Is he or isn't he alive?'

'I meant to say was. Oh, my God.' She now predictably broke down into an avalanche of tears, seconds away from soiling herself. What would become of her now?

Gross knew he had enough evidence already to condemn her to his bed that night, but he wanted to play the game just a little longer.

'So, if your carpenter husband died in a bombing raid, as you claim, why are you still wearing a ring? A beautiful single woman like you.'

'Please, it's the truth! I am going to Zagreb to inform his family about his death! You must believe me!'

'Must I?' Gross laughed wickedly. 'I will tell you what I think. I think you are the wife of a Chetnik traitor on her way to find him in Bihać. Am I correct?'

'No! Please!'

'Hauptman!' Gross now singled out the tallest of the two soldiers. Hauptman fumbled with a cigarette he had just lit and then stamped it out on the ground. Embarrassed, he rushed to his officer's side.

'Sir!'

'Take this treacherous whore and her friend to one of the trucks and secure them both. I shall interrogate them further when we get back to the camp. Do it!'

'Jawohl mein leutnant!' *Yes, indeed, my lieutenant.*

Hauptmann grabbed Maria by the arm and wrenched it viciously behind her back until she began to scream in agony. Before she could think of a way to fight back, Hauptman cruelly kicked at her feet, sending her sprawling to the ground.

'Get up and start walking to the truck, or I will shoot you.' Maria was sobbing hysterically, and Vuka wondered whether she was happy for the Germans to kill her right there, in front of everyone, rather than be subjected to further abuse. But just when Hauptman stood menacingly over her bruised body, ready to strike again, his eyes alit with cold-fuelled anger, Maria's friend, Ivana, heroically leapt in front of him and somehow managed to help the young woman to her feet.

'We are not resisting, so leave her alone,' Ivana cried defiantly at Hauptman and Gross. 'May God have mercy on your souls.'

Without saying another word, the two women, their arms wrapped around each other for protection, hustled their way towards the German convoy while Hauptman followed closely behind, never taking his eyes off them.

'See what can be achieved with a little discipline?' Gross laughed at the other soldier. He then turned his head towards Vuka and Dubravka. 'Now, what do we have here?'

In the midst of war, innocence and cruelty often dance together to the same tune. Perhaps this explained why Gross suddenly felt an indescribable sensation swell inside his stomach as his cold eyes connected with Dubravka's. He wanted to turn away from her gaze immediately— she seemed so out of place in such a desolate, unforgiving landscape— but he became temporarily transfixed by the sadness in her smile. It was almost as if, through telepathy, she had discovered every single atrocity he had committed in this ghastly country.

Who is this little girl? What does she want from me?

'Gross! Did you hear me, damn you?' Gross' destiny with his conscience was suddenly interrupted by the arrival of another German officer. And this one not only outranked him but despised him with a passion.

'Oberst Remer.' Gross snapped to attention. He released a vile-sounding 'Heil Hitler' because it was still the required ritual of all SS officers and because he also knew how much it would piss Remer off. 'What are you doing out here?'

'I could ask you the same question, Gross.'

'Picking through the entrails of the usual spies and whores, Herr Oberst.'

'Yes, your contribution to the war effort is greatly appreciated,' Remer retorted sarcastically. 'But this will soon become Partisan territory, so you and your men must leave here now.'

'On what authority?' Gross snorted. He was an SS officer, and even though Remer outranked him, he wasn't going to fall for his bullshit, either.

Remer unashamedly took one step closer to Gross' foul-smelling breath and stared into his truculent face. 'Listen, I don't have time for all this 'your dick is bigger than mine' crap. After what happened in Knin, where I lost half of my regiment, I am also not in the most agreeable of moods. The latest intelligence reports suggest that the Partisans are planning an attack on our position in the next six hours, and we have been ordered to establish a standing patrol alongside this road. So, if you even slightly attempt to get in my way, I will shoot you myself. Do you understand?'

'You dare threaten an SS officer?' Gross screamed. 'That's punishable by death!'

'So is rape and torture of innocent civilians, you sick pile of shit. I invite you to tempt me; nothing would give me greater pleasure.'

Without waiting for a reply, Remer turned his back on Gross, straightened his collar, and politely nodded at Vuka. They had spoken together several times at Mateo's restaurant; Vuka's command of German often impressed the homesick Swabian officer. Like her father, she despised all Germans but saw the relative decency inside Remer's heart. And now, by a stroke of incredible fortune, the same German officer who had saved her husband's life not so long ago was now smiling kindly at her.

'I trust no one has harmed you and your daughter in any way, Vuka?' he asked courteously.

'No, they haven't, Oberst Remer,' she replied respectfully. 'But that officer arrested two of my friends for no reason at all.'

'They are Chetnik whores on the way to find their husbands,' implored Gross angrily. 'I wish to interrogate them further.'

'For what purpose, Gross?' Remer interrupted. 'We all know about your predilections for young women. And I doubt whether your mindless interrogations have ever resulted in any real or imaginary military outcome.'

'The Chetniks were our enemy the last time I checked.'

'Well, you may need to check again. Not only did they fight bravely at Knin, but the high command, in their wisdom, have given safe passage for all Chetnik units to reach Bihać. We have also provided transport for their seriously wounded soldiers to receive treatment in Zagreb.'

'Yes,' spat Gross. 'I think it is disgraceful that we are helping these murderers and thieves. To also give them food and ammunition. My God, what are we thinking?'

'Perhaps you should take this matter up with the Führer yourself.'

After Gross finally lumbered away, cursing as he always did under his breath, Remer took Vuka by the hand and gestured towards his jeep. 'I will take you and your daughter to meet some people I know. They can help arrange the necessary transport to move you both to the Chetnik camp later tonight.'

'Thank you, Oberst Remer,' Vuka said. 'I don't know how to ever repay you.' She paused momentarily, testing to see whether her bravado could last the distance. 'But I do have one favour to ask. It involves my two friends, the women we just spoke about. They are also trying to find their husbands.'

Remer shook his head impatiently. 'Yes, yes, they can come with us, if that's what you are asking. Please, we need to leave now.'

Vuka quickly gathered her things before giving Dubravka a sturdy hug. 'God has smiled on us today, little one. Hopefully, we will see your father soon.' Dubravka nodded quietly and was just about to lift her backpack over her shoulders when suddenly a loud guttural scream streaked above the scything wind, followed by a bout of uncontrolled wailing.

'What the fuck is going on now?' Remer muttered under his breath.

He turned to find Vuka's little daughter pointing at a clump of trees. 'It's Bogdan!' she cried. 'They are hurting Bogdan!' Sure enough, two soldiers were pinning Bogdan's shrieking mother to the ground while another burly animal was dragging the young boy towards an open patch of snow-covered ground.

Vuka sighed and took Dubravka by the hand. 'This is not our concern, Dubravka.'

'But he's my friend.' Without any warning, Dubravka ripped her hand away from Vuka's grasp and began to rush towards Bogdan and his mother.

If I can get there before the other men do, I can save them both!

'Dubravka!' Vuka screamed. 'What are you doing? Come back here right now!'

Goodness knows what a fanatical SS soldier might have done to a young girl who brazenly sought to interfere with an arrest. It was fortunate for Dubravka that Nina saw what was happening and somehow managed to pluck her off the ground like an eagle does with its prey before she could make further headway. As she kicked her legs wildly and demanded that Nina release her, Vuka came bearing down on top of her and ordered her to be quiet.

Dubravka's frantic tears soon grew softer as she realised that there were one too many adults for her to contend with. She knew that without their help, she couldn't possibly save Bogdan from these evil men. So, cunning as she was, once Vuka gathered Dubravka in her arms, the little girl switched off her hysterics as if they had never happened and offered Nina a feigned apology in the sweetest, most timid voice she could muster.

'It's a terrible situation,' Nina quickly explained to Vuka now that Dubravka was seemingly compliant. 'Bogdan is half-Jewish by birth. His mother is a Croat, but her deceased husband was an Austrian Jew. She is safe for now, but the boy is not.'

'Is there anything that can be done?'

'Nothing. She understood the risks involved in undertaking this journey and what would happen if they were caught by the Germans. Now, please, you and Dubravka have been given a reprieve. Don't ruin it for a young boy you barely know.'

'She's right,' Remer said, suddenly appearing behind Vuka's shoulder. 'Forget the boy; we need to leave now.'

Vuka saw the desperation in Dubravka's eyes, and she suddenly felt incredibly helpless. For her daughter's sake and for all the children who had died in this horrible war, she had to try one last time. How could she look at Dubravka in the same way again if she didn't?

'Herr Oberst, he's just a little boy.' Just as she spoke, both Gross and Juric shuffled into view, much to the chagrin of Remer. They had more than a passing interest in what this upstart do-gooder would do next. In fact, they were almost willing him to be the hero and let the boy go so that they could denounce him later that evening to his commanding officer.

However, Remer wasn't a fool. Once in Smolensk, he had tried to save a family of Jews from the Einsatzgruppen and almost paid for it with a court-martial that would have destroyed his military career. Saving local women and children from being raped and murdered was one thing, but rescuing a Jew in such open circumstances was an entirely different matter. For the sake of his men, who needed his leadership more than ever, he wasn't going to risk it.

'There's nothing I can do. Vuka, please make your way to my jeep. We leave in two minutes.'

Despite their disappointment with Remer's decision, Gross and Juric began to laugh at his apparent cowardice before marching back towards Bogdan and his mother. Soon, as Vuka, Dubravka, Maria and Ivana somehow all managed to squeeze into Remer's jeep, a volley of rifle shots boomed across the sky. While no one dared say anything to her, Dubravka knew that Bogdan had been murdered. Her heart fractured like a broken vase. On the day where innocence and cruelty had played the same tune, it was cruelty, it seemed, that was destined to prevail.

Chapter Five

Bihać, Yugoslavia
December 1944

Anton stretched his legs across the top of his sleeping bag and immediately felt the pain torment him. He wanted to curse his agony with one loud scream but then realised this wasn't something military officers did in front of their men, unless, of course, you wanted to lose their respect. The shrapnel injuries to his shins he had sustained at Pađene were healing well, but the Chetnik doctor had warned him that the pain would remain with him in varying degrees for several months. It was a fate designed to destroy his spirit.

There were no battlefield hospitals out here in the wilderness where he could recover, just a daily concoction of morphine and other painkillers that thankfully dulled his senses. If Anton was honest, the diminishing supplies of morphine were probably needed for other soldiers with worse wounds than him. However, that was the privilege of command, and while he felt like shit, he wasn't going to reject it. Following the horrors of Pađene, he had become more anxious about surviving the war than he ever had been.

As a freezing wind attacked a nearby pile of fallen leaves, Anton reached over for his rifle and thought about using it as a prop to help him stand up. But just as he positioned himself onto his knees, a lone hand swivelled under his armpit and gently guided him back to the ground.

'Rest some more, my love,' Ilsa said softly. 'We don't need to get up just yet.' She sat down on the sleeping bag next to him and passed him a large steel cup of coffee. 'Here, I made you this,' she said with a smile. 'I should charge you for all the extra duties I do for you in your wife's absence.'

Anton grasped the cup with both hands and tried to laugh. 'Her coffee was never as good as yours,' he added before almost choking on Ilsa's latest sour ersatz concoction. While Anton knew the rules about women on the frontline, he wasn't giving Ilsa up for anything. They could remove him, if they wanted to. Besides, her Florence Nightingale routine had already saved many lives within the brigade, and she had become integral to his daily planning. No, Ilsa wasn't going anywhere, even if divisional headquarters kept demanding her return.

'Have you heard the latest?' Ilsa said, changing the subject. 'We are leaving tomorrow. There was a meeting last night between our lot, the Ustaše and the Germans. Apparently, they will give us safe passage if we agree to leave Croatia for good. I have heard rumours that Austria is a possible destination.'

'Austria?' Anton almost choked on his coffee. 'There is no way that Đujić will agree to that. Do they think we are stupid? The Russians will soon be at the gates of Vienna, from what I hear. We would be sitting ducks for the Bolsheviks. No, the boss is taking us to Slovenia, mark my words.'

'You may be right,' Ilsa agreed. 'But I was talking to Brigadier Spasic's adjutant this morning, and he reckons that when we do move, his brigade and ours will be the last to withdraw from our position. We are to act as a shield while the rest of the division gets a head start. Other Chetnik units will soon be joining us when they can.'

'The more the merrier,' Anton groaned. His legs felt so stiff that he now wondered whether he was actually suffering from frostbite as well. 'How's morale?'

'It's fine,' she responded. Anton doubted whether Ilsa would tell him otherwise. With every battlefield commander, there was always a nagging suspicion, after a setback like Pađene, that your troops had stopped believing in you. Perhaps he was imagining things because of his wounds, but he felt unnaturally distant with his men over recent days.

'They have gone through a lot over the past two months,' Ilsa continued. 'We have suffered over forty per cent casualties during that time. We are also losing men to typhoid every day. Pađene was an especially brutal fight, but thanks to your leadership, most of the old guard is still here.' Ilsa gently touched Anton on the knee in an effort to reassure him that everything she had said was true.

'Pađene was God's way of transporting the Devil's work to Earth. I hope that I never see anything like that again in my life.' Pađene was indeed a battle fought in the depths of hell. In horrific conditions, the Chetniks had been completely surrounded by the Partisans, who relentlessly bombarded them over several days with a withering cocktail of artillery and small-arms fire. Somehow, the Chetniks held their ground and then, against all odds, courageously broke through the Partisan lines. The fighting was brutal and unforgiving, and at times, hand-to-hand, but the Chetniks prevailed. As far as Anton was concerned, it was their finest moment of the war, and he was especially proud of how his men performed under such trying circumstances.

'The men are just grateful that they are alive, Anton.'

'For the moment, you may be right,' he began. 'But I am truly worried about the number of civilian refugees we are now carrying with us. It's a distraction our men can ill afford, especially when everyone else in Yugoslavia seems determined to kill us.'

Ilsa said nothing. She rarely raised the thorny issue of Anton's wife and daughter unless in jest. He had made the correct decision to leave them behind in Šibenik. As far as she was aware, he refused to contact them, even when people like Sukevic and Brontic urged him to do so. He either believed that their presence would make his leadership vulnerable, or he wanted to start afresh as a single man in another country. Either way, it was none of her business. She was living her life on the edge, and for the moment, she was prepared to share that experience with Anton. How long it would last was nothing more than a day-to-day proposition; after all, she could be dead herself by the end of that day.

Then everything changed in a matter of minutes.

Anton had just finished his coffee when Sukevic emerged from the tree line, his rifle hanging precariously over his massive shoulders. While most of Anton's brigade was heartily sick of the escalating violence, Sukevic was thriving in it. He had fought like a wild animal at Pađene, frightening even his own men in the process. Anton had lost count of how many Partisans Sukevic personally killed during the battle, only to be reminded by him afterwards. 'Forty-seven, Anton,' he kept saying, over and over again, until Anton finally believed him. At times, it seemed that Sukevic wanted the war to last forever.

'I have some news, Anton,' he said after he nodded politely at Ilsa. 'Some more refugees have arrived at our camp. Included in that lot are several dozen women and children from Šibenik.'

Anton froze as if he knew already what was about to come next. Perhaps he was living in a fool's paradise, and this day was always meant to catch up with him.

'And?'

'And your wife and daughter are among them.'

Anton dropped his cup on the ground and then looked desperately at Ilsa. 'That stupid woman. What the hell was she thinking?'

Ilsa didn't reply but knew immediately what she had to do. Her position was now untenable, after all. The commander of the brigade had to be with his wife and daughter, not some sex-crazed home wrecker like her. That was the curse of the 'other woman', she decided. Without saying a word, she calmly reached down to collect her bedding and weapon, then offered Anton a rueful look. 'Maybe your wife gets to make you that coffee after all.' She wanted to say something else, maybe a thank you for all the good times, but in the end, she couldn't think of anything that justified her sadness. Instead, she smiled pathetically at a lone hawk circling above them, before she and Sukevic shuffled off to the other side of the camp, leaving Anton to stew in his own guilt.

Chapter Six

Bihać, Yugoslavia
December 1944

The reunion between husband and wife was always going to be an eventful one. To ensure that the rest of the brigade didn't hear their argument, Sukevic suggested that Anton meet with Vuka in a small clearing behind the medical aid post. While some privacy was guaranteed, it was foolish to believe that the shouting wouldn't be heard.

'You bastard!' Vuka screamed when she first saw Anton emerge from the shadows. 'You were going to leave Yugoslavia without me! Just so you could be with your little whore from Split.'

'That's not true,' Anton pleaded, even though he couldn't make up his mind whether he was lying again or not. 'I always intended to find you once things became clearer.'

'Liar!' It went back and forth like this for at least an hour. Anton tried to hide his guilt by berating Vuka for risking Dubravka's life and bringing her into such a dangerous environment. But his desperate ploy wasn't going to work. Vuka was adamant that she had done the right thing.

'When you married me, it was forever,' she insisted. 'We are a family and need to stay together.'

The simple truth was that Anton didn't have a leg to stand on. His ranks were already swelling with the families of his soldiers; it was predicted that the division would soon be home to more than a thousand Serbian refugees. So, his argument that it was too dangerous for Vuka and Dubravka to travel with him was a hollow one, given the risks other civilians were also taking to be with their loved ones.

Indeed, Vuka refused to accept that having his family in such close proximity potentially compromised Anton's duties as a commander and his ability to make unemotional decisions in the middle of a battle. It made riveting discussion, sure, but who was he really kidding? Anton knew that his flagrant affair with Ilsa had already undermined his leadership in some ways. Most of his men, while adoring Ilsa for her medical prowess, were God-fearing Christians who had raised concerns among themselves about their commander's open adultery.

Displaying unerring moral leadership was the only way for Anton to keep such a disparate group of fighters together, especially when they faced the potential reality of death every day. Now that his wife had arrived, Anton couldn't risk alienating his men any further by carrying on with his affair. He had no choice other than to accept the new situation. However, he did have one warning for Vuka.

'While we are at war, my men come first. You must look after Dubravka yourself. Are we clear?' Vuka agreed to the condition as long as she and Dubravka were allowed to share his headquarters at night. Not only did she want to keep an eye on him, but she also wanted to make sure that by seeing her and Dubravka regularly, he would never again forget his true responsibilities to both of them. Vuka may have been viewed as the weak woman, the uncultured sister. In reality, she was as tough as nails and cunning as a fox.

Although Anton was not happy seeing Vuka again, that feeling definitely didn't extend to Dubravka. When father and daughter saw each other again for the first time, they hugged each other tightly until both of them ran out of breath.

At first, Dubravka was taken aback by her father's long, scraggly beard. Was that really Tata underneath that hair? Sensing her trepidation, Anton laughed and then explained. 'It's a Chetnik custom, my sweet. We will not shave again until our invaders are defeated and forced to flee our land.'

Once Dubravka understood, she grabbed her father around the waist again. 'I missed you, Tata,' she said tearfully. 'Please don't leave us again.'

'Of course, I won't,' a guilt-ridden Anton replied. Even then, he couldn't decide whether it was a promise he should have made or not.

As much as his life had changed, Anton didn't have time to reflect on his new marital circumstances. Over the next few days, he was completely preoccupied with supervising his brigade's withdrawal, reassuring his newly arrived civilians that they were safe and liaising with Đujić and the other Divisional commanders. Despite all this talk about high-level agreements with the Germans and the Ustaše, Anton was having none of it. He didn't trust anyone—not even his own people—and he considered every centimetre of ground in front of him as hostile territory.

Whenever they moved as a unit, Anton positioned his brigade HQ and his main body of troops at the vanguard of their formation. The civilians would always be deployed at the rear, protected by a small group of veterans led by Sukevic himself, who could respond quickly if they were ambushed from behind or on their flanks. It wasn't easy playing nursemaid to a bunch of mainly clueless women and children, many of whom were traumatised by their new living conditions, but Sukevic grasped his new orders with relish. Although he seemed to be an enabler for some of Anton's worst afflictions, even Vuka grew fond of the burly but dangerous Serb as he cajoled and organised his new flock.

By now, the brigade had more than a dozen children travelling under its protection, but there was no doubt that among the fighters, Dubravka was by far the most popular. Obviously, being the daughter of the boss helped, but her effervescent personality, natural kindness and childish beauty melted the hearts of even the most hardened veterans. Her playful innocence also brought a unique brevity to the brigade, and she had the remarkable ability of uplifting the spirits of everyone around her.

After a challenging day slogging through the never-ending snow-rimmed mountain trails, Dubravka's contagious laughter would often echo through the camp after dinner, undermining the natural weariness of the exhausted guerrilla fighters, many of whom had fallen into a maze of lost helplessness after the atrocities of Pađene. With her big, luminescent hazel eyes and mischievous grin, she would weave her way through the rows of tents, bringing about a sense of normalcy and warmth that many in the brigade had long forgotten.

Sukevic was particularly fond of her; burdened by the nightmares of his past and those of his future, he would often find solace in Dubravka's precociousness. At the end of every day, she would somehow find a new wildflower within the winter deadlands and then place it gently on Sukevic's bedding before he went to sleep. 'It will help you dream pleasant things,' she would often tell him.

Not a sentimental man by nature, the sight of the daily flower brought a touch of tranquillity into Sukevic's otherwise violent existence. While the stress of war never left him, Dubravka's antics reminded him that happiness could be found even in the darkest of times. Her innocent laughter and unwavering spirit became a beacon of hope, not only for him but for the other war-weary guerrillas who suddenly needed a new reason to survive the war.

Dubravka's charm even extended to the chain of command. Soon after Anton's brigade caught up with the rest of the division, Đujić, who had been recovering from wounds he had suffered during the Battle of Knin, paid an obligatory visit to the brigade. Normally, Đujić's presence would cast a nervous shadow across Anton's HQ. Anton was never really sure how Đujić felt about him, and this made every meeting between the two men increasingly tense. His Croatian heritage aside, Anton, for some reason, believed that his elevation to a brigade commander was borne out of political expediency and that Đujić wouldn't think twice about demoting him should the circumstances arrive. Perhaps it was just Anton's paranoia over-reaching, but even so, he begged everyone around him that night to be on their best behaviour.

However, someone had forgotten to tell Dubravka. As soon as Đujić arrived at the camp, she decided to greet him with a rambunctious version of the Italian National Anthem. Dubravka's joyful singing echoed loudly through the low-hanging snow clouds at the worst possible time, causing many of Anton's soldiers to stifle their laughter. While Anton stood at attention, ashen-faced, his hands shaking in panic, Đujić doffed his famous Chetnik cap and beckoned Dubravka to come to him.

'And what's your name, little one?' he asked with a perplexing smile.

'Dubravka!' she shouted. Anton, by now, was virtually shitting himself. *Who the fuck taught her the Italian National Anthem?*

'That's a pretty name for a pretty girl.' His shoulders then slumped wickedly as a speck of moonlight cascaded against his dirty beard. 'Do you know any other songs, my sweet?'

Dubravka put her hands on her lips and then released a smile so wide that it threatened to swallow Đujić whole. 'Yes! How about this one?' With a playful shake of her hair, she began to sing *Cetnicka Pesma*, a Chetnik song that Sukevic had taught her earlier that day. To the relief of Anton and Sukevic, who were standing nervously behind Đujić, he released a loud guffaw and then clapped his hands several times. 'Bravo! That's a much better song!'

After he and Anton crept away for several minutes for a secret discussion, Đujić soon re-emerged from the darkness and made his way directly back to where Dubravka was sitting. 'My poor child,' he began, his voice ladened with emotion. 'It is not right for a little girl to be out here in the wilderness. King Petar would be very proud of you. If he were here, I am sure he would give you a medal.'

'My Tata fights for King Petar!' Dubravka boldly declared, her hands raised in a mini salute. But by now, the commander of the famous Dinara Chetnik Division, one of the most feared guerrilla leaders in occupied Europe, who would soon be tried in absentia for war crimes by the Tito Government, had shuffled off into the night, barely saying a word to Anton or anyone else as he departed.

We can't be sure, of course, but perhaps Dubravka's purity had reminded Đujić of the world he had just lost. Even for a man of his bearing, it must have been a difficult concession to make.

Chapter Seven

Yugoslavia
December 1944

As Anton had predicted, Đujić had no intention of withdrawing to Austria. He had always planned to reach German occupied Slovenia via the Northern Dalmatian Coast and Istria. Đujić hoped that he and other Chetnik and Serbian nationalist commanders would join their forces for one last decisive battle against the Partisans. Đujić wrote to Pavelić himself requesting that he afford him and his army free passage as they moved, no strings attached. Perhaps the Germans placed considerable pressure on him, as he quickly agreed.

But like everything in Yugoslavia, the agreement wasn't worth the paper it was written on. In the manner of days, Đujić decided to change course. He didn't believe that the 'safe' routes offered by Pavelić adequately protected him against Partisan attacks. Instead, he proposed to reach the coast through the Lika region, involving some of the most mountainous and inhospitable terrain in all of Yugoslavia. To attempt this journey in the middle of a freezing, unforgiving winter, with the added responsibility of protecting civilians, was a huge gamble. And yet, it was one which Đujić felt he had to take.

Allegations of looting and violence followed Đujić's division as it marched through Croatia. This news soon caught the attention of local Ustaše forces, who were just spoiling for another fight with their mortal enemies. Before too long, all bets were off, and the Ustaše began to ruthlessly pursue the Chetniks across the mountains and endless valleys. Hundreds of Chetnik soldiers were killed as a result of these relentless attacks.

By now, Anton's brigade consisted of no more than three hundred fit fighting men—one small unit inside the six thousand soldiers that Đujić now had at his disposal. Anton's brigade often operated as an independent unit at the rear or extreme flanks of the main divisional advance. This made it a prime contender for an enemy ambush or counterattack. The constant stress of battle, combined with the extreme cold, little food and the burgeoning typhoid crisis, made daily life intolerable for Anton and his men. Something had to give, and when it did, it had tragic consequences for all involved.

The precursor to that horrible event was the controversy over Dubravka's newly acquired shoes. Despite Nina's quick work on that first day and the subsequent attention of the brigade's doctor, Dubravka's feet continued to deteriorate. She was just a little girl, after all, and her developing body was not made for ten-hour route marches through such unforgiving country. Sukevic tried to help out where he could, often carrying her on his enormous shoulders when things got too tough for her. But he was also the brigade's deadliest soldier, so much of his time was understandably focused on his military duties. Therefore, Dubravka often had to walk the horrendous ground by herself, much too proud to complain about the sharp, jagged rocks that regularly cut into the flimsy soles of her shoes. Sometimes, she was given a donkey to ride on when she was very tired, but the poor animal was old and crusty and, in fact, next to useless when traversing very high ground.

Vuka was naturally alert to her daughter's distress. For the first few nights after they left Bihać, she would make Dubravka take off her shoes and wriggle her little toes against the freezing winter air. Once Vuka carefully bathed Dubravka's feet with some water, she would rub them with some of the ointment that Nina had given her and then make her put on a fresh pair of woollen socks she had scrounged from another woman. By the time Dubravka was ready to collapse onto her bedding, Vuka made her repeat the one golden rule she always had to remember: 'Have your shoes close to your bed should we need to leave in a hurry.'

Of course, rules like that were meant to be broken, and on an exceptionally cold December night, just before Christmas, that's exactly what happened. The brigade was once again protecting the extreme left flank of the main formation. Over the previous forty-eight hours, they had engaged in several skirmishes with enemy patrols seeking to find weaknesses in Đujić's flanks. But on this particular night, just as most of the brigade had settled in their makeshift beds, the unmistakable sound of mortars screeched through the ghostly sky. This was the precursor to a full-blown attack!

With the ground exploding all around his HQ, Anton screamed out several impulsive orders for the brigade and its civilians to withdraw to a nearby ridgeline. In the commotion that followed, Vuka had bundled little Dubravka in her arms as quickly as she could and followed the trail of frightened guerrillas into the darkness. It was only when they reached their destination that Vuka realised Dubravka did not have time to retrieve her shoes.

This bordered on catastrophe. How could Dubravka expect to undertake the rest of this arduous journey barefoot? The next morning, when Anton realised what had happened, he was furious at his wife. Dubravka was Vuka's responsibility; he had made that abundantly clear to her when she first arrived at the camp. But now, on top of everything else he had to contend with, he was burdened with the thought of his only child walking through a winter hellhole without shoes.

How long can she last in these unforgiving conditions before she gets frostbite? Sukevic and some of the other men offered to carry Dubravka the following morning, but it was an impractical long-term solution that left everyone vulnerable.

Around midday, the brigade advanced towards a quiet little village that seemed largely unmolested by the war. Why or how, it didn't seem to matter. It existed as it always had for centuries, oblivious to the machinations of the outside world. Other combatants might have used this as an opportunity to engage in some looting, but Anton had implemented very strict rules about such things. His war wasn't against poor, innocent civilians, regardless of their nationalities, religious beliefs, or allegiances. Anton swiftly dealt with any of his men who disobeyed this edict.

As they entered the village, Vuka begged Anton to allow her to search for some children's shoes. She still had the money that her father had given her for an emergency, and there was no bigger emergency in Vuka's life at that time than finding footwear for her daughter. Incredibly, it didn't take her long to find a cobbler right in the middle of the main street. This was a miracle in the making! Taking Dubravka with her, she snuck away while Anton and Sukevic weren't looking and wandered into the tiny little shop. She was greeted by a feisty old man in his early seventies, whose flowing white beard and unplucked eyebrows reminded Dubravka of an out-of-work Father Christmas.

It didn't take long for Vuka's eyes to covet a lovely pair of brown children's shoes sitting idly on the cobbler's workbench that would have fitted Dubravka perfectly.

'How much do those shoes cost?' she asked furiously. 'I have plenty of money.'

'They are not for sale,' the old man replied defiantly.

'Please, look at my daughter's feet. We lost her shoes last night; all she is wearing now are her woollen socks. She can't spend another day like this.'

'That's not my concern. Those shoes belong to my granddaughter. I have just repaired them for her. They are not for sale. Please leave.'

But Vuka wasn't ready to leave yet. 'Surely you have other shoes that you could give your granddaughter?'

The old man laughed and then pointed to his empty shelves. 'Take a look. Do you see any spare shoes? We are in the middle of a war. I have no new shoes to sell or to give away to people like you. I fix the shoes and boots that are given to me by the townsfolk, nothing more.'

Suddenly, a noise came from the back of the store, perhaps a cat meowing or a door slamming; Dubravka couldn't be sure. Whatever it was, the old man became distracted and instinctively turned his back on her and Vuka. Perhaps it never occurred to him what a desperate mother would do for her daughter. Knowing that this was her only chance, Vuka snatched the shoes from the workbench without hesitation and held them tightly against her chest. 'Run!' she screamed at Dubravka. 'Run for your life!' Within seconds, they were tearing through a new layer of thick snow towards a puzzled Sukevic, not once turning back to see if the old man was following them.

Dubravka loved her new shoes. They were light and comfortable and didn't bite into the sores on her feet. She thought everyone would be pleased that she no longer had to walk in her socks, and to be fair, most people were. But for some reason, her father seemed angry about her new acquisition. He didn't say anything to Dubravka, of course, but later that night, she heard a furious argument develop between him and her mama.

'How could you steal those shoes?' she heard her father yell. 'After the orders, I gave to my men about not looting or stealing.'

'I didn't steal them,' her mama insisted.

'Don't lie to me, Vuka!' Her father was really yelling now. 'An old man began to harass some of my soldiers, claiming that a woman and her daughter had run away with his granddaughter's shoes. We both know that he was referring to you and Dubravka. How do you think that makes me look in front of my soldiers?'

'You seem to care more about your soldiers than you do about your own daughter.' Dubravka didn't want to hear what she heard next—the sound of a hand slapping a face, several muted cries and plenty of swear words. But when she woke up the next morning, her new shoes were still where she had left them under a nearby bush the previous night, and that was all that mattered.

By the end of that awful week, Anton had become completely frustrated with Vuka and her selfishness. The shoe incident had made him look stupid and weak in front of his men. The pair's constant bickering was also beginning to undermine his authority. And then there was Ilsa. Their relationship had become largely transactional, focusing solely on managing his brigade's casualties. She was still vital to his command-and-control system and the overall running of the brigade, but that's where it began and ended. How he missed her touch, her smooth and soft body and the ecstasy of their lovemaking. He tried to talk to her about how he felt several times in private, but she just brushed him away. 'You are a married man, Anton,' she would brutally say. 'And while your wife is with us, that's all you will ever be.'

For Vuka's part, she paid Ilsa no mind whatsoever. The two women had unintentionally crossed paths several times, but when they did, Vuka barely acknowledged her. As far as she was concerned, Ilsa was a whore who was socially beneath her. That she had tried to steal Vuka's husband behind her back further demonstrated her lack of morals and integrity. If she was somehow killed tomorrow by the Ustaše, Vuka would gladly dance on her grave.

Unsurprisingly, Ilsa felt the same way about Vuka. She thought that Vuka was an arrogant upstart who was both physically and intellectually inferior to her in every way and no match for a man of Anton's impressive qualities. At every opportunity, she sought to deride and undermine Vuka in front of other people in the brigade.

Naturally, the tensions between Vuka and Ilsa hung like a millstone around Anton's neck. As hard as he tried, he could no longer ignore the seriousness of the situation. His personal life had become too much of a distraction at a time when so much was at stake. He had already been wounded once at Pađene, and although he wasn't a fatalistic person, he knew that somewhere out there was a bullet with his name on it. He figured that his chances of surviving the withdrawal to Slovenia were barely fifty-fifty. Somehow, he needed to improve those odds. And that's when he decided to get rid of Vuka.

As fate would indeed have it, he didn't have to wait long before the perfect opportunity presented itself. Several days after the shoe incident, Đujić deployed his forces alongside a small valley while they sought food and medical supplies in a nearby village. Đujić ordered Anton to link up with several adjoining units and guard the southern approaches to their position. During that horrible afternoon, intelligence reports quickly emerged that a Partisan battalion was heading towards them. Anton's brigade was right in the firing line. As such, orders arrived that all women and children were to be taken out of harm's way and transported immediately to the village in several lorries.

For Anton, this was manna from Heaven. He sincerely believed that civilians did not belong inside a fighting unit like his. Now that the new order had been issued, he would plead with Đujić that, for their ongoing safety, Vuka, Dubravka, and the rest of the women and children in his brigade should continue to travel with divisional headquarters. Surely, common sense would prevail.

Unfortunately, Anton failed to predict Vuka's vehement opposition to such a move. As soon as she was told about the convoy, she flatly refused to go.

'You want to get rid of me so you can be with your whore!' she screamed at her husband. Not wanting to hear her parents argue again, Dubravka put her hands over her ears and pretended that she was in her grandfather's bomb shelter, listening to another one of his stories.

'Don't be stupid, Vuka,' Anton had responded audaciously. 'This has nothing to do with Ilsa. This is for your own protection.'

'Liar! You have been waiting for this opportunity ever since Bihać!'

The argument went backwards and forwards, with neither parent backing down. The last thing that Dubravka wanted was to leave her father again, but many of the other wives and children were now getting on the trucks. *Why is Mama so insistent that we should stay behind?*

'I have a bad feeling about this,' Vuka implored. 'I am scared that if we get on the truck, we will never come back alive!'

'Don't be ridiculous, woman!' Anton sneered. 'It's perfectly safe. Even your friends, Maria and Ivana, are going!'

'But I don't want to!'

Eventually, Anton completely lost himself in the chaos of his ferocious temper and irrationally reached for his pistol. Without even thinking how this might look to his precious daughter, who was watching him with frightened tears, he placed the tip of the barrel against Vuka's temple and stroked the trigger guard.

'You are taking our daughter and getting into that truck, or I will shoot you where you stand.'

Completely shocked by her husband's actions, Vuka sobbed violently before finally taking Dubravka's hand. 'This will be forever on your conscience,' she implored. 'God forgive you if anything happens to us.'

Ten minutes later, Dubravka was huddled in the back of the truck with her mama, while their friends Maria and Ivana fussed over the little girl's windswept hair. 'Here,' said Maria sweetly as she took out a brush from her bag. 'Let me untangle those knots for you.' As Maria brushed Dubravka's hair, she turned to face Vuka, who was looking glumly into the perpetually grey sky.

'What's wrong, Vuka?' Maria asked. 'I am very worried about you.'

'We don't belong in this truck,' Vuka replied. 'It's not safe.'

'There is going to be a battle here before the night is out. My Josip says that the situation is very dangerous. We are better off in the village than here.'

'We don't belong in this truck,' Vuka repeated again and again before she dropped her head into her hands and resumed her crying.

Throughout the passage of time, Dubravka could only remember bits and pieces from that afternoon. However, one thing that became permanently etched in her mind was the truck suddenly stopping for several seconds in the middle of a dirt track and her mother screaming at her to collect her bag. The next thing Dubravka recalled was her and Vuka rolling around on the frozen ground after they had jumped from the truck. There were whispers, some tears, perhaps a bruised knee or two, some shouting from Maria and Ivana in the distance and then a long walk back to the brigade camp. Vuka simply refused to go any further on that truck. Whatever witchery she possessed, she was going to follow its course even if Anton decided to kill her.

Of course, Anton almost did kill her. When he discovered both of them an hour later skulking near a tree, he turned into a virtual madman. Luckily for her, Sukevic and Ilsa quickly dispossessed Anton of his pistol before he carried out his threat. Incandescent with rage, he then cursed Vuka with every swear word in the Serbo-Croatian dictionary until there was no more air in his lungs to expunge. Defeated at last by his own perfidy, Anton slinked away to check his defensive perimeter while Ilsa, of all people, placed a calming arm around Vuka and made her and Dubravka a hot drink. Such was the calamity of war that brought together two mortal enemies, both competitors for the same man's heart.

Later that night, just before the Partisans attacked, word came down from the division that the trucks never made it to the village. The next morning, a search party finally found what was left of the convoy smouldering in fiery orange ashes barely two kilometres from Anton's position. It was a scene of disturbing horror. All the women had been raped and slaughtered with knives, their naked bodies mutilated in ways that can't be described.

The children also suffered a terrible fate, thrown into a nearby ravine and indiscriminately shot, nothing more than target practice for the shooters. It wasn't immediately clear who was responsible for this war crime—it could have been the Partisans; it might have been the Ustaše. Maybe it was the Germans. Does it even really matter? In the bigger scheme of things, atrocities like this occurred on a daily basis in Yugoslavia. What more could you expect from a country that had lost its sanity?

Vuka wept uncontrollably when, later that morning, they returned Maria's and Ivana's battered bodies to the camp. For a short period of time, they had been her friends—better friends than she ever had in Šibenik as a young woman or would ever meet in Australia as a frustrated migrant. But she didn't have time to mourn. That would come later. All she cared about was saving Dubravka from the monstrosities of war. From that day onwards, no one dared to get in her way, not even Anton. For on that cold, desolate afternoon, the tiny, fragile woman who was often called the black sheep of her family had stood taller than anyone else in the world.

Chapter Eight

Slovenia, Yugoslavia
January 1945

Vuka would later say that the last four months of the Second World War—January to May 1945—were exceptionally barbaric, even by Yugoslavia's epic standards. The civil war by then had evolved into a violent reckoning between Nazi collaborators who had brutally oppressed the local population during the occupation and those seeking their long-awaited revenge. In this nightmarish scenario, no quarter was given, and none was asked. It was warfare at its most primitive, leaving one belligerent in Montenegro to remark afterwards: 'If we ran out of guns and ammunition, we would have undoubtedly continued fighting with clubs and rocks.'

The brutality of war didn't matter much to Anton anymore. His sole focus was leading a disparate group of people beset by illness, fatigue and trauma across hostile territory to relative safety. Much had changed since the horror of the lorry massacre. Following an overwhelming display of grief from those impacted, there was a renewed determination by his soldiers to follow Anton into the pits of Hell, if necessary, in order to survive. No one blamed him personally for the massacre; they realised that he was only obeying orders and had put his own wife and daughter at risk in doing so. But woe and behold, any enemy soldier unfortunate enough to land in their clutches. Mercy was rarely contemplated, while death would be quick and brutal.

One of the immediate repercussions of the massacre was that it suddenly drew Anton and Vuka closer together, even if it was just for a short while. Although he felt like a proper cad for threatening Vuka's life like he had, Anton was eternally grateful that his wife had the courage and the sixth sense to do what she did on that awful day. The mere thought of potentially losing Dubravka in such brutal circumstances made him physically ill for weeks. Any possibility of reconnecting with Ilsa was now put aside, as Anton insisted that Vuka and Dubravka permanently join him in his HQ so that he could protect them. From that point onwards, they would live and fight together as a family.

The Ustaše and Partisans continually attacked Anton's brigade as it slugged its way towards the Dalmatian Coast and then to Slovenia. For Dubravka, who didn't fully understand how close she had come to being killed, being close to her father's side was all that mattered. The whirring sound of mortars screaming through the tree line or the distant clacking of machine gun fire never worried her as long as he was there to protect her. In her own childish way, she had learnt that the violence that surrounded her on a daily basis was something she had to accept. There was no point wishing for something better when reality had already decided her fate.

Besides, there was always a new adventure waiting for her just around the corner. Some days, she would be sitting next to her mama during a rest break, perhaps listening to Brontic tell one of his absurdly funny stories about his life in Italy, when a maze of rifle fire would smack randomly against the trees around them. Soldiers and civilians alike would jump into the air like frightened sheep, their panicked minds caught inside a deadly trance where every decision they made was the wrong one.

But once Anton and Sukevic appeared, an eerie calmness descended upon the flock. It was as if a switch had been automatically turned on, and everyone now knew what they had to do. Without saying a word, Dubravka would immediately leap onto Anton's left shoulder while he triumphantly waved his rifle in the air with his other hand. 'Follow me,' he would yell, as he trudged his way through the deep drifts of newly covered snow, firing at anyone stupid enough to get in his way. It was like a Saturday afternoon matinee movie but with real bullets and real consequences.

Afterwards, when the fighting was over, and the brigade undertook their battlefield clearances, Dubravka could be seen proudly scouring the ground with her father, examining the dead bodies that surrounded her with an eye for detail that only an innocent child could possess. 'They are enemy soldiers, Tata,' she would declare as she walked past a pile of half-decapitated bodies. 'There are no Chetniks here.' And Anton never once doubted her.

Most of the Chetnik units and their civilians arrived in Slovenia by January 1945. It was truly an incredible achievement, the stuff of legend that is still celebrated by the descendants of those Chetniks today. Unfortunately, the Germans who occupied that territory were not especially pleased to see them. They had no reason to trust the Chetniks, or any Serbian unit, for that matter. Even if they resupplied them with weapons and ammunition to fight the Partisans, how long would it take before they went running off to the Allies at the first sign of German vulnerability?

No, the Germans would disarm them first and then assess the situation. If they were satisfied that they could be trusted, perhaps they would be given some menial tasks, like protecting the local railway infrastructure against Partisan attacks.

The hiatus in activity came at an opportune time for Anton. He was physically exhausted and mentally fatigued from the stress of the previous four months. Together with his wounds from Padene and weeks of little sleep, his body's resistance to disease was at an all-time low for someone usually so fit and strong. As such, he was a ripe candidate for the typhoid outbreak that had decimated the Dinara Chetnik Division from the moment it left Bihać. It was no surprise, therefore, that Anton soon became its next victim.

The disease is caused by the Salmonella Typhi bacteria and is spread by eating or drinking food or water contaminated with the faeces of an infected person. During the war, typhoid was a significant problem for resistance forces due to poor sanitation and lack of clean water. Like most people who catch the disease, Anton's decline was a gradual one until he was suddenly beset by a high fever, chronic diarrhea and extreme tiredness. If there was one consolation, the division's medics had so much practice treating the disease that they knew how to make Anton comfortable during the worst days of his illness.

Dubravka was sad that her father was sick. She barely left his side during this time. Vuka reassured her that Anton would eventually recover, but when he started to lose his hair, even the normally phlegmatic Dubravka found cause for alarm. 'Please get better, Tata,' she would sometimes cry as she held his hand tightly. Whatever magic Dubravka contained inside her little fingers, it seemed to do the trick. After ten days, Anton's fever subsided, and he was able to sit up and eat some food. Everyone who had prayed for his quick recovery was equally relieved to see him soon walking around the camp, thanking people for their good wishes.

While Anton's recovery was a morale boost to his troops, an issue that had plagued him, Ilsa and Sukevic, for some time, soon came to a head. When Vuka first arrived at Bihać, she mentioned that Jelena had claimed there were Partisan spies in the brigade who were reporting on Anton's activities. At first, Anton wasn't overly alarmed by the revelation. He knew that the Partisans had infiltrated the wider Chetnik movement, often encouraging members to swap sides and join their cause. However, he was relatively certain that his own headquarters had not been compromised, despite what Jelena had revealed.

But ever since his brigade started their trek across Croatia towards Slovenia, he began to take the allegations more seriously. Something just didn't feel right—maybe it was a codebook that was found in a slightly different position than how he left it, or maybe it was a box of ammunition that was left open for the rain and snow to destroy its contents. And it always seemed that the Partisans knew exactly where and how his brigade was deployed, enabling them to harass his men almost daily. Anton especially found this concerning, given that information outlining the daily routes was closely guarded within the command structure and not widely shared.

Ilsa made no bones about who she felt was responsible. 'We have a spy in our midst, and it's him!' she would shout. 'I never trusted him from the first moment I met him.'

'Nonsense,' Anton would say. 'You have no proof at all that he has betrayed us.'

'I have seen him wander off at night by himself,' Sukevic intervened. 'Where does he go?'

'I simply don't trust him,' Ilsa had replied.

Anton then decided to consult the woman with the sixth sense. 'He's always trying to ingratiate himself with Dubravka,' Vuka said. 'That in itself is suspicious.'

Ironically, it was Dubravka's restlessness that eventually caught the traitor out. It was a cold, soulless night blessed with a rare, clear sky and a full moon. Despite the eerie calmness that had descended over the valley where the brigade had encamped for the last several days, Dubravka couldn't sleep. She had twisted and turned her body in several different directions over the past hour in an attempt to get comfortable, but still, she could not get rid of the tiny little pebbles that stabbed her constantly in her back. Frustrated, she decided to relieve herself in the nearby bushes, hoping that her indiscretion wouldn't wake her parents, who were lying together underneath a blanket next to her.

She first saw him just as she sprung to her haunches to readjust her woollen socks. A familiar figure silhouetted against a nearby pine tree barely ten metres away, staring at her through the moonlight. He was carrying his backpack and rifle and seemed to be going somewhere in a hurry. For a moment, their eyes connected through the darkness. As the man held his stare, he said nothing at first before offering Dubravka a knowing smile. Bereft of any other options other than to placate her, he then placed a skinny index finger across his lips. 'Shhhh,' he whispered several times before slithering into the tree line.

Dubravka didn't know the significance of what she had just seen but was smart enough to know that her father needed to be informed immediately. After all, she was his eyes and ears. 'Tata, Tata,' she pulled at her father's shoulder. 'It's Gospodin Brontic! He's running away!'

They found him an hour later, skulking inside a small cave. He tried to resist at first, firing a few shots aimlessly into the air, more in desperation than anything, before the force of numbers simply overwhelmed him. He was brought back to the camp to face Anton and Sukevic, blood pouring from a broken nose he had received during the return journey. Treachery was never rewarded by the Chetniks.

'Explain yourself!' Anton demanded angrily when Brontic was forced to kneel in front of him.

'Nothing personal, Anton,' he replied with a nervous grin. 'I like you very much and respect you as a leader. As much as I could, I tried to keep the shit away from you and your family.'

'Then why?'

Brontic shrugged his skinny shoulders. 'During my time in Italy, I saw the brutality of the Fascists firsthand. The beatings, the rapes, the murders. No one lifted a finger to stop them except for the Communists. They fought back against the madness; they refused to sit back and do nothing like the rest of them. Then the Italians occupied Dalmatia, and some of the Chetniks made a deal with these criminals. Imagine how I felt? For me, the Partisans were the only ones fighting a just war, so I joined them. The rest of you are just deluding yourselves, thinking that there is some honour in fighting for a monarchy that's abandoned you.'

'Pity you won't see your socialist utopia come to fruition,' snapped Ilsa. She was determined to be present when Brontic, her *bête noire*, made his confession.

'Ah, the Ice Queen herself,' Brontic laughed. 'Come to witness the final act, I see.'

'Wouldn't miss it for the world,' she replied sarcastically.

'That world would have been a much better place if they killed you in

Split. If I had my time all over again, I would not have lifted a finger to save your contemptible arse.'

Ilsa pondered whether to slap Brontic across his face in response to the insult. Instead, she decided that death was its own leveller. She considered him one last time with her cold, reptilian eyes before slowly walking away, laughing insanely at her latest victory.

Squeamish as he always was when it came to metering out punishment, Anton dropped his head into his chest and sighed. Deep down, he knew there was some truth to what Brontic had said. Where did this so-called moral victory begin and end? He wasn't sure anymore; that much was true. Perhaps in the cold, hard light of day, he never had been sure. All he cared about now was saving his men and family. That was the only way he could wash away the shame of defeat and live with himself.

'May God have mercy on you,' Anton whispered as he nodded his head towards Sukevic. He then turned his back on the traitor, his one-time friend and confidante, and stumbled mindlessly into a nearby clearing, his heart racing at the sound of the two rifle shots that followed. As he fought with his conscience one last time, Anton felt his stomach explode, and he soon fell onto his knees, retching out every last ounce of pride he had left. Only then, as he wiped the vomit from his chin, did Anton finally realise that he was meant to survive the war.

Chapter Nine

Isonzo River, Slovenia
May 1945

By April 1945, Nazi Germany was facing total annihilation, as the Russians swept towards Berlin and the American-led coalition overran the industrial heartland in the country's west. All across occupied Europe, the seemingly impregnable German Wehrmacht was in retreat, the thousand-year Reich proving to be nothing more than the demented dream of a madman. In a matter of weeks, the whole rotten system would collapse inside Hitler's lonely bunker.

In Yugoslavia, Tito and his Partisans, backed by the Soviet army, were now firmly in control of much of the country. After helping to liberate Belgrade, Russian soldiers actively broke into the city's houses and apartments, looking for women and girls to rape. That these unfortunate souls were technically on the same side as the Russians didn't seem to matter. When the famed Yugoslav partisan, Milovan Đilas, raised the issue with Joseph Stalin himself, the Soviet dictator was alleged to have said, 'Young guys are young guys, they've been through the war, and they need a little rest.' This was a tragic trend that would be imitated across Eastern Europe during those last desperate months of the war, especially in the German cities of Berlin and Königsberg.

The remaining German units in Yugoslavia, demoralised and exhausted, battled gamely against overwhelming odds as they made their own preparations to withdraw from the country. Although it would take a further month before the mass exodus started, Pavelić and his Ustaše cohorts also began to make their escape plans from Zagreb.

The Chetnik forces remained separated by the tyranny of distance;

Mihailović was trapped in Serbia; Đujić and Jevđević were ensconced in Slovenia, close to the Italian border, and Đurišić and his Montenegrins were still battling their way across Croatia to meet them. (Đurišić would eventually be captured and executed by the Ustaše in late April.) Đujić and other Chetnik officers begged Mihailović to leave his headquarters and join them in Slovenia, but the Chetnik leader refused, claiming that his forces would never survive the long march through Croatia. It was a fateful decision that would have tragic consequences for the Chetnik movement.

Instead, between March and April 1945, Mihailović and Dimitrije Ljotić, a Serbian right-wing idealogue who had initially been at loggerheads with the Chetniks earlier in the war, tried to organise a last-ditch alliance against the Partisans. They agreed that the Chetnik General Miodrag Damjanović would take command of the unified force and attempt to contact the Allies in Italy. However, their request to secure foreign aid for a proposed anti-Communist offensive to restore royalist Yugoslavia was largely ignored.

Following Ljotić's death in a car accident in late April, any thoughts of a coordinated attack against the Partisans finally ended forever. Damjanović's main goal now was to secure the safety of his troops before they were totally destroyed by the Partisans.

The urgency of the situation was amplified when the Partisans finally entered the contested Italian north-eastern border city of Trieste on 1 May 1945, ahead of the advancing New Zealand Army. In a last-ditch attempt to defend their position, the German-led forces fought ferociously, but it was all for nothing. The Partisans were too motivated, too well-equipped to be denied their place in history, even though the Allies eventually took control of the city.

Whether or not Anton fought at Trieste remains a mystery. Neither he nor Vuka ever mentioned the battle to their children on those rare occasions they discussed the war. What we do know is that the majority of the Dinara Chetnik Division, and the vast remainder of GEN Miodrag Damjanović's army and accompanying civilians, crossed the Isonzo River on 5 May 1945, surrendering to the British forces in the Italian town of Palmanova, fifty-five kilometres north-east of Trieste. Following the surrender, the army was disarmed and then transported to the Italian towns of Cesena and Forli, along with their families. They would eventually be interned at a large camp in the southern Italian town of Eboli, in the region of Campania, close to Naples and Salerno.

Anton's brigade was one of the last Chetnik units to cross the Isonzo River into Italy. On that warm spring afternoon, Anton surveyed the banks of the river, Dubravka by his side, his heart pounding in his chest. After everything he had gone through since he made that pact with Duško back in Split, he now stood at the precipice of a new life. Only one thing was left to be done—crossing this accursed body of water safely with his brigade intact. There had already been several skirmishes with Partisan units that morning, and they were expecting more that afternoon. It wasn't time to be complacent.

If he was truthful to himself, Anton had felt overwhelmed with fear ever since he woke up just before dawn. His war was nearly over, and they were minutes away from freedom, but everything seemed too good to be true. Even Dubravka, normally so cheerful and brave, seemed unusually tense. Perhaps the huge weight of responsibility he carried on his shoulders since Padene and the unnerving trek across the heart of Yugoslavia had now touched his daughter's soul. For her sake and everyone else he was responsible for, he needed to shake away his fears for one more day and lead from the front like he had always done.

Just as Dubravka bent down to inspect a funny-looking insect on the ground, the tranquillity of her moment was shattered. Rifle fire suddenly erupted from several points inside the dense forest situated behind the river, a volley of bullets ricocheting into the muddy sand around her. Anton, without having any time to think, grabbed his daughter by the shoulders and pushed her face into the ground.

'Stay still, Dubravka, and keep as low as possible,' he said calmly. 'Don't move unless I tell you. Understand?'

'Yes, Tata,' she gulped. For the first time in a very long while, she felt scared. But she was also determined to do everything her father asked of her. She wasn't going to fail him today, of all days.

There was more machine gun fire and more screaming. Anton's heart sank as he realised his brigade was caught in a crossfire. He always feared being attacked out here in the open; one of the basic principles of warfare was that you are at your most vulnerable when crossing an obstacle like a river. That's why he had deployed several three-man patrols in the forest to protect the routes into their position while they moved most of the brigade across the river.

But where the hell were they now?

Ilsa suddenly dropped down next to him. She looked pale and angry, her rifle pointed blithely at the forest.

'What the hell are you doing here, Ilsa?' Anton yelled above the persistent gunfire.

'What do you think I am doing? I am trying to help you.'

More bullets sprayed above their heads. Dubravka wanted to cry. Instead, she rolled her tiny fists into the ground in the desperate hope that her actions would somehow create a magic shield to protect her. Anton quickly turned to see if she had been hurt, and once satisfied that she wasn't in any immediate danger, he barked out some orders at several soldiers lying in front of him.

'See that little clearing at one o'clock?' he shouted.

'Yes, sir.'

'Concentrate your rifle fire there. Put every round you have into that area. Okay?'

Without responding, the men threw back their heads and began firing at the target. Meanwhile, Anton quickly picked Dubravka up in his arms and gestured Ilsa to follow him. Within seconds, they slumped safely behind a large, jagged rock. Somehow, the enemy was too distracted to see them.

'What the hell is going on?' Anton asked Ilsa. 'Where's Sukevic?'

'He's dead.'

An unearthly silence crept between them.

'No,' Anton finally whispered.

'I am afraid so, Anton,' Ilsa replied, tears streaming down the Ice Queen's face. 'I was standing right next to him when a bullet struck him in the forehead. He died in my arms. Then, somehow, I found you. I wasn't going to see two of my best friends killed in the space of thirty seconds.'

Anton wanted to cry like a baby, but he didn't have time. He could not allow himself to be overcome by grief, not while his daughter was shivering in fear next to him. He had a mission to complete, lives to protect. With a heavy heart, he rallied his soldiers to his position and then told them to follow him on his command. There was no option but to counterattack, he explained. If they stayed out there in the open for much longer, they would all be killed. And then, like the Devil himself, he jumped up as if impervious to enemy bullets and led a mesmerising frontal assault against the main group of Partisans sheltered at the edge of the forest.

The fighting was fierce and uncompromising, but the unity and resilience Anton had built in his brigade over the previous six months now prevailed. Although it seemed longer for those involved, the counterattack was over in barely ten minutes. Miraculously, apart from Sukevic and two of the patrols, which had been ambushed prior to the Partisan attacks, Anton's brigade suffered no further casualties. Sweeping through the forest at the conclusion of the fight, they countered thirty-five dead enemy soldiers. On this occasion, Anton didn't need Dubravka to identify them.

Of course, there wasn't time to celebrate. Undoubtedly, the Partisans would return soon with a larger force. They had to get everyone across immediately. Over the next hour, Anton's brigade worked furiously as they first escorted the remaining civilians to the other side of the river before the soldiers followed closely behind. Anton and Ilsa were the last to leave, as they did what they could to give Sukevic a proper burial. Remembering how much he loved Dubravka, Anton dug a hole in a nearby field of wildflowers and gently placed his huge body inside. Ilsa gave a short but heartfelt eulogy, and then the former lovers gave each other a deep hug.

'For such a violent man, he was the kindest person I ever met,' Ilsa sniffed. 'I would not have survived without him.'

'Neither would I,' Anton admitted. 'But I guess a warrior like him was destined to die this way. The last bullet of the last day of the last war.'

'Nonsense. He deserved to live more than any of us did.'

'Perhaps,' Anton said softly before taking Ilsa's hand. 'I know one thing—both of us also deserve to live after what we have gone through these past months.' He paused, staring one last time at Sukevic's grave. 'It's time for us to go.'

Once Anton had crossed the river into Italy, he slowly turned to face the land of his forefathers. A massive thunderstorm had quietly emerged from beyond the horizon and was threatening to explode on top of him. As streaks of brutal lightning scythed across the black sky, Anton was suddenly overcome with a sadness that ripped at his insides. Frightened beyond reality, his eyes slowly wandered to the field where he had just fought his last battle of the war. After adjusting his sight, he fixated on a lone tree, standing defiantly against the coming storm.

The tree seemed to reach into Anton's soul, and, for one ghostly moment, they prayed together for his everlasting redemption. Then, as if preordained by God, an arrow of lightning ripped through the tree's dry undergrowth, setting it on fire. Anton watched helplessly as the tree burned in cadence with the growling thunder, its smouldering ashes funnelling precariously towards the heavens. Finally, after all of his travails, he suddenly realised what he had never dared contemplate before that day—he would never see the country of his birth again. Without taking another breath, he lifted his rifle onto his shoulder, adjusted his backpack, and disappeared into the waiting rain.

Later that day, after Anton's brigade had surrendered to the British in Palmanova, Vuka and Dubravka sat quietly together inside a small courtyard next to the local hospital while British nurses busily attended to a number of elderly and sick refugees. They were both exhausted from the stress of the river crossing but relieved that, finally, the guns had stopped.

Anton didn't tell Vuka what happened when the Partisans attacked earlier that afternoon and how close Dubravka came to being killed. He was determined not to upset Vuka, given that she had been unusually sick over the previous few days, vomiting regularly in the mornings and evenings. It was almost as if Vuka was pregnant.

As she now bent over to light a cigarette, she saw Dubravka staring up at the cloudless late afternoon sky.

'What is it, Dubravka?' she asked softly. 'Is there something wrong?'

Having seemingly forgotten about her ordeal earlier in the afternoon, Dubravka gave her mother a wide smile, something that had been missing from recent weeks.

'Did you hear that, Mama?' she replied excitedly.

'Hear what?'

'The birds! The birds are singing again!'

No matter what would happen between them in the future, for this one glorious moment, mother and daughter stared into each other's eyes and laughed, knowing that at last, their horrible war was over.

Chapter Ten

Eboli, Italy
May 1945

Eighty years later, it is easy to forget the impact that the Second World War had on the generation that lived through it. Notwithstanding the enormous casualties—more than sixty million deaths worldwide, the dislocation and mass movement of people across vast distances, the breakdown of families and the trauma and utter madness of the Holocaust—the war reframed the whole concept of self-sacrifice and the differentiation between right and wrong.

Sadly, it has become trendy on social media platforms and at some universities to revisit the past with a critical, revisionist eye and blame those generations and the institutions that represented them for the perceived injustices and misalignments that continue to impact modern society. Iconic events like Anzac Day are criticised for celebrating war. Statues of famed historical figures like Captain Cook are derided and threatened with destruction. Older people are accused of being out of touch and responsible for all the ills of the world. Antisemitism is stronger now than at any time since the Holocaust.

While debates about the past should be had, one must always remember that history is an imperfect field. Things are not often what they seem. To make rushed, biased and uninformed assumptions about events that happened in another time without understanding the full context in which they occurred is dangerous. Not only do you run the risk of misinterpreting the outcome, but you will also fail to see the historical patterns or lessons that might apply to a present-day issue.

As Dubravka grew older, she would often contemplate these matters and bemoan the dangers associated with what she saw as the erosion of history. Given that the Second World War generation was slowly passing away, Dubravka wondered whether the lessons those people carried with them would be lost forever.

Dubravka was lucky that her own children and grandchildren respected her worldliness and character and would honour her values long after she was gone. But it annoyed her how much some people took for granted the world that was created due to the sacrifices of others.

Dubravka would especially focus on what she called her 'lost years' between September 1945 and August 1948—her time spent interned at the Eboli Displaced Persons Camp in Italy, followed by a resettlement camp in Germany. Like so many children of her age who survived the war, her earliest memories were not of going to school every day, shopping for a new dress, playing with friends or taking beach holidays with her family. Rather, her time was largely spent confined with thousands of desperate and traumatised people, trying to survive each day in the most basic of living conditions, their futures uncertain, their pride diminished. Somehow, though, Dubravka was able to rise above these challenges and set herself on a pathway to a better life.

By the time Dubravka, her parents and their Chetnik companions reached Eboli in September 1945, the World War that traumatised an entire generation had finally ended. Although the Allies had prevailed in Europe and the Pacific, the real work had just begun. Rebuilding a shattered European continent and managing a major refugee crisis was, of course, the immediate priority, but equal importance was given to the hunting of evil — ensuring those who had stained humanity through their heinous actions were brought to justice.

The Nuremberg trials would successfully prosecute those surviving members of the Nazi elite who had contributed to the atrocities of the Holocaust and other war crimes. Unfortunately, others escaped, never having to justify their wretched actions.

On 5 May, the same day that Anton surrendered to British forces in Palmanova, the Ustaše Government left Zagreb for good, followed by Pavelić himself. Many Ustaše troops fled to the Austrian village of Bleiburg only to be returned to Yugoslavia by British forces, along with a number of Chetnik escapees. Retribution by the Partisans was swift and brutal. Estimates vary, but some historians say the Partisans murdered over sixty thousand Ustaše and Chetnik soldiers.

As for Pavelić, he somehow managed to avoid capture on several occasions. Said to have accessed ratlines established by some in the Catholic Church, Pavelić eventually escaped to Argentina, where he would soon be joined by his wife and family. Controversial to the end, he was the target of an assassination attempt in Buenos Aires by a Serbian hotel owner in 1957. After Argentina agreed to an extradition request by the Yugoslav Communist Government, Pavelić moved to Chile and then to Franco's Spain before dying in a Madrid hospital in 1959 due to complications caused by his gun wounds. To his dying breath, he championed the creation of an independent Croatia. However, following his death, the Croatian separatist movement mostly distanced itself from him.

Upon hearing that Damjanović and his forces successfully made it to Italy, Draža Mihailović continued his war against the Partisans. Poorly equipped and suffering from illness, Mihailović's Chetniks were no match for the well-supplied and motivated Partisans. His forces dwindling, Mihailović went from mountain to mountain, continuing to fight while hoping that the Allies would see Tito for who he really was.

Unfortunately, it was nothing more than wishful thinking. The Allies may have grown frustrated with Tito over a range of military matters, but in the end, he was their man, and they were not for turning so close to the end. Abandoned by the Allies, a wounded and ill Mihailović was finally captured by the Partisans in March 1946. Accused of being a traitor and a collaborator, Tito had him executed not long afterwards following one of the most dubious political show trials of the twentieth century.

Despite the circumstances of his death and the accusations levelled at him, Mihailović remains a hero to many Serbs. His silent vindication as a critical wartime figure, particuarly in America, is supported by those who highlight his courage in saving downed Allied pilots during the latter stages of the war and his determination in preventing Nazi reprisals against innocent civilians. However, despite being posthumously awarded the Legion of Merit by US President Harry S. Truman for the actions he took in saving American lives, his legacy continues to be debated.

News of his execution cast a collective pall on the Eboli survivors. It was said that following his death, many Chetniks finally realised that they would never see Yugoslavia again. As for Vuka and Anton, they remained fierce Mihailović supporters for the rest of their lives.

King Petar never returned to Yugoslavia either. Tito didn't have any intention of including him in a future government. He was officially deposed by Yugoslavia's Communist Constituent Assembly on 29 November 1945. A new Communist Republic of Yugoslavia was announced on the same day. It was an especially cruel blow for those men and women who fought and died for the royalist cause. Unable to come to terms with this betrayal, King Petar eventually emigrated to the United States, where he developed an unfortunate reputation as a playboy. Despite attending royalist events in America, he rarely spoke out about the situation in Yugoslavia. He died in Denver, Colorado, in 1970 following a failed liver transplant. In many ways, his demise was the saddest of all the key wartime figures.

In the immediate aftermath of Palmanova, Anton took time to reflect on the reasons why the Chetniks had failed and what they could have done differently. He agreed with the commonly held belief that resistance groups only succeeded when their cause had the support of the wider population. Although he was fiercely loyal to King Petar, he also accepted that the Serbian monarchy was not popular in many areas of the country—especially in Croatia and Slovenia. Ordinary Yugoslavs wanted something different after the war was over, and Tito, the ultimate salesman, offered them a new way of life once victory was achieved. As a result, the Partisans fought with a unity of purpose that made such a victory inevitable, helped, of course, by the overwhelming scale of Allied support.

Perhaps Mihailović's cause might have benefited had he generated a wider patriotic call to all Yugoslavs, regardless of ethnicity, to join his Serbian warriors in fighting the evils of totalitarianism. As leader of a unified Yugoslav army, fighting for freedom and democracy in the King's name, his influence, especially with the Allies, would have been difficult to ignore. But alas, as Anton knew only too well, hindsight is a desolate cause, particularly in wartime.

Anton's soul-searching would continue for years to come, but he and Vuka faced more pressing issues once they reached Eboli. *What will happen to us now? How long will we be imprisoned? Where will we eventually go? Will the Allies send us back to Yugoslavia?* The last question would have undoubtedly preyed on the minds of the surviving Chetniks and their families who had risked everything to escape their beloved Yugoslavia. Let's not forget that the events of Bleiburg provided the blueprint of what the Partisans would do if they ever seized more Chetnik prisoners.

Thankfully, the same mistake wasn't made again. Some believed that Mihailović's status still had credence with the Allies, especially the Americans. There also existed within the Allied ranks a general sympathy towards the Chetnik forces—*after all, they were once our partners before being dumped by the top brass.* As a result, the Allies resisted all attempts by Tito to return the Chetniks.

The Chetniks and their families held at Eboli were now part of the massive resettlement process that was underway all across Europe.

Eboli's agrarian roots, lazy olive groves and relative isolation made it the perfect place to establish a displaced persons camp, despite the terrible destruction inflicted upon the town following the Allied invasion of Italy in 1943. The mild Mediterranean climate that greeted the internees was in complete contrast to the wintry, mountainous landscapes of Lika and Slovenia. After the living hell that was wartime Yugoslavia, Eboli, in comparison, seemed like a semi-paradise.

At its peak, Eboli was home to around fourteen thousand refugees.

The camp itself was littered with countless rows of newly built Nissen huts and canvas tents. The huts were usually reserved for senior officers and their families, while a hospital and several churches were also established. Despite rank having its privileges, most of the refugees were able to find passages of relative comfort inside the camp once they learnt to depend on each other.

While camp meals initially lacked diversity and quality, they were mostly hot and safely prepared. People could also purchase food and clothing at the local Eboli marketplace or through the inevitable black marketeers. Thankfully, disease and illness were carefully managed as camp doctors obtained access to new medical supplies. Movement outside of the camp was restricted at first, but soon the British guards allowed the Serbs to enter the town and mix with the locals.

While many townsfolk were still traumatised by the war, they were nevertheless welcoming of the new arrivals. As time went on, the British guards gradually became resigned onlookers, as the Serbs effectively managed every detail of camp life by themselves. Some of the camp's skilled workers even volunteered their services to the British army, undertaking a variety of reconstruction roles in the Campana region.

After the initial settling-in period had passed, boredom soon became the biggest issue for thousands of fighters who were used to living on the edge. They now had nothing better to do other than stare at the sun and contemplate their fate. To their credit, camp leaders reacted quickly. Church services were established, while the observance of Serbian cultural activities and festivals was greatly encouraged. Sporting events like intra-camp football matches brought excitement to the weekends, while regular theatre productions brought back memories of another, happier time.

Every effort was made to bring a piece of the old country back to a generation of people who most likely would never see the old country again.

The next big problem? Hundreds of bored and traumatised children. However, a school system was soon created, and children were taught basic reading, writing and arithmetic. It was hoped these tools would allow the children to assimilate into a new country when the time came. It wasn't a perfect system by any means, but it was all that they had. Anton and Vuka made sure that Dubravka attended lessons regularly. Anton was especially adamant that Dubravka's education should not suffer because of their challenging circumstances.

He need not have worried. Not only was Dubravka very smart, but she wanted to learn and didn't have any trouble adapting to her new environment. In fact, she very much looked forward to her lessons. She saw 'school' as an opportunity to have fun and make friends with children her age. It had its drawbacks, especially when she felt like playing in the sunshine, but as always, she lived for the day and never complained.

Maybe it was her sunny disposition and cheeky smile, but Dubravka soon became everyone's favourite. The British guards in her sector were especially enamoured with her and showered her with daily attention.

So much so that they even provided her with her own private room inside the family hut. Not having to share with a stranger made life so much more bearable.

Additional living space soon became a boon for the entire family. You see, Vuka was pregnant. How she and Anton had time to consummate a new baby in between all the arguments, Anton's typhoid, fighting Partisans, and being pursued across countless mountains and rivers in the driving cold was one of the war's great mysteries. But it was a reality they now all had to accept.

Dragan was born in early January 1946, one of the many babies delivered inside the Eboli camp. Dubravka, now five years old, was delighted to have a baby brother at first, even though it meant extra duties for her, like fetching and disposing of nappies and helping her mama put him to sleep. She understood the challenges facing her parents and tried very hard not to be an additional burden to them. Even so, she would get cranky at her Tata some nights when he accidentally woke her on his way to meet Aunty Ilsa in the hut next door. The strange noises the two of them made together often grew so loud that Dubravka was forced to press her mittens against her ears just so she could fall back to sleep.

Some old friends and enemies would soon find their way to Eboli. To Anton's great relief, his friend Duško, the man who had changed the course of Anton's war, appeared like a mirage one day in front of a medical aid post. The two old friends hugged each other like long-lost brothers before disappearing behind a vacant hut to have that long-awaited talk.

Duško's war had been a brutal affair, punctuated by treachery and regret. After spending much of 1942 in Mihailović's headquarters, he was tasked by his boss to improve the relationship between the wider Chetnik movement and the SOE. As fate would have it, he spent far too long with the Chetniks in Montenegro, regularly clashing with several different British officers about operational priorities. In between those disagreements, he was involved in countless pitched battles with the Partisans, almost losing his life when a mortar struck the side of his jeep during a withdrawal. How he survived was still very much a mystery to him.

After the Allies ditched the Chetniks, Duško spent the last part of the war in Switzerland trying to convince the American Office of Strategic Services (the forerunner to the CIA) that supporting the Partisans was a bad deal. At one point, he actually thought he was making some progress, with a smile here and a nod of the head there, but in the end, it was all smoke and mirrors. As far as Duško was concerned, the Americans were just as untrustworthy as the British. Not long after Germany capitulated, the OSS gave Duško twenty-four hours to leave the country.

After being guaranteed safe passage through Austria by the Americans, he was captured by a British patrol near Salzburg and ceremoniously sent back to Yugoslavia in handcuffs. Through his rat-like ingenuity, he was able to bribe one of his guards to let him go before they reached the Partisan camp—where he surely would have met his death—and then escaped into the night. Finding some other Yugoslav Army officers along the way, they somehow made it to Italy in one piece despite being chased and harangued by virtually anyone in a uniform.

'Then it was all for nothing, Duško,' Anton observed sadly.

'Probably not,' Duško noted dryly. 'But we still have our pride.'

'I'm not sure I even have that anymore.'

They then talked about comrades lost. Max, Sukevic and many more.

'Max was a tragedy,' Duško growled. 'We still don't know who betrayed him to the Ustaše.'

'A mystery indeed.' Anton swallowed hard. Why was Duško suddenly focused on Max's death? Was he hunting Anton for the truth? Waiting for that last slip of Anton's tongue that would finally give it all away?

'Any ideas what happened?'

'None whatsoever, but his brother has some theories.'

'His brother?'

'Yes, Yuri. I believe you have met him. Speaks very highly of you, by the way.'

Does he? Does he really?

'Yuri's here in Eboli?'

'Yes, he arrived with me earlier today. One of the last Chetniks to make it across the Isonzo River. Quite a brave lad. We spent a week together being questioned by the Yanks in Rome before being driven down here.'

'I see.' Anton felt like vomiting all over Duško's incredibly polished shoes, but somehow, he kept a straight face and a clean stomach. 'I look forward to seeing him again.'

'There's something else you should know, Anton.' Duško suddenly clasped his hands into a tight little ball.

What? More bad news?

'I met another man in my travels who knows you as well. Unlike Yuri, he's not your greatest fan.'

Anton sighed. It could only be one person. 'Ilic?'

'Yes, I'm afraid so. It seems that he has a vendetta against you.'

'What makes you think that?' Anton tried not to laugh at himself.

'Oh, the number of times he told me that he was going to kill you.'

'The man is a fool.'

'I agree,' Duško nodded. 'But he is a dangerous fool with important friends, even here in Eboli. So, watch your back.'

Of course, Anton always watched his back. You had to when men like Ilic were obsessed with justifying their actions during the war. His kind only saw life through their own vanity, where vengeance was the simplest of antidotes for their own self-inflicted misfortunes. But Ilic was a problem that could wait. A more pressing need for Anton was dealing with Yuri's arrival. For if a vengeance was to be had, Yuri's day of reckoning held a greater fear for Anton than anything else he had encountered in the war.

Chapter Eleven

Eboli, Italy
May 1947

After two years of incarceration, Dubravka had grown increasingly restless. She may have only been six and a half years old, but she understood, even at such a tender age, that another world was waiting for her. The desire to walk freely like other children her age tugged at every raw emotion she possessed. She didn't know exactly when her new life would start, but her dreams encouraged her to have patience. Indeed, her vivid imagination was the only thing that sustained her during those long, wasted days.

Of course, Dubravka's frustration was shared by those around her. The war had been over for two years, and most of the former Chetniks inside the camp desperately wanted to pursue new lives in whatever country awaited them. With the world now focused on the growing tensions between the Allies and the Soviet Union, an unarmed guerrilla force with little political or financial backing no longer presented a threat to anyone. It was time to move on.

Then came the announcement that shook everyone's world. After nearly two years of operation, Eboli was to be closed. Everyone would be transferred to resettlement camps in Germany. From there, several possible destinations awaited them—the United States, Great Britain, Canada and a remote country on the other side of the world called Australia. It would involve an exceptionally long process for sure, but at least the wheels were now in motion.

'We are finally leaving Eboli, Dubravka,' enthused Anton as he hugged his oldest child tightly. 'One day, you and I will eat hotdogs together in America!'

'What are hotdogs, Tata?' Dubravka asked with one of her iridescent smiles. But Anton was too caught up in his own excitement to hear her question.

Some people left earlier than others. As mysteriously as he had arrived in Eboli, Duško disappeared into thin air without ever saying goodbye. Rumours soon emerged that the Americans had whisked him away in the middle of the night to help them establish an anti-Communist spy network in Italy. It sounded like a pretty decent theory, Anton decided, but then, knowing Duško as he did, he could have plied his trade anywhere in the world. Nevertheless, he would miss his friend dearly.

Ilic was also on one of the first convoys to leave Eboli. Despite the warning from Duško, he had ignored Anton for much of their time together in the camp. It was obvious that someone in high authority, maybe even Duško himself, had read the riot act to the impetuous army officer. 'If you harm a hero like Anton in any way because of a stupid misunderstanding, prepare to suffer the consequences.'

As it happened, they had words with each other only on one occasion, ironically, once again on a football field when Anton decided to revisit the good old days and crunch Ilic from behind with a ferociously illegal tackle. Ilic had rolled around the ground for several seconds like the prima donna that he was before jumping up and threatening Anton with a curled fist.

'You mother fucker!' he had yelled. 'I will kill you for that!'

'Anytime, anywhere!' Anton had stupidly boasted in reply. Fortunately, the referee intervened, and a senior officer soon dressed both men down and forced them to shake hands. And that was the end of that.

Momčilo Đujić would eventually leave Eboli for Paris. Two years later, he emigrated to the United States, finally settling in California. Many of his loyal supporters soon followed. Easily the most famous of all the Chetnik leaders outside of Mihailović, Đujić helped establish the Ravna Gora Movement of Serbian Chetniks and became an outspoken advocate for the return of the Serbian monarchy. Despite failed attempts from Tito to have him extradited to Yugoslavia to face allegations of collaboration and war crimes, Đujić lived a long and prosperous life, eventually dying in San Diego at the age of ninety-two. Upon his death, thousands of Chetnik survivors mourned; they would admire him forever as the man who led them safely to freedom.

It was Đujić's impending departure that finally brought an end to the cantankerous romance between Ilsa and Anton, something that even a new son, a highly suspicious wife, and two years of incarceration couldn't contain.

'I have been seeing Đujić's principal aide, Stojkovic,' she told Anton brutally just before she left.

'Seeing him? You mean sleeping with him.' Anton's furrowed brows hid a deep hurt that he couldn't explain.

'I am not here to argue with you over semantics, Anton. I am here to tell you that Stojkovic has asked me to go to Paris with him and I've accepted. We leave this afternoon.'

'Just like that?'

'Just like that.'

Anton dropped his shoulders. He knew that it was wrong to emotionally blackmail his lover or dictate to her how she should spend the rest of her life. That didn't mean, though, that he wasn't going to try.

'What about us?' he whispered, placing a lone hand on her bare shoulder.

'There is no 'us', Anton. Not anymore, at least. Our bond was forged by the peculiarities of war, where we only had responsibility for ourselves. But whether you like it or not, you have always been a married man with a beautiful daughter and now, a new son. They are your future; I am your past. It's time for both of us to leave the war behind and start afresh. This is our last chance to make amends with the world.'

Their final kiss was as ferocious and passionate as their first, but it was conducted inside a pervading gloom that never left Anton to his dying days. When it was over, he wiped the tears from his cheeks, mumbled something under his breath, and then turned his back on Ilsa forever.

In later years, Anton's youngest son, Alex (out of interest and for the purpose of this account), would track Ilsa's whereabouts to Los Angeles, where she and Stojkovic owned a successful horticulture business. They had five children and lived a happy middle-class life until she sadly passed away from breast cancer in 1975. Those who knew her in Los Angeles swore that she should have been a Hollywood actress if only things had been different. According to the tributes, she died with her love for Yugoslavia and the monarchy, never leaving her heart.

Anton, Vuka, Dubravka and Dragan were among the last to leave Eboli for Germany. Travelling through Italy at the time wasn't without its dangers. The Treaty of Paris, signed in February 1947, had officially brought an end to the war between the Allies and the Fascist Italian state, but the mechanics of the treaty were not implemented until that September. This created a dangerous political chasm during the intermediary period.

A series of crises in May that crippled the ruling government raised the real possibility of a Communist uprising—an outcome completely untenable to the Americans and the British. Therefore, the prospect of anti-Communist refugees travelling through a country touched by Cold War revolutionary intrigue was not ideal. However, much to the relief of Anton and his family, their train journey, which extended through Naples, Rome, Verona, and then across the Brenner Pass to Austria, was largely incident-free. They were thankfully leaving Italy for good—or so they thought.

Anton had been hopeful that the dispersal of the Eboli refugees to various resettlement camps would break his nexus with Yuri once and for all, even though his concerns about Max's brother never did materialise. Rather, in Eboli, Yuri had followed Anton around like a puppy dog, worshipping him at every opportunity. 'I still can't believe you swam to Brač that night,' he would often remind Anton needlessly. It was as if Anton was the last remaining connection Yuri would ever have with his dead older brother. At a time when Anton wanted to forget about the war, Yuri's presence was a constant reminder of his darkest secrets and the threats that still hung over him.

Thankfully, Anton got his wish. Given that he was a single man, Yuri had been shipped to a separate camp in Germany and would soon be making his way to England. With Max and Sukevic now dead, Duško off playing spy games with the Yanks, Ilsa fucking Đujić's aide, and Yuri miles away from his orbit, Anton could finally make a clean break from his past. How long this respite would last before someone poured a bucket of shit over his head wasn't worth thinking about.

For Dubravka, the journey to Germany was the most exciting thing she had ever done in her short, tempestuous life. While most of the refugees on the train complained about the food, the unbearable, cramped conditions, the putrid smell of the old, urine-stained carriages, Dubravka spent her time with her tiny nose crammed up against the window, absorbing the wondrous scenery that surrounded her.

As the train rumbled through the heart of Italy, she was overwhelmed with scenic views of green, rolling hills, bountiful vineyards, olive groves and golden fields of sunflowers. Every time they entered a new town or village, she would strain her neck upwards as far as she could before catching glimpses of colourful houses, the odd medieval castle and picturesque squares full of red and yellow daffodils. It was like the war had never touched this unearthly paradise. Then, as if everything before it was nothing more than a prelude, the Brenner Pass left her gasping in amazement with its snow-capped peaks, deep green valleys and ice-blue rivers. What a time she was having!

It was a huge disappointment when they finally arrived at their destination in Germany and were ordered to board a truck that would take them to their resettlement camp. Dubravka panicked that she would become trapped once more inside an undefined purgatory without ever experiencing the freedoms she richly deserved. It was cruel and unfair, especially after she was given a glimpse of the outside world during the train journey. Although her Tata tried to console her, Dragan's constant crying and her mama's incessant complaining didn't make her feel any better. This wasn't the way a little girl should ever have to live.

The majority of the refugees who travelled to Germany hated their time inside the resettlement camps, especially when compared to the relative freedoms they enjoyed in Eboli. Much of this stemmed from the compulsory screening process that the Chetnik soldiers were forced to undertake before they could emigrate to another country. At a time when the world was still focused on the outcomes of Nuremberg, their British and American interrogators were determined to expose any Chetnik that may have been involved in war crimes. For some, it was a long and arduous process to prove their innocence.

Because Anton had made it through the screening process with little difficulty, initially, life for the family in the new camp was bearable. They were surprisingly given a large room on the second floor of a huge wooden house, which overlooked a sturdy walnut tree and a little playground where the camp children would often come to play. For the first time since she left her grandfather's house, Dubravka had a proper bed (albeit a basic one) and a soft pillow. And when her brother's crying became a little too much, there was a small room on the bottom floor of the hut full of children's books and toys to play with.

The only real concern that Dubravka had during those early days was the mean female guard who always seemed to pick on her. Maybe it had something to do with the walnuts she would pull off the tree with regular impunity before throwing them at the footpath below her. 'Do that one more time,' the German guard would bark, as she swept the loose walnuts into a dustpan, 'and you will feel my hand on your bottom.'

Dubravka understood enough German to know that the woman could be a dangerous foe if she wasn't careful. Things entered an untimely standoff between the two protagonists until the guard convinced Dubravka that if she ever entered the camp butchery by herself, she would push her down a hidden trapdoor that led to a horrible abattoir. It was here where 'naughty young girls were regularly turned into salamis.' Unsurprisingly, they became a lot friendlier after that discussion.

As life at the camp extended well into 1948, Anton grew more frustrated at his family's situation. It had been nearly three years since he surrendered his brigade at Palmanova, but here he was, still stateless and unsure about his future. He made it clear to the Americans and the Chetnik hierarchy that the United States was his preferred destination. As the months passed, some insidious piece of paperwork thwarted every attempt to get on a boat. Anton couldn't understand why his application was always rejected when other people who had made a less compelling contribution to the war seemed to be getting an easier ride. For the first time, he began to wonder whether his former Catholicism was finally working against him.

By mid-1948, a health crisis began to emerge inside the camp. Cholera, typhoid fever, measles and tuberculosis were rife. Of particular concern was the impact on the camp's children, many of whom were already suffering from various levels of malnutrition. One of the camp doctors who had befriended Anton didn't mince his words. 'Try to get your children out of this place before something we can't control kills them.'

That was easier said than done when the rejection slips to both the United States and Great Britain kept coming.

Anton was at the point of total despair when, out of the blue, an old friend came to visit him at the camp.

'As I live and breathe!' Anton exclaimed, shaking the visitor's hand. 'Major Stubbs!'

Stubbs smiled casually and then pointed at his epaulettes. 'Been promoted, actually. I'm a lieutenant colonel now.'

'A promotion well deserved, I'm sure.' Anton then looked at Stubbs cautiously. 'What are you doing here? It is a long way from England.'

'I came here to see you, actually. If you must know, I have been meaning to visit you for several months, ever since your old friend Major Ilic told me that you had survived the war.'

'Ilic,' Anton mumbled. 'The gift that keeps enduring.'

Stubbs laughed. 'He's quite the character.'

'That's one way of putting it.' Anton paused to cough several times. 'Even so, I am honoured that you still remember me.'

'How could I ever forget you? You were the only damn Yugoslav I worked with that was worth his salt. And Max, of course.'

'Yes, dear Max.'

A sullen silence gripped the room before Stubbs folded his arms and considered Anton with a gentle frown. 'I know what happened to him, Anton,' he said. 'It wasn't your fault.'

Stubbs' confession shocked Anton, even if he didn't immediately show it. He knew that sooner or later, someone would discover his awful secret. At least it was Stubbs, a man of integrity and someone Anton had grown to respect. 'I should ask you how you found out, but then I have a feeling you won't be able to tell me.'

'On the contrary, old chap, it was all rather routine. After the war ended, we wanted to find out more about Max's death. He was one of our top agents. During our investigation, we interrogated several Ustaše operatives in Austria, who were aware of the events that led to his execution. It wasn't difficult to draw some conclusions once we found out that you were arrested in Šibenik on the same day that Max was killed.'

'So, what now?'

'I don't think you're in any danger if that's what you're asking. As the US General Sherman once said, "War is hell." You decided to save a man's life, and it had horrific repercussions for another person. But I would like to think that most reasonable people would understand your motives. Perhaps even Max himself.'

'Does Đujić know?'

'Possibly. Probably. I don't know. But in the end, you tried to save the life of a Serbian Orthodox priest. As I said, most people would praise you for that.'

'But, nevertheless, you still have come to Germany to tell me this.'

'Only because I think you should reconsider moving to America. All of Đujić's people are joining him there. If you follow them, you will inevitably be dragged into their world, whether you like it or not. Perhaps some hard-nosed Chetnik who doesn't like you will eventually find out about Max and decide to blow what happened all out of proportion. Then what? Do you really want to face that situation?'

Anton shook his head. 'Of course not.'

'Then perhaps it's time for you to consider other options. I can get you and your family a guaranteed spot on a ship called the *SS Wooster Victory*. It leaves Genoa next Wednesday for Australia.'

'Australia? Really?' Anton briefly considered the pale blue sky above him and then dropped his eyes. 'Australia is so far away. What would I do there?'

'It's a young country that's modernising at a ferocious pace after the war. I am sure there will be many opportunities available for a talented man like you. And most importantly, it's as far away as one can be from Yugoslavia. You can start a completely new life without ever worrying about the past catching up with you.'

'And you can do this for me?'

'Yes. Otherwise, I wouldn't be here.'

'Why do you want to help me after all this time?'

'The British Government, well, the former SOE at least, owes you a lot, Anton. It's the least we can do after what happened.'

Later that afternoon, Anton consulted his doctor friend. He was emphatic in his response. 'Do it, Anton! For the sake of your children, don't even think twice about it!'

By the time he forced himself to have the conversation with Vuka, Anton had already made up his mind to accept Stubbs' offer. As always, Vuka was less convinced by her husband's intricate plans.

'Where do you want to take me now?' she screamed hysterically when he told her of his decision. 'It's the other side of the world! I will never see my family again!'

'No matter where we go, there is a good chance that we will never return to Yugoslavia. You have to accept that.'

'But I once read that deranged killers roam the Australian countryside while wild animals live in the main streets of the cities. It's not safe for our children.'

'Staying in this God-forsaken camp isn't good for our children either. We must take this opportunity now. Who knows when another one will present itself again?'

After she calmed down from the initial shock, Vuka also consulted the doctor. 'It's the only way, Vuka,' he explained calmly. 'I can't guarantee that Dubravka or Dragan will last another three months here, the way things are.'

As always, Vuka's maternal instinct trumped everything else in her life. Despite her misgivings about living in a country she barely knew anything about, she finally accepted that there was no other option but to take the offer and run. At least her family, which she had fought so hard to protect over the previous four years, would still be together.

'Are there hotdogs in Australia?' Dubravka asked wistfully when her Tata told her the news.

'I don't know, Dubravka,' he said sadly, realising at last that his American dream was over. 'I really don't know.'

There was an extraordinary flurry of activity once the decision was made. Within forty-eight hours, the family, together with Stubbs as their guide and benefactor, were on a train to the port city of Genoa.

Dubravka was thrilled to see the beautiful Italian countryside once again and spent the first day of their trip enchanted by the blossoming summer sunshine. Although she had never heard of Australia before then, she was excited that her life of living behind barbed wire was finally coming to an end.

Then early on the second morning, as Mama, Tata and the nice man from England were still fast asleep in their seats, she noticed something strange about Dragan, who was lying next to her. Without warning, he started to have a series of coughing fits that bellowed into her eardrum. They certainly didn't sound like any cough she had heard from him before. *I should wake the adults and tell them.*

'Jesus Christ,' Stubbs sighed. 'It's bloody whooping cough.'

'We are cursed,' Anton said bleakly. 'I can't believe our bad luck.'

'What do we do now?' Vuka sobbed as she cradled her sick little son in her arms.

'Nothing,' Stubbs finally said. 'You do absolutely nothing. Once you are safely on board and miles out to sea, you can then inform the ship's doctor about his condition. But until then, you must remain quiet and do what you can to stop him from coughing publicly.'

As plans go, it was a pretty crazy one, but incredibly, it worked. Once they arrived in Genoa to board the ship, Stubbs took control of everything. He was able to separate the family from the other passengers, and when it was time to board the *SS Wooster Victory*, he rushed them up the gangway before anyone even noticed.

'I don't know how to ever thank you,' an emotional Anton said as he turned to face the former SOE officer. 'We owe you our lives.'

'Just hurry up, Anton, for goodness sake.' As if especially choreographed for an epic wartime movie, Anton and Stubbs saluted each other solemnly while a swirl of band music played in the background. It was a fitting way for both men to say their final goodbyes.

After several hours at sea, Vuka could not hold her tongue any longer. Dragan was suffering from a severe fever, and his sudden coughing fits drew concerned looks from their fellow passengers. After a brief argument with Anton, who thought it was too soon, she demanded to see the ship's doctor. A kind-hearted middle-aged Italian man with a shoe-horn-shaped face and a wispy moustache, the doctor thankfully didn't judge her when Vuka revealed that Dragan had been coughing for most of the day. He simply jotted down some notes on a crinkled writing pad before beckoning to a nearby steward.

'This little boy has whooping cough,' he said matter-of-factly. 'We need to isolate him and his family immediately.' Within the hour, the entire family was locked away in their own private cabin, where, incredibly, they spent the rest of their journey to Australia in relative luxury. In years to come, Dubravka would always be grateful that her little brother conspired to catch whooping cough when he did, solely to give her a luxurious voyage.

*

On a warm November morning in 1948, after a journey that took almost three months, the *SS Wooster Victory* sailed quietly into Sydney Harbour, carrying within its hull hundreds of displaced people from all over Europe. They were part of Australia's large post-war migrant intake that would forever change the country's culture, values and way of life.

These conflicting cultures, of course, would initially spawn intolerable racism and isolation on many fronts, something Anton would first experience only hours later when handing over his family's immigration papers.

'Occupation?' the overweight, gruff official demanded.

Anton stood proudly. 'Marine engineer.'

The immigration official guffawed. 'Forget about that, mate. You're nothing but a labourer now.'

As Anton's thick eyebrows registered their disgust at that very idea, the immigration official turned to his colleague at the desk next to him and winked. 'These wogs. Nothing but whinging bludgers.' It was a comment that Anton would never forget for the rest of his life.

But for now, naïve to the additional challenges his heritage would bring, Anton was swept up in this joyful and historical moment; his family lineage would soon spread its roots in this fertile new soil.

Among the scores of excited faces who dropped their jaws in wonderment at their first sight of the Sydney Harbour Bridge, Anton tussled his windswept hair and studied the cloudless sky as the ship sailed into port. After his cursed existence during the war—the years of spying, trying to save Father Lukic, surviving the horrors of Padene, leading desperate people across rugged mountains and wild rivers, fighting for his life at the Isonzo River, and negotiating years of internment in refugee camps—Anton finally had the one thing he had always wanted. Hope. For as long as he lived, he would never have hope taken away from him or his family again.

Part Five

Reassessments

Chapter One

Eboli, Italy
October 2022

Whether it was a cathartic response to the questions I had carried with me for so long or just a symptom of my unremitting exhaustion, I began to cry as soon as I stepped onto the platform at Eboli station on a cool Saturday morning in October 2022. After avoiding my destiny for so long, I was finally about to come face-to-face with my family's history, and I was tormented with emotion. What I expected to find here, seventy-five years after my family departed to Germany, I wasn't sure, but its potential offerings had haunted me ever since I left Rome earlier that morning.

After I wiped away my half-frozen tears, I made my way to a small café attached to the station, where I was met by a local guide called Mario. He was your typically handsome thirty-something single Italian male straight from Hollywood casting; curly jet-black hair, ocean-blue eyes that sparkled in the sunshine, and a deep brown tan that would have made most men envious. He spoke excellent English with a raw, staccato accent, occasionally stuttering his words to emphasise a particular point. His company, however, was easy and polite, and as soon as we entered his red Audi Q2 (a present from his rich real estate father), we fell into a rollicking conversation about football.

After we briefly debated who would win the upcoming Champions League game between Napoli and Liverpool, he drove me towards the southerly edge of the town, where he explained in vivid detail the disposition of the camp and how Eboli must have looked in the mid-1940s. There were no distinctive reminders of the camp's former existence from what I could discern, but having examined a number of photos from a historical website before I left Australia, certain features, like the Montedoro spur line that surrounded the town, looked familiar. As we slowly walked through several cluttered streets towards the centre of town and the local marketplace, I felt touched by the town's simplicity and understated charm. It was hard to imagine that life for the local people had changed all that much since the war.

'Do the locals still talk about the camp?' I asked Mario softly.

'Not really,' Mario replied. 'Some of the old timers might discuss it with you if they are in the mood. We respect its place in our town's history, but by and large, it was a time to forget.'

'I understand,' I replied respectfully. 'Eboli suffered terribly during the war.'

Mario smiled. 'You know, Alex, I take hundreds of tourists around the Salerno district every year, and you're the first person I have ever met that has said something like that to me. Thank you for making that observation. Sometimes, I think the world forgot about Eboli's suffering.'

'The world forgets past suffering far too easily,' I said. 'That's why it's in such a mess today.'

'Amen to that.'

We soon reached Eboli's simple marketplace just as a police siren wailed in the distance. It was Saturday morning, and understandably, the area was thriving with weekend stalls hawking everything from fresh fruit and an assortment of flowers to the most intricate handicrafts. The crowd was gathering quickly, and the local stall owners were growing impatient. I reached into my pocket for some cash and bought a bag of peaches from a wizened old lady with a crooked smile—more to feel better about myself than anything else. Mario smiled at my generosity, then cheekily stole one of the peaches when I wasn't looking. 'Come, let's see some more,' he offered before taking a lazy bite of my peach.

As we passed through a group of children enjoying gelato, I stopped suddenly in my tracks and stared into the pale sun. I had become curiously afflicted by an attack of déjà vu. I couldn't remember ever experiencing such an overwhelming feeling.

Have I walked through this marketplace before? Perhaps on a previous trip to Italy?

Nonsense. You have never been to Eboli before.

But it feels so familiar …

Cut it out; you're scaring me!

'What is it, Alex?' Mario asked with a smile, watching my face in fascination.

'Oh, nothing really.'

'Quite the contrary. You feel that you have been here before, don't you?'

I wrinkled my nose at him. 'How could you possibly know that?'

'In my experience, most first-time visitors to Eboli who had relatives inside the camp get a similar eerie feeling. It's almost as if your family's past has found a way of catching up with you.'

We laughed together at the craziness of the whole thing before I offered to buy him lunch at a little restaurant just near the town square. Over coffee, he asked me whether I had found what I was looking for now that I had seen Eboli for myself. I told him truthfully that I wasn't yet sure.

'Perhaps that's an indication that it's time for you to forget the past.'

Rather than press the point further, Mario politely changed the topic, and we resumed our earlier conversation about football. With time to spare, we then visited the moving Museum of Operation Avalanche, which detailed Eboli's horrible destruction as a result of the Allied invasion of Italy. Afterwards, Mario drove me back to the station, took a few photos on my phone of me staring dolefully across the platform and then, like a concerned parent, ushered me onto the Salerno-bound train. I spent most of the return trip to Rome wondering what the poor guy made of my clumsy reconciliation with my long-lost family.

Later that night, I left my hotel near Termini Station and wandered down Via Cavour to have dinner at one of my favourite local restaurants. This was my third night in the Eternal City. I had made a last-minute decision to fly to Italy following the completion of my research in Croatia. I was already prepared to begin my return journey to Australia when, overcome with emotion after visiting the memorial at the site of the Jasenovac concentration camp, I felt an impulsive need to visit both Eboli and Palmanova.

So, without thinking through the implications, I tweaked my return ticket to Australia with the help of a friendly customer service officer, and then managed to strike a cheap business class deal with Air Italia to Rome. Given that my stay was coming to an end, I planned to catch a train to Venice in the morning and relax in that beautiful city for a day or two before travelling to Palmanova via Trieste. From there, I would take the train to Munich and then Berlin, where I would ultimately catch my return flight to Australia.

As I tucked into a plate of homemade ravioli, I reconsidered the question Mario had asked me during lunch and subsequently decided that my trip to Eboli had largely been a waste of time. Of course, it felt special to visit a town that played such a significant role in the lives of my family. But in reality, I obtained no additional insights into my overarching exam question: *Was my father's wartime service directly linked to my shooting?*

To be honest, I wasn't sure what could be found by simply walking through the town with a local tour guide. Through my research in Croatia, together with what I was told by Mum and Dubravka, I now possessed an excellent understanding of what Dad did during the war; his failures, his successes, and the people he pissed off along the way.

By the time he reached Eboli, my father was a man who had become sick of fighting and downtrodden by the insanity of Yugoslav politics. He had lost his family in Dubrovnik forever and witnessed many of his friends needlessly killed. He was then looking to turn a new page, to find a way of reclaiming his life without a gun being pointed at his head every day. From what I could tell, he did not make any new enemies in Eboli or Germany and seemed genuinely respected by everyone.

Of course, there was Ilic and his unhinged vendetta, and the whole thing with Max and Yuri, but those issues appeared to have been resolved once the family had left Europe for good. Dad was now his own man.

As I paid my bill and began the walk back to my hotel, I started to think about the comment that the immigration official made to Dad when he first arrived in Sydney.

You're nothing but a labourer now.

Those six words stung my father hard and had an indelible influence on his life. How do I know? Because he told me several times, especially when I became lost and desperate in my own life during my twenties.

'You don't know how it felt,' he once said to me when we lived in Redcliffe, a suburb north of Brisbane. 'To go through what I did, to lead men into battle day after day and to watch many of them die, only to have some ignorant Australian make fun of me.'

The one thing that stood out from our conversation was the extreme bitterness in his voice. And who could blame him? In some ways, I experienced that same ignorance myself when I was growing up. In Year Eight, we were asked to present in front of our class an anecdote about our parents. When it came to my turn, I proudly regaled some of Dad's wartime experiences. But when I mentioned the part about Dad carrying Dubravka in one hand and shooting a rifle with his other, my teacher angrily berated me for not taking the task seriously and inventing a bullshit story. The humiliation I felt that day remained with me for years.

So, Dad's reaction was perfectly understandable from my perspective; a classic example of a soldier who had faced death regularly during wartime, only to lose his identity once he returned to civilian life and a new country. I personally witnessed similar responses from many veterans I encountered over the years, especially those who had been medically discharged after returning from operational service. Feelings of loss and alienation, combined with an inability to readjust to normal life, are all contributing factors to the unacceptable level of suicide within our proud veteran community. If I was being honest, one of the main reasons I spent a significant part of my career working with veterans was a sense of obligation I felt towards my father and how he failed to deal effectively with his own wartime trauma.

As I stopped at a street corner to buy a gelato, I began to replay Dad's immigration interview over and over again in my head. There was something missing here, something screaming to be discovered. I just didn't know what. Then, after a few ill-considered slurps of my strawberry and mango gelato, it suddenly dawned on me. My father's arrival card!

Belinda had found it online through the Australian National Library just before I left Australia. It was a standard document of its type used in 1948 by immigration officials, recording the basic personal details of the new migrant. What Belinda and I had found interesting, however, was under the question of 'Religion', someone had initially typed 'Orthodox' before crossing it out with a black pen and writing 'RC' (Roman Catholic) in the space next to it.

I could only assume that these alterations were made by my father. But why would he do that? And at what stage did he change his mind and ask for that specific amendment to be made? Was it after he was ridiculed by the immigration official? Having spent so much of the war trying to convince himself and the Chetniks that he had converted to Serbian Orthodox, Dad suddenly decided that he was a Roman Catholic again? It all seemed very strange. This was the same guy who, four years before, had risked his life and the lives of his own family and Max by standing up for a Serbian Orthodox priest after he was arrested. The only reason I could find for his change of heart was that he saw it as a way of ingratiating himself with his new country by distancing himself deliberately from his Chetnik past.

For someone who had a basic understanding of how the spy game worked, it seemed to me that Dad, an experienced intelligence operative, was creating a new narrative or 'legend' for himself. Furthermore, throughout the time I lived with him, he never once marched on Anzac

Day with other Chetniks, nor did he ever join one of the many local Chetnik associations. On the very few occasions he spoke to me about his wartime service, he always referred to himself as a royalist fighter. It was as if he had completely disassociated himself with the word Chetnik. But why and for what purpose? And if I was right, did its repercussions eventually lead to Kandos and my shooting? Perhaps I was overreaching, but suddenly, I had a new line of inquiry to consider.

Chapter Two

Rome, Italy
October 2022

When I returned to my tiny hotel room that evening, I reached for my phone and found the mp4 file of a recorded interview that Belinda and I conducted with Dubravka several weeks ago as part of our investigation. As it stood, I hadn't yet taken the opportunity to review this important material. But if I were to progress my latest theory any further, I needed to reassess Dad's early life in Australia. And there was no one better to help fill those gaps for me than my oldest sister.

I fast-forwarded the recording until I reached the part where Dubravka started to talk about the family's arrival in Australia. She had just turned eight, and she had already spent half of her life crossing wild mountain ranges, being pursued by lunatics who wanted to kill her and being incarcerated inside several internment/resettlement camps. She had never attended a proper school, never watched a film in a cinema, never had a birthday party and never drunk a chocolate milkshake with her friends at the local milk bar. Her memories mostly involved death, destruction and despair, but she clung to a hope that the world would soon turn in her favour.

'Then, when we arrived in Australia, we were told that we were being sent to Bonegilla for two years. I cannot tell you how depressed that made all of us feel.'

The Bonegilla Migrant Reception and Training Centre was established in 1947 in response to the hundreds of thousands of migrants who arrived in Australia after the war. A former army barracks situated between the twin towns of Albury and Wodonga on the New South Wales/Victorian border, new arrivals were sent to Bonegilla to learn how to become valued citizens in their adopted country.

Despite that noble intent, the living quarters, which housed migrants from all over Europe, were basic and far from ideal; fit for service personnel perhaps, but not especially so for young families. According to my sister, the lack of ventilation inside these weather-beaten, timber-framed huts made life very uncomfortable. As a result, summertime could be excruciatingly hot at night, while winter often felt like a day trip to Antarctica. Most rooms didn't contain any partitioning, which meant little to no privacy for their inhabitants.

'Living in those huts wasn't especially fun,' Dubravka began, 'but as much as I can remember, life was significantly better than in post-war Europe. For example, there was a library for us children to use, as well as a cinema to enjoy. Sometimes, we even went on local excursions to the country. These were absolute luxuries for someone like me who lost most of my early childhood to the war.'

'How did Dad react to living in Bonegilla?' I asked.

'I can't remember anything that really stands out apart from our initial disappointment at being sent to another camp. I do remember that upon arrival, we were divided along national lines, so all the Yugoslavs were together. But for some reason, they also segregated the men from the women, which meant that most families, already anxious about living in a new country, were often split up. How ridiculous! In our case, Dad and our brother lived in one hut, while Mum and I were lodged elsewhere. But from what I seem to recall, both Mum and Dad were reasonably happy at first.'

I pressed pause for a moment and thought back to the time I had discussed Bonegilla with my mother several years before she died. I happened to be visiting the Army Logistics Training Centre at Latchford Barracks in Albury/Wodonga for my work with Defence when I suddenly realised that I was standing beside the old Bonegilla camp. Excited by this discovery, I called Mum on my mobile phone to tell her.

To my surprise, Mum was actually excited as well! In our ten-minute conversation, she told me so many stories about her life at Bonegilla that I simply couldn't keep up with her. Two things struck me at the time. First, she told me that she had virtually taught herself English by reading old copies of the *Women's Weekly* magazines. I found that especially funny, given her lifelong obsession with celebrity gossip. The other issue that stood out for me was far more serious.

'There were lots of Ustaše at Bonegilla,' Mum had said. 'Your father wasn't happy about that, and he told this to everyone who would listen. You know what he was like!'

I was already late for my next meeting, so I had hurriedly ended the call before she could expand on her statement further. What confused the issue for me was that Mum often referred to all Croats as Ustaše, even though she was an ethnic Croat herself. Was she talking about ordinary Croatian refugees who had escaped Communist rule or actual former Ustaše fighters? Sadly, I had never asked Mum for clarification, and she carried her answer with her to her grave.

I resumed Dubravka's interview and heard her speak for several more minutes about other aspects of her life at Bonegilla. I then got to the part that I particularly wanted to hear again—when I raised with her the issue of Dad's infamous conversation with the immigration official. Unsurprisingly, she had a different take on it than mine.

'Let's be clear, Alex,' she began. 'What happened to Dad also happened to most other migrants at the time. They were also humiliated and ridiculed and told that they no longer held professional qualifications and were, in effect, labourers. What you have to remember is that new arrivals were more or less indentured by the government. That meant that officials at Bonegilla could direct them to do whatever work was needed at the time, and what they needed mostly back then were labourers.'

'So, you think your father used it as an excuse to justify things when they didn't go well for him?' Belinda asked.

'Absolutely! Many of the people I just spoke about, regardless of their nationality and personal circumstances, shrugged off these insults, worked damn hard and achieved great personal success, becoming highly productive members of the Australian community. In the end, Dad's failure to reach the heights he had imagined for himself was down to him and no one else. Australia offered him a way forward, a second chance, and he never fully grasped that opportunity.'

Dubravka and I were never going to agree on this issue, that much was certain. But I fully understood her point of view. I could afford to be sympathetic to Dad's plight. Despite all the madness associated with our family, he gave me a relatively stable childhood and an education, and I felt obligated to him for that. But Dubravka's experience was different, and she saw right through his endless self-pity.

'As it turned out, we didn't stay in Bonegilla for very long,' Dubravka continued. 'I never understood why when so many other families were trapped there for the full two years. But by mid-1949, we returned to Sydney. Mum and Dad were absolutely ecstatic. Initially, we lived on a farm in Pendle Hill, near Parramatta. The owner was a lovely Croatian man who didn't care much for Yugoslav politics or what Dad did during the war. He actually turned his work shed into a temporary home for us, would you believe?'

'A shed!' I interrupted, laughing at the thought.

'Actually,' Dubravka continued, 'it wasn't as bad as it sounds. In fact, for the most part, we lived reasonably comfortably. Dad spent most weeks away, working on building sites and returning home on weekends. He also began studying to regain his technical qualifications. Mum found odd jobs here and there. We socialised a lot with other Yugoslavs and Dad helped them establish their own club. Given his war hero status and undeniable charisma, it didn't take him long to become club president, a role he kept for many years. So, at first, things looked promising for our family.'

Dubravka went on to describe her first day at school. Having never spent any time in a formal educational setting and barely able to speak or read English, she was extremely nervous when she entered her new classroom for the first time.

'I didn't know what to expect,' she admitted. 'I looked at all the other children in the room, and I thought they were going to eat me up.'

But she needn't have worried. She made new friends easily, and soon, her natural intelligence and willingness to learn shone through. Within three years, she was at the top of her class and exceeding in sport. Later, she became school captain and represented New South Wales in under-age basketball. Academically, the world was at her feet, but Dubravka's deteriorating family situation would soon conspire against her.

'Where to begin?' Dubravka said with a tinge of regret. 'Dad had two major weaknesses in his life—money and women. And when they came together, it destroyed everything in its path.'

As Dubravka explained further, Anton's best friend had a sister called Nada, who was married to a former Italian Army officer. From the moment Anton and Nada met, they created a sexual explosion together that couldn't be contained. Nada was stunningly beautiful, with a Marylin Monroe figure and an extroverted personality that left every man who knew her completely breathless and wanting more.

For Dad, the thrill of the chase was just as exciting as the actual sex act itself. Whereas Vuka, to him, was staid and boring, Nada was exciting and sensual. He had to have her, even if it meant losing everything in the process. And, of course, her sexuality and haughtiness brought back vivid memories of the one woman who had kept him alive during the war— Ilsa. In retrospect, Mum and Nada's husband never stood a chance.

Almost overnight, Anton and Nada began a highly passionate affair under the noses of everyone they knew. In fact, you might argue that they didn't even pretend to hide their lust for each other. They had it off in the cinema. They had it off on the beach. They even had it off in Nada's own house with her husband in the next room. It took cuckoldry to a new level. And then, when you thought Anton couldn't get any more 'pussy-struck', he sold the block of land he had bought for his family in Merrylands and moved them to Bankstown just so he could be near Nada.

But illicit affairs that cause so much collateral damage are always destined to fail spectacularly. And such was the case with this one. You see, Anton and Nada's husband suddenly decided to go into business together. They stupidly bought a new car on hire purchase to help them in their endeavours, even though neither of them had a driver's license.

Both men blamed each other for the ensuing accident, but whoever's fault it was, they somehow managed to ram themselves up the arse of another vehicle in broad daylight. Maybe the fact that neither man could really drive contributed to the situation. In any case, both cars were a complete write-off. Apart from not having driving licenses, neither man considered purchasing insurance either. In a flash, they were soon up for thousands of dollars in damages, money that neither of them remotely had. Faced with serious debts, the relationship eventually cooled. Love's never quite the same when you owe the other party lots of money!

The toll that Dad's madcap affair and accident had on the family was incalculable. Unsurprisingly, no one suffered more than Mum.

'What you have to understand, Alex,' Dubravka said, 'is that Mum always had mental health issues, even as a young girl. Add to that the traumas she faced during the war, Dad's secret life and other infidelities, their lack of money and the loss of her family, and you can understand why she fell apart when she found out about Nada. On top of that, in the middle of Dad's affair, she gave birth to our sister, Rosemary.'

Mum would suffer several mental breakdowns during this period and survived at least one suicide attempt. There was no easy ride back to normalcy for her; perhaps she never fully recovered from her ordeal and remained sadly tormented until the day she died.

As for Dubravka and my brother, the constant moving, the fear of being discovered by the authorities, and all the madness that went with their nomadic, dislocated lives had a debilitating impact on their education. All of my siblings are incredibly intelligent people, but while

Rosemary and I were blessed with a tertiary education, neither Dubravka nor my brother were afforded the same opportunities. Given her ability to structure an argument, analyse complex issues and recall details quickly, Dubravka would have made an excellent lawyer. However, in the middle of her highly disrupted senior year, she was offered a job at a bank in the city. Without even thinking twice about it, she accepted the offer immediately and left school. Together with her part-time modelling, she was making her own money for the first time in her life.

In an attempt to keep the creditors at bay, Dad decided to move to Cooma, inner News South Wales, in 1957 with my brother, where he joined hundreds of other migrant workers in building the famous Snowy Mountains Scheme, the largest engineering project in Australia's history. Meanwhile, our mentally unwell mother was expected to look after her new baby, Rosemary, by herself, while shacked up in the middle of suburban Sydney with little money and only Dubravka for support. Things inevitably grew too much for her, and after another mental breakdown, she was committed for several months in a mental institution.

'Finally, Dad returned from Cooma after a year away,' Dubravka continued. 'God knows why, but he tried very hard to bring the family back together. He still had debts that he kept running away from, and he still lived a mysterious life that no one was allowed to ask about, but he seemed determined to make things work with Mum. Gradually, we all got back together as a family, and by the early 1960s, we found ourselves in Lane Cove, on Sydney's north shore.'

'And that's where I came into it,' I said with a chuckle.

'Oh yes!' Dubravka laughed. 'But first, let's talk about the other important event that occurred around that same time. One Sunday afternoon, I was having drinks with my girlfriends at the Coogee Bay Hotel when this handsome Greek man sitting at a nearby table sent me a bunch of flowers. I played very hard to get that afternoon, but he persisted gamely over the next few weeks, and we soon fell in love. I then had to decide between a modelling career that was about to take off or marriage. I chose the latter. Sixty years later, and we are still happily together.'

'What a wonderful story!' Belinda said. 'And Alex was born around this time?'

'Yes, my youngest brother was born six months before our wedding,' Dubravka continued. 'And, of course, he should thank me for entering this world! I was the one who delivered him in our home at Lane Cove. The little monster that he was, he just popped out when we least expected it.'

'If Mum had her way,' I interrupted, 'I wouldn't have popped out at all. She wanted to have me aborted several times during her pregnancy.'

'You can thank Dad for that,' Dubravka said. 'He promised Mum, who mentally wasn't able to cope with the thought of another baby, that he had found someone to do the abortion, but like everything in his life, it was all a pack of lies.'

We all chuckled at that point of the interview before Dubravka talked some more about her wedding.

'It was so lovely,' Dubravka enthused. 'We had over two hundred guests, and Dad was beaming throughout the reception. He seemed to think that it was all about him.'

'There is something about European fathers and weddings,' Belinda said. 'It's the most important day of their life when they pass on responsibility for their daughter to another man.'

'Yes, you're right.' Dubravka laughed. 'And given his ego, he wanted to make a big splash as well, given all the important people he made me invite.'

'What important people?' I asked casually.

'I must have told you before, Alex. The Minister for the Army, John Gardner, attended our wedding.'

I pressed stop on the recording with a trembling finger and then stared outside my hotel window at all the hobos, the street tramps and the drug pushers congregating in front of Termini Station. At this moment in time, their lives seemed so much simpler than mine.

How the fuck did I miss that? Was I even listening to Dubravka that day? The army minister attended Dubravka's wedding? For God's sake!

I now had to face a new reality; perhaps Dad was involved in something much bigger than I ever thought. And as game changers went, this was likely to be the grandaddy of them all.

Chapter Three

Palmanova, Italy
October 2022

As I strolled past the lively Piazza Centrale in Palmanova for the tenth time that morning, I still didn't know what I was supposed to be looking for or how long I would stay before returning to Verona. I seemed to have been walking around in exaggerated circles for an eternity, hoping that some lightbulb moment would suddenly direct me to the exact location where the Chetniks had surrendered to the Allies in May 1945. This was definitely turning out to be one of those 'feel it and fuck it' trips into the unknown that I had become renowned for, where more often than not, I left empty-handed and thoroughly frustrated with myself.

Surprisingly, though, for a town that I had merely come to associate with the war, I was struck by its innocent charm and the beauty of its architecture, especially the magnificent Duomo church. Perhaps it was my Venetian blood, but I immediately felt a strange kinship with the local people who hurried past me, distant smiles toying on their lips. It was almost as if they had been expecting me.

But I wasn't there as a tourist. I was there as a son and a sibling to honour the place that saved our family and to consider the awful implications if Dad hadn't safely led his brigade across the Isonzo River that day. There was no question in my mind that Dad, Mum and Dubravka would have been killed by the Partisans had they been captured in Slovenia. It was hardly comforting to know that for want of a centimetre or two, our family would have been condemned forever as mere particles of dust swirling inside an unrelenting wind.

I battled aimlessly around the town for another hour, the echoes of the past beating louder with every breath. If I had any lingering doubts about the futility of my quest, now was the time to reconsider while here in Palmanova, where my family was given a second chance at life. But if anything, visiting the town had only reinvigorated my desire to find the truth. To quit now, when so much was at stake, would not only be dishonouring my family's past but also its future. And I was far too indebted to my own legacy to ever allow that to happen.

Twenty-four hours later, I was on a train to Munich, admiring the rolling green pastures of the Austrian countryside. I was doing my best to avoid thinking about my father until I was safely locked away in my hotel room later that night. Needing something more than the delightful scenery to pass the time, I tried to read some more of my book about Napoleon. But when I grew frustrated with the lunacy of his retreat from Moscow, I flung on my headphones and found the *Best of Duran Duran* on my phone.

For some reason, whenever I needed to escape my self-imposed apathy, a dose of Duran Duran often came to the rescue. My close friend, Luke, always insisted that my life could have been different had I taken an interest in Duran Duran at a much earlier age. Lately, I had come to agree with him.

But after I tapped away to *A View to a Kill*, *Girls on Film* and *Hungry Like a Wolf*, I realised that I had to face the inevitable sooner rather than later. I reluctantly turned my music off and reached into my backpack for a notebook and pen. Having the luxury of a first-class seat to myself, I stretched back and started to write.

The first thing I wanted to do was summarise all the key findings about Dad I had discovered during my journey so far. I scratched and scribbled for ten minutes before I came up with this exhaustive list:

- Between 1941 and 1944, Dad seemingly worked for the British SOE as a spy.
- He had a terrible weakness for beautiful women, having undertaken several disastrous extra-marital affairs.

- He made a long-term enemy of an influential Chetnik officer following a botched operation on the Island of Brač.
- At some point in 1943 or 1944, he changed his religion to Serbian Orthodox.
- He befriended a Serbian Orthodox priest and was arrested by local police when he publicly came to his aid.
- A close colleague was possibly identified and killed as a result of his arrest.
- He was forced to leave Šibenik in late 1944 and joined a local Chetnik unit, most likely the Dinara Chetnik Division, where he became a highly respected commander.
- His name appeared on several 'death lists' produced by both the Partisans and the Ustaše.
- He fought at the Battle of Knin and was wounded during the retreat from Pađene.
- He led his brigade across the Lika region of Croatia through Istria, Slovenia, and eventually to Italy.
- On the last day of the war, he fought a pitched battle with the Partisans before leading his men and civilian cohorts across the Isonzo River into Italy.
- He was a firm supporter of Draža Mihailović and ferociously denied that he ever collaborated with the Germans, the Italians or the Ustaše.
- He changed his religion back to Roman Catholic when he arrived in Australia.
- He raised concerns to the authorities about the number of Ustaše refugees residing in Bonegilla.
- He never joined any Chetnik association in Australia but was president of a local Sydney Yugoslav club.
- During his time living in Sydney, he accumulated large debts and was constantly running away from creditors.
- He maintained a secret lifestyle in Sydney, which he never

accounted for.

- The Minister for the Army, John Gardner, attended his daughter's wedding.
- After the wedding, he eventually moved the family to Kandos, two hundred and thirty kilometres west of Sydney, where he accepted a senior position at the local cement works. He left Sydney without telling his friends or Dubravka of his intentions or whereabouts.

If you looked at these events individually, it would be virtually impossible to draw evidential conclusions about my father with any confidence. But if I learnt one thing during my time in the Army Reserve and Defence, it was to 'never fight the green'. If something seemed obvious, then most likely it was. After I merged all of these disparate issues into one coherent storyline, a clear and uncontested pattern emerged of a man who continued his clandestine lifestyle well after he migrated to Australia.

To expand my reasoning further, I revisited the context of what was happening in Australia at the time. Between 1945 and 1963, more than fifty thousand Yugoslav migrants had moved to Australia. The majority of that figure consisted of Croatian nationals, some of whom hoped to continue the fight for an independent Croatia from the shores of their adopted home.

During the 1950s and 1960s, a highly nationalistic and anti-Communist Croatian movement began to prosper, comprising three right-wing organisations—the Croatian Liberation Movement (HOP), the Croatian National Resistance (HNO) and the Croatian Revolutionary Brotherhood (HRB). Their ultimate aim was to liberate Croatia from Communist rule through armed excursions into the Yugoslav state. To facilitate this, some young Croatian males joined the Citizen Military Force (today's army reserve) to obtain high-level military skills. At the same time, a number of secret right-wing Croatian training camps were also established in remote locations across the country.

For more than a decade, there would be bungled raids in Yugoslavia itself and a series of bomb attacks against Yugoslav interests in Australia.

Who was responsible for the bulk of those attacks continues to be the subject of controversy. Given the threat to internal Yugoslav security, its main intelligence service, the UBDa, slowly began to establish a foothold in Australia, and they did everything possible to foster public resentment against the Croatian community.

Claims were made that the UBDa was behind some of the terrorist plots initially blamed on the Croatian groups. Indeed, that became the central issue behind the ongoing controversy involving the Croatian Six, a case that I had recently become obsessed with.

In 1981, six Croatian Australians living in the New South Wales town of Lithgow were sentenced to fifteen years in jail for conspiring to bomb several targets in Sydney after one of the longest trials in Australian legal history. Following various unsuccessful appeals, the matter attracted ongoing media scrutiny, with several sources alleging that this was a classic UBDa sting operation. The New South Wales Supreme Court had recently ordered a review into the matter.

It took Australia's security organisations, such as the Australian Security Intelligence Organisation (ASIO), many years to combat the threat of Croatian extremism and dedicate appropriate resources to the problem. ASIO's overall handling of the issue and claims that they were hiding the identities of Croatian terrorists would ultimately lead to a highly controversial raid on its headquarters in 1973 by the then Labor Attorney General, Lionel Murphy.

But for the purposes of my investigation, it was important to note that the organisations involved in the surveillance of the Croatian groups, such as ASIO, the then Commonwealth Police and the Victorian and New South Wales Police Forces, all used informants within the Yugoslav community to provide them with much-needed intelligence. Was my father one of them? Did his involvement lead to my shooting in 1966?

To answer that question, I first revisited John Gardner's attendance at my sister's wedding. My family were extremely grateful for his presence and thought he was a lovely, dignified man. But even in the 1960s, politicians, especially ministers of the crown, had incredibly busy schedules. Given my own experience as a ministerial adviser, it would be extremely unlikely that a minister would accept an unsolicited invitation to a private wedding unless there was a good reason to do so. Why would Mr Gardner take a whole afternoon and night out of his precious diary unless he thought Dad was a worthy recipient of his time? What did he know about Dad that made him so important in his eyes?

Dubravka's wedding wasn't the only occasion that Dad's apparent connection with the military establishment had come to notice. During Year 10 (at the time, we were living in the Queensland town of Gladstone), I applied to join the navy via its midshipman program. If successful, I would complete my senior years in Jervis Bay, attend university and then undertake my naval training. Dad was absolutely delighted at my decision; I am certain he always felt that I wouldn't amount to very much, so to follow in his footsteps temporarily filled him with pride. To help facilitate my application, he suggested that we both meet with our local federal member in the neighbouring city of Rockhampton.

Honestly, I wasn't sure what Dad expected to achieve with this visit; there was no way on God's Earth that any politician would ruin their reputation by inappropriately influencing a navy officer selection process for some 'wog' kid he had never met before. This wasn't the nineteenth century when patronage from powerful politicians meant everything. I was just a skinny teenager from Gladstone with a reckless dream and an overbearing father who obviously had tickets on himself.

As we entered the politician's office, I was mightily embarrassed that we had the gall to make it as far as we did. But to my surprise, the Member for Capricornia greeted us warmly and then told Dad how honoured he was to meet someone of his stature and reputation. Considering that Dad was employed as a lowly boiler operator at the Queensland Alumina Limited (QAL) factory in Gladstone, it was a curious thing to say, but never once did I doubt his sincerity. I didn't pass my entrance exam, but on that sweltering hot day in Rockhampton, I learnt something new about my father that I would never forget.

The second incident happened many years later when I needed to renew my security clearance for work. Late one Friday afternoon, I had some paperwork associated with my clearance returned to me. Attached to my birth certificate, obviously by mistake, was a yellow post-it note containing some words scribbled in black pen. It took my eyes several minutes to adjust to the scrawled handwriting, but when they did, the result was clear as day. It read, '*Please cross reference with father's file.*'

My father's file. What file?

Without hesitation, I rang my contact officer to ask him about the note, but he tried desperately hard to deny its existence. When I finally had him cornered, and he accepted that he couldn't wriggle out of it any longer, the officer merely huffed down the phone and suggested that the note was put there in error. 'Just toss the note away and forget you ever saw it,' was his final instruction before hanging up.

As always, I did what I was told, but it was bloody hard to forget something that chipped away at my ego every day. Whether they liked it or not, the cat was out of the bag, and my curiosity would not be satisfied until I saw the file for myself. Belinda had already set the wheels in motion a month or so ago by submitting a number of Freedom of Information requests, but my patience was wearing thin.

When I looked at all the facts objectively, it was easy to conclude that Dad had some high-level connection with the government—either through Defence or the security establishment—that was so important even the occasional politician snuggled up to him when they needed to. In every respect, he was the perfect candidate to be an informer or some other kind of operative. He was an experienced spy, he had led people into battle, he had connections within the Yugoslav community, and he possessed more personal charm than he ever knew what to do with. As an ex-girlfriend once said to me, 'Your father makes you feel like you're the only person in the room when he's talking to you.'

I believed this: from the moment Dad entered Australia, he saw an opportunity to become the very important player he was in Yugoslavia by rebranding his past and looking for a new master. No, he wasn't going to be a labourer like they wanted him to be. He knew what he was capable of, what he could achieve when pushed to the limits. All he needed was to find the right people to indulge his fantasies. Having walked between the raindrops myself for so many years, I found it difficult to believe that Australia's security organisations wouldn't have rolled out the red carpet to acquire his services, given what was at stake at the time.

As the train left Austria for good and snaked its way towards Bavaria, I became thoroughly convinced that whatever Dad had been doing for the 'government' somehow blew back on me, an innocent four-year-old boy, on that fateful day in 1966. Perhaps it was a warning or a payback by Croatian extremists who found out that Dad was an informant. Maybe it was a sting operation by the UBDa aimed at putting the blame on the Croats for the shooting of a little boy. After all, given their alleged involvement in the Croatian Six terror plot and the recent announcement of a review into the convictions of the six men, could anyone totally rule out that scenario? And then there was the trip our family took to Lithgow two years after my shooting, when Dad mysteriously disappeared for two hours. *Lithgow once again.* It was all there, waiting to be revealed. All I had to do was to find Dad's security file, and finally I would know the truth.

Chapter Four

Canberra, Australia
November 2022

Sometimes, when you want something very bad and it fails to eventuate, the disappointment can be so intense that nothing else in your life matters. That's exactly how I felt a week later after Belinda broke the news that she had received a response to her Freedom of Information requests.

'And?' I asked impatiently as my eyes flittered in the coarse sunlight.

'There is no security file, Alex,' Belinda's calm voice floated down the phone line.

'What?' I exclaimed a little more rudely than usual. Having only been back in Australia for twenty-four hours, the severe jet lag I was experiencing had added to my foul mood. 'That's impossible.'

'I am sorry, Alex,' Belinda replied. 'But we ran the gauntlet, and this is the official line. There is not much more we can do.'

'But I don't understand.' And I didn't. *How could I have been so wrong?* Over the next few days, I replayed every conversation and reassessed every piece of information to try and find out what I had missed. But all that did was increase my frustration even more. For someone who believed that the 'green' was always correct, it simply didn't make any sense. None of it.

Even if Dad wasn't involved in any secret activities for the Australian Government, surely his status as a former Chetnik brigade commander warranted some form of official interest by the authorities after he arrived in Australia? And what about the politicians and that post-it note? Was all of that just one big misunderstanding? The whole episode hit me with the force of a bullet train, and I casually slipped back into those dark places I had promised myself not so long before that I would never visit again.

Two weeks later, I received a phone call from a friend who used to work with the police. A former colleague of hers had spent several years investigating the Croatian training camps during the sixties and seventies. He was something of an expert on the topic. He was getting on a bit, but he would be more than happy to meet with me. Did I want his contact details?

I was reluctant at first because, in my petulance over the security file that didn't exist, I told everyone around me that I was quitting the project. Not that they believed me. But after I gave it some more thought, I realised that an opportunity like this might not present itself again. So, I gave him a call, introduced myself and offered to meet him at a time and place of his choosing. He sounded particularly gruff and stand-offish at first—perhaps I had woken him up from his mid-morning nap—but soon, his tone became more accommodating.

'I would be happy to meet with you,' he said firmly. 'But it must be on my terms. No recordings, no photos, no emails, no texts, no notes and no public places. We choose a meeting place that I am happy with, preferably where there are no surveillance cameras. Do you agree?'

For a moment, I thought I was talking to the legendary British spy and traitor, Kim Philby. 'Sure,' I replied matter-of-factly.

'And you are to refer to me only as Albert.'

'Suits me fine… Albert.'

After some idle chitchat, we agreed to meet the following morning in Glebe Park, a public expanse on the eastern side of Civic, Canberra's central business district. For a person who wanted his privacy, it seemed a strange place for him to choose, especially given the many other options available in a city as secretive as Canberra.

Even close to nine thirty on a Thursday morning, it was full of young mothers with their hyperactive children, frantically trying to wrestle supremacy at the park's playground precinct.

It wasn't hard to distinguish Albert from the largely millennial crowd. He was a tall, gangly man with thinning grey hair who, despite the walking cane attached to his left hand, carried himself with a professional bearing that demanded your immediate respect. When he saw me walk towards him, he considered me with his suspicious blue eyes and then pointed to a nearby park bench.

'I am assuming you're Alex Gerrick?' he finally asked when we approached our seat.

'You assumed correctly.' We shook hands, and then he nodded towards a nearby café. 'I could do with a coffee,' he said bleakly. 'A long black, with two sugars.'

'The sugar will kill you,' I replied, stony-faced, mildly annoyed that he immediately assumed I would pay.

'I already have one foot in the grave, so tell it to someone who cares.' Fair enough.

'I will be back shortly,' I offered. Ten minutes later, I returned with his black coffee and an extra hot latte for me.

'Thank you,' he muttered before removing the lid to double-check that I had got his order correct. Obviously, a man who had inherited significant trust issues. 'Although I didn't recognise you at first, we have actually met before,' he finally said after taking a couple of sips from his coffee.

'Really? When?'

'At the Interpol Conference in Canberra in 1990,' he replied. 'You were working in the media relations area. We wrote a media response together about white-collar fraud—well, actually, you wrote most of it while I looked on and occasionally barked at you.'

Suddenly, his wrinkled expression grew in familiarity. 'Yes, I do remember now.' I smiled, as it had been one of those brief but rewarding collaborative efforts that I always enjoyed during my time working with the police. Generally speaking, I liked policemen and women, and they liked me. And if I remember correctly, the two of us had enjoyed a beer and a few laughs together later that night.

'We both got old,' I said ruefully.

'You got that right.' We talked some more about his career, his overseas postings and what he had been doing since retirement. Finally, he tossed his coffee cup into a nearby bin and folded his arms.

'I guess we didn't come here to reminisce, did we? How can I help you?'

I told him about my shooting, everything I had learnt about my father, my theories on who was responsible and the response to Belinda's Freedom of Information requests. He took each new bit of information in his stride as if he had heard it all before.

'I wouldn't get too stressed about the Freedom of Information stuff,' he finally admitted. 'Just because there is no security file doesn't mean to say any of your theories are wrong.'

'But the post-it note. I still can't get my head around what it said.'

'Well, maybe you should take some blame for that. You just assumed it referred to a security file that was opened when your father arrived in Australia, but they could have been talking about something else. A Defence file, an old army file, a Commonwealth police file, a New South Wales Special Branch file. The bottom line is that when they process a security clearance, they naturally look at all the relevant details connected to your past, including that of your family. So, if they found information about your father from another agency or source document, then of course those assessing your application would want to see it.'

I suddenly felt like a right idiot because that was something I should have known myself. 'But Dad wasn't just an ordinary displaced person,' I continued. 'According to him, he worked for SOE. He was a Chetnik war hero. Surely, there should have been some scrutiny of his background when he first arrived in Australia.'

'Two things.' Albert enviously gawked at my half-finished coffee before continuing. 'First, your parents arrived in Australia in 1948; ASIO, our main security organisation, wasn't established for another year. Second, I suggest you read the official histories of ASIO; you might learn something. The intelligence apparatus in Australia immediately after the war was a complete cluster fuck. So many right-wing extremists walked through the doors without barely a ripple of contention. Records of these events and conversations were rarely kept in an organised way or shared with other organisations. Even when ASIO was fully operational, they didn't have the appropriate resources to investigate the large majority of Yugoslav immigrants.'

I persisted. 'But someone must have known something about Dad and then recorded it. How do you explain things like the army minister attending my sister's wedding?'

'I can't explain them for certain. As I said before, we are talking about several different agencies that may have established a relationship with your father. But it is logical to speculate, given Gardner's presence at the wedding, that at some point, Defence or the Army department came into contact with him. Maybe he approached them himself, or perhaps the British military tipped them off, which can't be ruled out. He did do work for SOE, after all. Where this information was recorded in a file and who had access to it is something we will never know for sure, but if I were a betting man, I reckon it's either gathering dust somewhere in a Defence warehouse or has since been culled. Those are the breaks, I'm afraid.'

'Then I am screwed,' I said mournfully. Finished with my coffee, I also tossed the cup into the bin and then half-smiled at a pretty young mother who quickly walked past us with her two sons.

'Not necessarily,' Albert replied. 'Tell me, why do you think your father was an informant?'

I shrugged my shoulders. 'It just seemed logical to me. He had raised concerns about the Ustaše while at Bonegilla. My mother said that during those early days in Australia, they were both frightened of their ever-increasing presence. Dad still considered himself a patriot and maybe took it upon himself to shut down the camps. Or, more likely, he just enjoyed living on the edge and feeling important.'

'You must have something more than that.'

I sighed loudly. I had the feeling that Albert was playing with me, trying to determine whether I had some new piece of information that never came his way during his own career. Once I told him all, I was sure he would scurry off into the morning haze, and I would never hear from him again. For the first time since we began our conversation, I regretted meeting with him.

'Dad had a friend in Kandos called Misha,' I finally replied. 'Mum never liked him. I always remember her saying that he was an Ustaše supporter. She and Dad often argued about him, but then, they argued about everything. He was kind to me though, always bought me presents or gave me money. Whenever I saw him after I was shot, he used to ruffle my hair and ask me how I was. He was the only person who ever really showed me any sympathy about the shooting. I liked him.'

'You're still not convincing me,' Albert groaned.

'Perhaps this will. He was from Lithgow.'

'Okay, slightly better.'

'Maybe time has made me over-exaggerate things, but it seemed to me that whenever Dad went to see Misha, he travelled to Lithgow soon afterwards. It is only ninety kilometres away from Kandos, so it takes no more than an hour to get there.'

'Any idea who he went to see?'

'No. However, about eighteen months after my shooting, Dad took Mum, my sister Rosemary and me for a day trip to Lithgow. When he arrived, he dropped us off in the middle of town and told us he had to visit one of Misha's friends. We didn't see him again for another two hours. Mum was worried sick. When he eventually returned, they had yet another almighty blue, but none of us were any the wiser on where he had actually been or who he had seen.'

'I am still not sure where you are heading with this.'

'Fast forward to February 1979. I just came home from school and found Dad in the kitchen, staring at a cup of coffee. He had just returned from his day shift, and he looked white as a ghost. He barely said a word to me, muttered something to himself and then walked off to his room. When I asked my mother what had happened, she simply said that it had something to do with Lithgow. That night, I saw the news; you know the rest. That was the day the Croatian Six were arrested.'

Albert shuffled in his seat and tried to smile. 'You're reaching, Alex. The Croatian Six were not established locals with a long history in the area. They had only recently arrived in Lithgow before they got arrested. Sure, during the 1960s, some Croats worked at the Lithgow power station, but it wasn't a cesspit of extremism by any means. There were no training camps nearby, and there were no plots that were hatched by the locals, as far as I can recall. Suggesting that your father obtained intelligence on something that wouldn't happen for another eleven years is, if you don't mind me saying, quite preposterous.'

His words were delivered with such practical disdain that I jumped to my feet. I was ready to march right the fuck out of there without ever turning back. It was the first time since I started this whole damn thing that someone had actually questioned my integrity. It hurt like hell.

'Please sit down,' Albert said, pulling at my arm. 'I am not here to criticise you; I am here to put you on the right track.'

'What is the right track then?' I asked huffily after I resumed my seat.

'You've got this all back to front.'

'How?' I grizzled back at him.

'For a while, the Croats in Australia obtained an unenviable reputation for being the ultimate bad guys. Every time something suspicious happened, it was immediately blamed on them until we suspected that the UBDa was possibly behind some of these shenanigans. Yes, the Croatian groups did some stupid things. They planted some bombs, harassed and threatened people, rioted at football games and generally made nuisances of themselves. But to shoot a child in cold blood? Absolutely not. That was never in their DNA. If they had committed a crime like that, the regular Croatian community would have disowned them at the drop of a hat, as would the Australian Government. No. Supposing that your father was an informant of some kind, they would have come after him, not you. And in all my time observing these guys, I can't recall one Yugoslav informant ever being murdered by Croatian nationalists inside Australia.'

'What about the UBDa?'

'The same. They were ruthless for sure, but setting the Croats up by deliberately killing a little boy? No way. That wasn't their style, either. The risks of being found out would have been too great. Tito, at the time, was looking to improve relations with the West, not destroy them. Besides, the UBDa wasn't interested in former Chetniks like your father. The main game was to undermine the extremist Croats in Australia as much as possible. For both sides, the Chetniks were old news, nothing to worry about anymore.'

'Then what do you think happened?' I wanted to secretly use my phone to record him, but for now, I allowed my fingers to dangle loosely in my pocket.

'As I said, if your father was the main target, they could have easily taken him out in a small place like Kandos, and hardly anyone would have noticed. No, your shooting was personal, a revenge attack if you like. You took something precious of mine, and now I am going to take something precious of yours. I saw this play out numerous times during the decade I was involved with the Yugoslavs. Petty individual grievances from the war, betrayals that had only come to light recently, and differences of opinion that ended in violence. We all know how impulsive you guys can be when the blood boils and the red mist takes control of your emotions! Think about it. Your own father was concerned about a particular person and what he might find out one day. You should be looking at that possibility, not all that other bullshit we just discussed.'

'You mean Yuri,' I stated coldly.

'Yes. If I were investigating this case, I would try and establish where in the world Yuri was on the day you were shot. If you could do that, then I think you would get closer to the truth than you ever imagined.'

We talked some more about *The Spiders*, Marković and everything else that was bugging me. Albert abruptly advised me to ignore those obvious red herrings. 'Follow the Yuri trail,' he repeated several times before he wished me luck and quickly disappeared into a side street.

I should have gone straight home and mapped out my next plan of attack, but I was too driven with adrenaline. I had what I needed in my notebook, and so I jumped into the nearest taxi and ordered him to take me to the National Library of Australia. Once inside, I dropped myself down at the nearest terminal, pulled out my notebook, flipped it open and searched through for some names. The first one I found seemed the most obvious for some reason, so I stuck it in the search engine and eagerly pressed return.

Never in a million years did I expect to be hit with so many results. After all, luck had abandoned me so many times in my past. Why should it be any different now? And yet, here I was, reading the first of many, many entries. The words flew out at me from the computer screen. I was left stunned; I could hardly breathe. It was only after the kindly librarian asked me if I was okay that I somehow managed to ask her for assistance to continue my research.

Ten minutes later, I reached for my phone.

'Alex,' Belinda answered. 'At last. I have been worried sick about you.'

'Will you be home in an hour?' I asked excitedly. The first person I thought of who I urgently needed to chat with was Belinda; as the former detective who had shared this journey with me, it was essential to discuss these findings with her.

'Sure, what's the matter?'

'I will send you a video link shortly.'

I hung up, called a taxi, and ran out of the library as fast as my spindly legs could carry me.

Chapter Five

Canberra, Australia
November 2022

Once our video connection was established, I told Belinda everything about my conversation with Albert.

'When he said that I should find out where Yuri was on the day I was shot, an immediate thought entered my mind. Over the past six months, whenever I remembered names of people Mum and Dad may have mentioned in their conversations with me or with each other, I wrote them down in my notebook. I mean, you just never know when they might come in handy.'

'I agree,' replied Belinda softly. She looked immaculate, as she always did, even with a flickering internet connection.

'There was one surname I never forgot—I am not going to tell you what it is for your own protection, but let's call him Mr P. The real name is a pretty common Slavic name, to be fair. But there was a reason why it stuck in my head. In 1986, Dad stupidly bought a new car on hire purchase, and when he couldn't meet the repayments, he tried to sell it off to a second-hand car dealer under the illusion that he owned it outright. Of course, this was tantamount to fraud, but these things rarely worried my father.'

'Oh dear,' Belinda frowned.

'Anyway, I turned up one night to visit Mum and Dad, only to find the car dealer arguing with my father. Mum was in the background, of course, screaming and crying. What my father put her through. Anyway, after I spoke to the car dealer to find out what was going on, I walked back into their unit to find my parents in a heated argument. Then, out of the blue, Mum screams out, "Another man coming to our house because of your lies, just like Mr P in Lane Cove."'

'Lane Cove was where your family lived when you were born,' Belinda reiterated.

'Exactly. Anyway, on the way to the National Library, I started to wonder again who Mr P was and why he had been fighting with my father. Then I got this crazy idea. What if Mr P was Yuri?'

'I can see how you would make such a connection.'

'At the National Library, I searched the database for the phrase, 'Yuri P—arrival card' to see whether a Yuri P had ever entered Australia. As I said before, Yuri P would be a reasonably popular name, so predictably, a number of responses popped up for a whole range of reasons. But nevertheless, I decided to trawl through each entry one at a time. To my amazement, shock, horror, whatever you want to call it, I hit payload with the very first entry.'

Belinda looked as if she was about to fall off her chair. 'Are you serious?'

'Wait for it—Yuri P, a UK resident—entered Australia in April 1962!'

'When your family was living in Lane Cove.'

'Yes. The timing of Yuri's arrival in Australia and Mr P's visit to our home in Lane Cove align perfectly. It's too much of a coincidence. They must be the same person.'

'We will still need to do some further checking,' Belinda said.

I ignored her comment for the moment. 'But there's more. Given how all roads lead to Lithgow, the next thing I wanted to establish was whether Yuri P ever lived there during the mid-1960s. So, I asked one of the librarians for help, and she suggested that the best place to start would be the State Library of New South Wales. She showed me how to access their online database, and I began to filter through some keywords. Would you believe it? In a matter of minutes, I found several old company records from 1966 to 1967 indicating that Yuri P lived at the same address in Lithgow with another Yugoslav man whose name I won't reveal—but let's call him Niko S. They established a landscaping business that did work in country New South Wales, so they would have definitely travelled to neighbouring towns together.'

Belinda quickly consulted her own notebook, flicked a few pages, and then sat back in her chair. 'According to Matt, you told him that after you were shot, you saw two men in the car—a shooter and a driver.'

'Makes perfect sense to me.'

'So, what you are saying is that on the day you were shot, a man with a vendetta against your father was living barely an hour's drive away.'

'Yes,' I replied bleakly.

'Okay, let's assume that you're right and the Yuri P, who landed in Australia, was indeed Max's younger brother. How do you think the shooting went down?'

I took a deep breath. 'Let's speculate, shall we? We know that Ilic and Yuri both migrated to the UK after the war. I suspect that Ilic, given his background, remained connected with British intelligence, perhaps through Stubbs. Somewhere along the line, Ilic discovers the truth about what happened on the day Max was killed. This is the perfect opportunity to get his revenge on Dad after all these years. He either finds Yuri himself or Yuri approaches him; it doesn't really matter how they meet. Ilic embellishes the story in such a way that makes Dad totally culpable for Max's death. Yuri is so enraged that he vows to take vengeance as soon as he can.'

I reached over and swallowed some water from a glass placed conveniently next to my laptop. 'How am I going?'

Belinda offered me a smile and a thumbs-up sign. 'All good.'

'Eventually, Yuri makes it to Australia. As a UK citizen at the time, he can come and go as he pleases. He immerses himself inside Sydney's Yugoslav community, perhaps makes some enquiries with the police, and then discovers our address in Lane Cove. Sometime in 1962, he turns up at the house unannounced when Dubravka, Rosemary and Dragan are not there. He gets into an argument with Dad. He accuses him of being responsible for Max's death and demands immediate justice.'

I took a sip from my glass of water. 'While mum is crying in the background, Dad denies any culpability and orders Yuri to leave. Dad is distressed that the day he feared for so long has arrived, but he is not threatened easily.'

'Besides, his wife is about to give birth to a new child, and his precious daughter has just got engaged,' Belinda added. 'He plans to move on.'

'Until after the wedding,' I begin. 'With his debts still mounting, he now hears on the grapevine that Yuri is still in town, boasting to people that he's coming for Dad soon. For the first time, Dad is actually scared. He calls his contacts in the government, perhaps certain people in Defence who are aware of his background and begs them for assistance. Given his record of service for the British, they agree to help. They pull a few strings, twist a few arms, and eventually, a job is found for him in Kandos.' I coughed momentarily.

'While he waits for confirmation with the Kandos job, he packs the family up quickly without telling Dubravka where he is going, and they move to a variety of temporary locations around Sydney. Unhappily, he owes Dubravka money, too. Dad figures that if he doesn't tell her where he has gone, he won't have to repay her the money, nor can anybody looking for him trace him back through her. He wins both ways.'

'That's so sad that he turned his back on his own daughter after everything they went through together in Yugoslavia,' said Belinda.

'It does beggar belief,' I replied. 'But Dad was always running away from someone, even members of his own family.'

'Okay. What happens next?'

'Yuri is frustrated after Dad disappears but vows to find him. To make ends meet, he takes a job as a landscaper with his friend Niko S in Lithgow, unaware that Dad lives only an hour's drive away in Kandos. Somehow, he finds him, maybe by chance, maybe through the local Yugoslav network, who really knows? Under the pretence of looking for work, he and Niko S drive to Kandos with a .22-calibre rifle in the backseat of their car, hoping to find Dad and catch him unawares. They eventually locate our house, but there is no car in the driveway or any other sign that Dad is in the house.'

'It's the afternoon, your father is presumably at work.'

'Precisely. Just when they realise that very fact, I come prancing around the side of the house into the front yard. I wasn't wearing cowboy clothes as I was initially led to believe, but the combat uniform and plastic helmet that I used to wear almost every day. You have seen the photos of me yourself. I'm dressed like a soldier, together with my toy rifle and little army jeep, fighting an imaginary enemy. For some reason, maybe because he had a form of PTSD, this must have flicked a switch inside Yuri's head that led him to make a dreadful decision. The boy! We must kill the boy! An eye for an eye!'

'You think it was a spur-of-the-moment decision?'

'Almost definitely. Indeed, I would not be surprised if Niko S and Yuri P initially argued about it. As far as Niko is concerned, Yuri never mentioned anything about killing a little boy before they left Lithgow. This is not the Yugoslav way, not his way. But eventually, Yuri wears him down. He orders Niko to restart the car, and they do a lap of the block as a practice run. Niko secretly hopes that I have the wherewithal to go inside before they return a second time. But I don't. As I continue shooting imaginary Nazis in the front yard, I hear a sound, look up and see a car speeding past the house. Before I can comprehend what's happening, Yuri pulls out the rifle, thrusts it through the open passenger window and aims for my head. Bang! He shoots one clean shot in my direction, and I crumple to the ground like a sack of potatoes.'

Belinda folded her arms. She was no doubt critiquing every word I said, looking for the inevitable glitches in my theory. I still wasn't sure if I was totally convincing her.

'Thinking that they've killed me, they accelerate down the street and, with little traffic ahead of them, drive back to Lithgow undisturbed, hoping that no one has yet reported the shooting. When they arrive at Lithgow an hour later, Niko and Yuri argue some more. Yuri, who is fundamentally a decent person, is simply consumed with hate over the death of his beloved older brother but finally promises Niko that the vendetta is over.'

'Okay,' said Belinda. 'Let's fast forward a little. We are back in Kandos. You're receiving medical attention while your dad is talking to the local police. What then?'

'Dad is initially shocked like everyone else, but it doesn't take him long before he suspects that the shooting has something to do with him. Yet why would the Ustaše come for him now, after all this time? And since when did they attack innocent children playing in their front yard? It doesn't make sense. Then it must have hit him; it was Yuri! Who else? Only Yuri possessed the balls and the unremitting anger to do something like this. The police begin to ask him questions, but Dad is distracted and deliberately coy. The last thing he needs is for them to delve into his private affairs.'

'But they don't, do they?' Belinda reinforced. 'Somehow, it's decided that evening that the shooting was a likely accident caused by some kids.'

'That's right,' I replied. 'But we have been far too quick to blame the police for this indiscretion. They are completely exonerated in my view.'

'I agree, Alex. If you told Matt that you saw two men in a vehicle at the time of the shooting, that information should have been relayed to the police immediately by your father. And if it had been, they would never have ignored this evidence or put forward another theory without first initiating a proper investigation into those claims. In normal circumstances, you would have seen detectives from Mudgee or Lithgow at your house the next day, looking for the bullet and examining the front yard for other evidence.'

'Exactly,' I said. 'We can only assume that Dad never mentioned Matt's evidence to the police at all. A theory is then put forward about the possibility of some kids mucking around with a rifle, and Dad jumps on it. In fact, he's never been more relieved. It gives him the opportunity to handle things his own way, and no one needs to know any better. The legend of the accidental shooting is born, and I am forced to accept this nonsense for decades.'

'There is one thing that has bothered me from the beginning,' Belinda interjected. 'If your dad did believe that it was a deliberate attack, how could he have known that the perpetrators wouldn't return and try their luck a second time? It was a huge risk to take.'

'As I said, I think he was determined to deal with the issue his own way. He understood the Yugoslav community better than most. Perhaps he was confident that whatever forces were supporting Yuri would stop him from trying again. But he also wanted to be sure. That's when I think his friend Misha became involved. He had an extensive network and, through his contacts, they eventually tracked Yuri down.'

'Hence, all the trips your father made to Lithgow after the shooting,' Belinda added.

I nodded. 'I think it was a gradual process that evolved over several months, but eventually, Dad and Yuri agreed to meet on that day. He took us to Lithgow and abandoned us in town. In those crucial two hours, the two men somehow resolved their differences and agreed to move on without any further recriminations. A few months later, as the immigration records show, Yuri P returned to the United Kingdom for good.'

I stopped talking and gave Belinda a quizzical look. 'So, what do you think?'

Belinda's face showed little emotion before she eased back into her chair. 'It's an interesting theory,' she began.

'I can feel a 'but' coming,' I interrupted.

Belinda smiled. 'Look, I am a former detective, Alex. I was trained to focus on what I could prove in a court of law based on the evidence presented to me. Your theory has merit, but there are still so many issues that need clarifying. What I am trying to say is that much of what you have just presented is circumstantial. We need more than just that if people are going to take us seriously. We need to find the crime reports, check the immigration records, talk to a forensic expert, rattle some more cages. Now's the time to put meat on the bones, Alex. Trust me on this.'

I had predicted this response from Belinda during the Uber ride home, so I wasn't disappointed with her reasoning. If anything, it just confirmed how professional she was in her undertakings and what an important friend she had become. That's why what I was about to say was so difficult.

'I'm not sure if I can go much further with this.'

'What do you mean?'

'For the past several years, I have done everything possible to overcome my PTSD. It has been so bloody hard at times, but I was winning. I was just starting to enjoy the sunshine for one of the few times in my life when suddenly I fell into a dark void again. Ever since I returned from Croatia, I have been falling further and further into that abyss. I can't sleep, I can't focus, I can't... well, live. Just like my obsession with Martina, my obsession with this investigation is threatening to destroy who I have become and those I love. I need to end it now.'

'I understand, Alex,' Belinda said respectfully. 'I truly do.' And I had no doubt that she did.

'When we began, I knew that I was never going to get an answer that completely satisfied me,' I explained. 'All I wanted was something that made sense, something that I could hang onto inside my darkest dreams. And I think I found it. My concern is that if we progress this any further and we find evidence that contradicts my latest theory, it will set me back so much I may never recover. I need to have something that I can live with for the rest of my life, and out of all the possibilities, out of all the false lines of inquiry we have pursued, I can live with this one the most.'

Belinda and I talked some more, traded other bits of information, and then decided to wrap things up for good.

'If you ever change your mind, you know where to find me,' Belinda said with a friendly grin.

'I surely do.' For some reason, a tear flicked at my eyelid. 'Thank you for everything, Belinda,' I said with genuine affection. We both knew that nothing more needed to be said.

After I ended the video conference, I walked out of my study and into the adjoining hallway. My back was aching and my arms weighed like two lead balloons. Whether I accepted it or not, I was a physical and emotional wreck. I had put so much pressure on myself over the past twelve months with my book, searching for Martina, investigating my shooting and the endless overseas travel. And for what? Was any of it really worth it? I wasn't sure, to be honest, but I did know that my mind and body were beyond exhausted. Instinctively, I eyed off the double bed in one of our spare rooms, and ignoring Louie's sudden barking from outside, I belly-flopped onto it in one lurid motion. Finally, it was time for me to sleep.

Part Six

The Season
Of Thunder

Chapter One

Somewhere over the Pacific Ocean
October 2023

If *reincarnation is indeed real,* I sighed as I struggled to get comfortable in my seat, *I truly hope that in my next life I come back as a bird.* Apart from that one trip to London in 2022, it didn't matter where on the plane I was sitting or how tired I was, I could never seem to fall asleep for more than one hour at a time. Perhaps it was the curse of my tall frame, chronic bad back, overly sensitive bladder, or simply that I hated being confined in a small space with large groups of people. Whatever the reason, I always reached a point where the in-flight movies, the music on my phone or the book I was reading offered me little solace and I was left wide awake and restless, mulling over the mysteries of life inside a dark cabin full of snoring nobodies.

Such was my current predicament halfway through my flight from Sydney to Los Angeles. The trip didn't get off to a good start when the passenger sitting in the window seat next to me in premium economy decided to pull out some unfinished sushi from his bag moments after the seatbelt sign was lifted. Not only did his food stink the cabin to high heaven, but for some reason, it put every other passenger around us in a foul mood. A simple trip to the toilet suddenly became a scene from *Lord of the Flies*, as everyone argued and jostled each other out of irritation.

If that wasn't bad enough, several hours after the first meal, with the cabin in semi-darkness, this guy then had the temerity to ask me to turn my reading light off because it was disturbing him. Despite a kindly flight attendant coming down firmly on my side, the 'incident' took all the pleasure out of my book, so I switched off the light and began to sulk in front of my blank entertainment screen.

Inevitably, with nothing else to do and sleep seemingly impossible, my lonely thoughts soon began to focus on the events of the past year. Since closing down the investigation that afternoon with Belinda, my life had slowly returned to normal.

Free from distraction, I began to spend more time with my two charities—PTSD Australia/New Zealand and Animal Therapies Limited—and then found the literary spark to finally complete *A Season of Clouds*. Not content to rest on my laurels, and with the details of the investigation still fresh in my mind, I immediately embarked on a new writing venture. Incredibly, I was able to complete an initial draft manuscript of *A Season of Thunder* in just under nine months.

In a way, I should not have been surprised how effortlessly I had completed *Thunder* once I understood that this was what Brother Rojo had always wanted. All through the writing process, I felt his spirit guide my fingers as I typed out page after page in rapid succession. It was as if our conversation that day in Manila had mysteriously laid the groundwork for my eventual reconciliation with my family's past—a past that I never knew existed before now.

After ordering a coffee from a passing flight attendant, I allowed myself to wander back in time to that pivotal day in August 2001. Even after living in Manila for thirteen months, I still couldn't cope with the stifling Philippine humidity, the raucous sound of jeepneys that crammed the city's filthy streets and the endless grey smog that perpetually hovered around my face.

I was going to miss that crazy, fucked-up place more than I ever cared to admit. Sadly, it was my last week in the Philippines before returning to Australia via a two-week holiday in Europe. My time as a student at the National Defense College of the Philippines had come to an end, and I was about to start a new chapter in my life, armed with a master's degree in national security and a lifetime supply of incredible memories.

As I walked slowly towards Glorietta Mall in Makati, the main business district of Manila, the usual beads of sweat began to soak through one of the many fake designer t-shirts that I had bought locally for a pittance. Everything was so damn cheap in Manila—clothes, food, travel, and yes, even life. I had spent so much of my time in the Philippines rebelling against its madness before I realised that I was actually contributing to it myself. In that sense, it was probably a good thing that I was leaving.

Those misgivings aside, nothing could take away the life-changing experiences that had accompanied me on my journey. First, there was Sally, a vivacious American girl from New Orleans, with whom I fell in love almost overnight. She was unlike any woman I had ever met in my life up to that point, and she damn well knew it. But just when the romance of the century was about to blossom, Sally was called back to America due to her father's incurable bowel cancer. Although I had made a half-hearted attempt to visit her in the States during a break in the course, we never saw each other again. It was a story worthy of a 1930's Hollywood classic.

Then came the Second EDSA Revolution—a people's uprising that ousted President Joseph Estrada in January 2001. At its height, I was detained at gunpoint at the headquarters of the Armed Forces of the Philippines, Camp Aguinaldo, and almost got myself killed due to my own reckless stupidity. If that wasn't traumatic enough, several months later, while visiting the island of Mindanao to conduct research for my master's thesis, I was forced to watch on helplessly as a little Muslim girl in a remote village died from malaria.

I thought that I had reached my life's nadir after that terrible tragedy, but I was ultimately saved by an incredible man I met not long afterwards who dissected my soul like no other person before him. That man, of course, was Brother Rojo, an elderly, wizened Marist brother who had dedicated his life to helping lost sheep like me. He was the most amazing man I had ever met, and it was him whom I was about to meet for the final time.

I had intended to take him out to lunch at Makati's most expensive restaurant, but that was never his style. He was a simple man with simple tastes who valued your company more than he ever did the trappings of life. No, he would be content with a pot of his beloved lemon grass tea at a local cafe and maybe a cookie or two, if he was really indulgent.

We agreed to meet at eleven o'clock, and unsurprisingly, he was already sitting at an outside table under the shade of an umbrella, a white stained teapot in front of him. When he saw me, he perched his peculiar frog-like face momentarily towards the sun before extending his skinny hand to greet me.

'Alex, my friend,' he said happily. 'So good to see you.'

'Brother Rojo.' I shook his hand and then nodded at his tea. 'You can be very obstinate at times. I told you in my text that this was my treat.'

'You Australians,' he said with a broad smile. 'Always giving your money away. But I would be very pleased to have another pot if you're still keen on buying.' We both laughed, and I soon returned with his tea and a large flat white for myself.

'I have just returned from Baguio,' Brother Rojo said. 'My cousin Denny had business in Malaysia again, and so I kept Dulcie company for several days. Although I suspect she would have much preferred your company rather than mine.'

I smiled. Dulcie was Denny's beautiful, precocious twenty-three-year-old daughter. A few months earlier, I had 'baby-sat' Dulcie in her father's house while he was on a business trip to Malaysia. She absolutely loathed my presence at first, but by the end of the week, we had become besties. Dulcie then accompanied me as my guest during a recent foreign academic tour to Russia.

'How is she?'

'She is very well and sends her love. We spent most of our time talking about her trip to Russia.' He paused for a moment before winking at me with those strange, bulbous eyes of his. 'And a certain Australian, of course. I think she is quite taken by you.'

'Nothing more than a schoolgirl crush,' I said bluntly. 'I am thirty-eight, she is twenty-three. I have no doubt she will soon fall for someone else around her age.'

'You hope.'

'I know.'

We then talked about life in Baguio, the latest political situation in Mindanao and the overly steamy weather. As much as we could, we tried to avoid the inevitable discussion about my forthcoming departure, although we both knew that we had to broach the subject sooner or later.

'I am going to miss you, Alex,' he finally admitted. 'It was fun to unlock the heart of such an interesting man.'

I laughed. 'I still don't know what you found so interesting in me, but I owe you a debt of gratitude for leading me out of the wilderness. And, of course, for introducing me to the power of the Four Seasons.'

'I only showed you what was possible.' He grinned, exposing several yellow teeth. 'You were able to figure everything out yourself. Well, to a degree.'

I didn't want to take the bait at our last meeting, but I couldn't help myself. 'You still don't accept that Martina is the reason why I have been trapped inside the Season of Clouds for so long, do you?' We had argued several times about what he thought was my hastiness in blaming everything that was holding me back in my life on the guilt I felt about Martina. He wanted me to look deeper within myself, at the things that bubbled away nefariously every night inside my dreams, but I simply didn't have the patience anymore. It was so much easier to blame Martina.

'You will be relieved to know that I'm not here to talk about that today.'

'What then?' I asked curiously. It was obvious that he wanted to impart one last lesson before I went home.

'Do you remember what I said about passing through each season?'

'Yes, I do,' I replied. 'To be truly successful in the next season, you must first complete each of your learnings from the current one.'

'Excellent!' Brother Rojo clapped his hands. 'You have learnt something, after all.'

'Of course. You are one hell of a teacher.'

'I have taught you all I know; that much is true. But while we have talked extensively about your learnings as a teenager inside the Season of Fire and, of course, your current struggles inside the Season of Clouds, we have spoken very little about the Season of Thunder. Why is that, do you think?'

'I am not sure,' I replied testily after reflecting for several moments. 'Maybe I just don't particularly like my family.'

'Nonsense, Alex. We both know that's not true. You spoke glowingly about your brother to me when he visited the Philippines not so long ago. And you talk about your sisters all the time.'

'No, you're right,' I said. 'My siblings are good people, and they have all contributed positively to my life. I was thinking more about my parents.'

'And why is that?'

I wanted to tell him every aspect of Mum and Dad's dysfunctional lives—the arguments, the money problems, the lying, the domestic violence. Then there was all the other stuff that happened to me as a kid, like the shooting, things that no young child should ever have to experience. But we were running out of time, and I didn't want my final memories of Rojo to be trapped indefinitely inside my own deceit. Accordingly, there was only one issue I could bring myself to reveal.

'They let me down.' I then explained to Rojo what happened to me as a four-year-old boy in Kandos; how my parents never understood how much the shooting impacted my life and how they likely hid the truth from me, even when it was obvious that the story they perpetuated was nonsense.

'There's a lot of anger there,' Rojo said when I finished.

'Probably too much.'

'But before we can criticise our parents for their actions, we must always seek to understand the context in which they were made. You will find that nothing is ever totally black and white. I told you my own story about how my mother fell pregnant with me after being raped by Japanese soldiers during the war and then how she discarded me after my birth.'

'Yes, it was a horrible thing to do.'

'Was it, Alex? Oh, if you apply today's moral standards to the situation, then it probably was.'

Brother Rojo continued, perpetual wisdom shining from his child-like eyes. 'Admittedly, I thought that myself for a long time. But when I sat back and tried to understand the context in which my mother made that decision, I unreservedly forgave her. You see, she was a young woman with serious mental health issues who, in effect, had been blamed by those around her for her own gang rape. In the end, she did what she thought was right for her and for me. If you must know, I pray for her soul every night.'

I wanted to hug him to help ease his own self-inflicted pain, but that was not something you did to a Marist brother in the Philippines. So instead, I gently nodded my head and replied, 'But you are a far better man than I will ever be, Brother Rojo.'

'Oh, you're a good man, alright, Alex. That's why I know that one day, you will successfully resolve your issues inside the Season of Thunder, perhaps even write a book about your experiences.'

'You think so?'

'It is inevitable, like the next rain shower.' He looked upwards towards the thickening late-morning clouds and then smiled. 'But promise me that when you do, you will remember this conversation and be loyal to my faith in you. For your pursuit of the truth will undoubtedly set you on a troubling path, even though you will eventually prevail.'

Despite my reluctance to make any promises, given my record of breaking them so easily, what was I supposed to say?

'Of course, I will.'

'And remember, Alex,' he began, straining his neck across our table, almost in desperation. 'It's the context, do you understand? If you are to embrace the Season of Thunder with all your heart, then you must remember that it's all about the context.'

Chapter Two

Los Angeles, USA
October 2023

'This Season of Thunder stuff,' said Calvin, a local LA book publicist who had agreed to have lunch with me at a restaurant inside Century Plaza near Beverley Hills. 'Can you explain it to me again?'

'It's all about the context,' I replied confidently. I had already explained how the Season of Thunder—my childhood and my perception of my parents' relationship—had been the cooking pot that still bubbled and had set me on this investigative journey.

He gave me a quizzical look before gulping down some more of his enchilada. He was one of those hyperactive American go-getters who could only operate at a million miles an hour if he truly wanted to stay alive. As a result, eating lunch was a mundane, unnecessary task, something you forgot about ten minutes later.

'And the Four Seasons? What are they again?'

'The Season of Thunder, the Season of Fire, the Season of Clouds and the Season of Wisdom.'

'The Season of Wisdom!' he exclaimed. 'What sort of shit happens in there?'

'It's when you reach self-actualisation and eternal happiness.'

'Can I ask you a question, Alex?' Calvin said after he stuffed another chicken wing down his throat. That was now six for him and one for me.

'Sure.'

'Are you on drugs?'

'What?'

'You know, crack, cocaine, ice, heroin?'

'Of course not.'

'I won't judge you if you are. You're among friends here.'

'I assure you unreservedly that I am not.'

Calvin pulled out his napkin and then wiped the solidified ketchup from his three-day growth. 'You know, I read the first six chapters of your manuscript last night, and I goddamned loved it! You write a real rollicking yarn, kiddo.'

It had been about thirty years since someone called me 'kiddo', but I thanked him anyway.

'Just one small observation,' he added. 'You need to spice it up a tad. You know what it's like. Sex sells. Any chance that you and that Lottie dame can get it off for a few pages?'

'Absolutely not,' I retorted, almost spitting out the ice from my soft drink.

'Why the hell not? She sounds a real stunner.'

'Like, I'm married, and my wife, Miriam, will read the book? And so might Lottie and her husband, come to think of it.'

'Your point?'

I guess this was California, and I didn't really have one. Everyone seemed to be having an affair over here, even some of the derelicts on the streets! So, I nodded politely and promised myself never to repeat this conversation to either Miriam or Lottie, even under the threat of torture.

I had been in LA for almost a week, spruiking my forthcoming book, *A Season of Thunder*, to some local players in anticipation of its publication next year. Calvin was by far and away the most interested person in my work, even if he kept throwing hand grenades at me.

'You've got something here, Alex,' Calvin said excitedly before burping down his black coffee in record time. 'Not sold on all the weird shit about the seasons, mind you, but let's talk in a few months.' We shook hands until my arm almost came off, and then, as he darted out the door, I realised that he had left me with the bill. *Never mind.*

When I returned to the Huntley Hotel in Santa Monica, I exchanged my jacket and chinos for shorts and a t-shirt. It was a typically beautiful SoCal afternoon, and so I decided it was the perfect time to walk down to Venice Beach and catch a few rays and a dose of unfettered marijuana smoke. Soon, I was strolling happily through Santa Monica's Third Avenue promenade, listening to my self-made compilation of California-based songs on my phone.

I love California, especially LA. Dubrovnik may have been my spiritual sanctuary, and New York may have been my favourite city, but if I had my life all over again, I would have left Australia straight after university and made the City of Angels my permanent home. There is something about the city's eclectic madness that suits my restless personality, that makes me believe that anything is possible if I try hard enough.

For someone who had chased shadows for much of his life, LA was the perfect haven from which to escape their deceitfulness.

It was ironic, of course, that I had developed such an affection for LA and California when our family came so close to settling here after the war, like so many other Chetniks. If it had not been for Major Stubbs convincing Dad to choose Australia instead of the States, my life would have turned out differently. For a start, the events of Kandos would never have happened. Free from that burden, I could have grown into a more confident young man, willing to take on the world as I saw fit. What could I have achieved in my life as a result?

But that was the enduring riddle behind the Season of Thunder; it callously revealed those sliding door moments that you never knew about and then challenged you to make sense of them. Once that became apparent to me following my meeting with Marković in Copenhagen, I had no option other than to uncover the truth about my shooting, even if it meant facing some of my darkest fears and anxieties.

Although my journey had been preordained by the stars, I hadn't deliberately set out to either excoriate or exonerate my parents. That would have assumed that I had a right to judge them when I definitely didn't. Yes, I still felt betrayed by Dad and Mum over their reluctance to explain the shooting to me, but I now possessed a better understanding of their reasons, and the forces that shaped and motivated their own lives. Their decisions, their actions and their feelings were all by-products of a world that today's generation would barely understand. 'It is all about the context, Alex,' Brother Rojo had warned me, and this statement had resounded with me through time. Once I had examined the context of these events, it revealed everything I needed to know about my parents.

Dad was a complex man, shaped by an inherent belief system that slowly betrayed him over time. He was one of those rare people who was able to convince himself he was doing the right thing, even when it was obvious that he wasn't. This inability to take responsibility for his own actions, especially when it came to women and money, had a dreadful impact on the people who loved him. His treatment of my mother, especially those episodes of domestic violence, was, at times, appalling. However, he was also undoubtedly a patriot and a very brave man who stood up for the weak and oppressed. He successfully led his people safely to freedom. Above all, I remained proud of the way that he conducted himself as a guerrilla leader, refusing to succumb to the escalating violence against civilians that underpinned much of the conflict in Yugoslavia.

During my journey, I had travelled the length and breadth of Croatia and Italy looking for the answer to that painstaking question that bugged me from the beginning—what had motivated my father during the war? Why did he choose the path he did? After talking to so many different people and assessing so many different possibilities, sometimes to the detriment of my own integrity, I realised at last that it was always the most obvious answer: survival. Like most people trapped by a war they did not deserve, Dad was motivated by the desire to live a new day, free from tyranny and death. Maybe he chose a different path from what I would have taken, especially when it came to his treatment of my mother, but no one could doubt his bravery and resilience.

After my shooting, Dad worked for Kandos Cement Ltd as its boiler room manager for several more years. For a while, he liked to boast that he was the company's main man.

Then, towards the end of 1970, he had a falling out with his direct supervisor. The tension had been brewing for some time, with both men often engaged in public shouting matches in front of other staff. One hot summer afternoon, Dad's unpredictable Slavic temper finally snapped. After making threats in his manager's office, including claims that he could sabotage the factory at a whim, Dad stupidly tried to run him over later that day in the car park. Dad insisted that he had done it as a joke, but there was no way that excuse was going to curry favour with company management. Understandably, he was sacked immediately.

Three months later, we found ourselves in Redcliffe, Queensland, shuffling from one rental unit to the next while Dad searched for work. He quickly discovered that people weren't hiring workers who tried to run over their bosses with a car. Money started to get tight. Rosemary and I, much to our annoyance, were unable to attend school.

One day, Dad announced that he was going on a road trip by himself for a few weeks. We assumed it was to find work, but he never really explained to us what he was doing or where he was going. Mum flew into an incandescent rage, accusing him of running out on us. Dad barely said anything but simply dropped a few hundred dollars on the kitchen table for rent and food and told us he would be back soon. I can still remember crying in fear as he drove away on that fateful morning. In between tears, I wondered if I was ever going to see him again.

The next few weeks were particularly stressful as Mum slowly disintegrated in front of our eyes. Luckily, Rosemary, barely fifteen herself, had the maturity and courage to look after both of us. To this day, I still don't know how we survived. It was a credit to Rosemary that we did.

On his fifty-seventh birthday, Dad reappeared. He was in a buoyant mood, bringing chocolates for Rosemary, a new soccer ball for me and a huge bunch of flowers for Mum. He then made the stunning announcement that he had found a job in Gladstone at the local alumina plant; the family would be leaving Redcliffe as soon as the paperwork had been finalised. Initially, Mum was unhappy and didn't want to go—she had convinced herself that Gladstone was full of Ustaše waiting to kill her. But Mum's hysterics did little to sway Dad's decision. For a fifty-seven-year-old man who had just been sacked, he had no option other than to take the first job offered to him. A new life in Gladstone awaited us, propelling me headfirst into the Season of Fire. But that's another story…

Until the day he retired, Dad retained the respect and admiration of his work colleagues at Queensland Alumina, who not only saw him for the mechanical genius that he was, but equally appreciated his work ethic and generosity. Quite often, the words, 'He's Anton's son,' would confer special privileges upon me from the parents of some of my friends. For instance, when I made my A-grade cricket debut at the age of seventeen, the opposing captain, a notoriously tough nut on the field who worked with Dad, told his teammates as I came out to bat, 'I know this kid's old man. Let's give him his first run, and then we can get stuck into him.'

Probably the greatest achievement in Dad's life came just before he retired when he almost singlehandedly extinguished a blazing fire in the boiler-room where he worked. I was told years later that it was a close-run thing; if the fire had been left unattended for several more minutes, much of the factory could have been destroyed. Of course, other people helped save the day as well, but those I have spoken to who witnessed these events left me in no doubt who the real hero was.

'I have never seen personal courage like it,' one witness told me many years ago. 'He was like a man possessed.' Although I have no way of knowing, I would like to think that, at last, Dad had the perfect riposte to the immigration official, who offended him so much by calling him a labourer.

Dad died from oesophageal cancer in 1990, a condition possibly caused by the toxic fumes he inhaled from the boiler room fire. He was seventy-six. At the time of Dad's death, communism, a system that he had fought so strongly against, started to crumble across Eastern Europe. Dad went to his grave knowing that he had made his own contribution to its demise. However, I will always be grateful that he did not live long enough to witness the subsequent breakup of his beloved Yugoslavia and the brutal wars that followed.

By the time I finished my manuscript, I realised how much I had underestimated my mother when she was alive. The courage and determination she showed in keeping the family together at all costs was simply remarkable. Some might argue that her actions were selfish, that she put the life of an innocent child at enormous risk just to satisfy her own ego. But that is an overly simplistic way of looking at things. As she said to me one day, she could have easily stayed in Šibenik and experienced a relatively comfortable lifestyle with her family rather than chase Dad into the unknown. But she strongly believed that Dubravka needed her father, and she was determined not to let her down.

As we have seen, her resilience and willpower during those awful months came at a significant cost to her eventual physical and mental wellbeing. She never adjusted to life in Australia, and for a while, she would pine for the old days in Šibenik and the clear, warm waters of the Adriatic Sea. When she did return to Yugoslavia to see her family in 1972, she was meant to stay for six months, yet she only made it to three. Her wonderful sisters, at first buoyed by her return after nearly thirty years, apparently found themselves arguing with her every day, from everything about the war to the choices they made in their own lives.

From what I understand, they were heartily relieved when Mum eventually announced that she was returning to Australia ahead of schedule. In the years that followed her trip, I sadly never heard her utter Ruža's or Jelena's names again. Any fond memories she had about her life as a young woman in Yugoslavia were lost forever inside her growing bitterness.

Despite everything Dad did to her, the affairs, the arguments and the violence, Mum loved him with a craziness that, at times, was baffling. After he died, she cried and cursed his name for months before finally readjusting to her new life without him. She spent her remaining years in mental decline, supported by my sister Rosemary, arguing with the neighbours, seeing offence in every situation, and still believing that she had the best legs in Šibenik. After a short burst of dementia, she died in her sleep at an aged care facility in Brisbane in 2011. She was ninety-one.

The real heroine of my family's escape to Australia, however, was my oldest sister, Dubravka. Her courage as a little girl in the face of the unremitting maelstrom that attacked her with such incredible ferocity was inspirational. In many ways, it was her innocence and spontaneity that drove Dad forward during the bleakest times. She gave our father an additional reason to live at a juncture when he saw the war consume everyone around him. One wonders if he would have survived to lead his people across the Isonzo River had it not been for Dubravka's presence during that last battle and his overwhelming desire to save her life. If anyone deserved a medal from King Petar, Dubravka certainly did.

Unlike Dad, Dubravka embraced Australia wholeheartedly and never had any regrets about the choices she took. Given her incredible beauty, she could have been a model, jet-setting around the world with a flock of rich suitors pursuing her. Why, even the well-known Australian celebrity Bert Newton once stopped her in the street and offered her a modelling job. However, perhaps influenced by the over-riding love bequeathed to her from an early age by her grandfather, Mateo, family was always Dubravka's main priority. Her marriage to her husband, Michael, has lasted more than sixty years; it is a love that has endured many challenges along the way but even more successes.

During their time together, they worked hard, raised two beautiful, intelligent daughters, travelled the world, and remained true to their values. To their great pride, they saw their beloved daughters marry terrific men and have their own children. Only recently, Dubravka has become a great-grandmother to an amazing little girl called Jessica. One day, when she is old enough, she will no doubt read *A Season of Thunder* herself and learn about her great-grandmother's exploits during one of the worst periods in human history. Maybe that will give her the impetus to do something special with her own life.

Miriam once asked me whose side I would have taken in 1941 had I been alive at the time. 'No,' I replied. 'I will never answer that question.' As Igor said to me in Dubrovnik, everyone fights for their own reasons, and it's not for others, especially people like me sitting in my armchair eighty years later, to judge their calling. Context is indeed everything, but for a man who cherished democracy and personal freedom, I would have undoubtedly opposed anyone who attempted to take those rights away from me. I would have also railed against any form of violence and oppression directed towards innocent, defenceless civilians, especially women and children. Where that might have put me on the spectrum of adversaries during the Yugoslav conflict, I have no idea.

Although some historians would disagree, I firmly believe that the turmoil in Yugoslavia resulted directly from the failure of the Treaty of Versailles to read the room after the First World War. Establishing a country like Yugoslavia with different races, different cultures, different languages, different religions, and then saying to its inhabitants, 'Go and live happily together in peace', was either grossly stupid or dangerously naïve. If the world had only supported US President Wilson's Fourteen Points for peace and followed a pathway of self-determination for all nations, then perhaps a different history of the region would have prevailed.

Despite being an avid student of history and a keen observer of world affairs, I still struggle to come to terms with the collective horrors and atrocities of the Second World War. It simply defies description that certain countries and their citizens behaved in such a thoroughly callous manner towards their fellow humans. The sixty million people who died during those awful years, many of them civilians, remain a gruesome reminder of the futility of war and its tragic consequences.

However, the wars in the former Yugoslavia during the 1990s, the various conflicts in the Middle East and the Russian invasion of Ukraine in 2022, demonstrate that humanity continues to be stained by racism and terror. That innocent women and girls in war zones are still being brutalised by errant soldiers who see them as nothing more than booty and the spoils of victory is a sad indictment of how little civilisation has progressed since 1945. Stalin's comment about men needing their fun in war stains the world even today. It's time for all civilised nations to make a stand against this cycle of sexual violence and oppression.

And what of me and the discoveries of the past that continue to define my life? Although my shooting as a child made me a victim of a war I knew nothing about, I no longer bear any grudges or ill will towards anyone. My only regret is that I never met some of the other main characters in my family's incredible story: Dad's loving and caring mother, my grandmother; Mum's stern but honourable father, my grandfather; my brave and patriotic Aunty Jelena; and my serene and thoughtful Aunty Ruža. However, sometimes late at night, when the earth is perfectly still, I can often feel their heavenly presence drift in the cool air above our bed, urging me to seek the peace and contentment that has abandoned my life for so long. I look forward to the time when we can all meet in a different place.

I finally reached Venice Beach and grabbed myself a vanilla thick shake from a side street vendor. The young Vietnamese man who served me grinned at my 'I Love LA' t-shirt and asked me where I was from.

'Australia,' I replied with a cautious smile.

'A wonderful country,' he beamed. 'My cousins live in Sydney! Perhaps you know them?'

After I explained to him politely that Sydney was a very large city, I dropped a few extra notes into his tip jar and quietly strolled onto the sun-bleached sand. With an emptiness in my heart, I looked out longingly across the Pacific Ocean to another land that awaited my return. Despite my dreams of living in America, I still called Australia home and loved it with a passion. While terrible things happened to me as a child, such as the shooting, Australia also gave me the chance to prosper as a person, to maximise my abilities and to live a life of freedom and hope.

As I watched the first tentative streaks of sunset emerge across the distant sky, I finally understood what I had learnt from my experiences inside the Season of Thunder. They may not have been perfect people, but my parents, through their grit and determination, opened the door for Dubravka, Dragan, Rosemary and I to build a new world for ourselves. We each grasped the opportunities provided to us in our own special way, creating an environment for those we love to follow in our footsteps.

But as our stars begin to fade and a new generation stands ready to replace us, it is incumbent on my nieces and nephews and their children to keep Mum and Dad's legacy burning brightly in the years to come. In doing so, they will ensure that those of us who love freedom never forget the brave men and women who sacrificed everything to fight an insidious evil that threatened to consume the world.

Epilogue

March 2024

Nearly two years after my fateful trip to Copenhagen, Marković sent me a message under a false name via a social media account.

He wrote, presumably with the help of an AI tool to improve his English:

Mr Gerrick—First, I want to apologise for my unacceptable behaviour when we met in Copenhagen in 2022. It was wrong of me to frighten you in the way that I did, although to be fair, I was more scared of you than you ever realised. It didn't take me long to work out that you were a man of considerable ability, and my ill-considered reaction to your belligerence only made things worse between us.

I know that you quickly worked out my true identity; I could see it in your eyes. You can imagine my fear when I was initially told that a stranger was searching for Martina, the very same woman who had haunted my nightmares for decades. I wanted to meet this man, to work out how much he knew, and then put him off the trail forever. But when I saw that you didn't quite believe me, I panicked. Every move you made was one step ahead of me and my colleague, and to that end, I congratulate you.

This is not an attempt to seek your understanding or forgiveness, but I think about what we did to Martina, every day. It is no excuse, but back then, I was young, impressionable and indoctrinated. I soon realised not long afterwards what an animal I had become; how many women's lives, like Martina's, I had needlessly destroyed. That was why I have dedicated twenty-five years of my life to helping women who were brutalised by men like me have their day in court. In no way does that redeem my past, but it means that at least I have something to bargain with when I one day meet my creator.

Over the past twelve months, I have conducted my own search for Martina. Fate has sent me down many rabbit holes, more than you can ever imagine. But last week, one of my men found something concrete. He is confident that the person you knew as Martina runs a small seafood restaurant called Neptune's Table, situated along the main promenade in Marathon, Greece. I give you this information freely of my own will. Do with it what you please. I ask you not to try and follow me on this account; it will be disabled as soon you read this message. Since we last met, I have changed my identity several times, and so you will never hear from me again. I wish you luck.

M.

Naturally, the message took me completely by surprise, so much so that I had to re-read it several times to assure myself that it wasn't the result of some international scam. Of course, I worked out in my hotel room that night in Copenhagen that Marković was the man who Martina had referred to as the 'sergeant', the monster who had led her brutal gangrape in a farmhouse near Sarajevo in 1992. Her description of the sergeant, especially the distinctive half-crescent scar across his nose, had made his identification fairly obvious once I had time to think about it more clearly.

All things considered, I was pleased that he still carried a heavy burden for his crimes, especially given how unlikely it was he would ever be brought to justice. The mental and physical scars Martina had carried when I knew her could never be rectified by something so meaningless as Marković's personal shame. I, for one, didn't want to hear about his pitiful excuses and talk of redemption. As he alluded to himself, only God had the power to absolve him now.

Admittedly, I was rather disappointed that he had disabled his account before I had a chance to quiz him about my father. Why did he mention him at our meeting in Copenhagen? What did he know about his past that I didn't, and how? Could he have given me more information that helped deconstruct Dad's mystery even further? But within minutes, I tossed all of those questions aside and put them in my mental delete bin. As Albert said to me in 2022, Markovic's intervention was likely just a ruse designed to fuck with my head, just like *The Spiders* had done for nearly twenty years. It was time to finally leave this all behind.

It was only after I dealt with those initial issues that the magnitude of Marković's information about Martina's possible whereabouts finally hit me. *Is it true? Has he actually found her after all this time?* My initial response, being the cautious person I had always been, was to be wary of anything that Marković had to say about her. After all, he was a dangerous man with a dangerous past, with an undeniable propensity for violence. Was this his way of luring me to Greece for one last act of revenge?

After I thought about it some more, I quickly dismissed that theory. For a start, he had no way of knowing how I would respond to this information. There was also no guarantee that I would take the bait and travel to Greece, nor would he have any way of knowing my intentions about a trip if I kept them private. There was nothing in it for him to trap me now after these past two years. Once I examined every possibility, it seemed more and more likely that this was a genuine attempt to remove his own guilt about Martina's rape and the way he had treated me in Copenhagen. After years of hitting dead ends in my pursuit of Martina, I had a responsibility to consider this new information seriously and then decide what to do with it.

I quickly searched for 'Neptune's Table, Marathon' on my phone. A simple website popped up, and I excitedly clicked on the home page. Naturally, the information was in Greek, but when I turned the English filter on, it stated that the owners were Con and Isabella M. Isabella? I had always suspected that if Martina were alive, she would have changed her identity, perhaps many times. No, what I needed was visual confirmation.

Alas, as I clicked through a series of photos attached to the site, all I saw were images of fish, crabs, seafood platters and young people drinking Ouzo. I then clicked on to another site and saw some photos of Con and Isabella's daughter, Lara, a pretty young woman in her twenties with withering blue eyes and a deep olive complexion. I recalled Martina telling me that because of her rape, it was unlikely she could have children, but I couldn't rule out the possibility that some miracle had occurred or that Lara was adopted.

I scrutinised several more sites, but nothing gave me even the slightest glimpse of Isabella, not even a photo with Con. One by one, I then checked all the usual social media platforms for anyone called Isabella M who lived in the Marathon area. All I found was an old account that may have been hers but which offered no photos or posts. Another dead end? Absolutely not. It made perfect sense to me that if Martina truly wanted to hide her identity, she would drastically reduce her social media footprint. I always worked on my hunches, and my latest hunch told me that Isabella M was indeed Martina.

'The only way you will know for sure is if you see her in person,' Miriam said. 'Just go to Greece and get this over and done with for good.'

'I'm coming with you,' Lottie said during our subsequent phone call. 'If you think I am going to miss this opportunity when you are so close to finding the truth, then you're grossly mistaken.'

'What about your husband?'

'Kurt loves Athens. An ideal excuse for the two of us to take a well-deserved holiday.'

I boarded a flight from Sydney on a sultry April evening, and nineteen hours later, I found myself in Athens once again. It only occurred to me when I checked into my hotel that it was almost twenty-nine years ago to the day when I first visited the Greek capital, setting off a chain of events that had led me to meet Martina on Samos Island. How I had experienced the full circle of regret during that time.

After a long, post-flight sleep, I woke the next morning feeling refreshed. I did my customary tour of the Parthenon, then strolled effortlessly around the Monastiraki and the Plaka for a few hours. At two thirty, I walked back to the hotel just in time to greet Lottie and Kurt as they were checking in.

I was a bit nervous about meeting Kurt at first; I didn't know how much Lottie had told him about us, and there was always that possibility that things could quickly disintegrate into a pissing contest. Happily, nothing could have been further from the truth. Kurt was a tall, muscular man in his late fifties with a mop of brownish-grey hair that seemed to bend whichever way the wind was blowing. He reminded me of the famous German Liverpool FC manager, Jürgen Klopp, but without the beard. If he resembled Jürgen, he had to be a top guy, and unquestionably, he was. Without even trying, he made me feel entirely comfortable in his presence, and soon, the three of us were sinking some coffees at the hotel bar like we had known each other for years.

Later that afternoon, Lottie, who had lived in Athens for over a decade, drove us in her hire car to her favourite Greek restaurant in the seaside port of Piraeus. It was an excellent choice; the food was sublime, and the restaurant patio where we sat overlooked Piraeus' spectacular harbour at sunset. Halfway through the evening, emboldened by several glasses of red wine, I told Kurt and Lottie about Calvin and his suggestion on how I should make my book a little spicier. They both found it riotously funny, with Kurt soon giving his consent for me to proceed with any changes as long as he was allowed to write the scenes himself. It was that kind of fun night, and the only thing that was missing was Miriam's presence. 'Let's all of us catch up in Australia real soon,' bellowed Kurt after we paid the bill, and both Lottie and I knew he was deadly serious.

The next morning, the three of us had an early breakfast before Kurt bid his farewells just after eight thirty. I begged him to come with us to Marathon, but he simply shook his head. 'This is something you and Lottie need to do by yourselves,' he said. 'Besides, I have already planned my day around several museums.' He kissed Lottie goodbye and then firmly grasped my hand. 'I hope you find what you are looking for, my friend.'

By mid-morning, Lottie and I were on the road. Although it was barely an hour's drive to Marathon in peak traffic, we were in no rush. Neptune's Table opened at eleven thirty, so there was really no point arriving in Marathon any earlier. It was not our intention to meet with Isabella M if we could help it, but to observe her from a distance and then determine whether that person was the Martina we knew from Samos. Once we established her identity, we would then discuss whether we should directly approach her or not.

Our journey was relaxed at first, as the historian inside of me gave Lottie a lecture on the Battle of Marathon and its importance to the creation of the modern world. The more I spoke, the more I realised that Lottie probably knew more about the battle than even I did and was only listening out of politeness. When I finished yapping, a strange silence enveloped her, and I began to realise how important discovering the truth about Martina was to her as well. She only started to speak to me again in staggered whispers once we reached the outskirts of Marathon.

As we were well ahead of time, Lottie and I strayed into a small café several blocks away from Neptune's Table and nervously sipped at our coffees underneath a yellow pergola. The beach in front of us, the actual site of the Persians' withdrawal during the famous battle in 490BC, beamed under a cloudless, sunlit sky.

'Are you ready for this?' Lottie asked after we finished our coffees.

'Not really,' I said, trying to smile.

'You need to toughen up.' She inspected me with a dreamy expression, her fingers curiously twisting at a paper napkin, and then began to laugh. 'The pair of us never really get things right, do we? What makes you think today will be any different?'

'My intensive knowledge of the Battle of Marathon.'

She laughed again and then leant across the table to kiss me on the cheek. 'Okay mister, let's see if you're right.'

We paid our bill and soon began our journey towards Neptune's Table. Our plan was to cross the road and walk along the main beach until we landed directly opposite the restaurant. From what we discerned from its website, the restaurant mainly offered outdoor seating. And why not? They had awesome views of one of the most historic beaches in the world. We figured that if we did our best to remain conspicuous, we could carefully monitor the identities of those setting up the tables or serving guests. Hopefully, one of them would be Isabella M/Martina.

Once we reached our position, we tried to hide ourselves inside the shade of a telegraph pole. I have to admit, we must have looked pretty stupid squashed up against that pole in the middle of the day, staring into an empty space. Luckily, no one was really watching us.

After a few minutes, Lottie nudged me. 'Hold my hand,' she whispered.

'Why?'

'Because when you do, we will actually look like a couple walking along a beach, not two idiots pretending to be a couple walking along a beach.'

I grabbed her hand, and it melted into my fingers. 'See, that wasn't so bad, was it?' Lottie chirped.

'You're a piece of work. Has anyone ever told you that?'

'Quite often, but I usually ignore them.'

I tried to change the topic. 'What time do you make it?'

'Just on eleven thirty. They must be opening soon.'

Right on cue, there was movement from the station. A door was flung open, some chairs were being unstacked and several people started to walk in and out. That's when we saw her, a woman in her mid-fifties, balancing a cigarette in her mouth. She had jet black hair that was cut neatly to her shoulders, and the blue jeans and yellow t-shirt she was wearing covered a refined, slim figure.

'Is that her?' Lottie asked.

I inspected the woman closely as she flicked some cigarette ash onto the ground. 'It might be her,' I finally responded after several minutes of procrastination. 'I mean, I want it to be her, but I'm just not sure. What do you think?'

'She's a little slimmer than I remember, but everything else about her exudes an aura of familiarity.' Lottie stamped her foot, then released a huge sigh. 'I think it's her.'

I ran my spare hand through my hair. I always assumed I would recognise Martina immediately when I saw her, but there was something about this woman that was still holding me back. Maybe her smile was more crooked than I remembered, or it was the crisp sound of her laughter that didn't inspire any immediate memories. It didn't feel exactly right, but then again, it was twenty-nine fucking years ago. How could I possibly remember every little detail about her?

'I am about eighty per cent,' I finally admitted.

'Well, if you're not sure, then you know what you have to do.'

I dropped Lottie's hand, took one step forward with the intention of crossing the street, and then hesitated. The memories of my chance encounter with Martina in Samos all those years ago suddenly flooded my mind. The car ride on the first day we met, where we tested each other's patience, the trip to Ephesus where she told me about her rape, the final night in Samos when our two souls joined together for one cathartic moment, the day in Canberra when I deliberately ignored her frantic calls for help. Even just thinking about those events left me breathless with sadness and regret.

For the past eight years, I had become obsessed with finding her after discovering that she may not have committed suicide after all, a self-indulgent exercise that had slowly twisted my mind at a time when I should have been focused on my battle with the clouds. All I wanted was one opportunity to make amends with a woman whom I had betrayed during her hour of need, to receive her unreserved forgiveness and to finally eradicate the guilt that had consumed me for decades. But as I stood at the precipice of my atonement, I was suddenly confronted by a larger reality.

What's in it for her?

I pulled myself back from the road and drew Lottie closer to me until our faces almost touched.

'If you are going to make a pass at me,' Lottie joked, 'can you wait until we get back to the car? This is far too open, and people will talk.'

'I can't do it, Lottie.'

She grimaced, just as I knew she would.

'After coming all this way, you're going to give up now?'

'I am just not sure if I have the right to re-enter her life.'

'Of course you don't, Alex.' Lottie laughed before her face suddenly became serious. 'If that really is Martina, she has spent the last thirty years deliberately running away from the world with one aim in mind—to forget about that awful night in Bosnia forever. After doing so much to protect her own identity, your appearance will no doubt make her feel vulnerable and unsafe again. Who knows how she is going to react when she sees you.'

'Why didn't you mention this previously?'

'Because I care about you, Alex. I want to see you resolve this obsession of yours once and for all so that you can finally be at peace with yourself and enjoy your remaining life with Miriam. If that means hurting Martina, then I am happy to oblige.'

'Thank you,' I replied sadly.

'Any time, crazy man.'

'And so, what do I do now?'

'Basically, you have to figure out if you can live with eighty per cent, just like you did with your shooting.'

She was right about that, of course, but it didn't make things easier for me. Fifty per cent, sixty per cent, eighty per cent; what did it matter? Either way, I was about to play Russian Roulette with a woman's life just to satisfy my own selfish agenda, and I felt sick to my stomach even thinking about it.

Amidst my confusion, I averted my eyes back to the restaurant and saw eighty-per-cent-Martina rush through the cluttered chairs in the front courtyard to welcome some new guests—a young woman in her early twenties and two little girls, most likely twins. It didn't take me long before I recognised the young woman from the internet. Even from where I was standing, I could see the joy and love illuminate across eighty-per-cent-Martina's face as she greeted her daughter, Lara, and grandchildren with a flurry of hugs and kisses.

If this woman really was Martina, I couldn't help but admire the person she had become: a loving and caring parent and grandmother who would undoubtedly sacrifice everything to protect her family from the dangers that surrounded them. Whatever scars she possessed from her past, all that mattered now was the boundless love she carried with her into the future.

After my own recent life-changing experiences—chasing the mysteries of my shooting and uncovering my family's wartime legacy—a future filled with love was the only thing I had left. Who was I to deny that gift to someone else, especially the woman who had defined my life for so long? It was right at that moment when I realised I had no further business being in Marathon, not even for a second longer.

Lottie gently took my hand once again, her sapphire eyes dazzling in the Greek sunshine. 'It's your call, Alex. What will it be?'

Without replying, I gathered her into my arms, hugged her tightly to show my appreciation for the incredible support she had given me, and then slowly began to walk back to our car.

It was time to go home.

Acknowledgments

As stated in the Author's Note, *A Season of Thunder* is based on fact but written as a personal memoir with certain elements of the story fictionalised. It is not meant to be a definitive history of Yugoslavia, nor should it be treated as such. Rather, it's an allegory of the terrible events that occurred in that country during the Second World War and the Homeland War, and the cumulative impacts these conflicts had on me and my family. The book is the culmination of three years of research, including several trips to Europe, the United Kingdom and the United States, as well as countless hours scrutinising academic texts and reams of personal notes.

Despite the intensity of my research, to my frustration, some gaps in my family's story remain unresolved. Writing the book in the way I did allowed me to fictionalise resolutions to those gaps based on my intuition, historical knowledge and imagination. It may not satisfy some people who know the story of Yugoslavia better than I do or even satisfy some of my own friends and family members who perhaps have a different recollection of certain events. However, everyone is allowed to tell their own story, and this is how I have chosen to tell mine.

I am indebted to so many people who helped give this book life. I am especially grateful for the support provided to me by Roxanne McCarty-O'Kane and her team, who produced this book, Ocean Reeve Publishing who started the journey with me, and the countless subject matter experts I met during my travels overseas. A special thank you also to Nikola Lukich, who has produced an incredible book and website on life in the Eboli Displaced Persons Camp, which I readily accessed on several occasions.

This book would not have seen the light of day had it not been for the support given to me by my siblings and extended family, particularly my sister Dubravka, my wife Miriam and mother-in-law, Vereni, as well as my many friends in Australia and across the globe. Thank you.

The events that occurred in the former Yugoslavia during the Second World War still elicit controversy and raw emotions. Issues such as alleged Chetnik collaboration, the camps at Jasenovac and the treatment of civilians continue to be debated. During my research for the book, I discovered further information about the conflict that simply horrified me. It left me so distressed that I stopped writing for several weeks as I contemplated whether or not to finish the book. Consequently, I have refrained from including much of what I unearthed during that time. Sometimes it's best to let certain things remain in the past.

Having said that, I have tried very hard not to take sides and to be balanced in my description of certain events and key historical figures, supported always by various published works. The books I utilised often in my research included: *Britain, Mihailovic, and the Chetniks, 1941-42* by Simon Trew, *The Serbs* by Tim Judah, *Resistance* by Halik Kochanski, *The Fall of Yugoslavia* and *The Balkans* by Misha Gleny, *Tito's Secret Empire* by William Klinger and Dennis Kuljis, and especially the excellent, *Hitler's New Disorder* by Stevan K. Pavlowitch. I am also indebted to countless internet articles for background information. I encourage anyone who has an interest in the Yugoslav Civil War to read widely and develop your own conclusions.

While I consider myself to be a proud Australian Croat given my religion and parental background, I retain a deep affection for all Slavic people and their cultures. Hopefully, the Balkans have now entered a period of sustained peace, where everyone's rights and beliefs will be forever protected no matter what other forces are at play. Given the region's compelling but tragic history, it's the least these people deserve.

Finally, I salute my parents, Anton and Vuka. As for everyone from that incredible generation who fought and lived through the Second World War, they arrived with little and gave up a lot. Thank you, Mum and Dad.

Alex Gerrick, Canberra
November 2024

About the Author

Alex Gerrick is a former senior public servant, political staffer, Army Reserve officer and Not-For-Profit CEO. He holds Masters' degrees from the National Defense College of the Philippines and Deakin University, as well as several other academic qualifications in the areas of military and European history, strategic and international policy and industrial relations. In 2023, Alex established his own publishing arm, Alex's Books.

A Season of Thunder is his second book, having released his debut novel, *A Season of Clouds*, in February 2022. Alex lives in Canberra, Australia, with his wife, Miriam and loyal beagle, Louie. He is currently working on his next novel, his third and last in the *Season* trilogy, projected to be completed in 2026, as well as a fictional espionage series set prior to and during the Second World War, *The Farley Chronicles*.

alexgerrick.com.au

Also by the author:

A Season of Clouds: When only your past can save your future

* 9 7 8 1 7 6 3 7 5 6 1 0 6 *